THE PRISON STONE

The Red Horn Saga • Book One

J.R. MABRY

MICKEY ASTERIOU

Xenophile Press
1700 Shattuck Ave #81, Berkeley, CA 94709
www.xenophilepress.com

Printed in the United States of America
ISBN 978-1-949643-45-9 | paperback
ISBN 978-1-955821-72-8 | hardcover
ISBN 978-1-949643-46-6 | epub

BY THE SAME AUTHORS...

BY MICKEY ASTERIOU

Lake of Power

BY J.R. MABRY & MICKEY ASTERIOU

The Red Horn Saga

The Prison Stone • The Dark Field

Summoners' Keep • The Red Horn

BY J.R. MABRY

The Berkeley Blackfriars Series

The Kingdom • The Power • The Glory

The Temple of All Worlds Series

The Worship of Mystery

BY J.R. MABRY & B.J. WEST

The Oblivion Saga

Oblivion Threshold • Oblivion Flight

Oblivion Quest • Oblivion Gambit

GET THE BACK STORY...

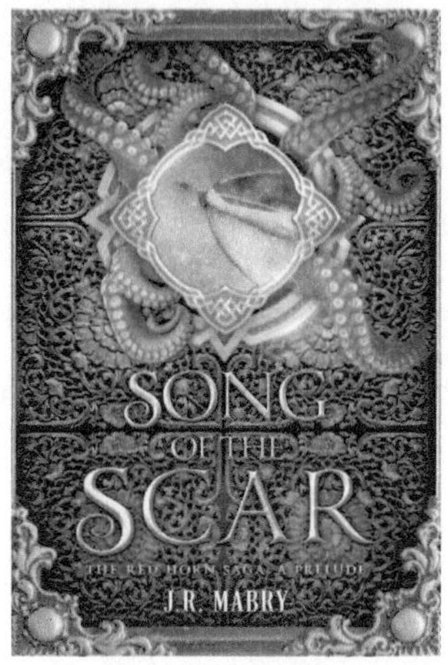

Read about the events that set the whole Red Horn Saga in motion. *The Song of the Scar* is a prequel novella available free when you join our mailing list.

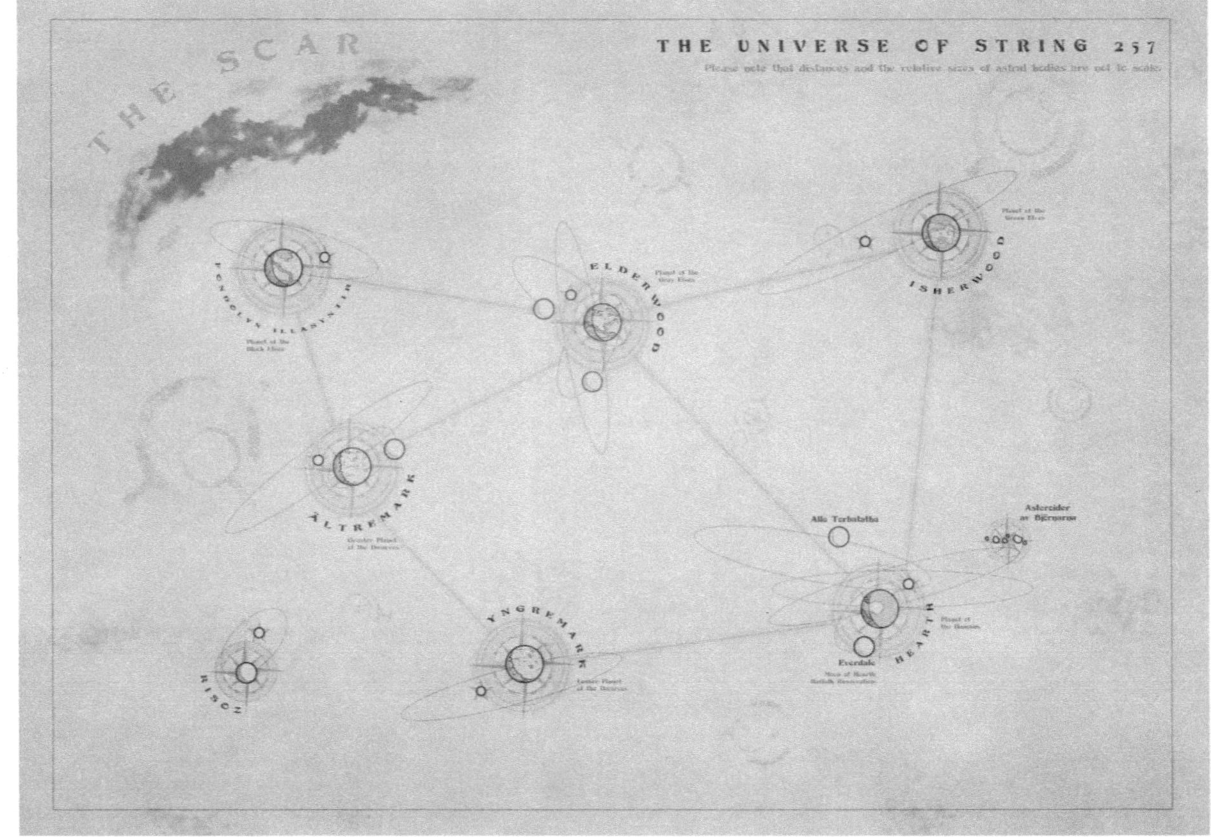
THE SCAR
THE UNIVERSE OF STRING 257
Please note that distances and the relative sizes of astral bodies are not to scale.
ELDERWOOD
ISHERWOOD
ÄLTREMARK
YNGREMARK
HEARTH
Everdale
RISCZ

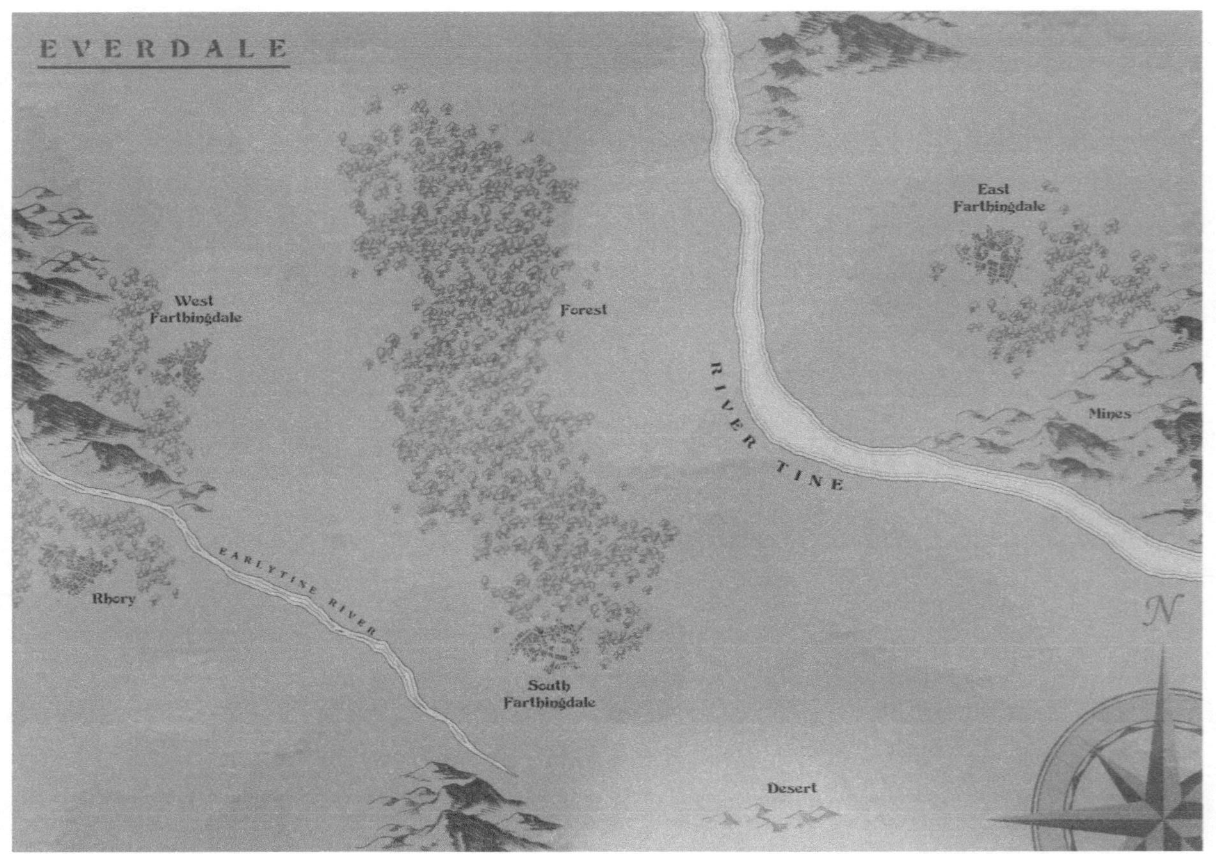
EVERDALE
West
Farthingdale
Rhory
EARLYTINE RIVER
Forest
South
Farthingdale
RIVER TINE
East
Farthingdale
Mines
Desert
N

CONTENTS

Prologue 1
Chapter 1 9
Chapter 2 28
Chapter 3 46
Chapter 4 64
Chapter 5 76
Chapter 6 95
Chapter 7 109
Chapter 8 124
Chapter 9 138
Chapter 10 162
Chapter 11 174
Chapter 12 198
Chapter 13 218
Chapter 14 230
Chapter 15 249
Chapter 16 264

Afterword 289
Dramatis Personae 293
Glossary 297

He roiled in the æther,
thrashing in his rage.
In the place of his birth,
he was a lesser being,
not respected or worshipped
—not as he ought to have been.

The spite he received from his own
fueled his anger
and made it a hot, dark thing,
ready and eager to incinerate
any who crossed him.

Samael, in Hearthentongue,
the Doom of All Bright Worlds;
Saklas, in the Dwarfentongue,
the Bringer of Death;
Ialdaboth, in the reckoning of the elves,
the Oathbreaker.

After many æons of contempt,
a scar opened between the worlds,
the work of a man.
A way opened into another universe,
where none was mightier than he.
He took it. He entered it.

He feasted upon the blood
of a billion bright beings.
He feasted until a more savory morsel
was presented to him.
Not only their fear,
but their awe, their worship.
He deigned to allow those who feared him
in their hearts and swore to him their fealty
the gift of their lives.
The others, he savaged without mercy,
roiling in his wrath from world to world.
Then he was banished,
the Scar permitting magic to pass,
but not him.
He found himself exiled,
not only from his own,
but from the universe
that worshipped and feared him.

There was a world where magic
could be invested in stone
A world where anything with a known name
could be sealed off and denied passage.
And so, due to the ministry of the summoners,
a stone was made,
the magic was summoned,
and the elder god extinguished
from the universe that feared him.

—*from* The Song of the Stone,
a free verse translation into Hearthentongue
from the original rhymed poem in the Elventongue
by Allas, Bard of Mywyck, 4th Age

PROLOGUE

{ String 257 }

A fissure wounded the face of the living rock, a cruel gash that looked like a smile marred by jagged granite teeth.

"What is that, father?"

Harclimar stepped back. His pick was raised, ready to strike, but he lowered it at the sound of his son's question. The truth was, he didn't know, but a trickle of cold ran down his spine.

His dark eyes narrowed as he studied the rock. There was much in dwarfish lore about the mood and character of stone, and Harclimar was well studied in his lore. The rock could tell you what forces had formed it, what it was composed of, what lay beneath it. And if your eye was sharp, the stone could tell a dwarf about himself—about his depths, the places he was brittle, and even the means by which the copper in his own blood would someday rejoin the metals still in the mountain.

"It could be many things," Harclimar said. He stepped away from the fissure and adjusted the lens of his lantern. He motioned for his son to step closer to the face of the rock. "But I want you to read it for yourself, *min kära*. What is the stone saying to you?"

Harcligan's eyes narrowed as he stepped closer to the rock face. His beard was wispy, just now beginning to jut beyond his chin. He was bright, but given to impulse. His father was grateful for an opportunity to invite him to pause and discern carefully.

He watched his son read the stone in the traditional way, from right to left, and then from bottom to top. "It is *gråstensten*," he said.

It was—a very common kind of stone, gray and strong, but brittle.

"But there is a glimmer of something else, just here along the lip of this seam. Realgar, maybe?"

"Could be," Harclimar agreed noncommittally. "We'll need to knock some out to tell."

"Well, if it is, the oyosin would say the combination augurs a tragedy just out of si—"

"The oyosin couldn't tell an agate from an arsehole," Harclimar interrupted him. "Tell me about the rock."

"The combination—if I'm right—probably means there's zinc around, too."

Harclimar grunted. "That is the lore, but in my experience it's as wrong as it is right."

Then Harcligan did something his father did not expect. He slapped the rock.

"Here, now, what are you—?" The rock could be chipped or hewn, but a slap was the traditional insult among dwarfs. To slap the rock was like slapping Father Mountain himself.

"Just...listen." Harcligan did it again.

Harclimar listened. There was an echo. His bushy brows bunched and his eyes met the eyes of his son. Harcligan smiled, showing his own jagged teeth beneath his nascent mustache.

"There's nothing in the rock to suggest a cavern behind it," Harcligan thought aloud, studying the rock face with new eyes. He turned to face his son. "How did you know?"

Harcligan shrugged. "It was just a feeling."

Harclimar scowled. He did not like the idea of affirming his son's impulsive nature, but he could not deny it had paid off in this case.

The dwarf raised his pickax and tapped along the fissure, listening. Finally, with one well-placed stroke, he smote the stone, just above the gash, and smiled with satisfaction as the rock gave away behind it, shards tumbling into darkness. Inserting the tip of the pick, Harclimar widened the hole, now punching at the rock, now pulling at it, testing the places it wanted to give and wanted to hold.

The dwarfs had more than six thousand words for rock, stone, and metal, ways to describe even the subtlest distinctions between them, and the variations within each species. But none of these words sprang to Harclimar's mind as he dug. He was one with the mountain as he tore at the seam, opening a way for passage, for discovery, for wisdom. Every dwarfish child was taught that there was no knowledge in the universe that could not be learned from the mountain, and the mountain was on the verge of a revelation—to him. Harclimar's pulse raced.

Soon the hole was wide enough to shine the lantern into it. Harclimar placed the lamp next to his cheek and felt the heat of it on his wide nose as he gazed into the gloom. He gasped.

"What is it, father?" Harcligan asked.

"Grab your pick. Dig."

The young dwarf did as he was told. He tapped at the stone with his pickax a few feet away from the hole his father had started and struck at the stone. It fell away from his ax with almost no effort. He struck again and again, pausing now and then to tug at the edges with his pick, testing as he had watched his father do.

Before long, they had widened a hole large enough for a small dwarf to step through. Just beyond it was a small cavern—a pocket in the mountain, it seemed to Harclimar, as he did not see any tunnels leading away from it. *It is too early to tell that,* he reminded himself. *The mountain likes to hide its secrets, just as much as it delights to reveal them.*

"Let me go in, father," Harcligan said. "I can fit easily."

It was true. His son was slim, as most young dwarfs were. They did not acquire their girth until their children arrived. The dwarfish saying was mostly true, "When a wife is with child, the whole family grows fat."

Harclimar nodded. "In you go, then. Make sure to test the floor."

"I'm not a fool, father." Harcligan looked momentarily wounded.

"No, *kära*, you're not. Love sometimes speaks with a sharp voice." That was another well-known dwarfish aphorism. "Forgive me."

Harcligan nodded his absolution, squeezing his father's forearm.

"Go in, and I'll hand the lantern through."

Harcligan passed his pickax through and tested the floor of the cavern. It was jagged but solid. He nodded at his father, and then placed one tentative boot on the lowermost lip of the hole they had made. His father hoisted at the young dwarf's belt, and tipped his balance inward. Harcligan stepped down and then reached back for the lantern.

Harclimar gave it to him. He fought down his own impulsive impatience. "What is Father Mountain revealing?" he asked.

"There are no tunnels. The floor is untrod. I feel dripping...from above."

Harclimar saw the shadows stretch ominously as the young dwarf moved the lantern around. "There is a shaft...straight above me. Its end is dark, but it is about three hands wide."

The divinatory implications began to rush through Harclimar's brain, and none of them were good. He pushed them aside.

"I...I think I see what you saw, father."

Harclimar closed his eyes and calmed himself. In his bones, he knew that Father Mountain was about to bestow a boon like none Harclimar had ever encountered before. His hairy ears twitched as he heard the scrape of a stone being lifted from its resting place. Harclimar opened his eyes to see a vision passing through the hole in the rock wall. With trembling hands he received it.

The stone was two hands wide, black as pitch and shiny. In the middle of it was a fiery red eye that seemed to be deeper than the stone was. The eye seemed to shine with a light of its own, but Harclimar knew that it must be an illusion. Somehow it was concentrating and refracting the dim, reflected light available. He longed to see it in the full light of day. He wondered if he would be able to tolerate its brilliance. He could not wait to find out.

"Is that all, son?" he heard himself call. *Is that all? What more could there possibly be?*

"I was right about the zinc," his son's voice said.

"*Knulla* zinc," he spat, unable to take his eyes from the treasure in his hands.

His son's face appeared in the rock wall's aperture, holding the lantern aloft. "What is it, father?"

Harclimar had an inkling, but did not want to get his son's hopes up. By looks alone, what he held was a special find, so rare he dared not speak of. He could feel its infrangible solidity, yet he feared that to express his suspicions would cause the rock to disintegrate before him. *Could it be?* he asked himself. *And how?* he added. *This stone should be hidden. It should not have been so easily found. Or*, he wondered, *was there a reason behind it? Was there a reason it had come to him?*

He would need to consult with a summoner, perhaps more than one. But whom could he trust?

"Father?"

"This," Harclimar voiced at last, "is a stone that can change the world." His world, certainly. If Harclimar was right, a find such as this one could make him a very rich dwarf indeed.

"Who would want *that*?" Harcligan asked.

"Many, my son," Harclimar replied, thinking only of the stone. "There are many—dwarf, elf, and man—who would desire this."

THE SUMMONER ELSORIN FAIRHAVEN lit a candle and sat down on his bed with a groan. For all his skill with magic, he was still growing old. He had done rituals to evade the creaking of bones, to soften the burning in his back, but to no avail. The common folk believed the summoners were omnipotent. "If only that were true," he whispered aloud to his empty room.

The summoners lived austere lives, yet, as head of the Order of Arrunwolfe, his room in the keep was larger than most. Summoners were not generally cloistered, but lived among the people, often peripatetic, travelling here and there as they were needed, relying on the hospitality of strangers. Some had familiars, some did not. And because the summoners were often effective at their arts, the people were generous. Elsorin did not live sumptuously, but he was comfortable.

Except for when he wasn't. The pain in his back was growing worse, and nothing he did seemed to help. He had resisted asking for help from the physic, seeing it as a sign of weakness. But he knew what the old lady would say—*not* coming to her was a sign of pride. She would not be wrong, but that did not make it easier.

Elsorin was just lifting his feet from the floor when he heard an urgent rapping on his door. "Horn of blood," he spat, and groaned as he stood. He reached for his cane and headed for the door. He was only halfway to the door when it swung open, which meant two things —it was his personal assistant, Riza, as no one else would dare enter unbidden; and that the matter was important.

Riza bowed, averting her eyes from his nightshirt. Her familiar, a mouse named Kibit, skittered under the hem of her robe. "I'm sorry, master."

"Yes, yes, yes. What's so important?"

"The oracle! ...The oracle has awakened."

"Oh." That was news indeed. The blind summoner Objor sat enthroned in the temple of the Keep, but he was usually motionless and silent. It was magic that kept him alive, and it was through magic that he beheld his visions. And the last time Elsorin could remember the oracle speaking, the order master still had hair on his head.

"Quickly, help me into my robe," Elsorin commanded, and Riza darted to the clothes horse near the foot of the master's bed. She was shorter than he—much shorter—but held the robe up as high as she could. Every now and then Kibit would skitter over his naked toe. It no longer bothered him. He had to stoop to put his arm through the sleeve, which made his back spasm, but he managed it. Tightening his cincture, he set his cane on the floor and pointed to the door with his chin. "Let's go."

Riza fluttered around him as he walked, rushing ahead to open doors, waiting until he passed, shutting doors behind him, then rushing ahead again, her mouse racing around her feet. The Keep was cold at night and Elsorin cursed the fact that he had not put on his slippers. *Too late now,* he thought.

The newfangled gas lamps stretched out at eye level along the corridors. They emitted a steadier glow than the torches used to, and with far less smoke. They had been a good decision. He had made a lot of good decisions, he realized. It was not for nothing that the Order of Arrunwolfe had elected him their master. He was worthy, and he knew it. He didn't lord it over anyone—at least he didn't think he did—but he had a keen sense of his authority and power. He had used it judiciously, and he was proud of what they had done.

The worlds of the bright races were thriving, in no small part due to the ministry of the summoners. Certainly there were those who disapproved of magic, but they were in the minority. Most people loved the summoners and were appreciative of how much easier their lives were because of them. They loved them because the order members were disciplined and principled. And it was *he* who made sure of that.

Elsorin felt a little winded by the time they made it to the temple. Riza rushed ahead to open the doors and strained against them. During the day they were always open. What purpose it served to close them at night, Elsorin did not know. It was simply what had always been done. That was a rule that could be changed. He made a mental note.

Grunting, Riza succeeded and Elsorin pushed past her, hearing the great doors shut behind them as Riza and her mouse flitted once more to his side, ready for whatever he might need.

He lifted his eyes to the dais where the oracle sat. He froze.

Objor the Seer sat bolt upright, his thin, atrophied muscles taught as a bow-string. His sightless eyes were wide, and the rheumy film that covered them seemed to glow. His mouth was open, and on his face was a look of abject horror. His familiar, a moth named Tepi, fluttered nervously about his head.

"What is it?" Elsorin asked. "What has he said?"

Two scribes sat at the base of the dais. It was their job to record anything the oracle uttered. One of them slunk down, his shoulders sagging, refusing to meet Elsorin's gaze.

"What's with you?" Elsorin snapped. "Let me guess—it has been twenty years since the oracle has spoken, and so you have no ink in your pot?"

The young man withered before him, squirmed in his seat, looked like he wished he could disappear. Elsorin turned his attention to the other scribe. "I trust you are better prepared?"

"I am, master," the young woman tried not to look superior. She failed. Her familiar, a ferret with enormous eyes, beheld the oracle with rapt attention. Every now and then it shuddered.

"Good. What has he said?"

The young woman looked down at her paper in order to report the words precisely. "The key has been found."

"Key? What key?" Elsorin scowled. "Is that all he said?"

The scribe met his eyes. She nodded.

The oracle stirred. Elsorin whirled about to face him, his muscles tense, his pains forgotten.

The oracle gazed off into some far part of space that only he could see. His jaw worked as if he were trying to get his mouth around an unpronounceable word. Finally, the words came.

"The unbreakable barrier...will be broken. There is a pinprick of light...it illumines the void. The prisoner writhes in the darkness...now he has hope. Oh...oh...woeful hope! Oh...oh...baneful hope!"

The oracle began to shake. He was standing up, and the stick-like legs beneath him could hardly support his weight. But stand he did. Tepi's fluttering became even more agitated. Objor held one bony finger aloft, his sightless eyes beholding a horror that he seemed incapable of expressing. "The tinder has been touched to the fire! Soon, the whole universe will be ablaze!"

Objor collapsed, his robes billowing as his skeletal frame crumpled beneath him, and his wizened head hit the stone dais with a sickening crack.

I

The Dale was soaked with brilliant sunlight, and Ellis reclined among the wildflowers. The meadow was so green it almost hurt, and Ellis breathed a deep sigh. Out of the corner of his eye, he saw his best friend Kit spinning. She was performing a dance traditional among the maids in Everdale, especially when they were looking for mates or families to join. It struck him as odd that she was doing the dance with only him in attendance. It also struck him as odd—no, truly off—that she was dancing at all. Kit did not *dance.*

Yet here she was. She was also smiling—and Kit did not smile. She was smiling at him. She leaned down amid the wildflowers and touched her nose to his. And then she cocked her head at just the right angle for a kiss, and he felt the whisper brush of her lips—

"OY! Slug-a-bed! So this is how the Royal Mail spends its money, eh?"

Ellis Sunderland felt a sharp pain in his side. He opened his eyes. The round face of Tubber Goodfoot was staring down at him. Tubber kicked him in the ribs. Then he did it again.

"By the Horn, Tubber! Stop it!" Ellis rolled away from Tubber as fast as he could.

"Wait until old Bracegirdle hears about this," Tubber said. "Sleeping on the King's farthing! You think *that's* the kind of lazy beastie they'll want for postmaster? 'Cause I don't." Tubber kicked him again.

"Tubber, I've nearly finished my route. What does it matter if I take a break? Everyone takes a break! You take yours in the pub."

"Oh, that's how it is, is it? Can't take responsibility for your own failings, so you have to lash out at yer betters? Oh, that's pretty, that is. Yes, sir, Bracegirdle will be very interested in all this."

Ellis wanted the postmaster's job so bad his back teeth ached. But Tubber wanted it, too, as did several other couriers in the Dale. Ellis was sure he'd do a better job than any of them, especially Tubber, whom he suspected was more interested in the prestige and the paycheck the position brought than actually improving Everdale's postal system.

The sun was directly behind Tubber's head, and Ellis had to squint to see him. Then his head blocked the sun completely and he was able to plainly see the look of satisfaction on his rival's face. He was also able to look up the young man's nostrils, straight into his sinus cavities. The sight made Ellis shudder and look away.

"Tubber, it was just a nap. All haffolk take naps. It might as well be required by law—along with second breakfast and tea-after-tea."

"Aye, you can try telling that to Bracegirdle." The young man looked around, then raised his boot to stomp Ellis in the head.

Ellis curled into a ball, issued a cry of protest, and raised his hands to ward off the blow.

But he needn't have bothered. Before Tubber's boot could come down on his face, the burly haffolk slapped at his neck. "Oy! What was that? Was that a wasp?"

He slapped again, this time at his head, and spun around wildly. Then he slowly backed away from Ellis.

Ellis lowered his arms and propped himself up on his elbows to peer over the wildflowers. Kittredge Cornfeather was striding toward them, slingshot armed and aimed—directly at Tubber's head.

"That was the tiniest pebble. The next one will be a rock. And the next one will split your swiving head like a melon. So if you like your face the way it is, you just keep backin' up."

Kit was short, even among haffolk, standing about waist high to man or elf. But she was among the fiercest creatures Ellis had ever known. She'd never encountered a weapon she didn't master, and Ellis was grateful that she counted him her friend.

They were friends—close friends—but he wished they were more. The images from the dream floated back to him, and he could almost feel the brush of her lips again—a feeling he had never experienced in waking life, nor likely ever would. Kit's affections tended toward tomboys like herself, leaving Ellis nursing a heart continually pummeled by unrequited affections but nevertheless grateful for her friendship.

"Now you turn yourself around, Tubber Goodfoot, and you walk on back to the village. You try something like this again and you'll be quarrying stone from your vacant head."

Ellis glanced back at Tubber, and saw his hands raised. He also saw him walking backward in retreat. Then he turned and began to walk briskly in the direction of West Farthingdale, throwing the occasional scowl over his shoulder.

Kit waited until he had rejoined the road before lowering her slingshot.

"That was close," Ellis said. "Have you ever thought of becoming sheriff?"

"I'd like that, I think. But you didn't need *me* to save you," Kit said, stowing her weapon in her shoulder bag. "One well-aimed kick in the groin would have solved your problems."

"I...didn't think of that."

"Obviously not. You know what the problem with you is, Ellis?"

"Uh...I don't make my bed?"

"You don't make your bed?" She raised one eyebrow at him. "Your *problem* is that you are too nice. You got no fight in you."

"That's not true!" Ellis feigned offense.

"'Tis true. When are you going to stand up for yourself?"

"Why should I?" He smiled. "I have you."

She narrowed her eyes. Then she rooted in her bag once more and pulled forth a wrapped bundle. "Mrs. Proudspindle's cheese." She tossed it to him. He caught it and unwrapped the rough cloth. Inside was a sweaty white cheese with red flakes in it. He sniffed at it. His eyes widened.

"It smells...wonderful."

"Wait 'til you taste it. Those specks are cranberries."

He tasted it, and instantly his mouth was awash in goodness. "That is the besht cheesh I ever ate," he said with his mouth full.

"Uh-huh. We've got the afternoon route to finish. So on your feet, unless you fancy delivering your packages in the dark."

Ellis stuffed the last bit of cheese into his cheek and stood. He slung his courier's bag over his shoulder and adjusted it so it was balanced for the long walk ahead of them.

Kit put her hand on the hilt of her longdagger and set out.

Ellis loved being with Kit every day, but at times, it hurt to watch her. She didn't dress like the other maids in the Dale. She wore the clothes of he-haffolk, but she avoided the gay colors favored by haffolk generally, preferring black, silver, and gray. This provided a striking look with her raven-black hair which hung just to her shoulders. Ellis sighed.

Kit was heading to the road with steady strides, and Ellis scrambled to catch up to her. They were at the edge of the meadow now, following a line of trees. Ellis shifted the weight of the bag and estimated that they had about two hours of work left to do.

Out of the corner of his eye, he saw movement. He turned his head to the left, and saw a small clearing. In the center of a circle of trees he saw a stag, standing stock still, staring straight at him. There was something strong, wise, and gentle about deer, and he loved to watch them. But there was something different about this stag.

Ellis froze, and time seemed to slow down. Suddenly it seemed that there was no sunlight, no breeze, no job to do, not even any Kit. There was just Ellis and the stag. Ellis cocked his head, not able to tear his eyes away. There was an oddness—not just about the moment, but about the stag itself—that he did not immediately grasp. Then he realized that the shape of its head was wrong—the antlers were only whole on one side. On the other, it looked as if they had been cut, or perhaps broken off in battle. He had heard that stags sometimes fought over their mates, locking horns in their efforts to best their rivals.

The stag seemed to be looking straight into Ellis' soul. It seemed to want something from him, but Ellis could not guess what it might be. Ellis' hands began to sweat. He wiped them on his trousers, but did not look away. Then, suddenly, the stag jerked back and bounded away into the dark shadows of the forest. Ellis' heart leaped to see the beauty of his movement, and just as fast felt the loss of the animal's absence and the magic of the moment.

"Yo, Ellis!" Kit's voice broke through his reverie. "Do I have to drag you to your swivin' route?"

EALON SUMMERFIELD RAISED his hand to shield his eyes from the sun as he surveyed the battlefield. For as far as his eye could see, men and dwarfs were locked in close fighting. Swords flashed, axes swung, horses reared and screamed, and the ground beneath their feet was black and slick with blood.

"I should be down there," he said aloud, his hand going reflexively to the hilt of his sword. "My place is down there."

Rear General Lord Sunhaven's bushy eyebrows raised. "I am surprised to hear it, Lord. Better that you are here, though. You may find yourself commanding battles one day, and knowing how armies move and react to orders will be a boon to you. Besides," he lowered his voice, "a man commands better if he is *alive*...if you take my meaning, sir."

Ealon turned his head away from the carnage to fix Sunhaven with a sour scowl. "You think I'm a coward."

"I think no such thing. I think you are a prince, and that your life is worth more than battle-fodder."

"And yet my brother—the king's heir—is down there."

"Aye, Lord." The old man turned his gaze to the battle. "Against my counsel."

"Yet you do not allow me to join the fray."

"I am charged—by your brother and by the king—to defend you."

"You are not a nursemaid. I don't need *you* to mind me."

"No, Lord."

Ealon sneered at Sunhaven's agreement, stated too quickly and with a hint of condescension. Ealon hated being patronized. In truth, he had no desire to be in the thick of battle. His skill with a sword was small, but his pride was a ravenous beast that needed constant feeding. What he truly hated was being told what to do, especially by his father or brother.

He had been groomed to rule in the event something happened to his brother Cormoran, an opportunity he knew may never come. *Although*, he thought as his eyes scoured the battlefield looking for his brother, *one can always hope*. But he found him, near the Summerfield standard rippling defiantly in the wind—a brilliant, semi-circular sun brooding over a dark plain. Cormoran was on his feet, sword swinging, bringing down foemen on every side with confident dispatch.

Ealon made a sour face and looked away. Their enemy today was Wybrook, residing to the northeast and sharing the coastline—and a petty kingdom which refused to bend the knee and pay tribute to the high king. They had bollocks, he had to give them that. But they did not have the numbers, nor the cannons, nor the dwarfs on their side—and there were no fiercer enemies than dwarfs in the grip of bloodlust.

He was growing bored of watching the fighting, just as he was bored by one petty insurgency after another, and by politics altogether. He loved the idea of power, he loved to make men jump when he commanded them, but the minutia of ruling made him want to stab out his eyes. He thanked the oyosii that such tedium fell to Cormoran and his father. It left him free to...

He felt a moment of vertigo. What *did* he do with his time? There seemed so little of it, but if he were honest, he would have to admit that he spent most of it playing nice at court, stumbling in his cups, hilt-deep in a whore, and seething over his brother. But he hated being honest, and he pushed the thought away.

He wished there was a way to best his brother. Cormoran had always been their father's favorite. It was Cormoran who got the attention, Cormoran who had been trained first in battle, Cormoran who had been schooled first in his letters and in diplomacy. The reasonable part of his brain pointed out that this must be so, since Cormoran was four years his senior, but such protests mattered not at all to the petty worm of his heart. Cormoran was born first, and Ealon hated him for it.

His eyes were drawn to color, and across the battlefield he noted the enemy general's camp, much like their own, perched at the top of the hillock just on the other side of the shallow valley. The hillock gave the enemy high ground to command from, just as their own camp had done. The hills descended into an extended valley to the right, but to the left there was a rim, a ridge that led through several stands of trees right around to his own camp.

Ealon cocked his head. He looked around at their own camp, counted the number of men. *Not many*...he thought. A plan began to form in his mind.

"Cormoran and the lords are holding their own," Sunhaven pointed out, "but we're taking heavy losses along our flank."

"Um...pardon me a moment, Lord Sunhaven. I need to find a stand of trees. 'Wine is only ever a visitor,' as they say."

"Yes, of course, my lord. There is a latrine behind the camp."

"I hate the latrine." His nostrils flared. "The smell offends me."

Sunhaven moved his head back and forth, accepting this answer. Ealon could tell he did not approve and probably thought the prince was being insufferably delicate, but he was wise enough not to say it.

Ealon gave the battle one last glance before turning and heading for the trees.

CORMORAN JUMPED BACK to avoid the follow-through of a dwarfish ax. "Sorry, my lord," Orfek Gravelhorn called over his shoulder.

Cormoran could hardly hold it against him. The dwarf had felled even more of the enemy than Cormoran himself had. There were few soldiers Cormoran could trust at his back, few who could match him, but Gravelhorn was one—even if his swing did go a bit wide at times.

Cormoran took advantage of the moment to get his bearings.

Looking around, mindful of any who might approach him, he pushed the visor of his helmet up and wiped the sweat from his chin on his silver gauntlet. He squinted at the sun's brightness, now no longer dimmed by his visor, and it seemed to him incongruously bright and cheery given the tragedy and blood seeping into his greaves.

He turned and chanced a glance at the general's camp, hoping to catch a glimpse of his brother—his troublesome brother whom he had promised father to keep safe. Cormoran felt a moment of panic when he did not see him. Sunhaven was there, Cormoran would recognize the man's large, stocky frame anywhere—but where was Ealon?

Probably lying down in the general's tent, taking a nap, he thought. It was a wicked thought, and even though he wouldn't for a second put such a thing past his brother, he pushed it away. Then, from the corner of his eye, he saw movement up on the ridge. He jerked his head to follow it and saw what was undeniably Ealon's distinctive gait—the young man walked on his toes, strangely. His younger brother was just entering a copse of trees, making for the ridge that surrounded the valley like the lip of a giant bowl.

"What is he up to?" Cormoran whispered aloud.

Just then he felt the wind of a blade and swung, taking the arm of an attacker off at the shoulder. He leaped, nimble even in his heavy armor, retaking his place at Gravelhorn's back. "Orfek, my friend, how do you fare?"

"I wish you'd bring me a real challenge, your highness," the dwarf called over his shoulder. "I'm starting to nod off."

Cormoran grinned. "Ealon's up to something. I need us to fight to the left flank to catch him."

"Horn of blood," Gravelhorn swore.

Cormoran took no offense. If anyone had earned the right to candor, it was Gravelhorn. "You lead, I'll follow, my lord," the dwarf said. "I always was partial to dancin'."

"You would let me lead?" Cormoran said, slashing his way forward.

"Try to find a more nimble-footed partner. I dare you," Gravelhorn growled, keeping close behind.

"Why does the last delivery of the day have to be to Rhory?" Ellis asked. His feet were already aching from the miles they'd trodden that day. He tugged on the strap of his courier bag, feeling the weight of the one package they had yet to deliver.

Kit didn't answer, and her mind seemed to be elsewhere.

"I mean, why shouldn't it be Rhory, after all?" Ellis countered his own argument. "Who am I? Why not give the unpleasant assignments to the napper, right?"

"Are you through?" Kit asked, a little too irritably. "This isn't a punishment, you thimblehead. It's just a job. It's the luck of the draw. Even if you *hadn't* had your little encounter with Tubber, we'd still be here, on our way to Rhory."

"I hate Rhory," Ellis said.

"I think even *the humans* hate Rhory," Kit agreed.

Rhory was a human outpost on Everdale—which was otherwise designated a haffolk reservation. It served as the administrative seat of the moon, connecting them to the Kingdom of Hearth, and it also hosted Everdale's ætherport. It was not a place one wanted to get caught in after dark, as the crowded streets were filled with those on their way from one place to another, many of whom, for various reasons, did not want to land on Hearth.

As they rounded a bend in the road, Ellis made out the border crossing ahead of them. There was a short line, as usual, for it took time to answer the questions of the border agents and obtain writs of passage.

Ellis sighed. "I'm tired of my life."

Kit rolled her eyes.

"I mean it," he said. "It's sunup and walk thirty miles and sunset and then do it again."

"You don't have to tell me about that. I walk every bleedin' mile with you."

"Nothing is ever going to change. I'm just going to be a courier, second-class, until my feet fall off."

"Don't be ridiculous. Your feet won't fall off. They'll just grind down to nubs."

"I want to do something important with my life," Ellis complained.

"I wish I could just leave all this behind and go do something...big. Something that matters."

"O! By the horn—will you stop whining?" Kit snapped.

"I'm not whining."

"You are. You make me want to crush the head of something innocent."

"Something that isn't me, I hope."

"Don't tempt me."

Ellis looked sideways at her as they walked. "You scare me sometimes."

"Well, you irritate me sometimes, so we're even."

They'd reached the border crossing, and stood at the back of the line. Ellis counted four travelers ahead of them. One was human, apparently finishing business in the Dale for the day and heading back to his home in Rhory. Three others were haffolk, two wore merchant's coats, and the other was wearing ordinary Dale dress, so Ellis couldn't guess why she might be crossing. *And it is none of your business*, he reminded himself.

A wooden fence made of rough-hewn timbers stretched as far as the eye could see. It came to about chest-high on the haffolk, and ran for many miles around the periphery of Rhory. Ellis wasn't sure if the purpose of it was to keep humans and dwarfs in or haffolk out. Perhaps it was both.

There was a large gate set into the fence, and a small guard house sat just inside on Rhory land. A wooden table had been placed about three paces in front of the gate, and two human guards sat at it. One, a thick-set woman in her middle years, had a pile of papers in front of her, and two spindles stacked with writs and receipts. Small, round spectacles perched on her nose, and her lips seemed frozen in a perpetual purse. A tight gray bun stuck out asymmetrically from one side of her head. The other human was sprawled in his chair, looking as if he might slide off in a sleepy stupor, one hand on the hilt of his sword.

As Ellis and Kit approached, Ellis withdrew his courier ID and held it up for them to read. The one keeping records slapped her partner's thigh. "Courier," she said. "I need Form 86E."

"Horn of blood, woman," he said, but he hauled himself to his feet and ambled back to the guard house. A moment later he returned.

"Name?" the woman asked.

"Ellis Sunderland, Courier Second Class, Everdale Post Office Number 27."

"Name?" The woman looked at Kit.

"Kittredge Cornfeather."

The woman looked back and forth between them. "You married?"

Ellis' face flushed and he began stammering.

"By the horn! No," Kit said. She rolled her eyes and shook her head, emphasizing the absurdity of the notion. "He's a whiner."

"I am *not* a whiner," Ellis protested.

"You're whining *right now*," Kit pointed out.

The woman put her hand up to stop them. She spoke once more in Kit's direction. "What is your occupation?"

The man returned and slapped Form 86E on the table, groaning as he dropped once more into his seat.

"Bodyguard," Kit said.

"Bodyguard?"

Kit put her hand on the hilt of her longneedle. "Bodyguard."

The woman's eyebrows rose. She looked at Ellis. "Is she *your* bodyguard?"

Ellis nodded vigorously.

"Well, all right then." The woman made a note.

"Did she say 'bodyguard'?" the man asked.

"She did."

"Is this what the world is coming to?" The man shook his head. "Not only do we have to live on this gods-forsaken d'race planet, not only do we have to lower ourselves by talking to the filthy creatures, now we have to put up with them giving themselves airs. Oooh, the d'race needs a bodyguard. As if a d'race could be fancy enough to need one, or *important* enough, like."

Ellis saw Kit stiffen. Haffolk was the name the Dale inhabitants used for themselves and was the respectful and proper term. "D'race," however, was a contraction from "mixed race," a word used only by humans and considered impolite at best—and an insufferable insult at worst.

"It's not what the world is coming to," the woman joined his lament, "it's where it bleedin' is."

"'Sooth," the man agreed.

"Let me see the package," the woman said to Ellis, making a "come" motion with her upturned hand.

Ellis removed a box about twelve inches square from his courier's bag and placed it on the table.

The woman eyed it suspiciously, noting the addresses of both the sender and the receiver.

"What's in it?" she asked.

"How should *we* know?" Kit snapped. Ellis noted her hand was tight on the hilt of her weapon.

Ellis was eager to mediate Kit's aggression. "We don't open the packages, I'm afraid. That's against the law. We just deliver them." Ellis wasn't telling them anything they didn't already know. Couriers passed through the border in both directions daily.

The woman turned to face the man. "I don't know about these two," she said. "Something smells off."

"I know just what you mean. You can smell a d'race a mile away." Then the man burped loudly.

"I'm not sure what to do about them," she tapped her fingers on the table.

"We're right here," Kit seethed. "We *can* hear you."

"If you'll pardon me," Ellis said. "But Hearth postal regulation 5, subsection D guarantees unimpeded courier service between reservation territories and Hearth municipal districts—which Rhory is, even though off-planet, subsequent to the Quintin Fieldmanor act."

The man nudged the woman, "Givin' himself airs."

"I see that." The woman turned back to the haffolk. She pointed to Ellis' chest. "That's a nice necklace."

Ellis' hand went to the medallion he wore—the same medallion he had been wearing since he had first been shipped off-world to Everdale.

"What is it?" she asked, peering at it.

Ellis' hand closed over it, holding it tight, covering the design.

"I'd like a necklace like that," the woman said to the man next to her.

"It'd look good on you, it would," the man nodded.

The woman looked Ellis in the eye and cocked her head.

"It's my birth medal," he said. "And you can't have it."

She narrowed her eyes. "Too bad, then. Well, our work is done here. Passage denied."

"For what reason?" Kit asked, incredulous.

"Suspicious package," the woman said. "Might be poison."

Ellis scowled at them. He shook the package. "That would be a lot of poison."

"Might be an explosive," the man said to the woman.

Ellis tossed the package on the table. It landed with a thud that made the man jump. He was losing his temper, which was usually Kit's response, not his. This time, however, Kit intervened. She grabbed the package and dutifully replaced it in the courier bag hanging from Ellis' shoulder. "We'll need to file a report," she said. "So we'll need your names."

The woman turned her papers over. "No, you won't."

Kit grew louder. "You are standing in the way of our delivery, and we'll need to explain why. Give us your names."

"Shall I call security over, to rough them up?" the man asked casually.

Eyes locked on Kit, the woman slowly smiled, as if to suggest she would like that very much.

Kit's jaw was set like granite, but she grabbed Ellis' elbow and steered him away.

"They're trolls," she said.

"I wouldn't be saying bad things about trolls, if I were you," Ellis cautioned.

"Come on," she kept pulling him, back through the line, away from the gate. "When I'm sheriff..." Kit trailed off.

"We have a duty to deliver this package," Ellis insisted.

"You're whining again."

"I'm not whining. I'm saying—"

"I know, and we *will* deliver it," Kit said.

"How?"

"Only one thing to do," she said.

"What's that?"

"Sneak."

❦

CORMORAN SWORE as he took the ridge. Orfek was gasping for breath behind him. Clearly the dwarf was made for battle, not long distance sprinting. The slope was steep, and Cormoran paused to let them both catch their breaths. "It's taken us too long," he confessed his fear. "We won't catch up to him."

"Aye, we might not head him off," Gravelhorn agreed, "but we may yet be able to clean up after 'im."

Cormoran didn't disagree with that. "Can you carry on?"

"My lord, it would take a lot more than this to slow me down."

Cormoran smiled sadly, his eyes moving to the battle raging beneath them. "My place is down there, not chasing after Ealon."

"And it's not my place to question your father's wisdom in sending him to this battle," Gravelhorn said, "but..."

He left it at that, and Cormoran nodded as he turned to follow the ridge and his errant brother. "My father's wisdom is sound—"

"'Course it is, lord," Gravelhorn said, too quickly.

"What I mean is, under ordinary circumstances, a king would want his son—even a second son—to gain experience in battle. You cannot lead if you do not fight."

"No, lord. 'Tis true."

"But there's no such thing as 'ordinary circumstances' where Ealon is involved."

Gravelhorn said nothing. His dwarfish legs had to work faster than Cormoran's own to carry him as far and as quickly. But he was the most dependable, loyal, indefatigable sideman Cormoran had ever known. Finally, the dwarf said, "Where the devil is he going?"

"My guess is to the rebel general's camp. See," he pointed back along the ridge to their own general's camp. "Both of our camps are along this ridge, just in front of the treeline. It's the only thing in this direction."

"Is he planning to single-handedly take out their command?" Orfek asked. "I mean, he has little enough skill with a sword." A moment later, he added, "Begging your pardon, lord."

"No, 'tis true enough. There are plenty who don't dare speak truth to their sovereigns, Orfek, but more should. We are far from perfect. We pretend we are gods, but we are often as blind as moles, and just as dug in. I cherish your candor."

"Thank you, lord," Gravelhorn said, although he did not sound very certain.

Just through a stand of trees, Cormoran saw the bright colors of the rebels' pavilion. He held his hand up, a gesture meaning both "halt" and "silence." Gravelhorn froze, waiting for further instructions.

Cormoran peered through the undergrowth and whispered, "We've got two guards in front. They don't look particularly wary—they're watching the battle and pointing as if they're betting on a tournament."

Gravelhorn grunted. "All the better for us."

"Indeed. Come." Cormoran slid to the left, deeper into the copse of trees, edging his way around to the rear of the pavilion. He squatted, moving more quickly than a man should in full armor, and more quietly. The copse came to an end just ahead, and Cormoran saw an open distance between the trees and the pavilion of about twenty yards. He also saw his brother, his black-clad backside turned toward them, peering through what appeared to be a hole in the tent.

"There's the bugger," Gravelhorn said, drawing alongside. "What in the Dark Field is he doing?"

"Trying to get himself killed, dammit," Cormoran spat. His mind reeled at how livid his father would be if he let that happen.

"Oh, I don't know about that, sir. Look." The dwarf pointed to a place a few yards in front of the truant prince—it looked like the grasses had been trodden down, and as Cormoran squinted, he could just barely make out the crumpled figure of a man. Some of the grasses were smeared with crimson.

Cormoran blew a gust of air through his cheeks. "Oh, my brother, what are you doing?"

"He's trying to single-handedly win the battle," Gravelhorn suggested.

"By flouting the most sacred rules of military propriety," Cormoran agreed. "How can we expect our enemies to fight honorably if we do not?"

Gravelhorn grunted.

"Do you see anyone else? Anything amiss?" Cormoran asked. Dwarfish eyes were sharper than human eyes, having been fashioned by the oyosii to see in the dark.

"All looks clear to me, lord."

Cormoran drew his sword and held it at the ready before him. "Then let us go." He stepped out from the cover of the copse and moved quickly over the brown grassy stretch toward the pavilion. He was almost upon Ealon when the prince, sensing movement, whipped around, dagger drawn. Ealon's eyes went wide at the sight of his brother, and Cormoran saw a series of emotions taking the field of his face in rapid succession—surprise, fear, anger... opportunity.

Wordlessly, Cormoran came up beside his brother, and signaled behind him for Gravelhorn to halt. Ealon turned back toward the pavilion without a sound and pointed at a small rip in the pavilion's fabric. His chin was inclined, as if daring Cormoran to question him, or challenge him, or—oyosii forbid—judge him.

Cormoran looked back at Gravelhorn, who stood close behind, ax at the ready. Were they alone, Cormoran would have hesitated to bend and put his eye to the hole. It would be as good as showing his brother his neck, and he did not trust Ealon not to take the opportunity to slit his throat. The thought made him sad. But he knew Ealon would try nothing with the dwarf standing guard. So he bent, exposing his neck to his little brother, and peered through the opening into the large tent.

At first, it took Cormoran a moment to figure out what he was seeing. He had expected generals gathered around maps, issuing orders to various runners, and arguing over strategy and tactics. Instead, he saw a fair-haired young man, dressed in ill-fitting armor, sullenly swishing a rapier from side to side.

"No, no, my young sir," came the weary voice of an unseen man. "Less elbow, I beg of you. Turn at the wrist. Always with the wrist. You must hold the blade in balance; it should feel an extension of your arm."

Cormoran shook his head in disbelief. A civilized country would have used such a pavilion to benefit its soldiers. There should be couches for relaxation, whoring for entertainment; yet these backwoods, rustic cowbedders were wasting it to train one imbecile child.

Rising, he moved away from the tent, gesturing for his brother to follow. Ealon reluctantly submitted, and the three of them crouched in the grasses not far from the body of the murdered guard. Cormoran could plainly see where the man's blood had spilt out onto the soil.

Cormoran removed his helmet and fixed his younger brother with a steely gaze. "What do you think you're doing?"

"Cutting off the snake's head," Ealon said with contempt, as if it were obvious. "Did you see the boy?"

"I did. Who is he?"

"He is the scion of the pretender, Avantir."

Avantir was the client king of Wybrook, and it was his army they were facing on the field that day. Wybrook was considered small, but its location up the coast, between Uther's land and the northern mountains of Untwold, gave it great influence. Two months ago, Avantir had declared its independence from the high king's throne. Obviously this was tantamount to a declaration of war. Battle had been inevitable.

"What's he doing here?" Cormoran asked.

"Not much at all, from what I could see," Ealon replied wryly.

"Let me rephrase," said Cormoran. "What are *you* doing here? What is your plan? If you have a plan."

"I was planning to cut through the fabric of the pavilion and slit the boy's throat from ear to ear." Ealon permitted himself a grin, but Cormoran saw little humor in the situation .

"And when the boy noticed you sawing away and cried for help? When the two guards out front rushed in? What then?"

Ealon's face fell. "Two guards?"

"You didn't surveil the front of the tent?" Cormoran asked, narrowing one eye. "And would slitting the boy's throat have been worth it, after the guards ran you through with their steel?"

Ealon said nothing. He looked mildly quizzical. Cormoran had rarely seen him at a loss for words. Gravelhorn buried his face in one hand and groaned.

Ealon brightened. "But *you* are here, now, brother. You and...your little friend there."

Gravelhorn looked up at Cormoran, an expression of shocked disbelief on his face. "My lord, would you remind my lord the princeling here that I am the Earl of Härgaladr?"

Ealon ignored him. "Between the three of us, we can take them easily."

Cormoran ground his teeth and balled his hands into fists inside his armored gloves. He concentrated on his breathing to still the storm of rage brewing within him. Finally, he fixed his brother's eye with his own and spoke in a measured and noble tone. "We might. But we won't."

Ealon's mouth worked, but no sounds came out. He pointed at the pavilion.

Cormoran continued. "We won't because such actions are ignoble. They violate the sacred trust of warriors. We will not do this wicked thing because even the thought of it dishonors our house."

Ealon opened his mouth to protest, but Cormoran held up his hand to stop him and continued. "The elder god was powerful, but he was evil, and the worship he demanded was evil. The oyosii defeated him by honorable means, and the conduct they require of us is honorable as well."

"You speak of fairy tale and myth," Ealon spat. "I speak of victory."

"What you intend would bring down our house every bit as much as defeat in battle. Which is itself all the more likely every minute Orfek and I are away from the fray."

"I do not understand you, brother. You are almost as young as I, and yet you cling to the ways of ossified old men."

"When those ways are noble, I do," his brother agreed. But he could see Ealon was having none of it. He changed tack. "Brother, listen. Think strategically. If you do this, what will happen?"

"Every client king on the planet with pretensions to independence will receive a fine warning of what happens when you cross the house of Summerfield."

Cormoran moved his head from side to side. "Or...every king will have reason to rethink whether allegiance to a house that is clearly corrupt and dishonorable is in his best interest. I can think of six royals who might band together to form an insurrection that would topple the house of Summerfield before winter arrives. Hearth might be torn apart—from a united planet under one crown to a squabbling assembly of nation states dragging our people into disorder and chaos. At best we might be looking at mass executions for the house of Summerfield and another interregnum. Did you ever think of that?"

Ealon's eyes flitted back and forth, taking in this information but saying nothing.

"No, it is clear that you haven't," Cormoran sighed. "The other kings look to us to lead. This is right and good. The Mountain and Plain Alliance, which binds the interests of men and dwarfs, also looks to us, not as sovereigns but as the wielders of power—not might alone, but *moral* power."

"If you are averse to killing him, let us capture him. Hold him for ransom."

"Is this your idea of compromise?" Cormoran glanced briefly to the sky. "Firstly, there is no way we could do it without detection. Women can scream, and I have no doubt the lad can as well. And secondly, there is no honor..."

He saw Ealon's eyes glazing over, as the youth readied for another speech. Cormoran shook his head and gave up. He glanced over his shoulder. "We have a battle—"

But the moment Cormoran looked away, Ealon was in motion. His brother did not see the dagger, did not see the quick arc through the air, did not see it bearing down upon the naked part of his neck.

2

Cormoran did not see his brother's lunge, only the widened eyes of the dwarf reacting. It was enough. Cormoran spun around, swiping his gauntlet upward toward his own neck—since that and his head were the only exposed parts of his body. He felt Ealon's blade connect with the gauntlet, and felt rather than heard it as it scraped down the armor covering his arm. With his left hand he reached around and tugged at his sword from where it hung on his right side, popping it out of its scabbard, catching Ealon in the gut with more force than Cormoran had intended.

The prince crumpled to the grass and rolled, clutching at his stomach, barely stifling a groan of protest and agony.

"Shhhh..." Cormoran hissed into his ear. "Unless you still want to face those guards. And make no mistake—I will let them *have you*."

Ealon's eyes shot daggers at his brother even as he struggled to gain his breath.

Cormoran sheathed his sword once more. He grabbed the black piping of his brother's doublet and hauled him to his feet. "If you want to do something to end this war, there is an honorable way to do it. But it is not here." He pointed to the battlefield. "It is *there*." He shoved Ealon in front of him, and gave his brother a kick in the seat of his britches. As they made for the tree line, Cormoran allowed more volume to his voice. "You can fight with honor, or you can huddle in our own pavilion. And then you'd better hope that our enemy has more honor than you."

❧

"SUNDERLAND!" Acting postmaster Elias Bracegirdle's voice carried above the din of the Everdale Courier Services offices.

"By the horn," Ellis swore. "What now?" But he left off sorting his route and padded quickly through the offices toward his superior. Bushy haffolk eyebrows raised as he passed, and a couple of the young women actually shrank as he passed them and then giggled. It was impossible to tell, from Bracegirdle's voice, whether Ellis was in trouble or just being summoned for some other, less fell reason. Ellis poked his head into Bracegirdle's office and tapped at the door. "You wanted to see me, sir?"

Bracegirdle looked every bit a haffolk nearing his seniority, having a round, portly frame, his trousers held aloft with suspenders after the old fashion, with spectacles teetering on the edge of his voluminous nose. Tufts of gray hair clung to the sides of his head and merged with the tufts coming out of his ears. At one time, he had been a stickler for order, but Ellis wondered at the disarray adorning his office now. Next to a picture of the Old Puck, a calendar hung askew, Bracegirdle's retirement date marked in large, splashy red digits. "Sit."

Ellis sat.

Bracegirdle did not look up at him just yet—he continued to scan several pieces of parchment in front of him, nodding and grunting occasionally.

Ellis waited, and he struggled to be patient. He was aware that his route was waiting, and the morning was not getting any younger. Kit would be wondering where he was.

Finally, Bracegirdle looked up at him, and he did not look pleased.

Ellis cocked his head.

"I received a complaint," Bracegirdle said.

Ellis looked away and sighed. "I was afraid of that. I'm sorry about the sneakin'."

Bracegirdle's eyebrows rose. "Sneakin'?"

"This isn't about the sneakin'?" Ellis asked, suddenly tense.

"Do I want to *know* about the sneakin'?" Bracegirdle narrowed one eye.

"Uh...probably not, sir. We just...we got the job done, sir." Ellis squirmed in his seat. He felt smaller than usual.

"Well, whatever *that* was about, *this* is not about *that*. I received a complaint from that idiot Goodfoot. Says you were napping."

Tubber, Ellis thought. He balled his hands into fists. *I'll get him back for that.* "It was first lunch break. Kit went to get some cheese from Farmer Proudspindle, so I took a short doze in the meadow."

Bracegirdle looked like he was chewing the cud. "That...sounds wonderful."

Ellis nodded, beginning to relax a little. "It was a typical day."

"Do you expect to take a nap again today?"

Ellis glanced back and forth. "I *hope* to."

"Good. Wish I could join you." Bracegirdle sighed and set the parchment aside. "Sunderland, no one cares what you do on your lunch break. There are no regulations in the courier's code about catching a quick doze in the middle of your route..."

"I hear a 'but' coming," Ellis said.

"*But*...this busybody Tubber Goodfoot has filed a *formal* complaint, instead of coming to me, which means—however spurious—it is now part of your permanent record and likely as not there will be a formal inquiry. The inspectors will be calling, no doubt. I'll go on record to say it's a pile of rubbish, of course."

"Thank you, sir."

"It shouldn't hurt you, except..."

"The postmaster's position?"

"Yes. I know you applied. And I know how badly you want it." The old haffolk looked around, as if to check to make sure there was no one in the tiny office. Apparently there was not, as he continued, in a lowered voice. "And between you and me, I think you'd do a fine job."

Ellis brightened. "Thank you, sir!"

"But this...complaint is not going to help your chances. It's ridiculous, but it's there. And among the seven applicants for the position, you are now the only one with a formal complaint among their files." He shook his head. "It's not good."

"But surely they'll see that it's sabotage. Tubber is going for the job, too."

"The complaint is anonymous, I fear," Bracegirdle shook his head.

"The snake!"

"Quite."

Ellis felt like Tubber had just punched him in the breadbasket. His ire rose, then collapsed in a pile of ashen defeat. "I didn't have a chance anyway."

"You can get more for your eggs than you're asking, Sunderland." Bracegirdle leaned back in his chair, making it squeak in protest. "The postmaster's committee will be making its decision soon, so if you want to counteract this...sabotage is a good word...naff naff naff..." He seemed to be going through his pockets. He pulled out a scrap of parchment. "Here. I wrote you a letter of recommendation. The clean copy is in your file." He threw the scrap on his desk.

Ellis snatched at it and his eyes went wide as he read. "That's...it's very kind of you, sir."

"It won't be enough," Bracegirdle confessed. "So I'm going to give you an assignment."

"Assignment, sir?" Ellis was not bad at his letters or maths, but he hated book reports.

"It's a prestigious assignment, so when you complete it, that too will be reflected in your file." He winked. "That *may* be enough."

"What sort of assignment, sir?" Ellis was truly curious now.

"Just came over the blips-and-squawks." The old haffolk shuffled through several sheets of parchment, trying to find the right one.

"Blips-and-squawks" was a code invented more than a thousand years previously by a dwarf named Hroffgar. It translated runes or letters into a series of shorter and longer beeps or clacks. The advantage of the code was that it could be transmitted great distances, even through space. It couldn't reach the next galaxy...but then they knew of no one who lived in the next galaxy. Within their own star system, however, and the next, and the one beyond that, it worked just fine.

He apparently found the right paper and adjusted his spectacles. He squinted, then his eyebrows rose higher than Ellis thought possible.

"Well, poke me with a witch's femur," Bracegirdle said. "I misspoke. Sorry, my boy. This didn't come via blips-and-squawks, this came via seerstone." He shook his head. "I didn't notice that before. I'm getting too old for this..." he trailed off.

If a message came via a seerstone, it meant one thing: summoners were somehow involved. Or perhaps there was a need for secrecy. Each of those prospects seemed exciting. Ellis had never met a summoner—at least not to his knowledge. Everdale was a moon of Hearth, so he had met humans aplenty. And of course, dwarfs were a ubiquitous and indispensable presence—nothing got done without dwarfish craft and expertise, unless it be on elf worlds.

Haffolk only existed because men and dwarfs in close proximity inevitably resulted in unexpected unions and unwanted offspring. The Everdale Haffolk Reservation was a beautiful place to live, and Ellis loved it, but no one was under any illusions about what it was—a place to hide the shameful, infertile children of human and dwarfish parents. So men and dwarfs were common visitors to the Dale, but summoners... Ellis' mind reeled with sudden fantasies.

"I'm going to give you this job," Bracegirdle waved the service order parchment at him, "even though Catspittle will moan about it like a goat in labor."

Ellis grinned. Everyone called Felix Axtiller "Catspittle" behind his back. It delighted Ellis that Bracegirdle did, too. Axtiller was the most senior of the couriers, and the most important jobs should, by rights, be his.

"What are you going to tell him?" Ellis asked.

"You leave that to me," Bracegirdle narrowed one eye.

Ellis liked the feeling of being a co-conspirator with his boss. He didn't even think the old haffolk liked him. "I'm your haffolk, sir."

"Good to hear it, Sunderland." Bracegirdle turned and fished out a file. Ellis squirmed internally, as it seemed to take the old haffolk an eternity to do anything. Finally, Bracegirdle selected a blank transport requisition parchment and, dipping his goose quill in ink, began to fill it out. "I'm sending you with some dispatch to Yngremark."

Ellis' eyebrows rose and he felt his innards twist. "Um...off-world, sir? I don't know about going off-world." Ellis felt suddenly faint. He'd been to every corner of the Dale, and he knew Rhory well enough. Ellis had never been off-world before, not even to Hearth, the home world of humans, the planet that Everdale circled as its satellite and celestial companion. His pulse quickened and he found himself unable to sit still.

"You have to go to the job, Sunderland. The job is not going to go to you."

"Yes, but...Yngremark..." he breathed. Yngremark was one of the two planets considered home to dwarfs. Of course, dwarfs could be found on most planets, but the dwarfish culture and architecture of their home worlds were famous. Yngremark had been the first dwarfish colony once they had become spacefaring, but now it rivaled the birth planet of the dwarfs, Ältremark, in its glory.

Bracegirdle sighed. "Look, Sunderland, I don't blame you. No haffolk wants to leave hearth and home and family and naps and second breakfasts—"

"No..." Ellis agreed.

"But you have an opportunity to shine, here, to pull out ahead of the pack, to advance your case..." he lowered his voice, "for postmaster, I mean."

Ellis gulped. He suddenly felt very small indeed. He gripped the wooden armrests of the chair he was in and steeled himself for what he was about to say. "Um...all right...when do we leave?"

Bracegirdle's grumpiness seemed to return. "We?"

"I...uh..." Ellis felt momentarily lost. "Kit usually goes with me—"

"Oh yes, the Cornfeather girl," Bracegirdle shook his head. "Someday she must contribute to society."

"Kit contributes a lot."

Bracegirdle's eyebrows rose, and gave Ellis a look that he took to mean, "Don't push your luck." The old haffolk removed his spectacles and rubbed at his eyes. "How does that girl earn her keep, anyway?"

"I split my pay with her," Ellis said.

"My dear boy, you make a pittance. This is all right with your family, is it?"

Haffolk "families" were not united by blood, but by chance. As soon as a haffolk child was born, it was whisked away to Everdale before it brought shame to any human or dwarfish clans and placed with a haffolk family by lot. For all their artificial origins, haffolk families bonded quickly and well. They were large, usually, often containing twelve or more 'folk of varying ages. Ellis' own family had seven people in it, at present, but they were past due for a new baby.

"Ever since Kit began to accompany me, I...well, sir, I don't get beaten up any more."

Ellis knew he was a bit of a runt—smaller and trimmer than most haffolk—a fact that was not lost on the likes of Tubber. Truth was, he was grateful for Kit, and hardly went anywhere without her.

"Well, you won't be needing her on this trip."

Ellis was about to protest, but Bracegirdle held his hand up to stop him. "I can't justify the expense of another travel requisition. I know the two of you are planted in the same pot, as it were, but this is one mission you'll need to take alone. Now, do you want this job or not, Sunderland?"

Ellis blinked. Inwardly, he was panicking. He had never been on a job by himself. He depended on Kit, not only for protection, but for emotional support. He was terrified of the prospect of going off-world without her. He swallowed and met Bracegirdle's eyes. "Um...yes, sir. When do we...when do I leave, sir?"

"Just after lunch, I should think."

❧

LIAGA THORNHEART WAS NODDING off when he heard the trumpets. His head jerked upright with a mild snort and he looked around quickly to see if anyone had noticed. King Uther seemed to be rousing himself from a nap as well, ensconced as he so often was in the window seat of the great throne room at Caer Trogan. The king loved to look out to sea, and the summoner wondered if perhaps the limitless possibilities of the waters and all the wonders that lay beyond them offered the king a balm for the mind. *There is a place beyond the dreadful minutiae of state*, Liaga summed up that balm, savoring the thought of it. But he suspected there was no place in the world of men, the two worlds of the dwarfs, or the three skyhavens of the elves where that was actually true.

Trumpets could mean any number of things, but listening closely for the song, Liaga quickly ascertained their meaning. The war party was returning, which meant the princes—if they lived—would soon be presenting themselves before the crown and making their report. The summoner was suddenly very much awake.

On the surface of it, his job was to advise King Uther, and to do what limited magic he had at his disposal for the good of the Kingdom of Hearth. His real job, however, was to know everything. He sometimes reported this knowledge to Elsorin, the head of his order. But just as often he kept it for himself. Knowledge, he had come to realize, was more powerful than magic, more advantageous than interstellar travel, more efficacious than the sword. Uther might wear the crown, but it was knowledge that made Liaga the most potent person in the throne room.

Uther called for a tonic, which the court physic brought to him with quick dispatch. The king then settled himself on the throne in readiness for his sons' arrival.

Uther hated the throne. He loved being king of Estenlan, and high king of all Hearth and its protectorates, but the throne itself was old, lumpy, and uncomfortable. He sat in it only so long as he had to. Liaga knew the king's heart, knew the old man would move back to the window seat as soon as decorously possible.

"The princes Cormoran and Ealon, your majesty," the doorkeeper called. Liaga moved to the right of the throne and stood with his hands behind his back. He did not stand straight—a kink in his spine from a riding accident in his youth prevented that. But he stood as straight as he could, an expression of pious expectation fixed upon his face.

The doors swung open and Cormoran entered first, as propriety demanded of the elder son. Cormoran took four swift steps and then knelt, bowing his head and offering his sword, tip to the ground. A moment later Ealon burst into the room behind him. Ealon did not bow, nor acknowledge the king or the court in any way. Instead, he strode with fierce dispatch toward the door behind the throne that led to the royal family's private chambers above. He slammed the door behind him.

Liaga's eyebrows rose at the indecorous display, and he watched the court keenly. Ealon's behavior was an egregious affront to the king, but as Uther ignored it, everyone else did, too. Cormoran rose, his jaw set and his countenance dour. He approached the throne.

"Father, I pray the oyosii have kept you well."

"I give thanks that the oyosii have kept you alive," Uther responded, "both of you. What news of the battle?"

"Surely you've received report by blips-and-squawks."

"Of course, but I want to hear it from you. Battlefield commanders either tell you what they want you to know or what they think you want to hear. Keep that in mind."

Cormoran nodded. It was not new teaching, and he knew the truth of it. "Avantir the usurper has been driven back. The cost was great, but his armies are vanquished. Wybrook is once again without dispute under the authority of the crown. Unity has been restored to Hearth, oyosii be thanked."

Uther nodded. Liaga was impressed. Cormoran had given a report that was free of almost all detail. Everything he said might be true, and probably was—Cormoran was no liar, Liaga knew. But there was much more that he was not saying. It was not Liaga's place to question the prince, but he made a mental note to inquire with his sources to obtain a more robust account.

But Uther seemed satisfied. "And how did your brother?"

"Father, we must speak...in private."

Uther looked around. The room was not packed with courtiers, as it often was, but there were a few of the more stalwart souls in attendance. Liaga counted six nobles and four servants, himself and the physic. Cormoran was right to be discreet.

Uther ignored him, however. "Was your brother not with us in battle?"

"Sunhaven prevented him. Or so he says."

"Sunhaven tries to protect him. He'd keep *you* out of it, if he could."

"Good thing I'm better with a sword than Lord Sunhaven, then."

It was a joke, but Uther did not smile. He seemed lost in thought, troubled by something just over his own mind's horizon.

"Ealon does battle with his own enemies, I fear," Cormoran laid his sword down on the steps of the dais and then sat on the steps himself. In one motion, he had gone from a subordinate presenting himself to his liege lord to a beloved son conversing with his father. "I tried to speak to him."

Uther grunted, but then waved his son's suggestion away. "No...no, I'll talk to him. Although I confess I am at a bit of a loss..." he trailed off, not finishing his thought. Liaga understood the king's frustration with Ealon, but he understood the dilemma of a second son even more, being one himself. "But first I must confer with the generals. Thank you for your...report." He clapped Cormoran on his armored shoulder. "You need a bath."

Cormoran did not dispute this. He smiled affectionately as he stood. He bowed to the throne, and exited toward the family's chambers.

Uther gathered his robes about him. "I'm off," he said.

Despite his best efforts, Liaga was not welcome in the war council. More than once he had made the argument that a summoner could advantageously advise on warcraft, but his efforts had been rebuffed. Not everyone trusted summoners.

As soon as Uther exited the throne room, Liaga turned and headed toward the royal family's chambers. A guard stood in front of the door. The man made to move, then stopped, clearly uncertain what to do. Liaga was a powerful counselor, but the man had a job to do. Liaga smiled patiently. "I need to speak to Prince Ealon. It is a matter of some urgency." That was not true, but the guard could not know that. The man hesitated a moment, then stepped aside. Liaga pressed the handle of the door and pushed it open.

Gas lights gave the hallway beyond a comforting yellow glow—even though the flames themselves were blue. The summoner had been in the private chambers before, and knew precisely where to head. He passed through the garderobe to the stairs which led to the second floor. He paused just outside the prince's rooms and lightly tapped on the door. A few moments later a servant opened it a crack and peered out.

"I would speak to the prince," Liaga said to him.

The door closed and Liaga counted seven before it swung open again. "The prince will see you."

Liaga had expected no other answer, and he pushed into the door without another glance at the servant.

"My lord is in his reading room," the servant said.

Liaga thought a moment, then headed east, ducking through a scarlet woolen curtain draped over a doorway—probably to keep the heat of the fireplace in.

The prince was sprawled on a couch, his foot on a low table before him, knee jutted in the air, higher than his head.

Liaga bowed. "My lord."

Ealon glanced up at the summoner, his face still a mask of anger and resentment. "What do you want?" he spat.

Liaga had always considered the prince the most interesting of the Summerfield house. Unlike Cormoran, he did not march in lockstep with his father's wishes. He did not dance the intricate cotillion of court propriety as his brother did, either. Ealon, sullen as he was, was his own man, and Liaga saw in him the promise of something neither his brother or father would ever possess—true cleverness. Liaga pretended to admire much and many, but cleverness was rare and anyone who possessed it was worthy of attention. Cleverness, after all, could be cultivated into wisdom, and who better to tend the king's garden than his summoner?

"I can see you are...not at ease. I am not your father's counselor alone."

"Anything I say to you will soon find its way to his ears," Ealon said.

"That is not so, my prince." Liaga smiled gravely. "Summoners are trained to value confidentiality. And I serve you as much as I do my lord the king—if you let me. It just...it seems as though a sympathetic ear might be of benefit to you."

Ealon narrowed his eyes. Liaga could tell Ealon was weighing whether or not to trust him. Finally, Ealon sat up and removed his feet from the table. "Forgive me, summoner. I am...not at my best."

"May I?" Liaga pointed to a nearby chair.

"By all means."

Much of the anger seemed to have drained from the prince, for now he appeared more troubled than angry. It was a welcome shift.

"Cormoran is a horse's ass. First that dolt Sunhaven refuses to let me fight, and then... Do you know I nearly killed the Wybrook scion?"

"Did you?" Liaga wasn't at all sure this was the truth, but now was not the time to question it.

"Yes. I had him right in my fist, but Cormoran wouldn't let me at him, or even ransom him. He...some nonsense about honor." He howled in rage. When he calmed down, he said simply, "I piss on his propriety."

"'Propriety is the skeleton of state,'" Liaga quoted the political philosopher Entwhistle. Ealon scowled at him. "But I take your point," Liaga added hastily.

"Hearth needs a strong hand to keep the peace. Hearth needs a strong leader. But father is...failing. And Cormoran...Cormoran is a stiff. If father dies, he'll just do whatever the council tells him to."

"'Tis true Cormoran lacks imagination," Liaga agreed, a little tentatively. Liaga was unsure just how much to reveal of his own opinions. Ealon could be mercurial, after all. At the same time, Ealon was the best of his options, he was sure. "But what Cormoran possesses, what is of great advantage to him, is equanimity."

"What do you mean?" Ealon asked.

"Emotion is a fine servant, but a terrible master," Liaga said, still cautious. "Emotion is like a horse—if it is unbroken, the horse is considered a danger and regarded warily. If a horse is even-tempered, it is trusted and put to good use."

"What are you saying?"

"I am saying..." Liaga paused, wondering if he was going about this right. He chose another metaphor. "The man who wins at a game of whist is not a man who shows his cards. He keeps his cards close to his chest, and only reveals them when it is advantageous to do so. He plays his cards, he does not allow his cards to play him."

"You are not talking about whist..."

"No, lord."

"You are saying that if I am angry I should not let the court *know* that I am angry."

"Precisely, my lord. Not unless the anger card is clearly to your advantage."

Ealon's eyes darted back and forth. "I will consider what you have said, summoner."

Liaga nodded. "I have one more piece of information that might advantage you, my lord."

Ealon's eyebrows rose and he fixed the summoner with a dubious look.

"My lord...forgive me for venturing into...religious questions, but... what is your opinion of the oyosii?"

Ealon blinked. Finally, he answered, "Besides their non-existence?"

Liaga laughed. He had expected contempt, but he had not expected that.

"We on Hearth have two epic lays," Liaga began.

"*The Song of the Scar* and *The Song of the Stone*," Ealon said. "I read them under master Tippleson. Dead boring. I liked the nursery versions better."

"Well, literary concerns aside, when Arrunwulfe brought the Red Horn through and created the scar, he accidentally gave the elder god access to our universe."

"*Blazing scarlet across the canopy of heaven / A gash of blood through which poured / The bane of elves and men*," Ealon recited.

Liaga was surprised. "Very good, my lord."

"Don't patronize me, summoner. I was forced to memorize whole sections of those turgid epics."

"I'm sorry, my lord. *The Song of the Stone* tells how the elder god was banished from our universe, even though the Scar remained."

"What of it?"

"Do you think that was just?"

Ealon cocked his head. "I have not considered the question."

"I invite you to consider it now, then, my prince. The elder god was banished because he did not play by the rules, he neither knew nor honored propriety, and what is more, he was more powerful by far than the oyosii."

Liaga could see Ealon thinking. The bait was dancing before him. It was time to set the hook. "Does it not make sense that the one who holds power should rule?"

"It does."

"Then by what logic did we deprive the elder god of the throne of heaven?"

Ealon stared at him, seemingly motionless, but Liaga could tell there was much going on within.

"I see a little of the elder god in you, my lord." It was a risky thing to say. The elder god was widely considered to be evil. Yet, Samael still had his followers, though most performed their worship in secret. Liaga knew this well, because he worshipped the elder god himself. "If Samael were to be liberated from his prison, he would need a man after his own heart on the throne of Hearth."

"The only way to end the elder god's exile is to destroy the Fängelsten." The Fängelsten was the Dwarfish name for the Prison Stone. One of the first—and greatest—acts of the summoners was to use the Fängelsten to banish the elder god from the universe. The stone had been given to the dwarfs for safekeeping, but that had not worked out as expected.

"But the Fängelsten was lost," Ealon said.

"Yes it was," Liaga said. "But I have it on good authority that it has been...recovered."

Osia Glenfallen struck the heavy oaken door of Summoner's Keep with his walking staff and waited. A raven perched on his shoulder and cawed into his ear. "Don't think too much of this, Jaq," Osia answered. "It will disrupt your digestion. And neither of us needs that."

Jaq pecked at the summoner's ear. "Don't yell at me," Osia insisted. "You're angry because I'm right. You're letting yourself get all worked up."

Jaq grumbled, a series of titters and caws. Osia struck the door again. A moment later, it swung inward, groaning on its great iron hinges. Osia peered into the gloom, waiting. He knew the rules. None entered without permission. An elderly woman with long, wavy hair and bright eyes emerged into the gap of the doors, a guttering candle in one hand. "Osia," she smiled warmly at him. "We've been expecting you."

"Of course you have," he said. "May I enter?"

"Since you ask so nicely." She pulled the door further inward, making room for him to pass. Imras seemed little changed since Osia had seen her last, nearly ten years ago. As guest master, it was her duty to make sure the legendary hospitality of Summoner's Keep did not fail. Seeing her, he was certain it would not fail him tonight.

"And a pleasure to see you, too, master Jaq," she said, giving a respectful nod toward the bird.

"Hel-*lo*," Jaq said. Then he said it again. Then he said it again.

"Enough," Osia told him.

"I have prepared a cell for you. It's a little larger than usual. This one has a chair for reading."

"Ah, Ogthar's old room," Osia said.

"The very one." Imras nodded and pushed the door closed behind him. "Come. You must be tired. How was the passage?"

"Harrowing. Dwarf magic may make the engines that can ferry us between the stars, but they can't stop the blasted ships from shaking."

"No. I hate the shaking," she agreed. "I hope it wasn't too bad." She turned and began to walk down a dim stone corridor.

"The cell isn't this way," Osia said. "It's been a while, but I do know my way around."

"The cell isn't, no, but the kitchen is. One thing about dwarf engines, the shaking makes for some...advanced digestion. You must be famished."

"I would certainly not decline a late meal," he agreed.

"I have it ready."

"You are the best, Imras. I don't care what they say."

She grinned at him. "I have heard that elven ships don't shake."

"'Tis true. They are smooth as glass."

"I wouldn't know."

"It is a rare thing to be allowed the privilege."

"But you have?"

"I have. It is because in dwarfish and human ships, the magic is in forging the engine—dwarfish lore, all of it. And by the horn, they do guard their secrets. But in elven ships, the engines *operate* by magic. It is no faster, but no slower. It is, however, blessedly calm."

"It sounds lovely," Imras said.

"Barring the elves, it is."

She burst out with a hearty laugh, then covered her mouth.

"Forgive me," Osia said. "That was...indiscreet."

"It also happens to be true," she said. "And if you can't be truthful with your friends..."

A few moments later, she turned the corner into the kitchen. She turned on the gas lamps and lit them. A warm glow filled the large room, and Osia's mouth filled with water in anticipation.

Jaq cawed.

"I'm sorry, Master Jaq, but I have no crickets in the kitchen, nor berries at the moment. The others' familiars eat mice and such, which are plentiful, if alive. I do have some stale bread. I hope that will do."

"Food," Jaq said. "Food. Food. Food."

"She is not deaf," Osia complained.

"Food."

Osia sighed. "He's as hungry as I am."

"You just sit yourself down, and I'll have a platter of cold ham and brittle cheese. There are only scraps of today's bread, but it'll go down just as well with the lime marmalade."

"You are too good for this place," Osia said.

Imras set a tankard of beer in front of him, along with a tiny cup of wine. Jaq leaped from Osia's shoulder to the table and immediately dipped his beak in the wine. He cawed.

"Take it easy with the wine," Osia cautioned. "Remember last time."

Jaq ignored him and dipped his beak again.

Imras quickly set out the meat and cheese and put it in front of Osia. Without waiting for the bread, he tucked in.

The ham was saltier than he liked, but it was smoky, and he

relished each bite. Imras next set out the bread, which Jaq hopped over to and pecked at.

"I was going to get you your own bread, master Jaq," Imras put her hands on her hips.

"We'll share," Osia told her.

"Good enough." She set a pot of marmalade beside him. Then she pulled a mug of wine for herself and sat across from him. Osia appreciated that she did not ply him with questions about his latest mission—she knew better. And she also knew that guests often needed time and quiet. Osia was suddenly grateful for the complex ministry she had and how well she performed it. There was a sad smile on her face as she watched Jaq pick at the bread.

"Rumor has it Objor has died," Osia said between mouthfuls.

"The rumor is not true, although Elsorin has done nothing to counter it. Objor suffered a failure of heart. He lives, but he is very frail. He sleeps in a bed for the first time any living summoner can remember. No one knows whether he will ever resume his post. Myself...I think he will not."

"I am truly sorry to hear that. I will look in on him before I go." Osia thought a moment. "The oracle is famous. He isn't beloved, but the *idea* of him is beloved—"

"Yes."

"I fear, if the rumors spread, people might panic," Osia said.

"People will."

Osia grunted. "But the truth about his condition might cause just as much panic. If people know he is failing..."

"I think this is the dilemma that Elsorin wrestles with. Among many others, of course."

Osia shook his head. "I am ever grateful not to rule."

"You are young, yet," she smiled.

He laughed at this. "Back to Objor, if you will. I heard he uttered a prophesy."

Imras looked away.

"Ah. But Elsorin is trying to keep that a secret, too."

"How much do you know?" Imras asked.

"Only what came over the blips-and-squawks. So...not much. Little more than dwarfish gossip."

"Dwarfish gossip is not as spurious as the gossip of men."

"It's still gossip. I want to hear it from the source."

"The source is dead."

Osia swallowed and smiled. "You'll do."

"You should ask Elsorin," she still wasn't looking at him.

He reached out and touched her wrinkled hand. "Imras, you know as well as I do that Elsorin will tell me only what advantages Elsorin."

"He is the head of our order."

"True, but his power is not absolute, as you well know. We must keep each other accountable."

"But it is his decision who should know what, not mine."

Osia grunted again and picked up some of the brittle cheese.

"He'll want to see you," she added.

"No doubt he will. But whether he will be pleased to see me is another matter."

"He sees you as a threat."

Osia did not need to answer. He let the cheese melt on his tongue and savored it.

"Food," Jaq said.

"Try a bit of the cheese," Osia told him. The bird picked at the bread. Osia rolled his eyes.

"You *are* a threat," Imras continued, "because you are a plain dealer. Not everyone likes you, Osia, but everyone respects you."

"I don't know about that—"

"It's true enough," Imras said. Osia could see she was struggling. He covered her hand with his and this time, kept it there. He waited until she met his eyes. He smiled. "You are my friend," he said. "I do not ask you to break your covenants."

She blinked. "Fine," she said. "Objor said, 'Soon, the whole universe will be ablaze...'"

3

"Summon the crown prince...and my enforcer."

"Of course, my lord," Liaga gave a curt bow and turned from the window seat in which King Uther sat staring out at the sea.

Uther did not know why the sea gave him such comfort, but it did. Probably he loved it because *she* had loved it, Melasenvia. The country she had come from was landlocked and the open water had held endless fascination for her. Once he had taken her aboard the royal yacht, for a clandestine tour of the harbor at night. He could not take her by day, for none could see them together. The boat's crew had been...expendable, and their lives were worth the one precious evening they'd spent together. At first, they'd watched the lights of the harbor as they bobbed and shimmered. Then they'd gone below deck for another kind of spectacle. But they could never be together. He was the high king, he must keep and enforce the law. And sometimes he loathed the law.

One boat had traversed the harbor by the time the King heard the clearing of throats. He turned to discover his summoner flanked by his firstborn and his enforcer, Daevis Ennisbrook.

Ennisbrook's face was scarred, though not from battle. Uther had once asked what had torn the man's face up, but his enforcer was an intensely private man who successfully evaded such questions. Uther had let it go. If the man wanted his scars to remain a mystery, what of it? He was an impressive figure, nevertheless, typically dressed in black leather from head to foot, his silver chain of office draped over his shoulders. A rapier hung from his left hip. Uther tried to think back...had he ever seen the man without his weapon? He could not picture it.

Uther took them each in, and they bowed in turn, Cormoran bowing the lowest. *He's a good and obedient child,* Uther thought. *Too bad he's not clever enough to be a good king.* "What hear you from Wybrook? Is Avantir licking his wounds?"

"I spoke to Avantir's summoner by seerstone, your majesty," Liaga said.

Uther's eyebrows rose. "And?"

"She says the man is properly chastened. She promises no more trouble from them. And she has given me her *personal* promise."

Uther cocked his head. "Meaning...what?"

"Meaning that should Avantir betray you again, he will not advance as far as his palace gate before he is brought down."

"She said that, did she? Avantir's summoner?" He looked pleased.

"She did. She knows where her loyalties lie."

Daevis looked skeptical. "I thought summoners had no loyalties, my lord."

"You wound me, sir."

"We wouldn't want that."

Neither man looked at the other during this exchange, and Uther felt tension thicken the air around them.

"Cormoran—"

"Yes, father?"

"I've been thinking about your brother's little...exploit."

Cormoran's eyebrows rose.

"If you hadn't stopped him, if he had secured Avantir's scion..."

Cormoran's face darkened.

"It was an evil deed, father. I could not let it stand."

"Yes...quite right you were, I'm sure. Still... His instincts were good,

I think. Liaga, what would have happened, do you suppose, if Ealon had succeeded?"

"The child would have been brought here under guard and made a ward of your majesty. We would have cared for him, ensuring that he would grow to love your majesty and would be formed by your generous influence."

"My *generous* influence..." Uther turned and looked back out the window. "And Avantir?"

"He would be very cautious, since he would want nothing to happen to his heir."

"Am I right in thinking he has another child?" Uther reminded him.

"A girl, your majesty."

"Hmm," he replied, with a look of distaste. "Still...people have put women on the throne before."

"People dress geese in bonnets and act out milkmaid rhymes at harvest festivals," Liaga noted.

"Ha!" Uther ejaculated. "Geese in bonnets." He turned back to his son and servants. "It would not have been a bad outcome," he said to Cormoran.

"Are you saying I was wrong to stop him?" A dark cloud passed over the prince's face.

"I am saying it would have been fine if you had not, and Ealon would have proven useful for something—which may have been good for him. It may have been good for us."

"But sir..." Cormoran was almost spitting. "It was not honorable."

Uther looked down at his hands, "I think perhaps a bit too much is made of knightly honor in a noble education, don't you, counselor?"

Liaga inclined his head and smiled obsequiously.

"What are you saying, father?"

"Who me? Eh...I'm not sure." The old man drew circles in one palm with the finger of his opposite hand.

"Father, are you feeling all right?" Cormoran asked.

"No! I'm feeling bored and grieved."

"Grieved by what?"

"Grieved that I have two sons, each of whom has received precisely half of what is needed to rule competently. You have the heart and your brother has the brains." He shook his head, and said to Liaga, "They never did learn to share."

Cormoran seemed to shrink. "Father, that is a...that is a cruel word."

"'No word is cruel that is true,'" Liaga quoted.

Uther pointed at his summoner and nodded. Then he turned to his enforcer. "We shall steer a middle path and thereby hope to reclaim some of the booty from Ealon's piracy."

Ennisbrook's eyebrows rose, but he said nothing. His leather gloves were clasped behind his back. He did not rock on his heels.

"You will journey to Wybrook, bearing a gift for Avantir—who retains the title of 'king' under the canopy of my throne."

Ennisbrook nodded.

"Once there you will inform the king of our kindness toward his scion. You will inform him that under the honor due to princes, we refused him the indignity of kidnapping."

"Very good, my lord," Ennisbrook said.

"Then you will inform him that, due to our great amity for the boy and our concern that he receive the finest education—as befits a future ruler—that he be tutored here at the palace at our expense and as our guest."

Cormoran's eyes widened. "Father—!"

Uther held his hand up to stop him. "Avantir will squeal like a boar with a spear in his back, I know. But he also knows I will be seated beside his beloved *kipper* every night with a steak knife at hand. He won't cross me again."

"You will provoke him!" Cormoran countered.

"He's lucky his head isn't ornamenting my castle wall!" Uther raised his voice for the first time. Cormoran shrank at the sound of it. Uther noted his son's response and, satisfied, turned to address his enforcer. "And that is a statement you are at liberty to circulate."

❦

OSIA ROSE to discover he felt hale and refreshed. "'Tis tremendous what a good night's sleep will do for a body," he said.

Jaq cawed.

"I warned you about the wine," Osia scolded.

Jaq cawed. Osia picked up his robe from where he had laid it aside the night before and brushed the raven fewmets from where they had collected on his shoulder. Then he pulled the robe on and stood. Jaq quickly flew to his preferred perch. He cawed.

"More wine will not fix it," Osia said. "You need water, and lots of it. Some grease would not hurt, either. And I can make you a decoction of willow bark, if you like."

Jaq cawed.

"Can you keep your balance, then?"

Jaq cawed.

"Not so bad as that, then. Good." Osia picked up his walking staff and felt at his face. "I need to shave one day soon." He sighed. "It needn't be today."

Jaq cawed.

"Elsorin, yes. I know how you feel. The chicken is dead, no good strangling the corpse."

Jaq cawed.

"I am not talking about a real chicken, no. It's an idiom, Jaq. A saying of the dwarfs."

Jaq cawed.

"Yes...me, too. Let's get this over with."

Osia opened the door of the cell and strode to the kitchen where a cold buffet had been laid out. Osia filled two cups with water and broke a piece of bacon into small bits for Jaq. Then he prepared a plate of bacon, bread, and cheese for himself.

He saw to it that Jaq drank more than his share of water, and coaxed him toward more of the bacon than the bird would normally enjoy. He was relieved to see a bit of the bird's brightness of eye return by the end of their meal. He was just rising when Imras entered.

"I trust you slept well," she smiled.

"Like a sack of root vegetables," he confessed.

"And Jaq?"

"A bit too much wine, I fear."

"Oh, I am sorry," she looked at the bird compassionately.

"It is his own fault. One morning he'll wake up and realize it wasn't worth it."

"I didn't just come to say good morning," Imras said. "Elsorin will see you as soon as you are ready."

"Thank you, my dear," Osia said. Jaq flew to his perch on Osia's shoulder, a patch on his brown robe stained white after years of use.

Imras gave him a quick bow and exited. Osia followed into the hall, but turned to head in another direction. A few minutes later he stood outside the order master's door. With the knot on the tip of his walking staff, he tapped on the heavy oak.

"Enter," came a muffled voice.

Osia pushed the door open and stepped inside.

Elsorin was at a low desk, what the elves called a "side desk," as there was no room for the legs beneath it. The order master was fond of elven affectations, as the artwork adorning his apartment revealed. Osia disapproved, but he showed no sign of it. A fire blazed in the hearth, filling the room with a welcome glow. Osia leaned on his walking stick and waited for Elsorin's attention.

The order master sighed and set his papers down. He looked up. "Is it not time to launder that robe?" he asked.

"Objor has fallen ill."

Elsorin looked down. "Yes."

Osia eyed the reaction closely, conscious of its pretense. "Were you there when he collapsed?"

"Soon enough after."

"A failure of heart, most likely." Elsorin pointed to a chair. "Where are my manners? Sit."

Osia sat. He looked at his order master, but his expression showed little. Time passed. Finally, he said, "I was hoping you would tell me what he said."

"Many have asked this of me, but the Oracle's messages have always only been shared with those who can understand them."

"I feel vaguely insulted."

"Receive it as you will," Elsorin replied dryly. "I will say only that it was a dire prophesy, which I admit I find troubling."

"What is more troubling is that Objor is the last of the oracles. He was always the most reliable, as well."

Elsorin did not dispute this. He looked away, staring into space.

Neither of them was young, but Elsorin looked to be far older. While Osia still had most of his hair and a strong frame, Elsorin was bald and had begun to stoop. He looked far frailer than Osia remembered from their last meeting.

"The unbreakable broken..." Osia said, after a long silence, as if thinking aloud. "The void illuminated..."

Elsorin's brow furrowed; his stare grew sharp. "How do you know this?" he demanded. "Where did you hear it?"

"It wasn't difficult to ascertain," Osia shrugged. "I asked one of the oracle scribes. Those poor souls are starved for conversation. As you might imagine, sitting there watching an old man sleep can be a tedious business."

"They are sworn to secrecy. Engaging them is a gross infraction. You know that."

"Oh, certainly. That's why all that I said was in jest."

Elsorin's glare continued. Osia waited for a reaction, but all he saw was a slight twitch in Elsorin's cheek. At length, the order master spoke again. "Jest or no, I shall be accelerating the rotation cycle of the scribes."

"Fair enough."

Elsorin reached up to massage the bridge of his nose. "Is there anything else?" he added.

"What does it *mean*?" Osia continued. "What do you suppose is 'the key' that 'has been found'?"

"I don't 'suppose'—I know. And the knowledge has kept me awake most nights since."

Then that was why the old man was looking so haggard.

He and Elsorin had never been close. He did not love the elder summoner, but he respected him. Elsorin did not share power as Osia would have preferred, and he loved secrets a bit too much. Yet Osia was bound by strong oaths. While his loyalty lay with the order rather than with Elsorin himself, it was because of his fealty to the order that he obeyed the old man.

Jaq cawed. The raven did not trust Elsorin, and Osia could understand that. The bird was an excellent judge of character, even when he was in his cups. Osia resolved to reserve his judgment until he knew all the facts. But he was pleased to see Elsorin's guard lowering, now that it was established there was no point in keeping secrets. Osia nodded his encouragement.

"I'm going to tell you something." Elsorin did not look at him as he said this. His voice was low, as if they might be overheard. In response, Osia leaned closer to the order master. "But you must not breathe a word of it, especially to men or elves."

Osia nodded his agreement. Jaq cawed.

"The Fängelsten has been found."

Osia felt a chill run from the crown of his head down to the base of his spine. He shuddered from the sudden cold, forcing Jaq to flap to keep his balance.

"The Prison Stone?" Osia repeated, using the language of men rather than its dwarfish name. "Are you certain?"

"Am I certain it actually *is* the Fängelsten? No. I have not held it in my own hands, so I have not been able to verify the claim." The old man nodded. "But the source is reliable."

"And what is the source?"

"Belorin."

"Belorin? Dwarf King Belorin of Yngremark?"

"The same. I received an encoded message from his chief lore master over the blips-and-squawks."

"What did it say?"

"Little. But enough. I have since spoken to him through the seerstone."

Osia waited.

"He was certain. He was also...shaken."

"I don't blame him," Osia said. "I can think of few objects of power so dire."

Elsorin nodded. Osia noted that his long beard had gone nearly white.

"What does Belorin plan to do with it?"

Elsorin did not answer right away. His gaze drifted to the fire, but he did not seem to actually see it. "It was better lost."

"We do not always agree, master," Osia said, "but we agree on this."

"Belorin wanted to keep it for himself."

"Of course he did."

"He thought of having it set into his crown, but it was too heavy. So he ordered the royal jeweler to set the Fängelsten into the breastplate of his armor."

Osia said nothing. There was no need to refute such egregious folly.

"He thought the notion of going into battle with the Fängelsten protecting his heart would cause his enemies to quail."

"That they would, but for all the wrong reasons," Osia said.

Elsorin nodded gravely. "I told the lore master what I thought of that idea."

"I'm sure you did. And did he listen?"

"He was in complete agreement. And...he succeeded in persuading the king, gods-be-praised."

Osia relaxed a bit. But not much. "And the stone?"

"I convinced him that the safest place for it was here at the Keep—in the vault below, beside the Red Horn."

Osia nodded his vigorous agreement. "There is no safer place for such a dread object in all the worlds of the bright beings. It is wise." Osia paused. "This is good news, surely. What disturbs you?"

"I recommended that an armed guard transport it, with summoners present, and with no less than five decoy ships."

Osia nodded his approval. "But?"

"But it is tourney season, and Belorin will not spare any of his troops, nor would he spare any of his fleet." The old man sighed. "They insist on sending it by courier."

Osia sat up, appearing to doubt what he had heard. "I'm sorry. Did you say *courier*?"

Ellis' short legs moved as quickly as possible as he headed toward the *Augmented Bovine*, the Mountain and Plain Alliance transport æthercraft. He clutched his courier bag close to his chest, looking around for any signs of trouble. But there were none. He had thrilled to visit the dwarf planet, despite the strain of its increased gravity, and to see its famed city Braka.

As he expected, the buildings were squat, after the fashion of dwarfs, but what they lacked in height, they made up for in riches. Each of the buildings he had visited, under the vault of the planet's surface, had been ornately adorned by jewels set into the very walls, and aphorisms from dwarfish philosophers and poets had been beautifully carved above most of the doors in the runic style. And these had been government buildings! He could only imagine what the palaces and opera houses and royal markets must have looked like.

But there was no time to explore. He had a job to do, and he was doing it with efficient dispatch. He looked up at the æthercraft. The hull of the galley was burnished copper, gleaming in the warm reddish glow of the landing cavern's torches. The æthercraft was not large, by Alliance standards, nor was it small. Besides the human captain and dwarfish crew, Ellis was sharing the ride with four dwarfs. In the cargo hold, he understood, were more than a thousand barrels of the thick, dwarfish ale called brunöl.

The stepladder into the passenger hold loomed before him. Ellis made sure his courier bag was in a solid position on his shoulder, and then reached for the ladder.

He was relieved to find the ladder made for dwarfish legs, which were close to the size of his own. He had found the ladder made for humans at the ætherport in Rhory almost impossible to climb. But this he was able to clamber up, and within a minute or two, he was being helped into the cabin by one of the dwarf stewards.

His fellow passengers were bantering with one another comically, as dwarfs will do, as they fastened the silver buckles on the leather straps that would hold them to their seats during the flight. Ellis sat near them, but not too near. There were plenty of empty seats, and while he didn't want to isolate himself, he didn't want to appear nosey either.

He set his bag down on the seat next to him and fumbled with the leather straps. One of the stewards paused as she passed. "You look like a diamond among the slag," she said.

"Uh...thank you?" Ellis offered. He had no idea what she meant, but being a diamond sounded nice.

"Having trouble making the buckles work?" she asked.

"They're...complicated."

The young dwarf woman grunted. "Complicated for d'ra—for a haffolk, maybe. Do ye mind?" She gestured toward the straps.

Ellis shook his head. "Thank you," he said as she sat near the bag. That made him nervous, and he reflexively reached for it.

"Oh, something precious, is it?" she asked.

"Uh...no, not really," Ellis lied. "Just a delivery."

"Must be an unusual delivery. We don't get a lot of haffolk couriers here."

That was probably true. Ellis had not seen another haffolk since he'd left Rhory. But he knew that haffolk couriers were famous throughout the Alliance for their dependability and discretion. Because of their low status in society, haffolk were often overlooked and ignored—an ideal situation for a courier who simply needed to get from one place to another with a minimum of fuss.

She fastened the buckle and tugged at the straps. "That ought to hold you, young one."

Ellis did not protest this. In all probability, he was older than she was, as haffolk reached their seniority more slowly than dwarfs did. "Thank you," he said again.

"I'm your cabin steward," she said. "So if you need anything, you let me know. My name is Gürhilde."

"You're very kind," Ellis said.

"I'll get you some brunöl," she said.

"That would be lovely," he said, and watched as she turned toward the galley.

Settling in, he took in the cabin's interior. Haffolk made most of their buildings out of wood, stone, and mud, so it felt unsettling to be surrounded by so much copper. There was nothing pretty about the cabin—it was fitted out for efficiency, not aesthetics, as most dwarfish interiors were, especially their work environments. It was all copper and iron, black rubber, thick glass, and more rivets than Ellis could count. The only wood he saw was the top of the table around which the nearby dwarf passengers were seated. Then he noticed there was a wooden tray in a vertical position beside him. He raised it up, and after some experimenting, figured out how to level it out to provide himself a small table top, even though he had nothing to set on it. It just felt better to have his hands on the warm grain of wood.

The steward returned in a moment with a stein of the brown sticky ale the dwarfs were so fond of, and he received it gratefully. "This is the last you'll see of me before the æthercraft is aloft," she told him. "D'you need anything else?"

Ellis shook his head and watched as she made the same inquiry of her fellow dwarfs. They responded with pleas for more brunöl and a quarter wheel of cheese, and he watched as she waddled to fetch them.

Ellis knew that many haffolk had an irrational fear of æthercraft, arising from traumatic associations from early childhood. All haffolk were torn from their birth parents and families. By law, dwarfs and men were forbidden to marry, but that did not stop them from fornicating. And fornication often led to *kipper*, as the dwarfs called their children.

When haffolk children were born—often to the great shame of dwarfish or human mothers—they were forcibly removed from their homes and sent to the reservation. There they could live out their infertile lives out of sight of the rest of the Alliance. The moon Everdale seemed to the haffolk a paradise, but to dwarfs and men it was a place of shame—not a secret, but not a place mentioned in polite society, either.

Fortunately for Ellis, when he had been transported to the Dale he was too young to remember. Not all haffolk were so lucky. None of his people were adventurous by nature, and few would willingly board an æthercraft, but at least Ellis was not traumatized by the memory.

It seemed like only a few minutes before they were space bound. The dwarfish engines roared as the craft climbed through Yngremark's atmosphere. Once safely in the æther, however, the craft began to shudder as the dwarfish engines, forged with magic that was theirs since the coming of the Scar, hurled the craft faster than the light of the stars.

Ellis had never had brunöl before. He sipped at it cautiously, and his eyebrows rose. He took a larger draught and licked his lips. Then he drained the glass and held it up for more.

Fortunately for him, Gürhilde was still strapped in and oblivious to his request. He put the glass back down and savored the fading taste of the nutty ale. Then he opened his courier pouch and withdrew a short stack of paperwork. Opening his travel writing case, he arranged his short quill and a spill-resistant ink pot and began work on the forms his office would need pertinent to this trip. It was a good use of time, he decided, and would leave him free, perhaps, to do a bit of sightseeing before his scheduled flight home.

The shuddering of the æthercraft subsided to a less dramatic vibration as they found their cruising speed. The sound of the dwarfs' laughter nearby made Ellis smile. He could understand snatches of the dwarfs' conversations, and he enjoyed their ebullient camaraderie. He longed to be part of it, and it made him momentarily homesick for his own family in the Dale.

Item to transport, the form required.

Confidential, Ellis wrote. That was not unusual. Much of their work was confidential, but any form with a customs section would ask, even if he was not obliged to answer—nor indeed even knew, as was the case now.

He was bored with his job. He knew it, and Kit knew it, and he suspected even old Bracegirdle knew it. But he was good at his job, and that gave him a feeling of pride. But a question nagged at the back of his mind.

A moment later Gürhilde walked by with a pitcher containing more brunöl. She paused and raised it, which he took to mean, *Would you like some more?* He cheerfully nodded and she filled his glass. "Can I get you anything else?" she asked. Her command of Hearthentongue was excellent.

Ellis cocked his head and thought a moment. Then he put his finger to his lips to indicate silence and waved her closer to him. She set the pitcher down on his table and took the seat next to him. "Yes, my friend?" she asked, a conspiratorial note in her voice.

"Can I ask you a...what might be a delicate question? About your people?"

She looked around, as if scared. Then he realized she was teasing him. "Of course," she said.

As all dwarfs were, she was squatter than most human or even haffolk women. This did not detract from her beauty, but was, in fact, an integral part of it. Ellis found himself mildly taken with her. Speaking in a low voice, he asked, "Do dwarfs have couriers?"

"Of course. We have a postal system that is the envy of the free worlds."

"Then why would your government hire a haffolk courier? Can you hazard a guess?"

She smiled sadly. "Yes, I can tell you this. But you must not judge us too harshly."

Ellis' eyebrows rose. "All right," he agreed.

"If we suspect there is gold in the ground, we feel compelled to dig it up."

Ellis nodded. That was indeed very dwarfish behavior.

"If we suspect there is treasure, we must discover it."

"Okay..."

"If there is a secret, we become obsessed with it until we know."

Ellis continued nodding, waiting for her to continue. But she just smiled as if that answered him.

"Uh..." his face pulled into a pained expression. "I'm still a little unclear on this."

She bit her lip. "I'll tell you a story."

"All right."

"Blöefonk was a dwarf in the second age, who was given an orb of light by the oyosii. They told him so long as he kept the orb, and kept it intact, he would be undefeated in battle, and our undisputed king. But Blöefonk had a problem—"

"What was that?"

"If he shook the orb, he could hear something rattling within it."

Ellis' eyes widened. "What was it?"

"He did not know. Was it a marble? Or a stone? Or a gold coin? Or was it a magic talisman?"

Ellis was on the edge of his seat.

Gürhilde continued, "The not knowing gnawed at him. It would not permit him to sleep. His servants and family would find him at all hours hunched on his throne with the orb in his hands, shaking it. He became so obsessed with it that he descended into madness."

"What happened?" Ellis asked.

"He finally smashed the orb, for despite all the good it would do for him, he could not abide not knowing what treasure lay within. Within a year, a rival clan conquered the kingdom, and his entire house was humbled."

"What a dire tale," Ellis breathed.

"And we," Gürhilde smiled sadly, "we are his children."

"That is why all your forms require you to disclose the contents of a package," Ellis pointed to his papers.

"Yes."

"So if you need something transported...clandestinely..."

"It is best if we get a trusted friend to do it for us." She glanced at his courier bag. "You don't have anything confidential there, do you?"

Ellis looked at his bag. He looked back at her face. He felt a moment of panic. Would she snatch up his bag and tear into the package? He felt the first tingling of fear in the tips of his fingers.

Then Gürhilde laughed and pushed him back into his seat. "I do believe I had you going, master haffolk."

Ellis chuckled nervously. "Uh...yes. Yes indeed."

"We are not maniacal, Mr. Haffolk. We're just...more curious than is good for us." She cocked her head, enjoying her little joke. Ellis wondered if she was about to kiss him. He hoped so. Instead, though, she leaned in and asked, in a slightly flirting way, "Are haffolk...curious?" She touched the top button on his shirt.

"Uh..." Ellis' mind raced. The question could have many meanings, and some were more desirable than others. But he decided to stick to the surface question. "No. Haffolk are decidedly *not* curious. Mostly, no."

"Well, there you have it," Gürhilde leaned away from him now and stood, taking up her pitcher again. "That is why *you* are here, then."

❧

OSIA DID NOT WAIT for the next morning to travel, and it was clear that Jaq felt his urgency. "Go!" the bird squawked, although he had trouble making the hard "g" sound, and more often than not, it sounded as if he were saying, "Dough!"

Osia understood, however. "Yes, yes, my friend. But I've a feeling we may be in need of a few items...and one of them I fear we may need for a little leverage. I'll need you to stand guard..."

It didn't take long to gather an æthersuit from the vestry. It was old, and its rubber grommets had begun to crack, but Osia reckoned they'd hold for another flight or two. Bundling it up and exiting the vestry, he nearly ran Imras down as he rounded a corner.

"In a hurry, are we?" she asked.

"You might say that," he conceded. "I have talked with The First."

"So you know all."

"I know enough. And I must make haste."

"I'll not ask what is in your pack, but you might want to add this to it."

"Food!" Jaq said.

"Precisely." She handed him a small bundle. "Journeybread and hard cheese. That should keep the both of you."

"I am greatly obliged to you."

"Off with you now. If you don't save us, no one will."

Osia laughed at the absurdity of the statement, but Imras was not smiling. She patted his cheek and turned, then retreated quickly the way she had come.

"We need one more thing, Jaq," Osia said. Retrieving the prize he had in mind without detection required stealth, but Jaq had a keen ear. No one saw them approach the treasury, and within a few minutes they had locked its door and strolled casually away with no one the wiser. With all possible haste, Osia headed for the stairs, the front gate, and the spaceport.

❧

It was not hard to secure passage on a ship, for any ship bound to any destination would suit Osia just as well. Within the hour, they were space bound. It was then that Osia called the oximorginon. The creature arrived almost instantly. The summoner felt a twinge of regret at having to call upon the beast. It was a great privilege and Osia did not want to abuse it. But he also knew it was his only chance of intercepting the Fängelsten before it left Yngremark. Hastily donning the æthersuit, with its large, spherical brass helmet, he stuffed his walking stick into the suit alongside his leg.

"We'll need to make you quite a bit smaller, Jaq. Will that be all right?" the summoner said. He could have just done it, but it seemed respectful to ask permission. Jaq squawked. Osia closed his eyes and connected with the Scar, the source of all magic. He knew there was a world in which changing size was possible, for they had done it many times. As he concentrated, the normally large bird shrank to the size of a sparrow. Opening his eyes, Osia gently placed Jaq on his own head before donning the helmet. "Mind what you do up there," he whispered, and ignored the bird's protests until the clamps were set and the rubber seals tested.

Stepping into the airlock, Osia pulled a lever and prepared himself. A moment later, the outer door swung open to the loud "phoop" sound of oxygen escaping into æther. At that same instant, Osia propelled himself off the far wall toward the brilliant shimmering of the summer stars.

He had not fastened lead lines, for he would not need them. Osia fought down a feeling of vertigo and hoped Jaq could do the same. The bird was prone to seasickness, and he fared little better in the æther.

Osia floated free of the ship and came face to face with the oximorginon. The summoner closed his eyes and reached out with his mind, imagining a world where he could speak to the creature mind-to-mind. And there must be one, for he heard the beast's reply—not in words, but in raw, unfiltered emotions.

He heard affection—for himself? Yes, for himself. It was a difficult thing to take in, yet Osia did not have the luxury of time. More emotions followed. A sense of obligation mixed with satisfaction. Good, then. The oximorginon did not resent the favor.

"Thank you, my friend," his mind said. He wasn't sure the beast could understand his language, but he hoped it would understand his meaning. "I promise not to abuse your kindness."

Jaq cawed in fright as the great beast unrolled before them, revealing itself to be little more than a tubular body with two great wings stretching symmetrically from either side of it. Osia's mind flashed on other, smaller creatures it reminded him of. It was similar to a bat, but its wings were larger in proportion to its torso, like a butterfly's. Its torso was also three times the length of a man or an elf, five times the size of a dwarf or a haffolk.

It was the only creature known among the bright worlds that could travel the vast distances between stars faster than the magic of elves could propel their æthercraft, or the powerful engines wrought by the dwarfs.

Osia spoke soothingly to Jaq as he watched the beast, its wings stretched as far as they could go, coming toward them. He floated straight toward the body of the beast, watching the stars wink out as the great wings occluded them. Then he felt the pressure as the wings wrapped around him, pressing him from all sides.

Then, held fast within the close-pressed darkness, he felt the rush of acceleration.

4

Suddenly, the shuddering began in earnest. Ellis gripped the leather armrests and pushed himself back into his seat, hoping to quell the worst of the shaking by merging with the ship, but it only made it worse. He leaned forward again, making as little contact with the seat as possible—it helped.

He caught the eye of Gürhilde, who smiled at him calmly.

"Okay," he whispered to himself. "She's not scared, so this is normal." But it seemed to him the entire æthercraft might shake apart at any moment.

The dwarfs noticed his reaction and pointed at him, laughing. "Don't dampen yer britches, little haffolk!" one of them called above the din in a thick accent. It occurred to Ellis that he was no smaller than any of the dwarfs, but he said nothing. He looked more like a human than a dwarf, and that might be what they were referring to.

A whine pierced through the rattling racket, and Ellis saw Gürhilde's eyes move back and forth. She wasn't smiling now. Now, he could tell, something was off. Gürhilde picked up a comhorn, holding it to her ear. Her lips pursed as she listened, and her face became grave. She replaced the comhorn in its holder and stepped forward into the cabin.

She began speaking quickly in dwarfish. She spoke for some time, and although Ellis could not make out much of what she said, he watched the faces of his four fellow passengers as they became, in turn, concerned, angry, and agitated.

Ellis opened his mouth to protest, but Gürhilde turned to him and continued, in Hearthentongue. "We're being ordered to stop."

"By whom?" Ellis asked.

"Hearth Royal Intelligence, apparently."

"Royal Intelligence?" Ellis breathed. The HRI was the premiere spy agency on the world of men. What had he stepped into? "Oh, fewmets," Ellis swore.

The whine continued and Ellis looked out of the portal to discover that the stars were no longer blurred, but stationary. The ship was still rattling, however, so it was clear they were still moving. But the shaking had lessened, and in a few minutes it had stopped altogether.

There was a clacking sound and Gürhilde picked up the comhorn again. "Ja?" Ellis watched her eyes carefully, barely breathing. She nodded and replaced the comhorn again.

She made another announcement in dwarfish, then turned to him. "I'm sorry to tell you this, but our flight is about to be interrupted. We're being boarded."

❧

THE ENFORCER IGNORED the scowls as he approached Avantir's throne. The men of Wybrook were a vanquished foe, and he could feel their enmity. *Did this one fight against us?* they might be thinking. *Did he slay my brother or my son?* He did not gloat, nor did their simmering antipathy make him feel uneasy. He accepted it and moved on. He had taken no pleasure in facing these same men on the battlefield, or striking down those who came too near his sword. He had done what his lord commanded—just as he was doing now, presenting Uther's message.

The afternoon sun streamed through the windows, casting a golden glow. Yet it was late, and the shadows were becoming long. The air was stuffy in the throne room, and Ennisbrook wished someone would open a window. He wanted to remove his black leather coat, or at least loosen the catch at his neck, but any such action would signal weakness, humanness, vulnerability. He chose to sweat.

Avantir eyed the Enforcer askance. *If only he'd used such circumspection weeks ago*, Ennisbrook thought, *there would've been no need to lose so many of his men.* Avantir remained silent as the Enforcer strode the length of the throne room and stopped at the bottom step of the dais. He gave the king the courtesy of a slight nod, rather than a bow.

"We are honored by this appearance of High King Uther's might in the flesh. But so soon? The terms have already been drawn up and agreed to. Pray, what else is there to discuss?"

"The high king," Ennisbrook began, "in a show of his benevolence, even to those who attempt to challenge him, has a new offer to be heard."

"And it is?" Avantir prompted, raising one eyebrow.

"That your son, Clendis, the scion of Wybrook, be his guest and live under his roof for a period of time during which—"

Avantir pushed up from his chair, standing quickly. The two opposing lines of guards in the throne room shuddered to attention, with a noise like a roar. "We shall discuss this in my chambers," Avantir announced, walking quickly to a side room. Ennisbrook followed.

The king spun upon him as soon as Ennisbrook crossed the threshold. "What is the meaning of this?" Avantir demanded. "You would kidnap my son? You would do this so brazenly?"

"I fear your highness has misheard me," Ennisbrook replied. "This is a gesture of good faith. Our High King Uther—to whom is due both your fealty and mine—wishes only the best for your family, and he knows exposure to his great court would be a boon to your son when his time comes to lead."

Avantir's eyes flashed, perhaps wondering if this was a threat.

"It would be a profitable learning experience," Ennisbrook concluded. It bothered him that he could not tell if he was convincing enough. He had never been known for his way with words, yet this was the mission assigned to him.

"It would be, yes. But then...why do I not trust you?" Avantir asked, walking away from the Enforcer before turning to look back at him. "Why do I feel that Uther would just as soon *kill* my boy as feed him?"

Ennisbrook's voice grew colder. "May I remind you that I am the emissary of *High King* Uther, and I will not suffer such insinuations to be made in my presence. Rest assured that your child shall come to no harm under High King Uther's tutelage."

"He swears it?"

"The high king swears it. As will I."

"That's good. That's good to hear," Avantir murmured, nodding. "I could not bear the thought of willingly placing him in danger. I would just as soon take his life myself rather than do that."

"That is unfortunate. The high king thinks well of your son, and he would not look favorably on marring something he has taken an interest in. Even by the boy's own father," Ennisbrook added.

Avantir stiffened slightly. "And now you use my boy against me," he murmured. "My boy is nothing but a game piece to you? A game of Cats and Rats—and who shall pounce first?" He sighed uneasily, emitting a sound like a growl. "It is a quandary. You threaten me through him, you threaten him through me. If he goes I fear I will lose him. If he stays I fear he will lose me. These are the stakes you present me?"

"The high king is aware this is a difficult decision for a doting father," Ennisbrook said, "and he extends an offer of one hundred fifty gold pieces to alleviate any burdens."

The king began to pace the room. The Enforcer let him take his time, though he found it tiresome and unbecoming that Avantir found it necessary to declare his thoughts out loud.

"This is vexing... You reach into my very family? You try to divide us, to play us against each other?... But to what end?... A bribe, but one with a certain appeal nonetheless... You use my boy as a weapon against me," Avantir declared, pointing at the Enforcer.

Ennisbrook was beginning to think he had failed at his mission, but then Avantir surprised him by declaring, "Ah, what can I do? So be it! I relinquish the boy to you. Let him stay with High King Uther and learn the ways of his household. *But*," he added, "let him reside with us one more night. One more night under his father's roof, in his own bed, and then you may take him upon the morrow."

The Enforcer nodded his assent. "It is agreed."

"Done," Avantir seconded, whereupon he stepped to a table and grasped a pitcher on a silver platter. He filled a cup with wine and raised it in salute to the Enforcer. "Here, sir knight, we celebrate an agreement with a drink." Ennisbrook noticed there was no move to fill a second cup, so he went for the pitcher and poured his own.

"Your health," Avantir said.

"To the high king," Ennisbrook said, noticing how Avantir, conveniently in mid-swallow, was unable to echo the sentiment.

THE OXIMORGINON MAY BE FASTER than any of the æthercraft of the bright beings, but the journey through the æther still took time. Jaq hopped around inside the brass helmet at first, and Osia was sure the bird would nick his face with that sharp beak—not maliciously, but inevitably, as he fluttered nervously. Eventually even Jaq had settled down, coming to rest on the concave bowl of the helmet just under Osia's chin.

There was no way to gauge their progress, as all three of the helmet's portals were covered by the great leathery wings, wrapped tightly around Osia's æthersuit. It was darker than midnight, leaving Osia alone with the sound of Jaq's breathing and his own dire thoughts.

His brain raced as he thought of the consequences of the Fängelsten's discovery. Much would depend, of course, on whose hands the fell stone ended up in. Osia cursed the dwarf king for his carelessness. On the other hand...there was a brilliance in treating it just like any other transport. The armed guard, the decoys, the summoners—surely that would have aroused suspicion and drawn attention. And yet, on balance, the prudence of it would have been preferable. One thing Osia knew: even without a guard, even without decoys, one summoner in attendance upon it was better than none.

Elsorin had given his grudging approval. The order master found it almost intolerable to admit that any idea of Osia's was good, and he had been loath to give his blessing. He indulged himself a thought for the estrangement between himself and his order master. Once they had been close. Elsorin had groomed Osia as his apprentice and eventual successor. Yet it had not turned out as the order master had hoped. Instead of obeying his every whim, the young summoner had turned out to have a mind of his own. Osia questioned the why behind things, including Elsorin's own motivations, and the elder summoner had found such impertinence irritating. And when, during the battle against the elf usurper Abyllon Tar, when Osia had disobeyed Elsorin's direct order, the tension between them became a rift from which they had not recovered.

It did not matter that, had Osia obeyed, he would be dead now, along with many innocent elves. What seemed to matter most to Elsorin was the affront. It pained Osia to think of it, even after all these years, but there was no avoiding the past...or the present awkwardness of their relationship.

It must have been hours later, but eventually Osia felt a rush of blood in his head that told him that they were turning or stopping, or that in some other way the oximorginon had changed course and the unavoidable effects of inertia were in play.

Indeed, the summoner felt the pressure around his æthersuit decrease, and through the front porthole, watched one of the creature's leathery wings unroll before him, revealing the twinkling brilliance of stars and the bright copper nautilus shape of a dwarf æthercraft. Beyond it was the vast red circle of the planet Yngremark, lesser seat of the dwarfs.

With a gentle push in the small of his back, the creature sent Osia spinning toward the airlock of the ship. Reaching out one stiff glove, the summoner caught at one of the handles and pulled against the inertia of his body, hauling himself toward the safety of the airlock.

The lock shut behind him, and he felt pressure once more on his æthersuit, but instead of wings, this time it was from the atmosphere rushing into the chamber. A brass gauge told him when it was safe to remove his helmet, and as soon as he did so, Jaq leaped into the air and stretched his wings, resuming his accustomed size and cawing loudly in protest.

"I know you don't like it," Osia said to him as he removed the suit. "We must often do unpleasant things in the service of the good."

Jaq cawed.

"It is *not* pious clapperjawing, it is the simple truth. And I'll ask you to watch your tone."

Osia set the copper helmet on the floor and cranked the lever by the inside hatch of the airlock.

As soon as the hatch swung open, Osia stooped and stepped over the gunwale.

He was met by two sword-wielding dwarfs of fierce affect, as if Osia's mere presence was an affront to them. But Osia was used to dealing with dwarfs. He drew himself up to his full height, which, when one included the hat he sometimes wore, was a formidable size in comparison with a dwarf. He held his walking staff aloft in one hand, and spread his arms wide to fill the space as much horizontally as vertically. He widened his eyes and stared down his nose at the dwarf guards.

Their shoulders had already sagged once they discerned their stowaway was a summoner, but this little dramatic display made the poor guards quail. Osia felt a stab of guilt, but he did not let it stop him. He flourished his arms as if to cast a spell, but then thought better of it.

Of course, magic did not work like that, but most people did not know this and it was often advantageous to play upon people's superstition rather than on actual magical theory or practice. A part of him hated deceiving people, yet a part of him enjoyed the play of it immensely.

When Jaq cawed at them and set to flittering around the room, the two guards nearly jumped out of their skins. They dropped their weapons and almost crawled over each other as they backed away, cowering.

Osia softened. *Enough*, he thought. "You are about to land at the main ætherport in Yngremark, yes?"

The two dwarfs nodded slowly, eyes wide. Good. The oximorginon knew what it was about, and had placed Osia before a ship going precisely where he needed to go, and within minutes of getting there.

"Here is enough gold to square my brief passage," Osia pressed a shilling into the hands of each of the dwarfs. "I trust that will find its way to the appropriate person?"

The two dwarfs looked at each other, then back at the summoner. Then they pocketed the coins. "T'won't be a problem, Mr. Summoner, sir," one of them said, in perfectly understandable Hearthentongue.

The other pointed to a seat with straps and buckles. "'Tis only cargo aboard, but...'tis probably safest for you to stay right here. It being we're almost there."

"I understand you perfectly, my bearded friend," Osia said, sitting. Jaq flitted to his shoulder. He began to adjust the straps and buckles. "Go on about your duties," he said, not bothering to look up at them. "I needn't trouble you any further."

❧

AVANTIR PACED IN HIS CHAMBER, his teeth grinding as he ran over and over the options in his mind. It was a mercy, he reminded himself, that his daughter was off-world at her studies. As with most princesses, she had been sent to be educated at a Women's House, living with those dedicated to the worship of the oyosii. Avantir did not know what he'd do with himself if Uther was able to lay a claim on *her*, to marry her to one of the two princes for instance.

Opening the door to his chamber, he called to his manservant, "Send for Graisellis. Immediately."

Graisellis must have been near, for his servant announced the arrival of his summoner only a few minutes later. She bowed before her king and he lost no time in relating Uther's enforcer's "offer."

Her lips puckered as he related the sour details. "This is an ill-wrought deal and I would counsel against it," she said.

"It is too late for that," Avantir said. "My hands are tied. I need to know what to do henceforth."

"I share your reluctance to treat with the high king," the summoner said. "I sense the ill-intent behind the offer. There are other reasons they want to take your son from you, but perhaps you can give your son a different reason to go."

Avantir was intrigued by her words, nodding for her to continue. "I have spoken to Liaga, Uther's summoner," Graisellis continued. "I have informed him that you are—my apologies—suitably cowed, following your defeat. They would never expect it if you attacked them."

"Are you blind for a seer? They routed us!"

"No. Not with your armies. You can attack them from within."

"You...you would use my boy as a weapon against *them*?" Avantir asked.

"My king," Graisellis began, "I know my truth is harsh, but you know yourself that your son is already in danger. Wouldn't it be better if you, through him, were given a way to strike first?"

His father's heart quailed at putting his son at risk, but he could also see the wisdom in her words. It would require much from his son, but its success could change everything. The vision of besting Uther, of taking control of the realm, of being on top at last, glimmered before him with tantalizing propinquity. It made his heart beat faster.

He knew his summoner spoke true. It was a daunting proposition, but this was an opportunity he didn't want to pass up. Dismissing Graisellis, he descended deep into the castle to consult with his chemists. He asked them for something odorless, colorless, and tasteless; something lethal and fast-acting. And by nightfall they delivered to him a metal flask, filled with a cloudy liquid derived from an oxide of preneurium, which Prince Clendis could hide among his things and take to the court of Uther, the so-called "high king."

Avantir found Clendis just before the young man was retiring for the night. He told his son of the adventure that would await him tomorrow, but he also told him about the metal flask. Avantir could see the worry on his son's face, even before Clendis's eyes began to fill with tears. By his own hand he was fashioning his son—the boy whom he had tried to shelter from battle—was being introduced to spycraft, assassination, regicide. The king's heart nearly broke as his son accepted the flask from his father. Staring at the flask the boy's head hung low, in uncertainty, perhaps, or dread. "You must use that, my son" Avantir began, but his voice failed him. "Use that... Use it on Uther when the perfect moment presents itself."

As Clendis listlessly turned the flask over in his hand, the father found himself examining his son's face. The strong neck muscles, the softness of his cheek, the delicate lashes that some young lass might notice. He focused on it with such intensity, it led him to wonder if this might be the last time he would look upon his scion.

His instinct was to throw his arms around the boy, to shield him; but he knew the time had come for Clendis to wage his own battle, to become a veritable weapon for his people, sent to strike at the heart of Uther's kingdom. "Our future is there in that bottle, my son," Avantir whispered. "Be as strong as I know you can be."

"Yes, father," Clendis replied, but his voice sounded timid and far too inexperienced.

"BOARDED?" Ellis whined. "We're being boarded? By whom, the HRI?"

She nodded.

Ellis looked at the package on the seat beside him. *It can't be me,* he reasoned with himself. *There might be lots of reasons why the HRI is stopping the ship. Perhaps one of the dwarfs there is a spy? Or a traitor?* His brain churned, but a part of him knew.

The boarding tubes clanked as they were positioned, and within a few minutes, Ellis felt a shudder beneath him which he didn't understand. A moment later a tall man of about thirty years entered, wearing a crisp military uniform. His hair was black as midnight, short, and he had no beard. His cheeks had a sharp angle to them, and his eyes were small and quick. Behind him was a dwarf with bushy red hair bursting out all over like the mane of a lion. His eyes were angry, serious, and appeared to miss nothing. His hand was on the hilt of his ax as if daring anyone to move or even to speak. In his other hand hung a small, metal travel case. It made Ellis wonder if perhaps the ship had been stopped simply so this latecomer dwarf could make his flight. But neither the dwarf nor the man appeared rushed or harried. In fact, the man took his time to appraise the cabin and its unsettled passengers.

"I am special agent Fineas Brill of the HRI, on assignment from his majesty the king. And this," he pointed at the dwarf beside him, "is special agent Tumnis." He flashed an ID too quickly and at too great a distance for anyone to read. "All you subjects of the Mountain and

Plain Alliance owe us your cooperation, by dint of your fealty to King Uther and his allied sovereigns among the dwarfs." He paused after this announcement, but no one challenged him. No one dared breathe.

"Are there any d'race aboard?" He looked directly at Ellis.

Ellis tried to shrink back into his seat, his hand going involuntarily to his courier bag.

"I see that there are. Madame steward," he turned to Gürhilde. "We will need a private place for my interview."

"This is a small ship, special ag—" Gürhilde halted, apparently catching the steely look in the agent's eye. "Right this way, sir."

"Mr. D'race, after you, please." Special Agent Brill gave Ellis a smile so nasty he shuddered.

Ellis fumbled with his restraints, but his hands were shaking too badly to work them. Gürhilde seemed to notice and rushed to him, quickly undoing the buckles. "Follow me," she whispered.

Ellis slung his bag over his shoulder and padded after Gürhilde. She led him through a dim, narrow passage, so narrow that Ellis wondered if the special agent would be able to traverse it. *That is not my problem*, he reminded himself. But when he glanced back, he saw that the human HRI agent was not far behind, although he was crouching and moving sideways with an awkward gait.

A moment later, Gürhilde and Ellis emerged in the engine room. Two dwarfs were there, naked to the waist, beards dark with coal dust. One had a shovel in hand.

"I have need of this room," Gürhilde said, in a voice that brooked no dissent. "Now."

The engineers glanced at each other and shrugged. One closed the blast door of what Ellis assumed was a backup furnace and pulled on two red levers. Then he rubbed ash from his hands and followed his fellow into the passage Ellis had just traversed, pushing past the agents with a curious stare.

Gürhilde stood near Ellis and placed a supportive hand on his shoulder. Brill moved into the center of the room, still stooping uncomfortably. After hitting his head on a brass valve, the agent opted to kneel, one knee to the floor. As he was bent over, Ellis saw a medallion swinging from a chain on his neck. His eyes widened and his hand involuntarily felt for his own.

His spine straight again, the agent regained his innate formality. His face radiated self-conscious power and an arrogance that Ellis immediately hated.

"So, my little friend, let's get down to business, shall we? You are a courier?"

Ellis nodded.

"Then we are not that different, you and I."

"We're not, sir?"

"No. We go where we are told by those above us. We are given missions we do not choose. We are...directed, are we not?"

"That is certainly true for me...speaking for myself, I mean. sir." Ellis' palms were sweating. He felt Gürhilde's hand squeeze his shoulder. Brill must have noticed the show of support, because he immediately looked at her and said, "Leave us." With one final squeeze, Gürhilde moved away.

Brill remained staring at Ellis, but then, after a length of time, he glanced over his shoulder. Presumably satisfied Gürhilde was at a sufficient distance, the agent at last resumed the conversation. "We have it on good authority that you are carrying an item of interest to the state, an item that could prove dangerous if it fell into the wrong hands."

"Dangerous, sir?"

"Quite. Of course, it might just be a rumor. That is why we are here. To investigate." He smiled. "I'm sure you want to keep people safe, don't you?"

"Of course, sir."

"And it isn't just human lives at risk. Dwarfs and haffolk lives, too, are in danger if this rumor should turn out to be true."

"Gods forbid it, sir."

His nose rose in a sneer. "Yes...the gods." He grunted. "The day the oyosii do anything for us, I'll quit the HRI and become a tanner."

The dwarf at his side guffawed at this, but then stopped quickly when he noticed he was the only one laughing.

"Please, your bag, courier." Brill smiled, but it was a smile full of teeth. "Now, if you will."

5

Brill stood with his hand extended, waiting for his prize. Ellis hesitated, feeling he should stand his ground, should demand a closer look at the agents' credentials, or maybe ask for a barrister to defend him. Kit would know what to do, he realized. But he had no way to reach Kit right now. His forehead began to perspire, his reluctance becoming palpable; but, seeing no alternative, he handed his bag over. It was slack, containing only one item: a rectangular box of dark wood, surprisingly heavy, engraved with minimal decoration and etched with a few dwarf runes, secured by metal bands and small locks.

The dwarf agent smiled, nodding in approval at its appearance. Brill handed the box to him and the dwarf's eyes gleamed. He gazed upon the box almost reverently before gently setting it on the floor beside him. Then, reaching off to the side, he grabbed a crate and swung it in place between the three of them, whereupon he set his travel case on it.

"My assistant," Brill explained, "is an experienced inspector of suspicious packages, with, for obvious reasons, a focus on objects of dwarfish provenance."

As Brill spoke, the dwarf flipped the travel case's latches and raised its lid. He removed a small device from the case, a narrow handle ending in what looked like needle points; and with it he easily unlocked Ellis' box. Agent Tumnis opened the box, showing the contents to Brill.

"What is this?" the human agent murmured. "Can this be true? Do my eyes deceive me?" He looked to Ellis. "All this botheration for a bit of *rock*?" He turned the box toward Ellis and the haffolk could see there was nothing within but a flat black stone with red streaks. "An interesting look, I grant you, but hardly a gemstone—so what's the point, eh?" Brill shook his head and then handed the box back to the dwarf. "But who are we to question the order-givers, right?" Brill added with a chuckle, which Ellis echoed half-heartedly. "Ours is but to execute them."

Tumnis set the box down. It was briefly obscured by the open lid of the travel case, but Ellis was reassured by the sound of the locks being snapped shut again, as they should be. This done, the dwarf passed the box back to Brill. Giving it a shake, showing it was not empty, the agent returned the box to Ellis, who received it in what he hoped was less than obvious relief.

"There," Brill said. "See? All done and nothing to it. Obviously some mistake has been made—but that is our concern, not yours. There's no need to hold you up in your...couriering... any further. You are free to go about your business, with our thanks for your patience and cooperation." The words were most courteous, but there was an edge to them that Ellis did not quite understand. Perhaps they sounded too rote. Perhaps this man was as tired of his job as Ellis was of his own.

The agent gestured ahead, signifying that Ellis should lead them, and they made their awkward way back to the cabin. Ellis found himself clutching the wooden box to his chest. It took him several moments to remember it was better concealed in his bag. Ellis regained his seat, the man and dwarf departed, and the ship began its shudder again. Ellis hardly noticed it, however, as he was shaking on his own.

THE SUMMONER'S landing was uneventful, save for getting a faceful of raven wing when the ship bucked on its springs upon contact with the stone of the landing pad. Jaq settled down and Osia began quickly setting to the buckles. Once free, he found the loading ramp and surprised everyone by pushing past the dwarfs unloading their cargo, ignoring their cries of, "Ah!" and "Hey!"

He didn't have time to explain his presence to anyone. He looked up at the ceiling of the grand cavern. He had visited Yngremark many times over the hundreds of years of its development, and it didn't take him long to get his bearings. As soon as he reached the street, he hailed an open carriage, and within minutes he was clopping away toward the castle.

Osia watched the streets as they slid past, but he didn't really see them. In his mind he turned over the dread possibilities the Fängelsten presented. He could think of no good outcomes. He shuddered. He wondered what kind of approach might yield some success with King Belorin.

Belorin was like most dwarfish royals, Osia mused. At turns, he was gregarious and brooding. He threw lavish parties but kept his secrets close. He was prideful and lusty—his appetite for women, gold, and power was formidable. Osia bit at his lip and wondered if he might use that to his advantage.

"Beer," Jaq said.

Indeed, they were passing a street vendor offering rough wooden tankards for a penny.

"You never learn," Osia sighed.

A few minutes later the carriage pulled up at a rock face that housed the servants' entrance to the palace, as instructed. Osia paid the man and tapping his staff on the cobblestones, set off with great, swift strides toward the servant's entrance.

Amazingly, no one challenged him as he entered. There was no question what he was, and probably little question of who. As summoners go, Osia was the subject of many a tale—many of which were true. Or true enough. He carried himself with an authority that brooked little opposition. And few people were willing to challenge a summoner, anyway. Even if they didn't know how magic worked, the fact that it did work was not disputed. The economies of the collected worlds of dwarfs, men, and elves depended on it.

Osia was sometimes known as "the young summoner," as opposed to Elsorin. It was true that he was younger than his order master, but far older than any living bright being, save some of the elves. He looked to be on the young side of fifty, and that was what people meant. He had been an ordinary man, once, born more than a thousand years ago, at the end of the last age. Magic had changed him, but his appearance was still that of a human of about five and forty years.

He wound his way to the throne room. At first, the guards crossed their spears to bar his passage. Perhaps it was his fierce affect, or his familiar with wings spread wider than the summoner's shoulders, or the fact that he charged straight toward them with no sign of slowing, but just as he drew near them, they uncrossed their spears and stood aside. He continued his charge into the throne room without slowing down.

"What's this?" King Belorin said, a grape halfway to his mouth. His black beard was wet with ale, and his dark eyes narrowed. They went wide when he recognized his visitor.

"Osia? To what do we owe this...honor?"

Osia halted three paces from the king and pounded his staff on the stone floor to announce his arrival. It was an unnecessary dramatic flourish, but it was the kind of thing Osia had found useful over the years. The sound echoed throughout the stone hall.

The king had descended from his dais for lunch at what was really a very modest table set to one side of the throne room. Osia recognized it as the table at which the scribes sat when court was in session. A sumptuous midday meal was set before him, which the king seemed to have only just begun.

"You have found the Fängelsten." Osia got straight to the point.

"One of our finest miners found it. 'The mountain gives up her treasure, a generous boon for the people under the earth,'" he quoted.

"That stone is not a boon," Osia hissed. "It is the bane of all bright beings."

"I thought it was the *salvation* of all bright beings," the King countered. "Or do I have my lore mixed up?"

"So long as that stone is left alone, you are not wrong, Belorin son of Belára. It keeps the elder god at bay, for the salvation of all bright beings. But it was best lost, where none could tamper with its purpose."

"It is a stone of great power," Belorin waved a turkey leg at him.

"It is a stone of dreadful power, which is why it belongs at Summoner's Keep. You were wise to agree to have it placed in our care."

"Was I?" Belorin narrowed an eye at him. "Why are you here?"

"I am here because I have heard you plan to transport the stone by simple courier."

"So what if I do?"

"No armed guard? No summoner escort? No decoys?"

"Time and cynicism has addled your brain. You worry too much." Belorin waved a hand. "I don't have time for such nonsense. The tourney season is upon us. If I called any of my officers away to *kipperset* I'd have a mutiny on my hand."

"It is only a mutiny at sea or in space," Osia corrected him.

"And it is impolitic to correct a reigning sovereign."

"Not when that sovereign is a fool."

Crimson colored the dwarf's face behind his beard. "You waste my time, summoner. If it was your purpose to shame me, you have failed. If your errand is to provide your precious 'summoner escort,' you are too late."

Osia's shoulders sagged. Despite his haste, he had been afraid of this.

"The stone has been packaged up, put in possession of a trusty haffolk courier, and is underway even as we speak."

"When is it due to arrive at the Keep?" Osia asked.

"Who said it is headed for the Keep?"

❧

THE SHIP BEGAN to shake again, waking Ellis. Wiping the sleep from his eyes, he looked out the nearest porthole and saw the planet Ältremark looming before them. Ellis had not been to the home world of the dwarfs before, but from his reading and travelers' tales, he knew it to be a grim, dark world dominated by rock and volcanoes. Yet upon this unlikely foundation, the dwarfs had built a formidable civilization —although it was mostly underground.

Ellis' eyes widened as he saw that, indeed, instead of coming down on a typical landing pad in a field, the ship was descending into a crevasse. Ellis saw great sheets of rock rise before him as the ship continued its descent. Finally, he felt the springs give as the æthercraft found purchase on solid ground.

The dwarfs seemed not to be fazed by this at all, and Ellis breathed a great sigh of relief. He succeeded in removing his own buckles this time, and clutching his courier's bag to his chest once more, he queued up behind the dwarfs, hoping to catch sight of Gürhilde once more. He brightened when she stepped into the cabin. She waddled over to him, and in a low voice said, "How are you, dear?"

"I'm fine."

"Rum thing, that was."

"Yes, but it's all right. Thank you for your support."

"It was nothing, my dear. Where will you go now?"

He pointed to the bag with his chin. "I'm to take this to the vault at the royal library, and then I'm off back to Everdale. Have you ever been to Everdale?"

"No," she smiled coyly at him. "But I'm sure it's lovely. And what will you do then?"

"Well, I hope to make postmaster." He stood just a little straighter as he said it. A part of him, he knew, was trying to impress her. But instead of looking impressed, she gave him the same look a girl gives a cute puppy. "I hope you do." Then she leaned over and planted a kiss on his cheek. "You be good to yourself, now, Mr. Haffolk."

Mildly paralyzed by the kiss, Ellis could only manage a squeak and a weak nod. Gürhilde patted his arm, and walked away down the corridor.

Ellis sighed audibly. "I could make a life with a girl like that," he said under his breath.

One of the dwarfs in the queue heard and his eyebrows bunched in indignation.

Ellis gulped. "Uh...if she were a haffolk, that is, of course, uh...oh boy."

The dwarf narrowed one eye at him as if to say, *I'm still not sure about you*, but he turned back to his fellows just the same.

Just then the great circular copper hatch opened, swinging outward and upward, and the dwarfs were stepping out onto the ladder. Ellis followed them, slinging his courier bag over his shoulder.

Once on the ground, he showed his paperwork to the customs officials, who seemed to have been waiting for him, for one of the officers gave him an escort. The officer waved for Ellis to follow, and struck off quickly and efficiently down a service corridor.

The dwarf was a little shorter than Ellis himself, with typically bushy eyebrows that were as brown as a squirrel. Although the dwarf's beard was long and luxuriant, the hair on his head was shaved close.

"I'm Ellis," Ellis said, struggling to keep up.

The officer said nothing.

"'I'm a customs officer. Nice to meet you, Mr. Ellis,'" Ellis said in a sing-song voice. The dwarf stopped and glared at Ellis.

"I'm uncertain about dwarfs and their sense of humor," Ellis confessed to the glaring officer.

"Are you mocking me, haffolk?"

"Decidedly not, sir. I'm..." Ellis realized he was about to really step in it. But with all that had gone wrong today he decided it probably didn't matter. Besides that, he was tired and not keen to tolerate rudeness. "I'm reminding you to be...polite."

The dwarf looked conflicted. Ellis half expected to be yelled at, but clearly he had struck a nerve. "You're right. My wife has been saying the same." The dwarf looked uncertain, then resumed his path.

It wasn't an apology, but it was something. A moment later, the dwarf said, "I'm Officer Nebblebit Charn of the Royal Customs and Planetary Protection Service. I am at your service." He did not look at Ellis as he said this, nor did he offer his hand, but Ellis took it as a mild victory in what was otherwise a dubious day.

The dwarf led him through a grand archway, its crown festooned with runes set in colorful tiles. They emerged onto a busy subterranean thoroughfare. Gas lamps were set into the stone walls and a string of bright lampposts illumined the street as far as the eye could see, giving everything a cheery golden glow.

Ellis' mouth gaped as he took in the enormous cavern. Above him he could see great looming jags of stone, and he wondered why they weren't falling on his head even now. He felt the hair on his forearms prickle and stand up straight. All around him dwarfs—more dwarfs than he had ever seen—bustled from one place to another. Some were in groups, laughing. Some pushed past him, heads down, hands in pockets, hurrying to their destination. Passing a pub, he heard songs spilling out into the street, and he couldn't help smiling. For all of Ältremark's strangeness, some things never seemed to change.

The shops lining the street were busy with customers, and Ellis wished he had the leisure to explore them. He identified a stationer's, a hearthweedist's, a chemist's, and several shops selling books and broadsides. Clothes stores there were in plenty, haberdasheries, and cobblers' stalls as well. No one seemed to notice him, and it seemed that there was scarcely a detail that he did not drink in.

"Do all haffolk drool?" Officer Charn asked.

Ellis wiped his mouth. "Sorry, Officer."

"We're going just through there."

Ellis looked up and saw the edifice of a large and impressive building. It wasn't a free-standing building—there weren't any of those. It was the façade of a building, its interior cut deep into the rock behind it. But the façade itself was a sight to behold, with large marble pillars and runic designs of such complexity that Ellis could scarce tease out where one rune ended and another began.

"What is this place?" Ellis asked.

"Can't you read?" Charn snapped, pointing to the runes. "It's the royal library. This way." Charn led him not up the stairs past the columns as he had expected, but through a small door to one side of the façade. *Of course,* Ellis thought, *the service entrance. It can't be behind the building, for there is no building, and how would we get there? "Behind" is deep in the earth.*

Once through the door, Officer Charn led him up a sloping ramp to an interior door, holding it open for him. Ellis passed through, ducking (although he needn't have done) and stepped into a large interior chamber. His eyes were well adjusted now, so that the gas lamps in the chamber seemed quite bright. The room had a series of counters and tables, most stacked with books or scrolls. Each counter and table had at least one librarian at work. It took him a moment to realize that the paneling on the walls was actually shelving.

Charn gestured toward one counter where an elderly dwarf presided. Her spectacles were thick, and Ellis could see them distorting the images behind them, so that every now and then, when the angle was just right, her eyes looked frighteningly large. There was a short line, and Ellis clutched at his bag as he waited. Charn stood by the wall near the entrance, surveying the chamber. *No doubt looking for suspicious types*, Ellis thought.

A few minutes later, Ellis was at the front of the line, and the she-dwarf peered up at him and waved him forward. Ellis placed his courier bag on the counter, but before opening it, placed his paperwork before her. "I beg your pardon, missus, but this delivery requires a second-level manager to take receipt."

The dwarf scowled at Ellis, but without a word turned and waddled away. A minute later, she returned with a dwarf who looked much younger than she. He was also thin and tall for a dwarf. In fact, if Ellis hadn't known better, he would have taken him for a haffolk. The young dwarf stepped up to the counter. "You needed a second-level manager?"

"I do. I have a secure package delivery from King Belorin of Yngremark." Ellis pointed to the papers. The young dwarf took them up and scanned them, examining each sheaf in turn. Ellis watched patiently as his eyes moved quickly over the lines. Then the young dwarf's eyebrows shot up. "Oh. *This* package. I was told to expect this package. This is a Very Important Package."

"Indeed," Ellis agreed. He glanced at the dwarf behind the second-level manager, who suddenly did not look so resentful.

"It requires an examination upon receipt," he said, pointing to a checkbox on the papers. He glared back at the dwarf behind him. "Ebba, I'll need the royal key ring from the safe. Ask postmaster Applewine to secure those for you, won't you please? And be sure to tell him that *the package* is here."

Ebba seemed almost eager now as she waddled away.

The young dwarf signed several of the forms, and handed two of them back to Ellis to confirm receipt. Others would be filed, and one would go to the office of blips-and-squawks to transmit a confirmation back to Yngremark. The manager ducked under the counter and retrieved a generous square of black velvet, unfolding it and draping it over the counter. He patted it. "You can place the package here."

Ellis reached into his bag and placed the box in the middle of the velvet square. Then he and the dwarf just stared at it as they waited. A heavy oak door opened and another dwarf emerged, followed by Ebba with her thick glasses. This new dwarf was elderly, and Ellis assumed he must be the postmaster. He had a ring with keys of various sizes on it. Also on the ring was the royal seal of Ältremark, bearing the emblem of a crossed hammer and ax topped by a shining crown.

"This is the one, is it?" the older dwarf asked.

"It is, postmaster, yes. The paperwork is all in order and complete. The only thing left is the inspection."

The older dwarf nodded, and then elbowed aside Ebba, who was hovering just over his shoulder. "A little room if you please, Ebba? No need to smother me."

"Sorry, sir." Ebba shrank back, and for the first time Ellis felt a warm feeling toward her, and felt sorry for her obvious macular degeneration.

Peering at the set through his own formidable spectacles, Applewine selected one of the smaller keys and began to unlock the tiny padlocks at the four corners of the box. Once that was done, the younger dwarf set to the straps. Then, having removed all of the restraints, the young dwarf exchanged a look with his superior, took a breath, and opened the lid.

Ellis blinked.

"What's this?" Applewine asked. "A piece of slag?"

"Slag?" Ellis asked.

The young dwarf upturned the box and a gray rock a little larger than Ellis' own fist fell onto the velvet, along with some pebbles of the same material.

Removing his spectacles, Applewine fitted a jeweler's loupe into one eye. He picked up the rock and examined it carefully, turning it over and over. Finally he set it down, replaced his spectacles and fixed Ellis with a piercing eye. "Is this a joke?"

"Joke, sir?" Ellis was taken aback, as much by the dwarf's tone as by the contents of the box. "No sir. Not at all, sir."

"Tifflebaumer, fetch the guards," Applewine instructed the young dwarf, who hurried away.

"Can I be of service?" Officer Charn stepped up beside Ellis. "Customs Agent Nebblebit Charn, at your service, postmaster."

"Agent Charn, I am relieved that you are here." The postmaster looked back at Ellis. "This young d'race has some explaining to do."

"That is not the stone I saw earlier," Ellis said.

"You opened a package under royal seal?" Applewine asked, almost spluttering.

"N-no sir! I would never do that," Ellis said. "There were two Hearth Royal Intelligence agents. A man and a dwarf."

"A dwarf?" Applewine narrowed one eye at him. "Working for the HRI?"

"Yes," Ellis said, beginning to sweat.

Applewine blinked. "I see. Tell me, did Arrunwolfe show up on your little journey, too? Perhaps the Queen of the Fairies served you tea?"

Ellis had no idea what the dwarf was talking about, but he could tell he was being mocked. Just then a squad of security personnel filed through a nearby door, led by Tifflebaumer—four sturdy dwarfs armed with axes, red sashes denoting their guard status draped over colorful vests. They rounded the counter and crowded around Ellis—not so close as to seize him, but close enough that he would not easily escape them.

Officer Charn held up one hand, ostensibly to counter the rising tension in the room. "Young sir," he said, turning to Ellis. "Perhaps you could tell us the story from the beginning."

"Yes," Ellis said. He wiped moisture from his forehead. "Uh...I picked up the package from the royal postmaster in Yngremark. Then I boarded the *Augmented Bovine*—"

"That is the name of the æthercraft you used to transport the package?" Charn asked.

"Yes. A...a...a commercial vessel, not chartered," Ellis clarified. "There were four other passengers, all dwarfs."

"Go on." Charn clearly enjoyed being in charge.

"Uh...en route we were stopped and boarded by Hearth Royal Intelligence—specifically an agent Brill." He looked up, trying to remember. "Fineas Brill, I think it was. And there was a dwarf, Agent Tumnis. I don't know if that is his first name or his last name." Ellis looked down and scratched his head. "Probably his last name."

"Go on," Charn repeated.

"Agent Brill said lives were at risk, and they needed to inspect the package."

"This package?" Applewine pointed at the box and the slag stone.

"Yes, sir." Ellis nodded. "They had keys, the dwarf did, and he opened the box, just like you did. But, sirs...they showed me the rock... or the stone...I'm not sure of the difference, begging your pardon, sirs. Anyway, they showed me the stone that was inside, and it was not *that* stone." He pointed at the slag on the velvet.

"It wasn't?" Charn asked. "What did it look like?"

"It was black, and longer than that one, and thinner, too. And it had a red smear in the middle of it, like an eye."

"Like...an eye?" Applewine scratched his chin through his beard.

"Yes, sir."

"Tell me, did this eye...did it sparkle or glimmer?"

Ellis, not seeing a difference, was unsure how to answer. "I beg your pardon, sir?"

Applewine sighed, as if calling upon his patience. Ellis had not considered it before, but dwarfs probably had a vast vocabulary when it came to rocks, and his ignorance of their terminology must make him seem like a simpleton. He could see it in Applewine's eyes, the way the postmaster was appraising him, trying to work out which word would trigger a helpful response. "Did it...*glow*?" Applewine finally asked. The room had grown dead quiet, and it seemed to him that everyone surrounding him was holding their breaths.

Ellis nodded. Suddenly everyone started speaking at once. Charn held his hands up and whistled—the loud obnoxious kind of whistling that only bullies seem to know how to do. In the resulting quiet, he turned back to Ellis. "After you saw the stone, what happened?"

"Agent Tumnis locked the box up and handed it back to me. Agent Brill said it was not what they were looking for and begged our pardon for the interruption." Ellis blinked. "He was very courteous...and kind of slimy...if you take my meaning."

"Other than your encounter with these...special agents, did the package ever leave your sight?"

"Never, sir."

Charn pounded the counter. "I'll check the flight log and interview the captain of the æthercraft," he announced. "Postmaster, I'll keep you in the loop."

Chaos erupted as everyone began speaking at once again. Ellis caught snatches of what was said, but since most of it was in Dwarfen-tongue, it just sounded like noise. This was all very confusing. First that human agent had found it ridiculous that Ellis was delivering a stone, and now these dwarfs were upset it wasn't the right kind of stone...or rock. And evidently this difference, small as it seemed, was causing great consternation.

Ellis shrank back from the counter, hoping to leave the arguing dwarfs to themselves. But just as he was backing up, he felt a dwarfish arm circling his neck, while two other dwarfs held his arms in a solid grip. "Hey!" Ellis protested.

"Officer Charn," Applewine bellowed above the din. "Will you please accompany Courier Sunderland to a holding cell at the Postal Inspection Service offices? We'll take it from there."

"I'd be delighted, Postmaster."

"A holding cell?" Ellis yelled. He tried to twist out of the dwarfs' grip, but they held him fast. "Why? What did I do?"

"What did you do?" Applewine cried. "You left Yngremark with one of the most valuable artifacts in dwarfish history. And when you arrived here you did not have it. That makes you our primary suspect."

"But I told you—"

"And we should let you waltz out of here, heading straight for the ætherport, straight for the safety of Hearth's jurisdiction, on the basis of your little story?"

"B-b-but it is a true story!" Ellis protested as the guards dragged him away.

"We shall see about that!" Applewine called after him. "In the meantime, I invite you to enjoy some dwarfish hospitality."

❧

THE ENFORCER impatiently waited in the dim courtyard. The sun had not risen enough to greet him, but he worried it quite likely would. He wondered if midday would come before the scion finally made his way down to start the journey. Ennisbrook had fed and groomed his steed while he waited; he had even seen to the scion's young horse. A quarter hour later, Clendis emerged, looking pale and nervous, blinking uneasily in the scant light. Behind him were several courtiers bearing bundles of clothing, along with a set of four attendants who were wheeling a cart weighted down in chests and more bundles.

The Enforcer stepped forward, causing the scion to shy away—not only shy away, but look away. Ennisbrook realized it was likely in response to his appearance. He well knew his rough and lined face was as much a subject of curiosity as it was of unease. There were some who claimed the lines were from a life lived hard; there were others who claimed they were scars from battle. Ennisbrook had never revealed their source and was not interested in doing so. It kept at bay those who were not worth dealing with and was not a concern for those that were.

The same held true now. The scion appeared uneasy with the Enforcer's appearance, and Ennisbrook did not care one whit. "Hold!" he called. "We will not be bringing all that with us."

"This is my clothing," the young man protested. "I will need it for my stay."

"Your pony cannot drag this much; and *my* mount will certainly not help you."

"But—"

"Bring one change of clothes for tomorrow. The rest you can

scrabble together when we reach our destination." Before the scion could object, Ennisbrook added "Never fear, you will find we wear clothing in Trogan as well."

The scion turned to his servants and reluctantly gestured by lowering a hand. The attendants responded by wheeling the cart back into the shadows of the castle proper. The courtiers closest to the scion's mount began loading the bundles onto the horse's back. The horse grew restless and Clendis was forced to grab his bridle and whisper calming words.

Ennisbrook watched the courtiers until his patience wore thin. "Enough," he stated, and the courtiers stopped with several bundles left to go. They looked nervously from the Enforcer to the scion, as if they feared they had made some terrible transgression. But the scion quietly made a gesture that shooed them away.

At last it was just the Enforcer and Clendis in the courtyard. Ennisbrook had expected Avantir to show up as well, to share parting words with his son; but the king made no appearance. *It is probably for the best,* Ennisbrook thought. *The king seems an emotional sort.* It was likely the royal highness did not want to appear unmanned and vulnerable in front of his subjects. If so, Ennisbrook approved; but he wouldn't be surprised if Avantir was looking down on them from some high window, witnessing the boy's departure with a tear-filled cloth to his face.

"Ready?" Ennisbrook asked.

The scion nodded but the expression on his face said otherwise. Ennisbrook led his steed away from the stables and into the courtyard, aiming for the entrance with its raised portcullis. Clendis followed, leading his pony. They tramped across the drawbridge and then met the road. They mounted their horses and ambled past the castle wall at a slow gait. A thick nest of trees immediately appeared on their right, with only a few to create any shade on their left.

Once Ennisbrook deemed they were sufficiently hidden from view, he stopped and dismounted. Clendis dismounted as well, uncertainly. The Enforcer grabbed one of the prince's bundles, unlaced it from the horse's back, and threw it into the trees that lined the road.

"My things!" Clendis cried, but Ennisbrook was already removing a second and third bundle and sending them to follow the first.

"Those are my things!" Clendis shouted.

"I told you that you would not need them," Ennisbrook replied, ignoring the boy's protests. "Let the ruffians take them. Let Wybrook be known for having the best dressed, kingliest waylayers in all the lands."

He suspected there were indeed ruffians in these woods, but he also trusted they had sense enough not to pester him. He wore the chain of his office across his chest, which all should surely recognize. It meant the rapier at his hip was not for show. It had been used before and was ever ready to be used again. He trusted this rapier and often relied on it as his only defense. But, there certain times, when he needed to be prepared for any enemy and any fight—times such as this, in fact—when he also strapped a broadsword on his back. The rapier was suited for stabbing and slashing; the broadsword was effective for an enemy's quick maiming or death.

Ennisbrook let a few bundles remain behind the saddle. He was about to continue when he saw that Clendis had retrieved one bundle from a ditch and was trying to return it. Angrily, Ennisbrook approached the boy, knocked the bundle from his hands, and struck him across the face.

"Mercy!" the boy cried, putting a hand to his reddened cheek. "You said I was an honored guest of your king!"

"Not yet," the Enforcer snarled. "Right now you are a parcel to be delivered and I will deal with you as I see fit." His threats seemed to have the desired effect. The boy was quaking.

Ennisbrook was a soldier, not a nursemaid, and he would brook no tearful child. He continued more softly, but without lessening his intent. "A word of advice, young prince. Do not cross me and all shall be well," he said, mounting his horse. They proceeded at an easy gait again. The sun rose and passed over them. Ennisbrook did not stop for a meal and was pleased that Clendis did not ask for one. Nor did they stop for an evening meal. As it grew dark, Ennisbrook finally called a halt. They led their horses into another wood, and Ennisbrook started a small fire. It would be a warm night and the fire was mostly for illumination. Ennisbrook gave the prince a few squares of journeybread, taking a short stack for himself. Afterward, the Enforcer rested his back against a tree trunk and closed his eyes, and Clendis tried curling up on the ground.

At first light, Ennisbrook prepared to continue. After a few minutes he clapped his hands loudly and woke Clendis. The boy wore a bleary expression, revealing how poorly he had slept. "We are going?" Clendis asked. "I have no time to wash?"

"You can clean yourself up once we get to Caer Trogan. I'm not wasting time looking for fresh water."

The boy approached his horse and gripped the saddle, but then stood there with his eyes closed as if he had forgotten how to mount.

Likely his muscles are still mush from sleep, Ennisbrook reasoned. Feeling what could have been a twinge of sympathy, he put his hands in the boy's armpits and assisted in raising him. But then he stopped. He had felt something puzzling and unexpected in the boy's right shirtsleeve, bound below the armpit. The shirtsleeves, he noticed, were loose and blousy. It had escaped him before, as the boy had worn a jacket, but those sleeves could hide much.

"What's this?" Ennisbrook asked aloud, clasping his hand over the object and tugging at it. Then he grabbed Clendis' shoulder and turned the boy to face him. "What is it? Remove it."

The boy's eyes sank and Ennisbrook saw color rise in his cheeks. Clendis reached within his shirt, dug a hand into the top of his sleeve, and tugged free a thin, unmarked metal flask.

"A closet tippler, are we?" Ennisbrook asked—an obvious joke, but there was no humor in his tone. The Enforcer unscrewed the cap and raised the flask to his nostrils. He detected no scent.

"Please," Clendis began. "It is nothing. It's the juice of the pelium plant—much beloved in our land."

"No," Ennisbrook said flatly. "It is clearly a poison. Intended to be used either on me or on the high king."

"No, my lord!" Clendis protested more strongly. "It is but a juice. I swear!"

"If it is but a juice, drink it now...in front of me."

Ennisbrook saw the slight hesitation in the boy's eyes, the struggle for a quick response. "But, great one," the boy stammered, "I only have the one vial—it was meant to last me through my whole stay."

The Enforcer almost felt like smiling. Paltry as it was, Clendis' reasoning amused him. But it did not sway him, nor distract him from the severity of the offense. "Drink it!" the Enforcer repeated, emphasizing the demand by drawing a dagger hidden in his belt. "Drink it now!"

Staring at the blade, the scion took the flask and slowly raised it to his mouth. His lips parted, as if to receive the liquid. Ennisbrook watched, wondering if Clendis would actually go through with it. And then the youth hesitated.

The Enforcer's tone grew cold. "Either the poison will kill you," he murmured, "or my blade will take you for threatening the life of my king."

Clendis' eyes raised, staring back at the Enforcer's. Lowering the flask, the boy replied just as coldly, "Then run me through, sir knight."

Ennisbrook maintained the stare. "You have made your choice," he stated. He might have felt a twinge of guilt at the thought of executing a boy, but the sudden resolve he saw before him assured him that, in this moment, Clendis had grown worthy of a noble end. The Enforcer nodded and approached. The boy's eyes lit up in fear and he tried to back away. He bumped against a tree and the Enforcer was on him, grabbing Clendis' left shoulder, securing him against the tree.

"Please, sir," Clendis said, panic rising in his voice. "I am the son of a king."

"You are a danger to *my* king," the Enforcer hissed. "Don't betray your honor. Stand and take what you have brought upon yourself."

Clendis' back rubbed against the tree as he struggled to free himself. The Enforcer put his weight against the boy's shoulder to steady him, before driving the dagger into the scion's chest. Any strength of spirit faltered as the pain struck. A whine grew into a scream, as Clendis channeled all his defiance into volume—until the Enforcer wrenched the blade sideways and ended it. He pulled the dagger free and let it fall point first into the ground, to be wiped clean later. Dragging the body by its shirtfront, Ennisbrook found soft and uneven ground farther ahead. He dropped the body and, with his foot, shoved it so that it tumbled down a steep hill, coming to rest at the exposed roots of a tree.

6

The novelty of being in the great halls of the dwarf king had passed. Ellis decided he did not like being underground. Much more than that, however, he did not like being locked in a cell underground.

Every bone in his body was tired. He tried to estimate how long it had been since he'd slept, but the mathematical chore of estimating, given all the time changes en route to the different worlds, left him baffled, and eventually he gave up. "It's been a rum long time," he finally said aloud. Then he yawned.

Yet there was no way he could sleep. For one thing, he was cold. For another, he was frightened. The cell was very small, even for a haffolk. It was long enough for him to stretch out, but only just. There was a porcelain waste tube in one corner, and he was careful to lie with his face far from it.

There was no light, save for that coming through a small window the size of Ellis' hand cut into the heavy oaken door. A steady dripping noise could be heard, although Ellis could not tell where it was coming from. "At least there's nothing dripping on me," he murmured. "That's something to be thankful for." The stone on which he lay was many degrees colder than the air, but he had been provided no blanket. *If I were not so beastly tired I would stand,* he thought. But he *was* beastly tired. Despite himself, his eyelids began to droop.

He tried not to despair. In his head he ran through every step of his journey, again and again. And no matter how many times he ran through it, he could not see how he could have done anything any differently. He had followed protocol and procedure to the letter. He had executed what was in his control perfectly. And what had been out of his control...that was what bothered him. *Might I have been cleverer with that agent, Brill? What ought I to have said?* he wondered.

Worst of all, however, were his fantasies of what would happen to him. Would the dwarfs condemn him to years of hard labor underground? Ellis couldn't imagine a life without seeing the sun, any sun. He couldn't imagine a life without second breakfasts or afternoon naps or tea or...Kit. His hand instinctively went to a little leather pouch around his neck. Opening it, he drew forth a single tiny feather—brown, with a pattern in white radiating from its rachis. The feather had fallen from her hat band one day when she stopped by his house. Later, he had found it and put it in the pouch to keep it safe until he could return it to her. But he had never returned it. It was the one part of Kit he could claim as his own, and he found he could not relinquish it. He held it to his nose and breathed in, hoping to catch even the tiniest whiff of her scent. Instead, it smelled like bird, but it was close enough.

Replacing the feather in the pouch, he had another dreadful thought. What if the dwarfs put him to death? *Do dwarfs do that?* he wondered. He didn't know. He knew humans did that, though. It was clear that the dwarfs felt robbed of a very great prize—a prize put into his keeping, under his protection. Shame nearly overwhelmed him as he contemplated his failure. He bit at the knuckle of his right hand, not feeling the pain of it.

But he found no ready answer, and tired as he was, he found himself turning and tossing on the dark, cold stone of his cell. *What could I have done differently?* he asked again. He really did not know...and his mind began to cycle through the steps of his journey again.

Ellis must have eventually drifted off, for he was awakened at last by the loud clanking of iron as a ring of keys struck the iron plate that housed the lock of his cell's door. He woke enough to hear the tumblers turning and squinted against the light as the door swung outward. He sat up and pushed himself against the far wall, momentarily blinded and unable to tell what was happening to him.

As his eyes adjusted, he saw that he was not going to be dragged from the cell...not yet, anyway. Instead, someone was coming in. Not a dwarf. A man. A large man, too large for the cell. He entered, stooping, and then squatted in the place where Ellis' head had been mere moments before.

It seemed that the man folded himself in half, but as Ellis blinked and got more of his bearings, he saw that the man was sitting with his back to the wall opposite him, with his knees drawn up so that they were nearly has high as his head. And did he have two heads?

No, he decided. There are two heads because there are two beings. A human head and a bird's head. The man's head was noble, with a long nose and deep eyes that told stories without words needing to be said. They were sad eyes, and old—older than his face appeared to be. His hair was short and black, and he wore a gray one-piece robe with obvious bird droppings covering one stiff shoulder.

The bird was larger than the man's head—a large black crow or a small raven, Ellis could not tell which. The bird's eyes flitted back and forth, and it moved its head to take in their surroundings. There was an intelligence in its eyes that frightened Ellis a little.

"Goodness, my little friend, what a mess you've landed yourself in," the man said.

"Who are you, sir?" Ellis asked. The bird's eye was piercing...and ominous. It suddenly occurred to him that the man might be the dwarf king's equivalent of Uther's enforcer—a man all creatures feared.

"Have you come to...to kill me, sir?" There. He'd said it out loud. *Might as well get the worst of it out in the open*, he thought.

The man laughed. It was not a maniacal laugh, or menacing in any way. It was an honest, full-throated laugh, the kind you welcome from a friend by firelight at your own hearth.

"No indeed, friend haffolk. I have not come to harm you, but to help you." The man's eyes were kind and his smile sincere. "And to answer your previous question, I am called Osia by most bright beings."

"Food," the bird said.

"And to Jaq, here, I am the One Who Feeds." He grinned, showing Ellis a wide mouth full of whole, gleaming teeth. It was an impressive set of teeth, Ellis had to admit, for he had rarely seen a mouth that did not lack some teeth, and none where all the teeth were white, except in the very young. Haffolk were a little too fond of sweets, which did no favors for their smiles.

"You have not heard of me, then?" Osia raised his chin and looked down his formidable nose. "Pity. I wonder if my pride ought to be wounded." He grinned. "Well, so much the better, I say. No expectations to live up to. One does not always get a clean slate."

Ellis had no idea what the man was talking about. But he was comforted by his kind tone. Too many questions were running through Ellis' brain, but he did not know where to begin. Yet his mouth opened and one emerged. "What do you want with me, sir?"

"Want with you?" Osia placed his finger along the side of his nose and tapped. "Want with you, want with you. What do I want with you..." Then he seemed to know and brightened. "I think I would like a story."

"A story, sir?" This seemed an odd place and an odd situation for a story.

"Yes. *Your* story, if you will. I want to know everything that happened since you left the ætherport at Rhory."

Ellis blinked. "Oh," he said. That was a story he could not stop unreeling in his mind, over and over. Perhaps it would help if he could say it out loud. "I can do that. But if you'll beg my pardon, sir, I don't know you, or for whom you work, or what designs you have upon me. If I tell you my story, how do I know you won't use it against me?"

"I suppose you don't," Osia said.

"Oh." Ellis truly didn't know what to do now.

Lines bunched at the corners of the man's eyes as he smiled. "Perhaps I need to introduce myself better than I have done, eh?" He held out a long-fingered hand, which Ellis hesitantly took and shook. "You may call me Osia, as I said. I am a fellow of Summoner's Keep, second in seniority only to Elsorin, our master."

Ellis' eyebrows shot up nearly to the top of his head. "A summoner, sir? You're a summoner? And not just any summoner, but...a powerful summoner?"

"Power is...relative. But I *am* a summoner, and of some reputation, if I do say so myself."

"I haven't heard of you, sir."

"Quite. And that is why, among other reasons, you charm me."

"Food," the bird squawked.

"I am here because the item you were delivering is of great interest to the Keep. I am also hoping to secure your release and get you home. But to do that..." he leaned in closer, "you must tell me your story."

Ellis nodded. *What do I have to lose, now?* he thought. He cleared his throat and began.

He started out by saying only the rough outlines, but the summoner kept interrupting and asking for details, so Ellis adjusted his storytelling, including every detail he could remember. Throughout it all, Osia reclined against the far wall, not looking the slightest bit comfortable, but not complaining either. That was left to Jaq, whose entreaties for food continued sporadically throughout the tale. When Ellis had finished, the summoner was still rubbing the side of his nose with one long finger, his eyebrows bunched in thought, and his thin lips pursed.

After several minutes had passed, broken only by the sound of dripping water, the summoner said, "Well, Mr. Sunderland, you have had a time, have you not?"

Ellis nodded. In the saying of it all aloud it became clear to him that, whatever had gone awry, the fault lay with no one but him. It was his assignment and his responsibility. He was an agent of the Royal Mails. The Kingdom had put its trust in him, and he had let all and sundry down.

"A tale like that requires a pipe," Osia said. "You don't have a pipe, do you?"

"I don't, sir."

"That's all right. The dwarfs frown on smoking underground."

"I don't blame them, sir."

"Quite right..." The summoner's voice descended into mumbling. "Tell me more about this Special Agent Brill. He was a man. He was tall—tall for men or tall for haffolk?"

"Tall even for men, sir."

"Black hair, you say, and short cut?"

"Black as your bird there, sir."

"And his nose—large or...?"

"Normal size, I should think, sir."

"Weight?"

"He was lean, sir, like yourself. No bird, though."

Osia smiled. "No, I wouldn't think so. Tell me about his accent."

Ellis had not thought of the man's accent. He looked up as he recalled it. "That was strange, now that you mention it. Most law enforcement officers use middle-speak, as the merchants do. But this one was high-spoken, sir, as if he were noble."

The summoner's eyebrows rose. "You don't say? Didn't you think that was strange?"

"I confess I didn't think much about it in the moment. There was too much else that was queer."

Osia nodded. "Can you think of any other detail? Anything at all. It doesn't have to seem important."

Ellis frowned, thinking hard. His hand went involuntarily to his birth medal. And touching it, he remembered. "The medal."

"Yes?" Osia inclined his head. "Medal, you say?"

Ellis clutched at his birth medal. "This medal was with me when I was adopted. It's all I have from my birth house."

"This is not unheard of. People are often sentimental when surrendering their haffolk *kipper*," he said, using the dwarfish term. "They want to give them something to remember them by, even if they're too young to remember. May I?" He held his hand out for the medal. Noting Ellis' hesitation, Osia added, "I will give it right back to you, my little friend. You have my word. The reputation of my order stands upon it."

Ellis wrestled within himself, but finally drew the chain over his head and handed it to the summoner.

He watched Osia's eyebrows leap to the top of his head as he studied the medallion. Ellis knew every detail by heart—a flaming sun with three apples floating inside it, forming a triangle. "My dear boy," the summoner said, after a close inspection. "Do you know what house you are of?"

"No sir. I was hoping that...well, maybe someday I'd be admitted to the royal library and I'd make a search for it."

"You won't find it there, I'm afraid," the summoner said.

"Do you recognize it, sir?" Ellis breathed, trying not to sound too eager.

Instead of answering, Osia simply turned the medallion over and over in his hand, studying every detail. When at last he spoke, he said, "Do you know that many nobles have two names?"

Ellis had no idea what this had to do with his medallion. "Uh...no sir."

"They do. They have a public name and a secret name."

"That's a queer thing, sir. Why is that, if I might ask?"

"There is a theory of magic that says if you know someone's name, you can wield power over them—magical power."

"Is that true, sir?"

"Oh, without a doubt," he nodded. "So the nobility seek to keep themselves safe by a ritual in which they designate the public name as an alias—even though this is the name that is on the birth certificates—but establish the secret name as the *real* name, known only to the child's parents."

"Oh." Ellis did not know what to make of this information, nor why it was relevant. "That's very interesting, sir." He scratched his head. "And, uh...does that work? I mean, sir, does that keep them safe?"

"No. Not really. A name is a name, and anything people call you attaches a handle of sorts to you. In fact the public name is more magically efficacious than the secret name, because—" he shrugged and chuckled, "—well, no one *uses* the secret name." He shook his head. "No, it's a bunch of noble foolishness."

"I'm not sure what that has to do with my medallion, sir, if you'll pardon my saying so."

"Oh! Quite right. I'd almost forgotten, you are such a pleasure to talk to. So just as nobles have a public and a secret name, they also have a public crest and a secret crest. The public crest you will find on their stationery, on their battle standards, on their coat-of-arms. But the secret crest...well, that you will not find anywhere except well-hidden, on their own persons." He handed the medallion back to the haffolk. "That, my dear Mr. Sunderland, is a secret crest."

Ellis' eyes went wide. "A *secret* crest."

There was a joyous glimmer in the summoner's eyes. "But tell me what the medal has to do with your story."

"Mr. Brill, sir, he had a medal, too."

"Did he?" Osia cocked his head. "So he *is* high-born."

"And not just that, sir. He had *this* medal."

Osia's eyes went wide. "This medal? The same design as yours? You're certain?"

"Quite certain, sir."

Ellis could see the summoner's mind racing as his eyes moved back and forth, but he said no more about it. After several minutes, he groaned and pushed himself up off the back wall. Stooping in the tiny cell, he extended a long-fingered hand to Ellis. The haffolk took it reflexively and shook it. "Well, my young friend, take courage. I'll go and see what I can do. Regardless of what you hear, it is possible to talk sense to dwarfs."

"Are you going to speak for me, sir?"

"I will."

"And do you think...I might get to go home?"

"I promise nothing, but...as much as the dwarfs want to punish someone, I think it quite clear that you intended no malice. And I think they know it, too. But do get some rest, and try not to twist your brain into a knot of worry, for it will not do you a jot of good."

"I will sir. Thank you sir."

And with that the great oak door swung shut with a clang and a boom that echoed for what seemed like eternity.

Ealon descended the final ridge and looked around. Twilight was falling, but he had timed his arrival well. He pulled on the lead, and the goat kid with him clambered down beside him, bleating. Ealon set down his pack and scanned the landscape, feeling a thrill of satisfaction. This was Asura Varr, the table of the elder god. Once, when Hearth was formed, it had been the pit of a volcano. In the last age, it had served as the primary place of sacrifice to the elder god—the place where unwilling victims were offered to appease the appetite of the deity.

The blood of thousands—perhaps hundreds of thousands—had seeped into the rock here, and indeed, the rock had a red-black tint to it. The setting sun made the effect more pronounced, no doubt, but Ealon immediately felt the morphic resonance of the place. It felt at once holy and malign. It was as if he could hear the screams of the ancient victims still, echoing eternally off the canyon walls, their blood crying out from the ground. Power radiated from the porous rock beneath his boots. He knelt and felt the ground. Was it his imagination, or did it pulse beneath his fingers? It pulsed, he was certain of it.

No man was there to see the look of triumph on his face, nor did he wish to be anything but alone in his moment of triumph. He would share it with none. This act would be his and his alone. This bold triumph, this fell glory would fall on only one head. If he could not wear the crown, he would wear this.

He tied the goat to some scrub and then cleared a place on the rock for a fire. He quickly collected some brush, then pulled a tinder box from his jacket. Within minutes, a tiny flame was crackling. He added some small branches, and before the sun descended from sight, the varr was lit by a leaping fire.

Having tended to the fire, he stretched to his full height again and turned to his next task. He must prepare the ritual. This was the one part of his plan he felt less certain about. Liaga had given him detailed instructions. The summoner had even offered to conduct the ritual for him, and had looked crestfallen when Ealon declined. But he had nevertheless offered copious guidance.

Yet Ealon was neither a priest nor a summoner. Metaphysical rituals formed no part of his princely training, nor had he ever taken even a passing interest in theology or magic. Where talent and experience and education failed, raw courage and a single-pointed will must prevail. He recalled Liaga's instructions from the beginning and began the preparations.

Pulling a tin of sulfur from his pack, he paced off a seven-pointed star, trailing the powder behind him. Once complete, he could see the yellow design in the firelight quite clearly. The star of summoning—a symmetrical design for an asymmetrical number. Ealon did not understand the purpose of that, and it had taken some practice with a stack of parchment to master the star with a free hand. Yet Liaga was quite insistent about it, and Ealon kept at it until he had mastered it.

The final result was not, in fact, perfectly symmetrical. But Ealon did not think he could do better. Next, he took a tin of oxidized iron and shook a few grains into his hand. They appeared bright red in the fire light. Looking to the stars to establish his directions, he created a circle just inside the southernmost side of the star, shaking out the iron filings with quick flicks of his wrist. This was the circle of safety. Once the ritual began, it was the one place Ealon would be protected from...from whatever he hoped to unleash.

Rubbing the last of the iron from his hands, he walked to where the goat was tethered. Taking a length of cord from his jacket, he jerked the kid's legs from beneath it and ignored its bleating protest as its body hit the rock with a resonant thud. Holding it in place with one hand, he quickly began to wind the cord around its thrashing legs.

He'd always felt the elder god had been poorly treated. The victors write history, of course, and ever since he was a boy he wondered what the true story was. There were two sides to every conflict, he knew, but no one told the elder god's tale from the perspective of Samael.

"Samael," he said the name aloud. That was the name of the god, the name few deigned to utter and all feared. Yet Ealon felt outrage and pity at the sound of it. He felt a kinship with this god. He had long ago rejected the oyosii with their petty rules, their propriety, their precious piety, and most especially their almost complete non-involvement with daily life. Samael, at least, had ruled. It might have been a dread rule, if the tales were true, but no one doubted his existence or his power.

This was truly the god of his heart. A god who had been rejected, as Ealon had. A god deprived of his throne, as Ealon himself had been. A god who would wreak vengeance on any who dared stand against him, just as Ealon would.

Having bound the back legs, Ealon turned his attention to the front. Ignoring the panicked, persistent bleating of the animal, Ealon imagined the look on Cormoran's face when he learned of his little brother's triumph. It was a look of horror. Ealon enjoyed the fantasy immensely. He thought of his father's face, and saw appreciation and perhaps even admiration in the old man's eyes—a rare sight that he longed to behold again. The high king would approve of his boldness, his courage, his creativity, even if it wasn't a plan he himself would have set in motion.

Picking up the kid, he felt its muscles thrashing against its bonds, the helpless form writhing in his grip. He felt a rush of pleasure surge through him. *This is the feeling I most crave,* he thought. *I want to hold the world in just this way.*

Having never been to Asura Varr before, he had expected there to actually be a stone table. Perhaps there had been, once. Probably the oyosin had destroyed it long ago. But it made little difference. The rock floor of the varr itself would be his table. Stepping carefully, holding his victim fast, Ealon entered the star, careful not to disturb the sulfur marking its periphery. Walking up to the circle of protection, he laid the goat just beyond it—close enough to reach from inside the circle, but not inside the circle. It would be food for the god, the Dark Lord's first meal after his centuries-long exile. He would be hungry.

Ealon felt a stab of fear as he examined the circle of protection. Would simple iron filings be enough to protect him? He did not know. If the elder god were truly hungry, how could a simple kid be enough to sate him? Ealon knew little about the ways of religion or magic, and indeed was unclear on the difference between the two, and did not know which category his actions this night fell into. But not being an oyosin or a summoner, he decided it did not matter and he did not much care. What he cared about was the fact that a victim lay before him, the fire raged to his left, and darkness loomed to his right. Behind him lay all of history and all that was unknown.

Stepping carefully over the design he'd drawn, he pulled the last needed items from his pack—a flint knife, a dwarfish rock hammer, and the Fängelsten. Straightening up once more, he turned toward the circle of protection. He breathed deeply, steadying his nerve. Ignoring the struggling, protesting baby goat, he stepped over the iron filings into the circle.

He knelt with his knees just inside the circle and placed just beyond it the knife, the hammer, and the stone. His altar ready, he closed his eyes and centered himself. *This is a holy moment,* he thought, and for the first time in his life, he felt what holiness must feel like. It felt portentous, infinitely large, and mysterious. It felt like touching time or eternity. It felt like touching *power*.

And suddenly, once again for the first time, he understood a tiny bit of the appeal that religion and magic had for the mindless masses that cared about such things. He felt a glimmer of empathy for them, and it impacted him with the force of a revelation. "This is power," he said aloud. "I understand power." There was still much about the endless droning minutia of piety that he didn't understand, or want to understand...but he understood *this*.

He thrilled to feel it, and his mind leaped to fantasies of his imminent triumph. *I will be revered as the Lizard King is revered*, he thought. *I shall be feared as Rasha, the Render of Flesh is feared.*

His heart pounded in his chest. His hand shook slightly as he picked up the stone knife. The goat's eye connected to his own, as if it understood, as if it were pleading for its life. It had stopped bleating but was panting heavily, clearly terrified. "No need to be frightened, little one," Ealon said, feeling a fleeting sympathy for the little creature. "It will all be over in a second."

And with one quick motion of the knife, the thirsty rock of Asura Varr once more tasted blood. Ealon heard a raspy gurgle as the kid's blood spurted and pooled before him, spreading quickly over the ground. "Your supper is ready, my lord. Now to release you from your prison."

He picked up the hammer, and was surprised to find another eye fixed to his own—this one the swirling red eye in the heart of the Fängelsten. It seemed to be moving, as if he were watching the life of a galaxy unspool before him, with time accelerating, or perhaps beyond time altogether. Unable to look away from the eye, he allowed it to hold his own, but still he brought up the hammer, swung it high behind his head, and then brought it down with all the force his arm could muster. The eye shattered into an explosive rain of shards.

One of the shards flew into Ealon's eye. Clutching at it, he howled, rolling on the ground, suddenly heedless of the circle of protection, and forgetting for the moment all of his great designs as he clawed at his face, writhing in agony.

❧

Samael roiled still. A thousand years of wrath burned at him. Relentlessly he pounded on the seal that kept him from his adopted universe, thrashing his great tentacled arm against the barrier. But always it held, always it denied him, always it cut him off from the only place where he had been a god. For a thousand years he pounded. For a thousand years it barred his way...until this day. For a moment, the writhing stopped. The great beast reached out one great, quivering tentacle, itself as large around as a moon, and pushed at the place where, only moments before, there had been an impassable seal against him.

The seal was gone. The tentacle passed through. He withdrew the tentacle again. His rage momentarily forgotten, his gelatinous body, the size of a star system, quivered in hope. Dare he think his passage clear? Was it yet another trap, set by the summoners against him? Might he follow the passage to his doom? Or...he dared not even think it...might those who worshipped him still have found a way to secure his liberation, his freedom, his return to the throne of heaven?

He hesitated. But he feared to hesitate too long. The passage might close again. He quivered in his indecision. But he did not consider long. Any chance was better than exile. Any worship was better than the contempt of his betters. Any world was better than this one. Resolved, he reached forth his tentacle again, and his wonder and hope was swallowed up once more by wrath and the lust for revenge as his great, writhing body and the region of desolation that surrounded him slipped into the gap, crossing between worlds, sliding into the universe where he was universally feared and sometimes worshipped.

Home, he thought of it. The place where he was the most powerful and dread being among all others. A place where his fellows did not shun or mock him. The place where creatures cowered before him. A place ripe with the savory blood of bright beings. He quivered as he slipped fully into its space. He reached out his tentacles, feeling the space around him, the familiar odor of its æther, deliciously cold and redolent of spoor and seed. There were living things here. Many, many living things. And they all feared him.

He was a god again. He would rule again. And he was thirsty for blood.

❧ 7 ❧

Osia rested his head in his hand as the æthercraft shuddered toward Hearth. The passenger cabin was full, and on flights as long as this one, alternated from being very much like a rowdy pub to being like an old warmaster's long house with everyone sleeping piled up together under the chief's animal skins.

There were no animal skins here, but the cycle was definitely in the sleeping mode. Jaq lay in Osia's lap, beak open, twitching now and then in sympathy with his dreams. Normally, Osia had no trouble sleeping. He had been an ordinary man once, but that was in the last age. He did not need sleep now, but he enjoyed it, and partook regularly as he partook of wine and his pipe.

But there was no sleeping for him now. There was a knot in his stomach that caused him pain, and his teeth ground anxiously. Something was amiss, but he did not know exactly what. The missing Fängelsten was enough to keep him awake, but there was something more...as if he was waiting for the other shoe to drop, as the men of Hearth liked to say.

He glanced at Ellis, whose head bobbed with the shaking of the æthercraft. A warm feeling came over him that he did not quite understand. *There is something special about this one*, he thought. *There are depths to him invisible to the naked eye, and secrets follow him that none suspect.* But he suspected. Nay, he knew. Deep in his bones, his intuition told him that whatever storm was coming, this little one would be at the center of it. *I must keep him close,* Osia thought. *Better, I should make use of him.* What that use might be he did not know, but he was used to trusting his intuition. In the many hundreds of years he had served bright beings it had not yet failed him. This little one might be headed back to Everdale, but it would not be the last Osia would see of him—he was certain of that.

Osia yawned, and his eyes began to close. Sleep would, indeed, feel good after such an eventful day. He began to drift.

Then suddenly, Osia's eyes snapped open and he leaped to his feet, head whipping from right to left. Jaq cawed in protest, and with a great flurry of wings, succeeded in avoiding a tumble to the cabin floor at just the last moment. For no reason Osia could divine, the knot in his stomach had plummeted into a bottomless pit, and he thought he heard a cry of agony—or perhaps it was triumph—that pierced the distance between the stars. *I have been dreaming,* he told himself. *It was just a nightmare.* But no, something had changed, something portentous, something fell and dreadful. He bent to peer through one of the portholes, yet saw nothing but the æther whipping by and the distant light of stars blurred by their speed.

"I feel like something or someone dear to me has just died," he whispered to Jaq, who flew to his shoulder but did not continue his complaint. "Or perhaps like a world is ending."

"What?" asked Jaq. "What? What?"

"I do not know what it is, my friend," Osia answered him. "But I fear it is nothing good."

Objor's eyes snapped open. He thrashed upon his bed and cried out while his familiar Tepi fluttered about his head. His attendants ran to him and raised the alarm. The great bell in the Keep began to sound, rousing the summoners from their sleep.

Riza entered her master's chamber, followed by the scurrying of her mouse familiar. Gently, she shook Elsorin. His eyes fluttered open, then he rubbed the sleep from his eyes and sat up. Then he heard the bell. Throwing off the bedclothes, he demanded his robe. Riza was ready with it, and he threw it on as he walked. Riza stopped him at the door, handing him slippers. He cursed but he put them on. Turning out of his rooms into the hall, she could barely keep up with the old man. He ran to where the seer was convalescing, not bothering to acknowledge the small crowd that had gathered outside the door. He pushed past the assembled brethren and went straight to the bedside. The physic was there, feeling at the old seer's pulse.

"What happened?" Elsorin asked no one in particular.

"I'm not sure," the physic said. "It might have been another seizure of the heart."

The seer's eyes were open and his hand was held aloft, as if reaching up to heaven.

Elsorin reached out and clasped the hand in his own, bringing it to his breast. It was cold, and he held it against his robe to warm it. Objor turned his head toward the master summoner, and his eyes seemed to focus. "Master," he said. Tepi continued to flutter nervously around his head.

"I'm here, Objor. What do you see?"

"I see our doom returning from exile. I see his great fell body slipping in between the worlds. I see him feasting on the blood of dwarfs and elves. Fire!" The old man shouted this last word with such force that his skeletal frame shuddered and went limp.

"Physic?" Elsorin asked.

"He lives. But he sleeps."

Elsorin nodded. He patted the old man's hand. He stood. He faltered.

Fortunately, Riza was beside him, one hand on his back protectively. She caught him around the middle and stopped his fall. The physic's eyes went wide and he nearly tripped trying to get to his master. Riza laid Elsorin out on the stone floor of the seer's tiny chamber, now impossibly crowded. "Back!" she shouted. "Everyone but the physic out!"

Riza was not a person of any rank among the summoners, but none dared disobey her in the moment. The assembly backed up, out of the cell, but continued to peer into it, crowding the doorway.

Riza lunged for the pitcher standing on the little table near the seer's bed. Fishing a handkerchief from her pocket, she poured water onto it and then dabbed at her master's face. Her familiar looked on anxiously, whiskers twitching. A moment later Elsorin stirred and his eyes opened. "What am I doing on the ground?" he asked.

"You are not on the ground, but on the floor," corrected the physic.

Elsorin scowled at this answer. His eyes flitted to Riza's face and looked relieved. "Don't tell me I fainted."

"You fell," she said.

"That is little better," he said. Then his eyes went wide. He had remembered. "Objor?" he tried to sit.

Riza gently pushed him back down. "He's sleeping."

"He may have had a stroke," the physic said.

"He is being dramatic, master. The seer sleeps, that is all." She scowled at the physic. His face soured in offense.

"This is the least of our troubles. Falling...is the least of our troubles." His eyes flitted back and forth as he raced through the implications of his thoughts. "If the warning in the message of the oracle is plain, then our ancient enemy has returned. The Fängelsten must have been destroyed, or somehow compromised. The magic that has kept Samael at bay is no more. Our safety is gone. Our children will once again be...the food of a dark and cunning god." He struggled to sit up, but this time pushed Riza away when she tried to stop him. "Fetch me a seerstone," he said.

❦

INDIÉL WATCHED with increasingly wide eyes as Cienith began her dance. She was the daughter of their guest, Lord Illuvium of the House of Endilla, resident ambassador from Elderwood. Indiél knew he was there to discuss intolerably dull matters of state, but there was nothing boring about Cienith. Her skin was dark, as all the Gray Elves were, her body lithe, and her silvery, shimmering shift just revealing enough to make Indiél's breath catch as Cienith kicked one leg into the air and spun around.

There was no music, nor did Indiél miss it. The vision of Cienith spinning in the center of the Hall of Nobles was sufficient in itself. The hair on Indiél's arms stood up as gooseflesh erupted on her skin. She was suddenly keenly aware of the moisture of her own lips, and wondered what Cienith's might taste like.

And then, as suddenly as it had begun, the dance ended, with Cienith coming out of a spin at the foot of her father's smallthrone. Indiél's father, King Eoche, clapped exactly three times for the performance, and then looked away from the young elf maiden who had just given her all. Cienith might have taken offense, but she barely seemed to notice Eoche. To Indiél's disappointment, she hardly seemed to notice her, either, but instead simply bowed, eyes to the ground, and withdrew from the room.

Lord Illuvium made up for Eoche's coolness with his own spirited response. But if he was offended by Eoche's lack of enthusiasm, he did not betray it. Instead, he turned to Indiél and smiled, "Perhaps *your* daughter may entertain us, now?"

Indiél was expecting this. Although the elves had years ago derived from their magic the ability to send sounds and images great distances, including stage plays and even operas, private performances were still the entertainment of choice in polite gatherings of noble elves—chamber dramas, dance, and solo musical offerings. Being called upon to entertain was one of Indiél's primary responsibilities in the royal household, and she had been schooled in art, dance, dramatics, and music from her earliest days. "Would you prefer a sonnet or a sonata, my lord?" she asked, flitting her eyelids at him coquettishly.

"I am quite partial to poetry," he said. "We have many fine poets among the Gray."

"I have read many of your poets, my lord," she said. "Who is your favorite?"

His dark face looked down, and she could see that one of his ears ended in a jagged point, having been torn in battle long before she was born. "I am most fond of an ancient poetess by the name of—"

She held up her hand. "Let me guess," she said. "Gehednilar, the duchess of ice."

"Yes," his face broke out into a broad smile. "You surprise me, my lady."

"Her 'Shorter Song of Fallow Fields' is a favorite of mine," she confessed.

"Let us hear it, then," he said. He might have been merely being polite—it would have sufficed—but unlike her father, she could tell the man really wanted to hear her performance. She stepped out from behind her father's smallthrone—every room had one, save for the throne room where the greatthrone sat—and bowed. But just as she was opening her mouth, the door opened and a page entered, more quickly than usual.

The king noticed this too, and sat up. As the page approached, he bowed. Eoche cocked his head, turning his ear toward the young man. Indiél studied her father's face as the news was related. His eyes narrowed and his lips stretched into a thin line.

"A dwarf ship? In orbit around Isherwood? What can be the meaning of it?"

"May I speak openly, your majesty?" the page asked.

"Yes, yes," Eoche waved at his daughter and Lord Illuvium. "They are in my confidence."

"The dwarfs are communicating by Hroffgar's method."

"It is their primitive way," Eoche sighed.

"Blips-and-squawks?" Indiél giggled.

"Yes, my lady," the page answered.

"And what do they say?"

"The message was still coming in when I was dispatched."

Just then another page, dressed identically to the first, pushed open the door to the room and bowed, his fair hair flowing over the silver-blue collar of his doublet. This page handed a note to the king, who took it and studied the parchment.

"Father?" Indiél prompted.

"It is no ordinary dwarf. It is King Belorin himself."

Lord Illuvium looked surprised. "King Belorin? He is a rough fellow. What business would he have here?"

"He accuses us of stealing something from him."

"Preposterous," Illuvium huffed.

"Quite, quite," Eoche drummed his fingers.

"Father, what are you supposed to have stolen?" Indiél asked.

"It doesn't say."

"This is an affront to your honor, your majesty," Illuvium reminded him, quite unnecessarily, Indiél thought. She could already see the clouds gathering over her father's face. He was grave at the best of times, but he was insufferable when wroth.

"Send this message to the lesser King of the Dwarfs," Eoche said. This confused Indiél for a moment until she remembered that Belorin was King of Yngremark, the smaller of the two dwarf worlds. It had not been an insult. Her father continued, "Your accusation is absurd and needs not be answered with any utterance but the blistering bite of a lightning gun. Yet, as you see, we are gracious and give you the boon of an answer."

The first page had pulled forth a small pad and a stubby pencil and was scribbling furiously.

"You offend our space with your presence, even as you offend our honor with your assertion," Eoche continued. "You will turn your ship back toward dwarfish space immediately and we shall, in our great mercy, forget this exchange has happened. Any further accusations, or indeed, any further communication, will be seen as an act of dwarfish aggression—"

"Father," Indiél stepped forward and curtsied. "If I may offer a small word to season the stew?" She hoped the cooking metaphor would soften her intrusion. It had the desired effect.

Her father inclined his head to her, peering at her from over his thin, prodigious nose. "You have some wisdom to offer, daughter? In the presence of our peer?"

She understood. It was one thing to offer him advice when they were alone. It was quite another to do so in front of a noble. "I beg Lord Illuvium's pardon for my impertinence..."

Lord Illuvium had also inclined his head, but there was the slight trace of a smile on his dark lips. She would have been happier if Cienith were still with them, but she was confident that the tale of her boldness would find its way to her. And perhaps then, the gray maiden of the Endilla would notice her.

"*But…*" her father continued. "You were saying?"

"Father, it is an impolitic response. If your goal is to send King Belorin back to his people, this will not accomplish your goal."

"Nonsense. Aggression is the only language dwarfs understand."

"Father, have you ever read dwarfish poetry?"

"What absurdity! Dwarfs lack the poetic sensitivity—"

"You are wrong, Father."

She heard Lord Illuvium gasp and saw Eoche spear her with one eye. Whether she would see daylight for the next week depended on the delicacy of her next words. "Dwarfs write poetry that is rough—'tis true—but it is also thoughtful, playful, and often profound. You think them empty-headed ruffians, but as Telios tells us, 'If your view of your enemy is inaccurate, then your enemy has the upper hand.'"

Illuvium's eyebrows rose. "Your daughter reads Telios?"

"His daughter has memorized Telios," she responded, although she felt a little embarrassed to have done so. Telios was known as "the poet of war," and even people who did not care for poetry knew a little of him, or at least a few of his aphorisms. She turned back to her father. "As Telios also says, 'A cautious word diverts destruction.'"

"How can a single dwarf ship bring destruction?"

"'There are many roads to ruin,'" Illuvium quoted. "Telios again."

"I wish you would both stop."

"It's hard to argue with Telios," Illuvium pointed out.

"It's impossible to argue with *her*," Eoche pointed at his daughter with his chin. "Very well, how would *you* answer this dwarf king?"

"I would sympathize with his obvious distress and offer him your hospitality. Share a meal with him, show him that your hands are open and empty, and perhaps he will leave a friend rather than an enemy."

"We have no dwarf friends," her father spat.

"We have the opportunity for one now," she said.

Her father rolled his eyes and then looked at Lord Illuvium. "Your daughter does not interfere with affairs of state, I trust?"

"She does not, my king."

"I envy you her."

Indiél scowled. That had stung. But she held her ground. Eoche's eyes moved back and forth, and Indiél guessed he was running through all the possible outcomes of the various approaches to his problem. Finally he looked up at her and glared darkly. "Have it your way, daughter. 'Another friend is more advantageous than another enemy.' You see? I can quote Telios, too."

"That is not Telios," she narrowed one eye at him. "You just made that up."

For the first time that evening, she saw her father smile.

THERE HAD BEEN no need for dwarf architects to choose the location of Caer Trogan. The promontory that jutted into the water was broad, strong, and raised, providing a strategic and defensible location for a high king's castle. Its back to the sea, a large, boisterous city had formed in front of the castle, spreading out like an apron. Walls had been erected to embrace and protect the homes and businesses of the town. The poorer denizens were forced to construct their own shelters outside the walls, building shacks and hovels and creating what soon became known as the more dangerous parts of town.

On either side of the promontory harbors clung to the coastland, where food from the ocean or and merchandise from the other coastal cities were imported or traded. At one time, the brave sailors of Estenlan, Wybrook, and Untwold had spread out upon the ocean, in search of other continents with which to trade. It was the advent of æther-travel which proved these voyages had been in vain. There were no other continents. The planet of Hearth was a huge blue orb covered almost entirely with water. The only other land to be found was on the far opposite end of the world, in the form of a relatively small island chain, remote but lushly verdant.

At one time, the ships trading commodities up and down the coast would unlade their goods into the Caer by way of tunnels. But by Uther's time those tunnels had been sealed up, in the name of preserving the castle's defenses. Not only had these tunnels allowed for the possibility of unauthorized ingress, they had the potential to flood during storms. Nowadays, all goods coming from the harbor needed to be transported up roads at either side of the promontory, heading either to the Caer's gate or, farther, into the city of Trogan. The Caer was immense, with walls of smooth, well-cut stone. It was broad, but the promontory afforded a strip of land on either side and a sizeable grassy field behind.

It feels good to be outdoors, Uther thought, standing behind his castle. He liked the sound of the wind as it stirred the tall grass, he enjoyed the coolness of the breeze, and he was hypnotized by the blue of the bay and the silver sparkles on the great sea beyond. He did not even mind that his aim was off today. He called for another set of birds, raised his crossbow, and missed both of them. The wind was too strong and sent his arrows too high. Off to his right, though, two sharpshooters took them down. They then turned to their king and enthused, "Good shot, sire!" and "Excellent shooting, my liege!"

Uther gave them a polite nod, muttering to himself, "How pathetic. You're seriously not fooling anyone." He had no idea where this tradition got started, but he found it sad and demeaning. Having others shoot your targets for you must have come from the weakest and most sniveling in his ancestry. He hated the tradition and those who started it.

He raised his face to the skies, begging for patience, as well as taking in more of the breeze. The thought occurred to him that he could quite easily dismiss the sharpshooters. He could end the tradition right now...but then that would mean his misses would be too obvious. If he sent another arrow into the bay, the birds would be able to freely cross the sky, obviously and undeniably.

He started at the realization. Could it be? Was he as weak and as vain as the worst of his line? He looked to the castle, grateful for an interruption to his thoughts. He saw movement and recognized his enforcer making his way down the field. A runner proceeded him. Even though the Enforcer was recognizable, this unkempt young man was compelled to run wildly ahead in order to drop to his knee and announce to the high king, "Daevis Ennisbrook, to see your majesty!"

"Yes, yes. Thank you," Uther replied. The young man rose and ran just as madly back to the Caer. Ennisbrook continued onward, ignoring the runner's commotion. Uther waited to speak until they were a few feet apart. Ennisbrook bowed, Uther murmured, "Rise," and the two stood face to face. Not for the first time, Uther noticed that the lines and scars in the Enforcer's cheek were more pronounced in the sunlight. "So...is Avantir's scion installed in my household?" the King asked.

"About that, my liege," Ennisbrook began. "The boy did not make it."

"Ha! Avantir didn't have the guts to let his precious boy out of his sight?"

"No, your majesty. I was forced to kill him."

Uther froze for a moment. "You jest."

"No, my liege, I do not. The boy is dead."

Uther paused again, needing more time for this news to sink in. Realizing where he was, he turned to the others and waved his arm. "Away with you. Give me room!" he shouted angrily. The two sharpshooters walked away, keeping a respectful distance between king and cliff.

"Swiving gods, Daevis!" the king growled. "Must every interaction you have end up with someone being slain?" Uther shook his head in bewilderment. "I trust you had good reason?"

The Enforcer drew out a metal flask and handed it to Uther. He knew better than to think Ennisbrook was sharing a beverage. The king twisted the cap off the flask and waved it under his nose. Then he delicately poured some out on the ground. Instantly the weeds by his feet smoked and withered.

"How did you discern this was poison?" Uther asked, astonished. "I smelled no odor."

"To be honest, I did not. But upon finding it I dared the boy to drink, and he refused."

"Then Avantir sent him to kill me?"

Ennisbrook nodded.

"Once again," the king continued, "you have saved me from destruction. We have a sticky situation with Avantir, granted, but he is digging his own grave as I ken it. We must expect some response, though it is unlikely through battle. His army is routed—even he can see that." Uther raised a finger. "But does he have enough pull with the other families? Will the loss of his son be enough to get other armies to side with him? We must drown out his tale of woe, Daevis. It is *our* story the people must hear. We need to make sure that everyone knows Grendel—"

"Clendis."

"Clendis—what kind of name is that? It sounds like an internal organ—that Clendis was sent to us as a spy with designs to murder us. Let's see Avantir try to drum up sympathy on that! I'll need a chemist to study the poison, too. Perhaps it's from some plant known only in Wybrook. That would help with the story. In fact, let's make it that. The poison came from Wybrook alone, and if Avantir has a problem with it he's as good as admitted his guilt."

"There are other ways to attack us than through armies," Ennisbrook said.

"Yes. Yes. Good point. They don't send us food, do they? But textiles—*that* they give us. We must stop the importation of all goods from Wybrook immediately. For all we know they can be dosing their goods with this Wybrook poison in an attempt to kill us all."

Uther's mood had changed considerably. He had to remind himself that at the bottom of this was the death of a young royal. "The boy? Do you have his body?"

"It has been disposed of," the Enforcer replied.

"All right. Very well," Uther said, distractedly. "I must be back at the castle. We've got some rumors to spread."

"If I may, your majesty—a suggestion." Ennisbrook raised a finger.

Uther raised a great hoary eyebrow in return.

"I think what we need is a bard. Your majesty might commission a song to tell the tale of the poisoner prince. It could be completed before last bell tonight—I know a songster who is speedy with a tune. On the morrow, we will employ every bard in the capital and send them out to the four corners of our kingdom, and into our client kingdoms as well."

"We will *indeed* call the tune," Uther nodded, his face breaking into a smile for the first time since their meeting began. "Very well. Employ your bards." He gave a loud whistle, attracting the attention of his sharpshooters as well as the retainers with their bird cages. "Enough of this," he shouted at them. "To the castle."

❧

"YOU MAY WAIT HERE, SUMMONER," the page said, bowing with respect.

Osia bowed in return and relaxed a bit as soon as the door was shut. It was the first privacy he had experienced since he had felt the... what would he call it? *The change,* he decided. Something had changed. He knew not what, only that it was dreadful.

Uther liked to keep people waiting, Osia knew. He believed him to be a competent king at heart, with genuine concern for his people, but he also had a temper and a petty streak common to humans in power. *Common to bright beings,* he corrected himself. *Every ruler I have met has been a petty creature.* The thought made him sad, but only because he truly cared for them. He sighed.

There was a gift in the wait, however. Osia pulled the velvet bag containing his seerstone out of one of the large pockets of his robe and loosened its drawstrings. Jaq cawed in recognition. "Ever since I felt... the change...I have also felt Elsorin's presence," Osia explained to his familiar. "Not exactly his voice in my head, but as if he were standing behind me, waiting for an opportunity to speak."

The bird cawed his understanding. Osia sat in one of the chairs furthest from the bright window, as light made viewing the seerstone difficult. Holding the stone in his lap, Osia shut his eyes and connected with the Scar. He reached out with is mind, summoning the influence of a world where speech through the stone was possible. He knew it would be there, and found it easily. When he snapped open his eyes, a distant mist swirled in the stone before him. To aid his viewing, he narrowed his eyes, softening his focus. That helped enormously, and in moments Osia saw the ghostly face of Elsorin his master floating as if deep beneath the stone's dark surface.

"Master," Osia said aloud. He did not need to speak aloud, but it was easier and he had no reason to believe he was being spied upon.

"It is a fell day, Osia," Elsorin said.

"I feel it," Osia agreed, his visage grim.

"Any being with a thimbleful of magic feels it," Elsorin agreed.

Jaq cawed.

"Even Jaq feels it, apparently," Elsorin added.

As he had so many times before, Osia wondered why Elsorin had taken no familiar. There was a saying that one should never trust a summoner without a familiar, and yet one of those "solitaries" was the head of their order—just another of the paradoxes magic was rife with. "What does it mean?" Osia asked.

"I was awakened by Objor. We thought he was having another piercing of the heart."

"Is he well, then?"

"Not well, but not in any danger that the physic can detect. Still... he uttered another oracle."

"It regards the Fängelsten?"

"The old man did not mention the stone...but it is hard to imagine that the two are unconnected. What have you found?"

"The stone was found...then stolen. The courier was played like a back alley game of walnut shells."

"With the Prison Stone as the pea," Elsorin growled.

"Precisely."

"Do you know who did the playing?"

"I am investigating that now, but...I have my suspicions."

"And they are?"

"Suspicions. Until they are more than that I'll not impugn any bright being."

Elsorin grunted. "Very well. You will inform me of your findings."

"I will," Osia agreed. His eyebrows bunched. "Master, to what end has the stone been stolen?"

"You ask because you do not want to admit what you already know."

Osia said nothing. "*That* is what I am feeling, isn't it?"

"I expect that it is. I feel it too."

"If whoever took the Fängelsten has destroyed it, or *disempowered* it somehow..." Osia breathed, "Then our doom is upon us."

"I am loath to call upon the oyosii to help us," Elsorin said, through gritted teeth. "But I may yet do so today."

8

There were others. The sound of the ancient words, faint on the wind, had reached them though separated by layers of stone. The message had penetrated the rock, and lying in darkness they found themselves stirred. For hundreds of years they had waited for the return of such sounds, for his name to be said again. And they heard it, on this very day.

Deep in the caves and fissures under the varr they had remained hidden, biding their time, waiting for this day of days. The incantation had roused them, made their blood run faster. Hungry grins had returned to their faces; their limbs yearned to fight again. The war for which they had been brought here had been waged long ago. They longed for another fight; they had forgotten how much. For too long they had kept themselves apart, foraging by night, not straying too far in their foraging.

They should be fighters—warriors. It was wrong for them to cower in darkness. It was against their nature. But they knew they needed to protect themselves, to keep themselves ready for the eventual war. They had been brought here, eons ago, to destroy the humans; but somehow the humans had harnessed some unforeseen magic which had driven away the masters, had shut off their greatest master from them. They were orphaned. Bereft of orders, they had been forced to hide. They knew their masters would be able to return—their power must be greater than the humans'—so all that was needed was to wait. Magic must wane, they knew, so they had to keep themselves ready. Close by and ready. Waiting in the shadows—waiting for today.

Of all the beings that would aid them, they were confused to see that their deliverer was a human. It seemed implausible, but it was he who had said the words—he who had caused the quake which roused them from their stupor. The lightning flash, the thunderblast were unmistakable. They had heard the sound of the old words, had recognized the call. It stirred in their breast. It made them want to shout out, *We hear your words. We are born today.*

After the blast, the varr was quiet again. The air was still. The only tremble was in their limbs, ready to grip old weapons again. A few of them crawled tentatively to the lip of the fissure and looked out upon the varr. After centuries of secrecy, the impulsive instinct for action had been repressed. Now they looked upon the world warily. *It is no longer safe*, they thought, *to go out before nightfall.* To do so would be to let themselves be seen, to give themselves away. But they were roused now. The spoken name had quickened them, had given them hope, had roused their hunger. After such as this the battle would be renewed—it must! They could slay warriors in great masses again, rather than stray shepherds who wandered too far afield.

Your word is great. Our fists are strong.

Strange as it seemed, this human would make it so. Three of them took the old armor plates and strapped them to their chests. Then they stepped out into the still air. They warily crossed the varr and approached the motionless human. As they drew nearer they saw he was lying on his back. His arms were askew; his right palm was facing up.

The first one leaned on his ax handle as he lowered himself to one knee. He was called Cragga and was respected for his many kills. Half of the human's face was obscured by a crust of blood, but Cragga ignored this. Instead he placed his thick, oversized hand on the human's chest. The others waited. Cragga felt his hand rise and fall.

"It breathes," Cragga said in Orcentongue.

"It is one of their young," said the second, dismissively. Stargha's voice was strangely reedy for such a hulking figure. "How could it know how to wake the old one?"

"Does that matter?" said Cragga, still on one knee. He jabbed a huge knuckle into the side of the prone body, but it did not wake. "It knew enough. It said the name."

The others nodded and grunted their assent. This human had said the name; that alone was reason enough to treat him differently. Words echoed in the air as if called aloud. *We stand strong. We are yours.*

Cragga shoved his massive hands under the human's legs and back, lifting the human as he rose to his feet. "You are taking him with us?" Stargha asked, reaching out to support the human's dangling head.

"Praltuda will want to see him," Cragga said. "He will find out what this human knows and why the name was said. And then we will learn when the war will resume. When Samael will call upon the Scrum once more."

"Great is his name," they said together. *We await you. We are ready.*

"How do you hold this?" Stargha said, uncomfortable at cradling the human's head.

Cragga brought his forearm farther out, hoping the head would rest on it. Then he changed his mind and slung the human over his shoulder. "There," he said.

"That looks better," Stargha said. "Even if he *does* know our ways, he is still a human. I'd rather *you* touch him."

A lone bird soared overhead. "Quick," said Grazzak, the third of the group. "Let us get back underground before we are discovered."

"Yes. Let us get to Praltuda. He will see."

We are the Scrum. The Scrum will strike.

INDIÉL WATCHED her father's face carefully as the dwarf vessel completed its landing in the field south of the palace.

"It is frighteningly primitive," he sniffed. "It's a wonder they survived the journey."

"Father," she admonished him with a lilt of her voice, "best manners. This is an opportunity."

"An opportunity for looking like fools," he said. "What will the other houses say?"

"They will commend you for your hospitality and diplomacy, if they have any brain at all."

The stars were blindingly bright behind the great, hulking copper vessel, dominated by the blood-red gash of the Scar. Large lamps, powered by lightning juice, flooded the landing field with harsh but serviceable light. The dwarfish æthercraft rocked forward on black rubber-tipped landing rods, and Indiél could hear the distant clacking of gears as, somewhere deep in the bowels of the ship, someone must have been turning a crank. At first she could not divine for what purpose, but slowly she saw the prow rise until the ship was perfectly level.

"I trust Lord Illuvium will not feel neglected," she inquired.

"He and his will be off for Elderwood early tomorrow. I doubt you'll have occasion to see them again before they go."

"Pity," she said.

Her father looked sideways at her and raised one eyebrow. "You know...soon you must marry. These...dalliances—"

"And I'm sure he understands emergencies of state," she interrupted him. "Lord Illuvium, I mean."

"I'm sure he does."

"He won't hold it against you." Her voice was firm.

"No," he agreed, narrowing his eyes.

New motion attracted Indiél's attention. A round port opened. It was surrounded by a silver plate, held into place by perfectly symmetrical rivets. Once again, she heard a clacking noise, but of a different timbre. Moments later, a ladder proceeded from the ship just below the open porthole.

Out of the corner of her eye, she watched her father straighten his silver suit coat and adjust his cravat. He then stood straight and still, assuming the air of every proprietary dignitary.

"Here he comes," her father said, out of one side of his mouth.

A dwarf's hindquarters emerged from the porthole and pinwheeled in the air momentarily until finding purchase on the ladder.

Her father sniffed. "Ugh. The indignity."

The dwarf then descended rather quickly.

"No, I think that is a guard," Indiél corrected him. "You see, he has an ax across his back, and a cap on, with an insignia of some sort."

"Hm," her father said.

Another pair of legs emerged, only this time they were not clad in hose, but naked, covered only intermittently by the whipping train of a dress.

"Oh, my," her father said, the disdain in his voice thick as treacle.

This dwarf had a bit more trouble finding the ladder, but after a bit, succeeded. Descending rapidly, Indiél saw that it was a young female. She was squat, as all dwarfs were, but she was not fat. Her dress clung closely to her torso, and the way the wind whipped at it only increased its allure. The dwarf's hair was auburn and surprisingly short, bobbed so that it hung just below her jaw.

Reaching the bottom, she looked around, disoriented. Seeing the guard, she went to stand by him. Safely within arm's reach of him, she started to look around. She spied Indiél and her father. Indiél waved.

"Here he comes, then," her father said.

Looking up once more, she saw new legs emerge. These found the ladder easily, and within mere moments, had descended more quickly than Indiél would have thought possible. The dwarf king adjusted his crown, placed his hand on the young she-dwarf's shoulder and gave a curt nod. Then he turned and began to stride directly toward them.

As soon as he was within speaking distance, her father raised his voice and said in Dwarfentongue, "You are well met, Belorin King. You honor us with your presence."

"Very good," Indiél whispered.

"I *have* done this kind of thing before, daughter," he whispered back.

King Belorin stopped several paces away, a wary look in his coal-black eyes. "What's your game?"

"Game?" her father spread his hands. "I'm sorry, brother king, but I do not understand."

"You understand a good deal more than you're saying," Belorin huffed. "Fine. Play your games. We have time to tease out the truth."

Eoche and his daughter exchanged a cautious glance.

"This is my daughter, Brennar," Belorin waved in the direction of the young dwarf, who stepped up beside her father and curtsied.

"She's studying Elventongue and blackmailed me into letting her come."

Close up, Brennar was even prettier than she was from a distance. Indiél found herself intrigued. Then the young dwarf opened her mouth, and spoke her greeting in perfect Elventongue. "*Osrantine il lillia, noth ramaskir tourratith*."

"*Ostrantine il illia,*" Indiél responded, "*noth assurapith don*."

Brenner gave a respectful nod, but looking up again, locked eyes with the elf princess. Indiél felt her knees grow weak, and her breath caught in her throat.

"Shall we stick to Hearthentongue as a neutral medium of communication?" Eoche asked.

"We shall give the humans cause for airs," Belorin grumbled, "but it seems expedient, as I speak little Elventongue and you probably speak less Dwarfentongue."

"Probably," Eoche agreed.

"Well, this bodes well for your negotiations, doesn't it, father?" Indiél whispered. "Look how well you're getting on already."

Her father ignored her. "I imagine you must be tired from your journey through the æther. Allow our page to show you to some apartments worthy of your royal station." He waved at the night sky, at the Scar. "As you can see, it is late here, and my daughter and I were about to retire. I beg you, be our guests tonight, and I hope you will break your fast with us on the morrow. Then we can address the grave matter on which you have come. Will that be acceptable to his majesty?"

It seemed to Indiél that the dwarf king seemed shocked and entirely disarmed by her father's generosity. She guessed that such treatment simply did not fit into the universe he knew. It would be inappropriate for him to be belligerent after so gracious a greeting, and it seemed to leave him without a script. He looked up at Brennar, fumbling for words.

Brennar stepped forward. "You are so kind," she said, in equally perfect Hearthentongue. "And yes, the flight was long and...turbulent." She rolled her eyes. "They always are." She smiled again. "So your offer of a suite where we may rest is most welcome. We thank you."

"We'll have some food and our best bottle of night elixir sent over straight away. Please follow Elniath, here," Indiél nodded at the page. "I look forward to seeing you both in the morning."

Brennar grabbed her father's arm and steered him toward the page. Still looking wary and uncertain, he allowed it.

"Good night, Belorin King," her father said.

"Good night," the dwarf huffed.

Once they were inside, Indiél turned to her father. "You did very well, father."

"I pretended he was High King Uther. That way I would be respectful, yet still retain a bit of disdain."

Indiél laughed out loud, taking her father's arm and leading him toward the palace. "If you're not careful, you'll make friends of them."

"I would never live it down."

❦

AT FIRST AVANTIR WAS INSULTED. Word was that the ruffians in the surrounding woods were wearing royal fineries. He knew Uther's enforcer had ransacked Clendis' belongings; perhaps that was how his clothes had wound up shared between thieves and cutthroats. But now this latest news left him shaking. Maybe it was from anger, maybe fear, but it took an effort to speak steadily.

"Say that again, if you would." Avantir addressed his sub-commander, for the commander of his soldiery had perished in the recent battle against Uther.

"We have received word, my liege," the man said uneasily, "that the scion has been captured. That he is being held captive in the wood."

Avantir shifted, finding no comfortable spot in his throne. "And, pray, who brings you this news?"

"His name is Clumfero," the sub-commander said. "One of the wildmen of the wood. The one said to be their leader."

Avantir raised a forearm to his head, letting out a great cry without even knowing it. The sub-commander looked about questioningly. He hoped the king's summoner, Graisellis, might intercede, but she remained where she was, standing behind the throne. However, the sub-commander's adjutant stepped forward, willing to continue.

"Your majesty, they tell us that if you give them enough money they will release Prince Clendis to you."

Avantir's head rocked from side to side, as a moan erupted from him. "No. No. No," he said, rising to his feet. "Enough! I wish to hear no more! I will not suffer this outrage."

As if his eyes cleared, he glared at his commanders. "How dare they set hand upon my son!" he demanded, as if the two men could answer. "How dare they keep him from his royal seat and demand money for him! Furthermore"—Avantir's eyes wildly beseeched the very air about him—"how could these dirty brigands have bested Uther's Enforcer?"

He turned his back on his commanders, clinging to the arm of his throne. The two soldiers remained in place, exchanging a look of uncertainty. There had been no word of dismissal, and the king appeared to still be talking. "Word has come to them?" Avantir said to himself. "Word has *come* to them? How bad have things become that my soldiers are loath to go beyond their castle walls? How badly have I administered that we have no money to ransom my own son? I should call my council to order but I know those indecisive fools would never come to any consensus." He pushed himself up, standing straighter, and turned toward his commanders again.

"No," he continued. "The time has come to undo what should never have been done." His voice grew louder, as he pointed at his sub-commander. "Take your elite force and penetrate the woods. Bring back any of the brutes you can find. Then hold them for interrogation."

The men seemed heartened to have been given an order. They bowed and departed. Graisellis, his summoner, stepped forward but Avantir would not look at her. "Begone from me," he said, thrusting his palm out. "I need none of your help." The summoner bowed her shaggy head and departed as well.

Avantir left the throne room and entered a small antechamber. His attendants tried to follow but he closed the door on them. The room contained only three chairs and a small table. Avantir picked up a chair and tried to smash it against the table, but the chair would not break. The chair legs were only gouged, yet he deemed the exertion sufficient enough. He opened the door and the attendants darted away as if they had not been listening to his tumult.

Within hours some grimy, hairy brute had been caught and dragged to the castle. He was thrown into a subterranean cell and Avantir hurried to look at him through the grate in the heavy oak door. "Do whatever you must," he told his men, "go to any lengths to learn what you can from this fiend. Find the prince and learn who is responsible for such an offense."

The king had assumed he would enjoy hearing one of his son's captors being tortured, but he had less tolerance for it than he expected. He went up to the ground level and tried to ease his mind by wandering through the gardens. But when a page informed him that there was news, he hurried back to the cell.

Graisellis was there before him. "Your majesty, you might —" she began, but again he ignored her. His men looked uneasy as well as they stood around their prisoner, but Avantir entered the cell and dismissed them. He was now alone with the wildman. He was not worried, for the unkempt barbarian was chained to his chair. Nor did he feel pity for this wretch, though heavily wounded and soaked in blood. He cared for nothing but news of Clendis.

"Go ahead," he said, his voice sounding gentle and patient. "Tell me what you told them."

And the wretch, speaking in gasps and groans, explained how the scion was *not* being held hostage. Clumfero hoped to get some money from the king before it was revealed the scion was already dead. His body had been found in the southern end of the woods.

The king's voice remained as steady as before, though tears spread down his face. "Again," he coaxed. "Tell it to me...again." And as the man repeated the story, Avantir stepped closer, reaching out and wrapping his hands around the man's neck. He felt the solidness of the throat within his grip, and—with another cry escaping from him—he squeezed until he crushed it.

When the king emerged from the cell he ordered all available soldiers to infiltrate the woods and set them ablaze. No mercy would be shown. Everyone residing in the woods, as well as the woods themselves, would be consumed in fire. The raging in the king's soul would be made manifest in the wildfire outside his castle. Let all about him be reduced to cinder and ash. Avantir hoped thereby to scald the remorse which perfused him, to sear the careening guilt he felt for damning his son to an unavailing death.

❧

EVEN THOUGH FREE of dwarf-world gravity, Ellis climbed down the ladder of the æthercraft feeling like he had hundred-pound weights strapped to his legs. Stepping to the ground, he looked around and blinked. It was twilight in Rhory, and the grimy city was just beginning to come to life. Just a few blocks away from the ætherport were the taverns, and he could already hear the reels, jigs, and whoops carrying over the humid evening air. For all the merrymaking, however, he did not feel merry.

He moved through customs quickly, as he had nothing to declare and there were few people aboard the merchant transport ship that ran hourly between Hearth and Everdale. Just inside the ætherport's waiting room, he saw a friendly face, one hand on the hilt of her longneedle and another working a toothpick.

"How was the job?" she asked, a little too casually. She didn't look him in the eye, and her affect was cool.

"It was disastrous," Ellis sighed.

"Course it was. You bleedin' left me here."

So that's it, Ellis thought. *Well, she has a right to be peeved. We're partners, after all, and I abandoned her*. "I'm sorry, Kit. They wouldn't let you go."

"*You* didn't have to go," she said, finally meeting his eye. "You could have said, 'Either she goes or get someone else.' Say it with me, it's easy: 'Either she goes—'"

He looked away. This was the last thing he wanted to deal with right now. "Kit, I *did* have to go. By the horn, Kit, I'm up for a promotion, for the postmaster's job. It's not like I could have turned a major assignment like this down—how would it look?"

"It would look like you were a person who possessed a scrap of loyalty, that's how it would look." She spat. "Even if you don't."

"No spitting in the terminal!" called a porter in Kit's direction.

She ignored him. "C'mon, it's a long way back to the village."

He slung his empty courier's bag over his shoulder and she handed him a piece of journeybread with a very smelly cheese smeared on it. He took a bite and turned to follow her as she set off for the border. It was delicious, but he didn't taste it much, so lost was he in his own thoughts.

Kit was not the chatty type, but despite her anger at being left out of the assignment, he could tell she wanted to hear about it. She kept glancing at him as if she were going to ask a question, but then thought better of it. Finally, he said, "I wish you *had* been there."

"Why?"

"Because you would have...you wouldn't have...it wouldn't have..."

"Oh, horn of blood, man, spit it out."

"It was terrible, Kit. I was...terrible. I'll probably be fired."

"Fired?" Kit stopped and looked him full in the face for the first time since he'd landed. He could tell that, hurt feelings or no, she was concerned for him. "What happened?"

"I picked up a package at Yngremark. Then we were boarded by pirates...I guess they were pirates. They stole the package, but I didn't know that until I made the delivery—"

"How could you not know that?"

"Because they said they were HRI and they had to inspect the package."

"And you fell for that?"

"I...how could I know they weren't HRI?"

"For one thing, HRI doesn't inspect packages. Postal inspectors inspect packages. For another thing, you weren't in a Hearth jurisdiction, you were in dwarfish space."

"But the Alliance—"

"Is a joint cooperation of powers—it doesn't mean that the various law enforcement agencies just piss away their jurisdictions willy-nilly."

"Oh." Everything Kit was saying made sense. He didn't know why he hadn't thought of it in the moment. It had all happened so fast, and he had been intimidated by the pirates, as he'd come to think of them. "I wish you had been there," he said again.

"I wish I had been, too."

Tears welled up in Ellis' eyes. "Oh, Kit. I made such a mess of things. I'm so sorry." He threw himself at her, and she stumbled under the force of his bear hug.

Righting herself with a quick step backward, she hugged him back, awkwardly, and patted at his back. "It's...oh, swiving horn of blood. It's okay. I forgive you."

This made him sob audibly.

"Stop that. People are staring," Kit said. "Can't you wait until we're past the border to fall apart?"

"Sorry," Ellis said, wiping at his eyes. "I just..."

"I know, I know," Kit said, double-timing her steps in the direction of their home. "Just...not in front of the humans. It's humiliating."

"They're dock workers and prostitutes," Ellis said, looking around.

"So what? You know what they think of us...even the lowest of them think they're better than us."

Ellis bit his lip and wiped his nose on his sleeve. They didn't speak again until they were past the border and safely on the broad road into the wood that would lead them to the Dale.

"Do you really forgive me?" Ellis asked.

"I really forgive you."

"Really? You're not going to give me the cold shoulder tomorrow?" Ellis asked.

"I might. A little. I'm still angry," Kit said.

"That's fair," Ellis reasoned. "But you'll get over it?"

"I'll get over it. Just don't...don't do it again."

Ellis nodded, but felt a warmth in his chest he had not felt for days. He couldn't stand the thought of being out of Kit's graces. There was much in his life he loved, and loved fiercely. But of all the things he called his, he loved her the most. And deep down, he knew she would never be his. Not in the way that he wanted.

But she was his friend. And she was devoted to him. His Aunt Tully had often told him, "A half pie is better than no pie, my dear." Kit's friendship was a delicious half pie, but no matter how long their friendship lasted, he knew he would always long for the whole pie.

"Speaking of not doing it again..." Kit started. "If you do get this job, what happens to me?"

"Oh, that's easy—chief of security, or postal inspector."

She made a face. "Too much responsibility."

He stopped, "Well, what would you want to do?"

"Security guard, right there at the central post office."

Ellis nodded. "That's easy. But...why wouldn't you want to make more money?"

"I don't give a goat's teat about money. I care about you."

Ellis gulped. It was the closest Kit had ever come to expressing any affection for him at all. He squeezed her shoulder and resumed his pace. "But this is all just dreaming. I'm not going to get the job."

"Who says? Who're they going to give it to? Tubber? 'Tis a jest."

"Not Tubber. They're not idiots. Maybe Spindlethorn or Hamfoot, though. I just know for certain it won't be me. In fact, once I have a chance to debrief with Bracegirdle, I'll probably lose this job, too."

"Well, we'll find out tomorrow. They post the new jobs at noon."

Ellis sighed, so deeply that it seemed to rustle the dark, friendly trees that lined both sides of the road.

"It can't be that bad," Kit said.

"I can't think of anything—anywhere, happening to anyone—that is worse than this."

"Now you're just being overly dramatic." Kit stopped. "What...is that?"

She pointed to the sky, visible just between the trees reaching over the road.

"Is it the Scar?"

"Maybe—but it's brighter than the Scar usually is. Redder, too."

Ellis glanced up and saw it. "I have no idea."

Kit scowled. "New events in the heavens are never good news."

"Who says?"

"The *Summoner's Almanac*."

"That thing is fit only for use in the outhouse."

"Where do you think I saw it?"

"Do you think that's true, though?" Ellis asked.

"We'll find out soon enough, I reckon."

9

King Belorin sniffed at the food in front of him. "What is it?"

"It is a typical elven breakfast, my lord," Eoche responded. "Grilled fish with elb tubers and prunes."

Belorin looked up at his daughter, a slight look of panic in his eye.

"Fish is a novelty for us," Brennar explained, as the servants set out their breakfast. "Not many species live in the caverns, and they aren't worth eating."

Eoche was watching his brother king with obvious amusement, which made Belorin frown.

Brennar lifted a forkful of fish to her mouth and chewed. Her eyes went wide and she cocked her head. Then she greedily cut off another bite. "Father, you'll be surprised. It's quite good. More tender than the meat you're used to." She looked at Indiél and smiled. "And the seasoning is sublime."

The princess Indiél smiled back at her, looking shy, and...was she blushing? Belorin did not know how to interpret that. He cut a piece of the fish and speared it, but it broke apart and fell back to his plate before it got to his mouth. "It's too tender even for that, Father. Use the fork like a shovel, think of the meat as coal."

That worked better. Uncertainly, Belorin chewed. Then he stopped.

Then he chewed again, his eyes moving back and forth. "It's...not evil," he said.

Brennar burst out in a laugh. "No, father, it is decidedly not evil." She shot Indiél an apologetic look.

"And what is this?" Belorin said, picking up the long, narrow glass filled with golden liquid.

"We call it *vissa*, your majesty," Eoche said. "It is considered delightful."

He sniffed at it, but was so low to the table that he found getting the glass to his lips without hitting the stem on the table impossible. He turned so that he could handle the glass without the intrusion of the table. He sipped and his eyebrows shot up. "It has bubbles." He sneezed. Then he sneezed again. Eoche glanced at his daughter with a look of...what? Tired patience? More amusement? Something of the sort. Belorin set the glass back down.

"Yes, brother king," Eoche explained. "The *vissa* is effervescent, a kind of wine, so light it almost defies gravity."

"It's queer. And it tastes queer."

"It is delicious," Brennar pronounced, taking a sip herself.

"Might we to our business?" Eoche asked.

"What? With the women present?" Belorin asked.

"Is that such an absurdity among the dwarfs?"

Belorin narrowed his eyes. Was this a trick?

"I often find that my Indiél has astute observations," Eoche continued. "In fact, I imagine that if I listened to her more often, my kingdom would run a good deal more smoothly."

Indiél bowed her head momentarily, accepting the compliment.

Belorin huffed.

"Alas, that is not our way," Brennar admitted. "We need examples such as your own to help us...evolve in our thinking."

"We most certainly do not," Belorin countered.

"Well, then, tell us a bit about life on Yngremark," Eoche said, changing the subject.

They made small talk throughout the rest of the meal. Once the last of the plates had been taken away, tea was brought forth. Eoche held up his hand. "The ladies will take tea in the cloister. We will take ours in the Room of Meeting."

Immediately the tea service was whisked away. Indiél stood. "I believe that is our cue. Princess Brennar, may I show you around the gardens?"

"I would like that," the dwarf princess replied. "Not as much as talking matters of state, of course, but I will take some consolation in it."

Belorin's countenance darkened. His daughter was teasing him, which never pleased him, but pleased him less in the presence of the high-minded fair folk. Once the ladies had retired, Eoche stood and waved toward a door. "This way, please, your majesty. Now that we are rested and fortified, I believe we have much to discuss."

Belorin rose and trotted toward the indicated door. He was relieved when, once through the door, Eoche walked beside him, since he had no idea where he was going. He was afraid that the elf king would use his wrong turns and befuddlement as a source of amusement—it was, after all, a very elven thing to do. But instead, Eoche continued to surprise him with his forbearance and consideration.

It was all too much. Belorin stopped and faced the elf. "What's your game?" It was a repeat of his question from the previous night, but it still nagged at him.

Eoche stopped and blinked. His face was a hard, inscrutable shell. Dwarfs wore their emotions like cloaks, colorful and for all to see. Elves, however, had a reputation for cool calculations. They had emotions, but they would rather die than reveal them.

And both races, Belorin reflected, were too proud for their own good, which just complicated things.

"I will admit, your majesty, that when I first received your message, my first reaction was one of scorn, and my impulse was to rebuff you."

"And what was your second impulse?"

"To listen to my daughter."

Belorin blinked. "I never listen to my daughter."

They turned and began walking again, side by side.

"And how would you characterize your relationship with your daughter?" Eoche asked.

"I'm afraid I don't know what you mean," Belorin huffed.

"I mean...are you close? Does she confide in you her feelings, her hopes, her anxieties?"

Belorin scowled as they walked. Elves were so closed, he had not actually considered the depths of their inner lives. Come to think of it, he hadn't considered the depths of Brennar's, either. "No. Does your daughter?"

"Less and less, I fear. It seems that one of the aspects of becoming a young woman is secrecy."

Belorin grunted. "*That* I have noticed."

"She's a lovely young woman, your daughter," Eoche said. "And she seems astute. I congratulate you on rearing a person of such fine qualities."

"Uh...thank you...I think," Belorin said, still deeply distrustful of such odd elven niceness.

Eoche opened the door to a splendidly appointed room, large enough for a small gathering, but small enough to not feel oppressive. A roaring fire was lit in the hearth, and two comfortable chairs were set before it, facing one another. A single block of wood was in front of the chair on the right, which Belorin immediately understood to be a step to allow him to reach the chair without aid. He stopped short of it, feeling unexpectedly grateful and welcome.

A servant was pouring tea. As the kings approached, he bowed and withdrew.

"Do you sweeten your tea?" Eoche asked, sitting and picking up a pair of tiny tongs.

"I don't drink tea, normally," Belorin. "We consider it a woman's drink. But I'll not rebuke your kindness. Make mine the way you take your own."

"Slightly sweet, then." Eoche placed what looked like a jagged, crystalline stone in a cup and poured the brown liquid over it. Then he placed it on a small table to the immediate right of the dwarf king's chair before tending to his own.

Belorin sniffed at it, but did not lift the cup.

Eoche picked up his saucer in one thin, almost translucent hand, and his cup in the other, his little finger extended delicately.

"Now, good king of our friends, the dwarfs—" Eoche began.

"Oh, just stop with the nonsense," Belorin said. "It gives me the grumbles in my gut."

"Very well," Eoche gave him a patient smile. "You wanted to speak to me about a matter of some urgency."

"That's better," Belorin said. "It is not my habit to dine with thieves, so I find myself in a fistfight...within me."

"You feel...conflicted. I know the feeling." Eoche gave him a slight, compassionate smile. "But by thieves, you are referring to my own person?"

"I am." Belorin's eyes narrowed.

"And just what am I supposed to have stolen from you?"

"You know very well."

"Let us pretend, for the moment, that I do not."

"You're going to make me say it, aren't you, you—?"

Eoche held forth one slender finger and Belorin stopped. "We have built some good will between our houses this day. Let us not dash it so eagerly."

"I don't understand what you are playing at," Belorin confessed.

"It may very well be that I play at nothing, and that you have misjudged me."

"I doubt that very much." Belorin's words fell one by one, like stones.

"You may well doubt it, yet that would not stop it being true, if true it were."

"This is a logic puzzle, then?" Belorin asked testily.

"It is not, brother king. Since you accuse us of games, allow us to suggest a game, since we seem to be at a bit of an impasse."

"A game?"

"Indeed. Let us play that we are not suspicious of one another. Let us say we are...if not friends, then *friendly*. Let us say you are troubled and are inclined to share that trouble with me. I can break out the *hrrok*, if you like."

That, Belorin had tried. *Hrrok* was an elven liquor that was universally hailed and could be found on the worlds of any bright beings.

"It is too early for that." Belorin waved away the notion. "I hesitate to play your game, as I suspect you are using me for sport."

Eoche waved around the room. "And for whom is the sport intended? My dear brother king, let us both note how deep runs the distrust, nay, the enmity between our kinds. We cannot even talk with one another."

"I don't trust you," Belorin said plainly.

"Nor I you," Eoche admitted. "Thus...the game."

Belorin looked from side to side. "There are no elf nobles watching this bit of theater, through a mirror or something?"

Eoche shook his head slowly and patiently. "There are, for one thing, no mirrors in this room."

Belorin looked around. *That* was true. "No peepholes?"

"My dear brother king, this is where I conduct my most intimate conversations. Why would I suffer there to be peepholes?" Eoche looked down his thin nose at him.

"All right, all right. To the game, then."

"To the game," Eoche relaxed visibly.

"I...uh...we...had one of our most precious relics. Well, it had been lost. But then we found it. In a mountain. As often happens, you know."

Eoche nodded, sipping his tea.

"And, uh...it was a find that...well, concerned all and sundry."

"That sounds like a momentous event, finding a lost treasure. Even among elves...if another elmirill were to be found, it would cause some consternation."

"Yes, but this..."

"What was it?"

"The Fängelsten."

Eoche dropped his teacup, spilling tea down the front of his shirt and crashing into pieces on the marble floor. "I'm sorry...do you mean the Prison Stone?" Eoche asked.

"That's what the men call it, aye. We found it."

"And...pray...what did you do with it?"

Eoche did not bother to clean up his shirt. He did not call his servants. He was, instead, sitting on the edge of his seat. More than that, the elf king looked genuinely terrified. Belorin scowled, suddenly uncertain. *Have I misjudged this elf?* he wondered. *Could it be?*

"I reported the find to High King Banniffe, of course, and was instructed to transport it to the Royal Library on Ältremark."

"I would think that Summoner's Keep would be a better—"

"Everything is clear in hindsight, aye." Belorin looked down at his hands.

"Surely you sent it under royal guard? With a contingent of summoners?"

"Nay, it was felt that such a show would only attract attention. It was felt that...keeping a low profile was the safest...and cheapest...way to go about it." Belorin looked at his feet.

Eoche, king of the Green Elves, rose from his seat. Belorin raised his eyes, but when he met the eyes of the elf king, he felt smaller than ever. "And is this the treasure you accuse me to stealing? You *lost* the Prison Stone?" Eoche stretched out one long, thin finger, pointing at him. "You greedy, ignorant fool."

"I...I...I...what?" Belorin stammered, taken aback by the sudden shift in the elf king's demeanor.

The brown stain had seeped down the whole frilly front of the elf king's shirt, but he did not seem to notice. His eyes were ablaze and his face was wroth. "Do you know what you've done?"

"I...I've done nothing! The Fängelsten was *stolen* from us. I thought you...that *you* took it."

"You did not just lose the Prison Stone, you empty-headed rock-crawling excuse for a beard, you have lost the one thing that keeps this universe safe!"

"Safe?"

"You are too young to remember," Eoche drew himself up to his full height, looking down the length of his nose upon the dwarf. "But I was there. I was witness to the evil the dark lord wrought upon the worlds of the bright beings. I saw whole star systems shudder before him and perish. I was present when the summoners sealed the magic into that stone, and when they banished his fell hide, tentacles and all!"

"Those are *legends*." Belorin narrowed his eyes. He would not be treated like a child.

"The stories are no less true for being old. I am older. And I witnessed it with my own eyes."

Belorin did not know what to say. He knew elves were long-lived, maybe immortal if not felled by ax, fire, or sword. But the tales were too incredible to be true.

"I knew something was amiss." Eoche looked away, as if searching out some hidden shadow in the room. "I felt it. It may be that whatever the stone held at bay is already upon us." He turned and flashed daggers at the king of the dwarfs. "And I blame you."

OSIA HAD TIRED OF WAITING.

"Food," Jaq said.

"Soon enough, my old friend. First, we will see the high king, whether he will it or no."

"Food."

Osia stood and pushed open the large double doors that led to the waiting room. He then strode to the throne room, ignoring the protests of the pages and porters who noticed him.

When he arrived at the great oak entrance, two guards blocked his way with crossed spears. Jaq stretched his wings wide, creating the unsettling effect that the summoner's head was sporting black wings on either side. Then Osia raised his staff as if he were about to strike them, and his other hand made as if to gather energy for an attack.

It was more theatrical foolishness, but again it worked. The guards quailed and the crossed spears faltered, one falling with a deafening clatter to the stone floor. Osia gathered himself to his full height and spoke in his most commanding voice. "I am Osia, second among the summoners. I will speak to High King Uther this very minute. I will also require guards and will possibly need to make an arrest. You will accompany me."

The two guards looked at one another. It was one thing to fail at their jobs; it was quite another to be appropriated for an important mission. They nodded and fell into line behind him as he strode through the archway.

At the end of the vestibule was another enormous double door. Osia pushed the doors open with such force that they struck the stone on either side with a resounding boom.

Uther was in his preferred seat by the window overlooking the bay. Cormoran was near his father, but Liaga hovered near the throne, as if gravitating to the real source of his loyalty. The high king seemed to be in mid-conversation with his son and summoner, but all froze as Osia approached. Osia noted how Liaga seemed to shrink as he approached, draping a light cloak across his opposite shoulder and stepping back into the shadow of the throne. Cormoran, however, increased, standing tall and meeting Osia's approach with an open and curious face, despite the summoner's breach of protocol.

Uther's face, however, darkened, as if he saw the summoner's presence as a threat to his authority. Osia was approaching without permission, without being summoned, which did indeed threaten the order of things. Osia decided in the moment that he would not make mention of it. Instead, he set immediately to his task.

"I see one of your sons, Uther King," Osia began. "Where is the other?"

"My sons are grown, summoner. They are also princes. They do as they please."

"And what if doing as they please breaks your law?"

"What?" the high king asked, scowling.

"And what if it breaks your treaty with the dwarfs and threatens the Mountain and Plain Alliance?"

Uther opened his mouth, but nothing came out.

"Pray tell me how I have offended, summoner," Cormoran bowed his head, but remained upright, "and I will repent and make my amends."

Osia's face softened. "I have no quarrel with you, my prince. Your heart is stout and constant as a stag, and every bit as noble. I look forward to the day when I treat with you."

He looked back to Uther, narrowing one eye. When Uther said nothing, Osia struck the stone with the head of his staff. "Uther King! Present your son, the prince Ealon."

"You may summon many things from the rip in the heavens, Osia, but you do not summon my son or my obedience."

"This has too quickly moved to the shaking of fists." Cormoran held up his hands. "Summoner, please tell us why you wish to speak to my brother the prince. Perhaps if we understood your urgency, we would share it."

Osia almost smiled then, nodding his head. *His father does not see it,* he thought, *but this man will make a fine king*. "Apologies, your majesty, dismay and danger consume me."

"Pray, inform us of your disquiet." Cormoran raised a hand as if to take Osia by the elbow, but then lowered it. The gesture was enough.

"I do not want to alarm your majesties, but the Fängelsten has been found."

Osia waited, gauging the reactions of the others. The high king's eyes widened, as did the prince's. Liaga slunk further out of sight.

"The Prison Stone is a valuable treasure," Uther said, "and a dangerous one."

"Indeed it is," Osia said. "It alone keeps the Dark Lord imprisoned." Osia knew that was not actually true. It simply kept Samael from entering this universe. In truth, the elder god was free to go anywhere else. The fact that he cared nothing about any of the universes at his disposal only spoke to his mad obsession with regaining what had once been his and his alone—the throne of heaven. But the statement was true enough, and for the moment he deemed the colloquial theology the most effective.

"Fire!" Jaq said piercingly.

"It is being kept safe, I hope," Uther said, one eyebrow raising. Osia knew the high king's ire was tipping into actual interest, which would be a help to him.

"If it were, my king, I would not be here." Osia watched the alarm play out on Uther's face. He stood from his window seat and began to pace. Osia continued, "It should have been sent under appropriate guard to Summoner's Keep to be held under ward and seal alongside the Red Horn."

"Yes...that would be the best place for it." Uther nodded, agreeing with the logic. "So what happened? Where was it found?"

Osia chose to answer the second question. "It was found on Yngremark, by a miner teaching his son the craft."

Uther's eyes narrowed. "Let me guess: The dwarfs elected to keep it for themselves."

Osia nodded grimly. "You have guessed the whole of it. En route to Ältremark it was stolen."

"By whom?" Uther's eyes looked unnaturally large. He pulled at his beard with one hand, and the other began tapping at his formidable belly.

"That...is what I am here to determine," Osia said. "The planets of every bright being are in dire peril, your majesty, and every moment of delay moves us closer to our doom. Given our current... situation, petty dominance games—such as making me wait for hours—do not serve us, they do not serve your kingdom, they do not serve the other bright beings we trade with, even if we do not love them."

It was the wrong thing to say. Osia realized that immediately. He had intended a mild chastening that he hoped would make Uther more responsive and cooperative. But he watched the high king's countenance darken and harden into a mask of indignation.

"Fire!" Jaq shrieked. Everyone ignored him.

"My king," Osia said, in a softer tone. "I wish only to speak with your son. Briefly."

"You think Ealon had something to do with this?" the high king asked through clenched teeth. Finally, he met Osia's eyes, and Osia read in them the truth. Osia did not know for certain that Ealon was culpable, but he was certain that the high king feared it, even suspected it.

Liaga moved out from behind the throne, "Let us not be hasty with our accusations. Slander against a prince might be mistaken for treason."

Osia nodded in Liaga's direction. "I make no accusations, Liaga. My intent is to make an investigation. If there are prosecutions to be made, the evidence will make them, not I."

Liaga bowed obsequiously, but held up a finger. "Surely, however, you do not seek to prosecute...whomever is guilty...in a summoners' court? Elsorin's authority extends only to those taking vows with our order, not to the laity, and surely not to princes."

"I said nothing about a summoner's court, and you know it," Osia felt heat rising up his neck. He willed himself to be calm.

"Fire!" Jaq shrieked.

"Jaq, please," Osia whispered. He needed to focus, and his familiar was not helping. He turned back to Liaga. Just the man's presence made his skin crawl. "In truth, I care nothing about prosecution. I care only for finding the Fängelsten and securing its safety before..." He did not finish the sentence. A part of him knew the truth: It was *already* too late.

"My summoner is right." High King Uther strode to his throne. He climbed the dais and turned, causing the tails of his coat to flourish dramatically as he sat. Placing both hands on the armrests, he made his pronouncement. "You did right to bring this to our attention, Osia summoner, and we owe you our thanks. But you are hereby relieved of any responsibility to investigate or mete justice in any capacity. We are the High King, and you have heard this from our own lips."

Osia looked down.

"Fire!" screamed Jaq.

"Quiet that damned bird!" Uther shouted.

"Shhhhh," Osia shushed, still looking at the floor.

"The situation is indeed dire, and the matter will be taken up by the civil authorities, as is fitting for a criminal act. We will conduct this investigation."

Osia said nothing.

"You are dismissed." Uther ended the audience.

Osia bowed, backed up, and having put the distance between himself and the throne required by propriety, turned and walked through the archway, past the bewildered guards, and into the long and ornate hall.

"Fire!" Jaq yelled in his ear.

"You did not help," Osia said, as he descended a stairway.

Jaq cawed.

"Don't deceive yourself. All you did was stoke his ire."

Jaq cawed.

"I'm not blaming anything on you. I'm just saying you *didn't help*."

"Food," Jaq changed tack.

"Fine," Osia said, and made a detour past the kitchen. After procuring a handful of fruit and a pocketful of nuts for the bird, he once more resumed his course for the front gate.

Osia was almost at the grand entryway when he heard a double clap. Osia slowed and looked in the direction of the sound. He saw an oak door set into the stone, opened just enough to reveal Cormoran's face.

Osia halted and looked around. He had no escort, and the grand entryway seemed to be otherwise deserted. "Hold your tongue," he commanded Jaq, and turned toward the door.

The summoner slipped through and closed it behind him. The room was neither small nor large—Osia could see by the many hooks set into long timbers running the length of the room that they were in a place where dignitaries left their coats, weapons, and other valuables while at the castle. Apparently, no guests were expected, for the room had no guard.

"I apologize for my father," Cormoran said.

"A donkey cannot shorten his ears," Osia reassured him. "Your father is simply being himself, and can be no other."

"Be that as it may...the situation grieves me." There was a sound out in the hall. Cormoran's head whipped in its direction. "We haven't much time."

Osia nodded.

"I know you are not going to just stop trying to find the Prison Stone," Cormoran said, "no matter what father says. You can't. You mustn't."

Osia nodded, waiting.

"I want to help you...if I can."

"What I did not get to tell your father, I will say to you: I know that whoever did this was from your house," Osia said grimly.

"How do you know this?" Cormoran asked.

"I..." Osia opened his mouth, then thought better of it. He began again. "I cannot tell you that."

Cormoran's eyes widened with offense, but a moment later softened. "I understand. This is the nature of investigations. You have sources that must needs be protected."

"Quite so," Osia agreed. "One thing that would be very helpful would be a rendering of your brother. A fine ink drawing of him, perhaps, or...I dare not hope for a *vakerbild*."

A *vakerbild* was a recent dwarfish innovation that could capture visual images on a thin sheet of copper. The elves had something similar, able to capture colors as well, and reproduce them onto paper, but the elves shared their secrets with no one.

"Father has a *vakerbild* of the both of us, taken at the tourney last year," Cormoran nodded.

"If you want to help me, secure it for me, and let me take it with me."

"I will," Cormoran said. "Wait here."

Cormoran paused at the door, stood straight, put his chin in the air, and exited.

"When that man comes into his magnitude he will be a king worthy of service," Osia said to Jaq, "If he has a kingdom left to rule."

❧

THE PAIN WAS ALWAYS THERE. He tried to ignore it but it would not relent. In his dream state he imagined he could sleep long enough to outlast it, but it was still there when he woke. *Why won't it go away?* he thought. *Why isn't this over with?* He refused to give in to it. He refused to open his eyes. To do so would be to concede to it, to admit to it.

Now that he was more aware, he realized he could *not* open his eyes. The right eyelid felt like it was sealed shut, but the left eye felt like it had been replaced with a burning coal. As he fully woke, the pain grew more intense, building until he was ready to shout in anger.

Shouting might prove difficult too, for he noticed trouble with his breathing. His chest ached and he was only able to take short, shallow breaths. If he tried any harder he would hear a wheezing sound in his chest. He slowly raised his left arm, bringing his hand close to his face. He feared the result, but he simply had to feel why his face felt so hot and sore. He tried to be as delicate as he could, bringing his fingers closer and closer. What his fingertips met felt soft and wet.

Is that my face? he thought in alarm. Or was it, more likely, something *on* his face? He pressed a little harder, and as soon as his fingertips touched his eyelid a volcanic surge of pain ripped through his skull. This time he did cry out.

And now his fingertips began to burn.

Gritting his teeth, panting so loud it sounded like whimpering, he used his right hand to attempt touching the right side of his face. Thankfully, this was not as bad. In fact, gently rubbing the area, he was able to coax the eyelid open and he got his first look at his surroundings.

He was in a cave. He was against one wall, on a smooth ledge of rock. He vaguely remembered an explosion, and the thought occurred to him that he'd gone right through a rock wall and was inside some mountain. But no, this room-sized cave was lit with torches. He must have been *brought* here.

"Hello?" he called out, trying to ignore the painful vibrations in his head brought about by speaking. His limited vision throbbed. He used his right elbow to prop himself up, but the strain hurt his chest. He sank back in a swoon, with a loud gasp. *What is this?* he thought. *What has happened to me?* He had shattered the Fängelsten, had he not? He should have unleashed great armies, gained incredible power... Why was he whimpering in the dark, feeling like a prisoner?

"Hello?" he tried again, but the pain washed over him and overwhelmed him. The fingertips of his left hand still felt hot. *What is on my face that would do that?*

He was lying on some hard surface — he could tell that. Some crude poultice had been applied, ineffective as it was. Obviously he was being "cared" for, in backwards fashion. But he knew not by whom. The rocky surroundings suggested he was still near the varr — perhaps under it — though he'd been led to believe that no one lived in this area.

As these thoughts swam in his head, he became aware that he was moaning to himself. He moaned with each exhalation, and the repetition again comforted him in some strange way. He focused on this for a while, eager for the distraction; and it took him a few moments to realize someone had joined him at last.

"Someone is here?" Ealon asked, unwilling to turn his head for a better look.

"I am Cragga," said a tall cloudy figure. "I brought you here. You are well now? The healers have tended to you many hours."

"They did?" Ealon sneered. It sure didn't feel like it. He couldn't imagine feeling *worse* than this.

"Praltuda will see you soon. He is our leader. You will like him. He serves the honored one, too."

Ealon struggled to raise himself, wanting to get a better look after all. Through the slit of his right eyelid Ealon beheld a man-like figure, but taller than a man, even though he stood hunched over. His clothing was crude and only covered his lower extremities. His shoulders were broad, his arms were massive. Maybe it was a trick of the light, but his skin appeared to be an unnatural dark gray. His black hair was long, and his face...looked about as bashed in as Ealon assumed his own must be. This Cragga also appeared to have two large teeth, like tusks, which jutted out from his lower jaw...but that might be a trick of the light, too.

"What has happened to me?" Ealon asked. "What do your physics say? Why am I in such pain?"

"You were touched by the dark one," Cragga said. "It is much for one to handle."

"What's wrong with my eye?" Ealon was not sure he was ready for the answer, but he was compelled to ask.

"I do not know. But you have looked into the great dominion; likely, your eye was overcome."

Ealon heard someone else enter. "Why all this talking?" said an older-sounding voice. Ealon turned his head slowly to see a slighter figure, with white hair. He wore a shawl over his shoulders, but Ealon could see the skin on this one was close to a pale purple.

"Are you the healer?" Ealon asked.

"I am one of them, yes," the second figure said.

"Tell me, please. What has happened to me? To my eye?"

"Your left eye is of no use to you," the healer said flatly. "When the

Stone was shattered, it shattered your eye. But what of it?" the healer added brightly. "It is a small ransom."

"It pains me horribly," Ealon said. "Can you give me something to ease my suffering?"

The healer swiped his fingers in a bowl and approached Ealon with a handful of what looked like mud. Ealon wasn't sure because his attention was turned toward the hand itself. It was not a human hand, but appeared to have only three large fingers and a thumb. Ealon lowered himself back onto the slab and the healer spread the mud over his face. It was blessedly cool, but Ealon still winced as the weight of it pressed against the left side of his face.

"What is this?" Ealon murmured. "What have you given me?"

"It's more of the soothing poultice we give to our warriors," said the healer. "We have used it before on you. On your face and in your chest."

"*In* my chest?" Ealon asked, his right eyelid opening again. "You *fed* this mud to me?" Maybe that explained the wheezing. *They stuffed so much mud in me there isn't room for air.*

He felt soothed by it at first, but now his face under the mud started to grow warm and burn. "What is happening?" he asked. "This doesn't feel right."

The healer leaned in close. Ealon could see the flattened nose, the strong wrinkles alongside his mouth, the strange yellow eyes. *Who are these people, these brutes?* he wondered. The word "orc" occurred to him, but he dismissed the thought. That name was the stuff of myth and childhood frights. *These beings can't be orcs,* he told himself, *no matter how much the name might suit them.*

"It's starting to hurt. Take it off me. Take it off!" He could hear the panic in his voice, coming out in an adolescent whine—but he did not care. "It's burning me!"

"I've never seen a reaction like this," the healer said to himself, still leaning over Ealon, studying him rather than saving him.

"I don't care!" Ealon screamed—pain be damned—"Get it off me!"

In his desperation, he reached up to start clawing the mud away himself—but now his fingers started to burn. Finally the healer returned, pouring something over Ealon's face. Some of the liquid passed through his lips, and he was relieved to find it was something familiar to him: water.

"It's remarkable," the healer said, continuing to talk to himself. "There was no reaction before, but it's different now."

"Maybe if you had some medicine for *humans*?" Ealon groused. It was fairly obvious he was dealing with some new race here, orcs or not, and he would just have to accept it. "Do you have anything like that here?"

The healer stared at Ealon and then reached out his strange flipper-like hand. Before Ealon could react, the fingers were on his face. The weight against his pain almost made him swoon, and then it grew much worse as the healer spread his fingers and forced the left eyelid open. It felt like he was ripping the skin apart. In some other situation he might have deemed it a sign of weakness to scream, but he did not care about that now. He howled loud enough to drown out the healer's comments.

"Yes. I should've known. His body is weak and there is a great infection in the eye socket. There is no sense in leaving the eye meat now. Here, hold his head up." Cragga advanced to place a large flipper-hand behind Ealon's head. And the healer returned with what looked like small metal spoon.

"What are you doing?" Ealon howled. "Give me medicine for the pain! Give me laudanum first!"

"Shoo, shoo," the healer said, perhaps in the way he might coo at a child. "It will be over soon. This should help you."

Ealon squeezed his right eyelid shut, praying this would somehow shut him off from what was about to happen. He felt his left eyelid open wider and then screamed in agony as the spoon skidded over the eyeball to find purchase behind it. The healer tugged hard, scooping the eyeball out, and Ealon could feel the tug and rip of the small fibers being severed within the optic nerve. *This is insane!* his mind screamed. *This can't be happening! Make it stop! Why am I not passing out?*

He could feel blood seeping out onto his face, running past his ear. "Lower the head," the healer said and Cragga gently set Ealon's head back onto the smooth ledge. "We might clean the hole," the healer added. Ealon did not know what to expect next, and he screamed anew as hot oil was poured into the eye socket.

"You really must stop causing such a disturbance," the healer said, gaining an edge to his voice. "I am trying to help you."

Ealon grew quieter, but only because all that howling wearied him. Instead he started to whimper. The healer used some kind of rough cloth to swab the eye socket out. Ealon prayed that his ordeal was finally over, that this so-called healer would finally stop torturing him. He heard the healer remove himself, and Ealon's whimper lowered into a soft moan, a repetitive noise which seemed to comfort him or at least distract him. *At last it's over,* he told himself. But then he heard the healer close by again. His left eyelid was yanked open and he felt hot wax being dripped over the wound to seal it.

His face tightened, his mouth opened, but he could not scream anymore. All of it compounded into a pain too great to be expressed in anger. All that came out was a high-pitched croak. His body went slack and he became aware he was finally, mercifully starting to black out. He heard the healer say, "Good. He sleeps finally... And you said *this one* was the great deliverer?"

❧

ELLIS HEARD the knock at the door, but didn't remove the pillow from atop his head. Since returning from the Rhory ætherport, he had barely budged from his bed.

"Is he here?" he heard Kit's voice inquire.

"Oh, 'e's 'ere, all right, wat's left of 'm," his Aunt Tully said in her thick Pravis accent. Tully wasn't really a blood relative—no haffolk lived with blood relatives. Village councils all over the Dale reservation assigned incoming infants to existing "families." Ellis remembered no other family but this one. "Go in, love. Maybe you can rouse 'im. Although if my meat pies can't dislodge 'im, I don't see 'ow you'll do it."

A moment later the round door to his room swung open.

"Ellis," Kit said.

Ellis ignored her.

Kit grabbed the pillow and tore it off his head, throwing it to the floor.

"Hey," Ellis protested.

"They're posting the jobs," she said.

"It's our day off. And I'm sick," he said.

"That's a pocketful of fewmets if I ever heard it," she said, dragging the bedclothes from atop him.

"Hey," he protested again.

"At the count of three, I will pull up your nightshirt and force your legs into your trousers," she warned.

"All right, all right." Ellis forced himself upright and groaned.

"Have you talked to Bracegirdle?"

"No."

"You haven't filed a report?"

"I haven't left the house since I got back. And *it's our day off*."

"It's noon. Put your pants on."

"Kit, there's no reason—"

"Now!" She lifted his trousers from the chair back, where he had lain them aside the night before, and threw them at him. He caught them and pulled them on without standing. She threw him a tunic. "You're not going in your nightshirt."

He removed the nightshirt and pulled on the fresh tunic. It was a deep saffron color, made by Aunt Tully just a few months before. It was one of his favorite tunics, but this day it did little to cheer him. "Let's get a little daybeer in you, and some sausage. You'll feel better, I promise."

Ellis scowled. Kit was being uncharacteristically maternal. It made him wary, as he suspected the care and concern was a thin veneer. If he resisted, it would quickly be replaced by scorn and abuse. That motivated him, as he generally liked to stay on Kit's good side. He stood up. "All right, all right. I'm up. I'm dressed."

"Eat," she said, holding the door for him.

"Love, you're a right miracle worker, you are," Tully raised her hands to heaven as they entered the kitchen. Ellis' little sister Agnes was at the table, cleaning beans, while he could hear his other sister

Beatrice banging away at something in the mud room. His Uncle and brothers were obviously out, at work or play.

Without asking, Kit went to the pit cooler and withdrew a pitcher of daybeer—a watered-down ale, bitter and amber colored, that was the traditional haffolk beverage during the working day. She poured a mug and set it in front of Ellis before turning back to Tully. "Sorry Auntie," she said, apologizing for Ellis. "He's not himself. Do you have something left over from breakfast?"

"There's a meat pie set aside for 'im, wrapped in a cheesecloth in the pit cooler there. You just missed it."

"I see it," Kit said, kneeling over the cooler. She reached her arm into the hole in the floor, but it was just a bit too short. She strained, and then succeeded, pulling the pie up by its cheesecloth. She stood and plopped the pie in front of Ellis. "Can you eat it like that, or do you need a plate?"

"Um...a plate?"

Kit rolled her eyes, but fetched a plate and threw it atop the pie.

Ellis turned the plate over and put the pie on it properly. Then, pausing to let the oyosii smell the aroma, the spiritual essence of the pie, he tucked in. As he ate, he found his appetite returning.

"That's more like the Ellis we know," Tully said, sitting next to Agnes and reaching for a handful of beans.

Ellis noticed Kit looking at the window, no doubt marking the arc of the sun in the sky. Kit didn't say anything, but he knew she wanted him to hurry. He washed the pie down with the mug of daybeer and wiped his mouth on the sleeve of his tunic.

"Ready?" Kit asked.

"No," Ellis said.

"Too bad for you," she said, marching to the door and holding it open for him.

"Ellis needs to hold on to that one," Tully said to Agnes.

Kit scowled at them. Then she scowled at Ellis. He moaned again, but stood and shambled toward the door. He passed through and she slammed it behind them and set out for the market square. "Stop lagging," she said.

"We *just* left," he complained. "I haven't had a chance to lag."

"I can tell you are *going* to lag," she said. "So don't."

"What is your hurry?" he asked. "The jobs will be posted all day."

"And if you get the job, you'll need to claim it *before* anyone can file an objection. If you have the seal of office and the key to the building in your hand, no one will dare oppose you."

She was right. That was exactly how things worked in the Dale. Haffolk were generally conciliatory people, but they would bog themselves down with bureaucratic nonsense given half a chance.

"I'm sick," he whined.

"You're not sick," she said. "You're embarrassed. And you're scared."

She was right on both counts, Ellis knew, as she usually was. He was embarrassed about his failure in delivering the dwarfs' stone. And he was terrified to look at that board. And he certainly did not want to face Bracegirdle.

Haffolk worked a ten-day week, with three days off. Some people preferred to lump all of their days off together, while others scattered them throughout the week. Ellis worked four days on, two days off, three days on, one day off. Today was his one day, but he found it impossible to enjoy it.

Yet it seemed a merry enough day on the surface of it. As they walked toward the marketplace, the village was bustling. The sun was nearly at its zenith, bright and too cheery by half for Ellis' liking. Their neighbors passed them with smiles and nods and "howdy-do's" that would have warmed his heart on any other day.

As they approached the market square, Ellis saw a gaggle of people standing around the posting board, and more were coming. Ellis guessed someone from the post office had just tacked up the results.

"This is foolish," Ellis said. "The day before yesterday I might have had a chance at this...but not now."

"It's not done until it's done," Kit said. Normally, a saying like that would have amused Ellis, but today it simply irritated him.

"There is no question that *it's done*," Ellis said with finality. "And I don't have to look at the board to see that."

Kit turned on him and for the first time that morning looked him in the eye. It was not a friendly look. "Listen up, you wilted excuse for a leaf—you respect yourself less than half as much as twice the people here. And you doubt yourself more than half the folk around you have ever done, and I'm counting everybody."

Ellis tried to work out exactly what she was saying, but he had never been very good at his numbers. "Um...what are you getting at?"

"I'm saying, if you had a crossbow you'd shoot yourself in the foot," she turned on her heel and made a beeline for the posting board.

Ellis looked down, imagining a crossbow bolt sticking out of his boot. It might as well have actually been there, because he felt frozen to the spot. He lifted his eyes, however, and they followed Kit as she elbowed her way to the front of the gaggle that was hunched over and peering at the parchment of new assignments.

Ellis saw Kit lean in, too, saw the ponytail at the back of her head move from side to side as she read. Then he saw her shoulders sag. She looked down. Then she turned on her heel, ducked out from under the gaggle of sign-readers, and marched back to where he stood. She did not look him in the eye.

"Told you," he said.

She shifted from one foot to the other, a sign of agitation.

"Who got it?" he asked. "Tubber?"

"No, thank the gods," she said. "Spindlethorn got it."

"Jess is a good egg." Ellis nodded. "She'll make a fine postmaster."

Kit finally looked at him. "You're taking this well."

He shrugged. "It's not like I didn't know it was coming. And at least that idiot Tubber didn't get it."

"That is a small victory," she conceded.

"Thank you," he said.

She narrowed her eyes at him. "For what?"

"For caring enough about me to drag me down here. Even if it was for nothing."

"You can get more for your eggs than you're asking, Ellis."

"I hear that a lot," he said.

Just then a small boy bumped into him. "Man gave me this for you," the boy said, stuffing a wad of parchment into Ellis' hand, then running off.

"What?" Ellis asked. Then he called after the boy, "What man? And do you mean a human—?" But the boy had disappeared into the crowd. Ellis had not recognized him.

Ellis looked at Kit. Her eyebrows were high on her head and her mouth was pursed. "Well, don't just stand there, what does it say?"

He unfolded the parchment scrap and held it up to catch a good light, as the market was located in a clearing surrounded by trees. "Meet me after second dinner in the Slug and Lettuce. Keep it quiet. Signed, Your traveling companion." Ellis read. Then he froze. "I'm supposed to keep it quiet." His eyes flashed back and forth.

"Who is your traveling companion?" Kit asked. She narrowed one eye, and Ellis believed she actually looked jealous for a moment.

"Uh...you are, of course."

"Then who is this?"

"I have no idea."

"You're not going to go," she said. It wasn't a question.

Ellis didn't answer.

"Yo, Sunderland!"

Ellis turned. "Horn of blood," he swore.

Bracegirdle was waddling toward them through the crowd.

"Courage," Kit said, squeezing his arm.

Bracegirdle was upon them within moments.

"There you are, Sunderland. I've been looking for you."

"It's my day off, sir."

Bracegirdle raised his chin and peered through his spectacles at Kit. "The Cornfeather girl," he said with undisguised distaste.

Kit scowled at him.

He turned back to Ellis. "Your hair looks like a badger's den. Combs these days are both inexpensive and efficient. Not like when I was a boy."

"It *is* my day off, sir."

"My office, now."

"But sir, it's..." Ellis trailed off, as Bracegirdle had turned and was already waddling back to the post office. "...my day off."

10

Uther paced in his private chambers. He rubbed at his head where the crown chafed it. He poured himself another glass of wine and added three drops of laudanum, as he did most nights, at his physic's behest. He knew that in about an hour, he would know blessed relief from the stress and the worries he shouldered daily. It was this evening time—this time for relaxation, for oblivion—that made his days endurable. He downed the cup and heard a rap at the door.

"Enter," he said, and turned to face his enforcer.

Daevis Ennisbrook closed the door behind him, turned and went to one knee.

"Rise and have a cup of wine with me," Uther said.

"Thank you, your majesty," Ennisbrook said, standing.

Uther poured a cup and handed it to him. The Enforcer received it, but did not drink.

"Daevis, tell me what you think about my son."

Ennisbrook's eyes narrowed. "Which son, sir?"

"Oh yes. Right. My *younger* son, Ealon."

Ennisbrook blinked. He set the cup on the table and put his hands behind his back. He looked at the floor, brooding. Finally, he said, "I am unsure of how your majesty wishes me to answer. And I do not wish to displease your majesty."

"Oh come now, Daevis. You have been my enforcer for ten years. You have earned the right to speak to me with candor. Especially when I command it." He met his enforcer's eye, then looked away and shook his head. "I...I fear I do not see him clearly. I wish to know how another...someone whose judgment I trust...someone like you..." He took a sip of wine. "I want to know how you see him."

Ennisbrook squared his shoulders and lifted his chin. The scars on his face glowed in the firelight. "Very well, your majesty, but I pray you will not hold it against me, and I ask you not to repeat what I say to another."

"It's that bad, is it?" The king sat in the chair at his table and put his head into one hand, shaking it slowly. "It *is* that bad."

"No father wants to see the rot in his child, I am sure."

"Rot, is it?"

"It is a figure of speech, your majesty."

"Go on. Tell me plainly. Tell me...as if I were not the king."

"Very well, your majesty. From my observations, Ealon has the will of a boy and the body of a man. He acts as a child would, impulsively. His emotions alone drive his actions, and...they are not good emotions, my king. He is bitter and resentful. He sees himself as victim to everyone around him. And he has no sense that his own actions have anything to do with how people treat him."

Uther raised his head and blinked. "I...tell me more of this."

Ennisbrook cleared his throat. "Ealon wants people to love and fear him, in equal measure, simply because he is a prince. But the truth is, as you know well, common men judge princes by their justice and their quality of heart, not by their station or some vague right bestowed by the oyosii. Princes have no innate *right* to the respect of their peoples, they must *earn* it. Ealon has yet to learn this fact."

"No, we have power, though, 'tis true. We can command the body, but the one thing we cannot command is the heart. That's a rum thing."

"It...you might see it as a gift from the oyosii, your majesty."

"Eh? How so?"

"It is the one thing that might keep a king honest."

Uther looked at his enforcer as if seeing him for the first time. "You speak like a philosopher, Daevis."

Ennisbrook smiled. "I studied moral philosophy at the university, in fact. I wanted to teach, at one time."

"And tonight you instruct me."

"I would not presume, your majesty. I simply...answered your question."

"You have done more than that. You have helped me peer around a corner where I have feared to look."

"If you do not mind me asking, your majesty...to what end?"

The king felt the first faint nodding effects of the laudanum. He welcomed them, but he knew there was not much time before he would cease to make responsible decisions for the evening. "Drink," he commanded. "A man who doesn't drink makes me nervous."

Ennisbrook retrieved the cup from the table and sipped at it. He set it back on the table and gave the king a curt nod.

"Eh...you give me compliance, when what I really want tonight is a companion."

Ennisbrook's face softened. He pointed to a chair. "May I, your majesty?"

"Ai, gods, sit, man. So long as you drink."

Ennisbrook sat, pushing his rapier unconsciously to the side, clear of the table leg. He picked up the cup, held it aloft before Uther as a toast, and took a healthy swig.

"That's better," Uther said.

"If your majesty will pardon me..." Ennisbrook leaned across the table and fixed Uther with an intelligent eye. "To what end?"

"What?"

"Why do you seek my counsel about Prince Ealon?"

"The summoner was here from the Keep. Osia."

"The one with the bird?"

"That's him. The fellow comes across as stout of heart, but...every time he speaks, I quail inside." He looked up. "I trust only you with this, Daevis."

"I will prove worthy of your secrets, my lord, I assure you."

"You always are." The king tapped his fingers. "He came asking after Ealon. A fell thing of power has been found...and stolen."

"He suspects Ealon?"

"He didn't say as much...yet he did."

"Have you asked the prince about it?"

Uther narrowed one eye. "I have not. Because I cannot find the prince."

Ennisbrook sat upright. "What mean you?"

"I mean that the prince is not in his chambers and has not been seen for days. I mean that we cannot find him and do not know where he has gone."

"This is a dire state for the house, my lord. The prince could be in danger, or dead, or captive. And given what has happened to Avantir's son..." Ennisbrook's eyes moved back and forth quickly. "Do you think—?"

"No, it is too soon. I have yet to send a messenger to Avantir with the news. To be honest, I haven't figured out how to word the letter."

"So it isn't revenge." Daevis drummed his own fingers on the table. He took another sip of wine, seemingly unconscious of it. "Where do *you* think your son is? In your father's heart?"

Uther swallowed but did not look at his enforcer. "I think he is hale of body, but not of mind. I think he lives, but is not free."

"Do you mean to say he has been captured by an enemy power?"

Uther shook his head. "I mean to say that he is a slave to his passions."

"I understand, your majesty."

Uther looked his enforcer in the eye. "I do not know what he is up to, but I fear it is not noble, nor is it something that would reflect well upon this house. Find him, Daevis. Find him and stop him and bring him back here to face my discipline."

Ennisbrook stood. "I will find him, your majesty. But if he will not come willingly?"

"Then bring him...unwillingly."

"SIT," Bracegirdle commanded.

Ellis slid into the chair in front of the old haffolk and sank as low as he could go, shoulders bunched higher than his ears.

Bracegirdle sat with a flourish and peered at him over his spectacles.

"Yes, you would do well to writhe, young man."

"I didn't get the job," Ellis said.

"No, you didn't get the bleedin' job!" Bracegirdle shouted. Others in the post office stopped and peered through his door. Bracegirdle got up, waddled to the door, and shut it with a bang.

Returning to his desk, he resumed his scowl. "How could you possibly turn in a performance like you did on your route from Yngremark to Ältremark and expect to advance?"

"I can explain, sir."

"Oh, can you?"

"I can."

"I'm listening."

"Uh...what do you know?"

"This came over the blips-and-squawks." The supervisor threw a short sheaf of parchments at him. The transmissions were recorded in a tight, neat hand, and followed all the appropriate protocol. Ellis sank even further as he read.

"You *lost* the package." Bracegirdle's voice dripped with disdain.

"Not exactly. The package was stolen. See?"

"So says a steward."

Ellis rifled through the pages. "Isn't there an affidavit from the pilot? We were boarded."

"In a position of responsibility...*one must take responsibility*." Bracegirdle was sneering at him now. "That is why you didn't get the postmaster job."

"How am I responsible if I'm hijacked and swindled?"

"A farthing must fall into some pocket, Sunderland. It fell into yours."

"I...I don't want that farthing, sir."

"And yet you will carry it. And it is *yours* to carry."

"I don't think my pockets are big enough."

"No one else is going to carry it, my boy."

"Um...we're not really talking about farthings, are we, sir?"

Bracegirdle sighed an exasperated sigh, pulling at the strands of hair left on either side of his head. "You were sent on a job. You did not complete the job. You *failed* at the job. That is the whole of the story."

Ellis said nothing. He looked at a scuff on the knee of his trousers.

"And now...the Royal Library has filed a brief in an Alliance court, asking to be heard on the matter of compensation. For a Very Important Item." He threw another piece of parchment at Ellis.

Ellis caught it and skimmed it through. He didn't understand a word of the complicated legalese.

"I don't understand, sir."

"It means if the courts agree to hear the case, the Royal Mail—*our* Royal Mail—may be on the hook for millions of pounds...all thanks to you."

Ellis bit his lip and squirmed in his seat, feeling nearly as small as a grown haffolk could feel.

"Am I fired, sir?"

"That...will be up to the new postmaster, not to me," Bracegirdle said.

"It's gone that high up, has it?"

"It has."

Ellis nodded, but could not meet his supervisor's eyes.

"So until then," Bracegirdle continued, "consider yourself on probation. From this moment on, you are relieved of your regular route. You will check in every day and I will personally select assignments that I deem...ungoofable."

"Ungoofable? Is that a word, sir?"

"It is, and it means a job that *even you* can't muff up."

"Yes, sir."

"I'll be checking your 'in' times and 'out' times. And I'll also be checking your paperwork. Personally."

Ellis looked away, so uncomfortable that at any moment he feared he would writhe out of his chair in shame. He gripped the chair's hand rests, just in case. The old haffolk took off his glasses and rubbed at his eyes. "You mind your p's and q's, don't lose any more packages, and in a year or two, you might well regain enough trust to earn back your old route."

"If Kit had been allowed to—"

Bracegirdle slammed his desktop with the flat of his hand. "Don't you try to put that farthing in *my* pocket, you toadlyish excuse for a haffolk."

"No, sir. Toadlyish. Quite right, sir."

Bracegirdle fitted his spectacles back onto the bridge of his nose and looked at the first of a sheaf of parchments sitting atop his desk. "Get out of my sight, Sunderland."

"Yes sir." Ellis almost slithered out of the chair. He headed for the door, but before opening it, he turned back. "Um...thank you, sir."

Bracegirdle blinked, but did not look up. "Whatever for?"

"The Yngremark assignment. It was a gift, I know. You were trying to help me. You probably went out on a limb to get me that assignment. And I let you down."

"A good courier can read the skies," Bracegirdle said. He looked up at him. "You always could read the skies, Sunderland. I'll give you that much."

Ellis nodded, turned, and let himself out the door.

❧

INDIÉL CLASPED her hands behind her back as she strolled in the garden beside Brennar. The top of the dwarf princess' head barely reached beyond her navel, but she appreciated her sturdy beauty. What surprised her more, though, was her cleverness.

"Do you often accompany your father on state visits?"

"Is that what this is?" Brennar laughed. "I thought my father just wanted to strangle someone."

Indiél responded with a laugh of her own. "Well then, is your father often in a mood to strangle someone?"

"Daily."

"And are you often party to it?"

"Rarely. And...I rarely get to accompany him, to properly answer your question. I was amazed he permitted it this time." She seemed to muse for a bit before adding. "I have my ways of influencing him."

"I think I know exactly what you mean," Indiél said, in a voice that was slightly conspiratorial. "All my life I've heard how diametrically opposed our cultures are—dwarfs and elves. For some reason, it's less important to distinguish ourselves from humans, although you do hear it. But everyone is always going on about the inferiority of dwarfs. I always wondered if it were actually true, or if perhaps it was a story we told ourselves just to help us feel superior." Brennar looked up at her and she held the dwarf's eye. "Now I suspect it was just a story."

The cloister garden was losing the last bit of dew to the sun, which was already midpoint to its zenith. Indiél paused to smell a bright spray of *vesse*, and motioned for Brennar to do the same. The dwarf princess' eyebrows rose. "It smells of clove."

"It does."

As they resumed their walk, Brennar said, "We tell similar stories about you." She laughed. "Not you personally, of course, but about elves."

"And what do dwarfs say about elves?"

"Do you really want to know? You won't be offended?"

"Pish," Indiél said. "I doubt you could say anything worse than I have thought."

"Very well, but I'll say you provoked me. We say that elves are arrogant, full of themselves, self-absorbed as a race."

"All true," Indiél confessed. "Every bit of it."

"And what do elves say about dwarfs?"

"You really want to hear?"

Brennar reached up and gave Indiél a playful slap.

"All right, all right," Indiél laughed, "We say you are prideful, emotional, and reckless."

"Guilty as charged," Brennar responded.

The two locked eyes and burst out laughing. Brennar put her hands to her mouth and shook her head. "We could get into trouble, talking like this, don't you think?"

"Why? Because we're probably the only dwarf and elf who have ever told each other the truth since the oyosii crafted our bones?"

"You jest, but you point to a sad truth." Brennar looked down.

In the middle of the cloister, a large fountain rose. Indiél watched as beads of spray caught the sunlight, creating a miniature rainbow before them. A few ducks pecked at the grass near their feet. "This is where the real diplomacy is happening," she said.

"Yes." Brennar reached out and took her hand.

Indiél felt a thrill run through her. Could it be that the dwarf princess was attracted to her? Or was it merely wishful thinking and an overactive imagination? Her hand-holding might only be a sign of solidarity, or maybe friendly affection. Whatever it was, Indiél thrilled to it.

Brennar let go and turned around. "This is a very beautiful garden... but I confess I'm not much for gardens. What do you do for sport?"

"Sport?"

"Yes. Do you hurl javelins, perhaps? Or throw axes? Or perhaps you play Oplicot?"

Indiél burst out laughing. "Oh dear, no. Nothing like that."

"Oh." Brennar looked a bit sheepish for a moment. "Well, do you cook? I mean, I know you *have* cooks, but sometimes I cook for fun."

"No, but I'd love to join you in that sometime."

"I know," Brennar said. "Let's fix our fathers lunch."

"What?" Indiél was slightly taken aback by Brennar's enthusiasm, but she didn't want to stop it.

"We can start now and be done before they break." Brennar leaned over and snatched up one of the ducks. Before Indiél even knew what was happening, the dwarf grabbed the screaming duck by the neck and whirled it about her head until the screaming stopped.

Indiél froze, her eyes wide, her mouth speechless.

Brennar reached into her short hose and drew forth a jeweled blade. With a confident and practiced flick, she severed the duck's head and grabbed it by its feet, draining its blood onto the grass. "Show me to your kitchen and let's see what kind of herbs you've got."

"I—I—" Indiél couldn't get any more words past her throat.

"What's wrong?" Brennar asked, the excitement draining from her faster than the duck's blood. "Was this a pet? Oh, that would be a horrible mistake."

"No," Indiél managed. "No pet."

"Well, that's a relief then. To the kitchen!" Brennar said, stomping off.

Before Indiél could say anything more, she heard a deep voice echoing off the cloister walls. It was not a pleased or pleasant voice. It took her a moment to realize it was Brennar's father yelling.

"—this instant. Where is my daughter?"

The dwarf king suddenly burst into view, his face red, his wide nostrils snorting. "Brenn-AARRRR!"

"Here, father," Brennar said, looking suddenly small in comparison with the magnitude of her father's apparent wrath.

"To the æthercraft, at once. We'll have no more elven prickishness!"

Brennar and Indiél exchanged a panicked, sorrow-filled look. Brennar handed the duck carcass to the elf princess. Indiél did not know what else to do in the moment but simply receive it, holding it at arm's length and raising her nose to the air.

King Belorin snatched at his daughter's hand and jerked her toward the cloister's ornamented archway. "They're all but foppishness and trickery."

"Good bye," Brennar threw over her shoulder.

"Good bye," Indiél responded. She looked at the severed head of the duck, resting on the grass, gazing sightlessly at the sky.

❧

Avantir walked through a haze. It could have been the smoke that still filled the air. Perhaps it was the obscuring blur from his watery eyes. But mostly it was the confusion that blanketed his mind. Why was there such a clamor without the castle? Why was there so much shouting? Why were so many people running about? Why was there such a smell of burning in the air?

The king made his way to the lower levels, trying to find a familiar face among the crowds. "Someone tell me what is happening," he cried out. "Are we being attacked?"

One of his soldiers, a man named Querrin, saw him and rushed to his aid. "Your majesty," the man said, daring to take the king's arm. "You must not be here. Come with me and—"

"Unhand me! Get away from me!" the king shouted, pushing the captain away as if he were being attacked. "Where are my guards? Seize this man!"

"Your majesty, let me help you," the captain tried again. "I am one of your guard."

Avantir took a second look at the man before renewing his shouts. "Then why are you here?" he cried. "Do not hide in the shadows! Get out and defend the castle, you traitor!"

"Your majesty, please. I fear you are under some strain." Looking around, the captain saw another member of the guard and waved him over. The second man took Avantir's other arm, and together they tried to gently turn the king back the way he had come.

"No, no," Avantir said, more quietly. "I do not want to go back. Take me outside. I must see what is happening."

"It is dangerous, sire. It is best to stay indoors."

"No, lead me out, I beg you."

The two guards exchanged a glance and then drew the king to a nearby door leading to an access corridor. A light at the end of it revealed a way out, a narrow opening, a service door where only one could pass through at a time. It was bright out, and Avantir's old eyes had trouble adjusting. He pulled his arm away from the guard, shading his brow with it. There was no greenery to absorb the sunlight; it had been reduced to soot and ash. The air was very hot and stank of smoke. The castle wall on this side was scorched black. "My home," Avantir murmured. "What has become of my keep? It is a ruin." Avantir looked about him. "What sorry legacy will I be leaving the prince now?"

The two guardsmen exchanged another worried look.

Avantir suddenly became more agitated. "The prince! My son! He was in these woods!" He broke free of his escort and started marching over the rough ground.

"Your majesty! Sire!" they called, chasing after him. With great determination the king made his way over the uneven ground and around the thick black limbs that used to be the forest. The area closest to the castle had been reduced to cinders, but further along were the remains of trees and many hearty, thorny bushes which had somehow survived the conflagration. These provided an obstacle for the king, but advantageous cover for those the king had wished to destroy.

Before the guards could react, seven men sprang onto the ruined plain. One of them grabbed the king, forcing him to the ashen ground. Others attacked his escort, but whether they restrained them or killed them, Avantir could not tell, as his attacker pulled a black bag over his head, tightening it at his neck. Unseen arms hurled him to his feet. He stumbled, but caught his balance, even as his assailant poked him with the dull end of a spear. "Walk!" the unseen man commanded. Avantir tried but stumbled again. He writhed as he found himself lifted from the ground.

II

Tubber Goodfoot swerved in his path, not to avoid the sleeping dog, but to meet it. He gave it a swift kick to the ribs and smiled as the surprised animal yelped and dashed away, looking fearfully over its shoulder. There were few enough occasions for sport along his route, and he rarely passed up such an opportunity. As he approached his next stop, Punter's End, he fished in his bag for the small bundle to be delivered—four letters of various sizes, bound together by rough twine. Looking around to make sure he was not being observed, he quickly sorted through the letters. One looked like a bill from the gas utility—Tubber recognized widow Shadowlasher's neat script. She was the only person in the billing and receiving department there, so he had little doubt about it. That letter would yield him nothing. Two appeared to be announcements—thinly disguised adverts. The fourth was more interesting, however.

Looking around one more time, he pulled this last letter, the largest, from the bundle and held it up between his eye and the full light of the sun. He narrowed his eyes and tried to make out what was in it through the envelope. Seeing the telltale circle typically found in the corner of a pound note, he grinned. "This one need not find its way home just yet," he said out loud, though quietly, to himself. Later, he would steam the envelope open and "inspect" the contents. Hopefully the letter inside would not mention the pound note. If, as he hoped, it did not mention it, the letter would find its owner on the morrow. If it did mention it, it would be disappointing all around, as some letters just get lost in transit—more's the pity.

Tubber placed the letter carefully into a back fold in his courier bag, where none but he would find it. Just then he saw movement out of the corner of his eye. It was the Dale, so quick movement of any kind was unusual. Looking up and squinting, he saw his friend Powdy Grumblethorn running in his direction. Tubber slung his courier's bag over his rested shoulder and waved.

Powdy inclined his head in greeting and kept running until, out of breath and gasping, he nearly collapsed at Tubber's feet. He reached out for Tubber's arm to steady himself, and Tubber grasped at his hand and held him up. "What is it? What news?"

"The postings," he said in between gasps.

"Yes, yes, out with it," Tubber said.

He wanted the postmaster's job so badly he could taste it. He knew the competition was strong, and in his more honest moments would agree that there were better haffolk in contention for it than he, but the lure of the power, the influence he would have over the Dale as postmaster was almost intoxicating. People would call him "Postmaster Goodfoot," an honorific he had carved into the tabletop at the Slug and Lettuce tavern, just to see how it would look.

But Powdy was still doubled over, hands grasping his legs just below the knees. He knew his friend was out of shape—in fact all of his friends were. Tubber was probably the fittest, by dint of the miles he walked every day on his route. Powdy put one finger in the air, and then, still heaving, he rose and looked Tubber in the face.

Tubber knew, instantly. It was not a triumphant look. Powdy shook his head, his face grimacing—but more from lack of air than from the news. "Sorry, boss," Powdy said. "You didn't get it."

"Swiving horn of bloody blood," Tubber spat. "Who did? It was that weasel Sunderland, wasn't it?"

He hated Sunderland. Ever since grade school when the too-good-for-tattling Ellis had bested him in an astronomy contest, he knew the little grub had it in for him.

Powdy shook his head. "No, not...not Sunderland. Jess—"

"Spindlethorn? Jess Spindlethorn? That wee lass?"

"Aye."

That took Tubber by surprise. He hadn't expected a she-haffolk to get the job. It just seemed...wrong. It was hard to know how to position himself to take offense at it, however. That would require some pondering.

"How in the blazing Scar did I get bested by a girl?"

"She's a smart one," Powdy commented, his breathing finally slowing down.

Tubber ignored him. He placed his forefinger on his lips and tapped. "It must have been sabotage. It's the only explanation."

"Sunderland was talking to Bracegirdle...before he went off-world."

"Was he now?"

"Telia saw him. It was some long conversation, she said. He was in his office for a quarter hour or more."

"Was he now?" Tubber's brows knit together darkly.

"He just got back, you know. Word is, his job didn't go well."

Tubber wasn't sad to hear it. He would have to find out more about that later. But in the meantime... "See if you can find out what Sunderland said to Bracegirdle, eh?" Tubber clapped his friend on the shoulder. "If we can't get the job...the least we can do is get revenge."

❧

AVANTIR RESISTED the indignity of being carried, like a boar to roasting, but he also realized there was nothing he could do about it. At last, it had come to this: he was too old and weak to defend himself. He heard scuffling behind him, a disturbance with many snarled threats, which he took to be his escort trying to break free. But they must be as restrained and helpless as he was.

At last he felt himself settled onto a low, shallow seat. His hood was removed and he found himself sitting on a log as black as charcoal. His surroundings were dark but there was light coming from behind him. He turned as far as he could and saw he was in the mouth of a cave — a shelf of rock above them but with a floor of dark soil. The cave was filled with a smoky haze, most likely from the fires his soldiers had started and not from the small fire which had been set in front of him. Though seated, he could tell the cave had a low ceiling, as his captors were hunched over. Another one emerged from the shadows, a burly man with a thick black beard and long mustaches which ended in carefully groomed curls. His hair was slick and the firelight made it shine, presumably from perfumed oils. What made the man's demeanor most curious to Avantir was that, despite the menacing surroundings, he seemed to be in high spirits. There was a glint in his eye which seemed out of place.

The man was already bending low, but then he struggled to bow even more, sweeping an arm out theatrically. He spoke with a deep voice. "Your majesty. I have often wondered if we might meet some day."

"And who are you, my good man?" Avantir asked.

"You are king of the castle. I am king of the wildmen. I am Clumfero."

"*You*!" Avantir cried, struggling to get up. Immediately hands were placed on his shoulders, forcing him back down. "You murderer! *You killed my son*!"

"I see it is your grief talking. I understand it, but you could not be more wrong, great king. I did not kill your son." Avantir, in his frustration, had begun to weep. Clumfero repeated his words louder, the better for the king to hear them. "I did *not* kill your son. He was dead when we found him, I'm afraid to say. Surely you may condemn me for using the discovery to ransom money from you—and you'd do well to, I don't deny it. But, as you certainly know, a king must do everything he can for the good of his people. I was simply making what I could out of the situation presented to me."

"My son!" Avantir cried. He hung his head low, but his weeping had stopped.

"Your grief hurts my heart, great king," Clumfero said. "I have sons, too. To lose them would surely rend my soul, as it has yours. But if I may, you must accept that he is dead, my lord. Burning down the forest will not make him come back."

Avantir raised his tear-stained face. His eyes locked on Clumfero's and his voice was steadier than it had been in many days. "You say you did not kill Clendis."

"Yes. His life had already been taken. He was left in the woods for us to find."

"Who would do such a thing? Who say you?"

"It was the right-hand man of High King Uther. The one they call the Enforcer. We saw him take the prince's life and leave the body behind."

Avantir's head dropped again. "Damn him," he said in a whisper. "Damn him and damn them all. All of them." There was a long silence, as the king struggled with his emotions, taking many loud and tattered breaths. Finally he spoke again. "What did you with the prince? Where is his body?"

"He sleeps here, great king. We buried him in the shelter of this cave."

"Then you have treated him better than I. For in my madness, I would've charred his remains in fire."

Then Avantir raised his head again, his shoulders rising, his back becoming straighter. It looked like his kingly bearing was returning to him, there in front of everyone. "Untie me," he declared. "There will be, I assure you, no repercussions for my treatment here. But I — and my escort — must return to the castle. There is business to attend to."

"Great king," Clumfero said, nodding. "I will do as you ask. But, you must promise to let my people stay, unencumbered, in that part of the forest that remains. If you agree to that, you can stay in your castle, we can stay in the forest, and we need never meet again."

Avantir did not agree out loud, but he did not speak against the proposition. He nodded, and, smiling, Clumfero gestured for his men to free Avantir. They helped the king to his feet, unbound his guards, and escorted them to the mouth of the cave. Stepping back into the sunlight, Avantir saw his castle was still within view. This cave was not much farther than where they'd been attacked. The two guardsmen helped Avantir back, but he walked with a stronger gait and a surer foot now. The air was still a haze, but the haze was gone from his mind. He had a purpose now. He had sworn vengeance on the wrong man. Clumfero meant nothing to him. It was now Uther and the house of Summerfield he vowed to destroy.

❧

EALON WAS unsure how long he lay on the hard rock. It felt like only a few hours, but it must have been longer, since the pain had lessened to a tolerable level. His head still throbbed, his face was extremely tender, but the shortness of breath was gone and he had more mobility in his limbs.

He heard a noise and two figures entered. One was presumably the gray-skinned one from before, followed by a similar brute with dark-red skin. They were both hulking, muscular, and intimidating. Between them they carried a pallet of two poles connected by woven straps. They roughly shoved it under Ealon and then rolled him onto it. He was tempted to protest their rough treatment, but he realized they were transporting him somewhere, and he would rather be borne upon this stretcher than forced to walk.

Ealon was carried from the cave into a long tunnel which was also lit by torches. He passed voices and activity and assumed there must be other caves off this tunnel. Perhaps he was passing people's homes; perhaps he was passing through a whole underground city of these brutish creatures.

The noises drifted away, but his bearers continued onward. He was unaware of any turns or whether the passageway forked to one side or the other. At length the roof of the tunnel—which he had been staring at—vanished, replaced by darkness. As his bearers set him on the ground, he could tell by the sound that he was in a huge cavern. He rolled onto his side and saw he had been transported to some place recognizable as a throne room, vast and impressive—except that the walls and ceiling were jagged rock. The floor was level and smooth; ahead of him were steps leading up to a large dark chair, lit by braziers on either side. A figure sat in the chair, silent and unmoving. Unlike most of the beings here, this one was draped in a robe. The top of his head was bald, but his white hair was long, as was his beard.

"Rise," Cragga muttered to Ealon. "On your feet. Bow before Praltuda, king of the *Ūnna-kar.*" Ealon was too slow to react, and Cragga jabbed him with a foot as heavy as a club.

Ealon was unsure if he could stand, but he managed to push himself up so that he was kneeling. Cragga grabbed his elbow and Ealon was able to rise to his feet.

Praltuda, the great lord of the Scrum, watched them as they approached. He sat motionless, but after a long moment he tilted his head to the right. His body then followed as he shifted against his armrest. His eyes were large and dark, Ealon saw. His mouth was stretched forward, similar to a beak; and as he spoke, Ealon was taken aback at the unexpected number of ugly dark teeth.

"I am told it was you who spoke the name of the most honored... you, who sundered the Prison Stone."

"Yes," Ealon said. "It was I."

"'*My lord*,'" Cragga hissed.

"Yes, my lord. It was I," Ealon offered.

"Yet weren't you, earlier, filling our halls with screams, wailing like a babe without a breast?"

Ealon had assumed he was about to finally gain the recognition he felt entitled to, but here he was being insulted—with his bearers openly laughing at him. "How," Praltuda continued, "could such a pathetic weakling gain possession of the Fängelsten, I ask you?"

Ealon quivered at the insult. First they torture him and now they ridicule him? He pulled his elbow from Cragga's grasp and forced himself to approach the throne. The lord leaned forward, intrigued by what might happen. "I gained possession," Ealon began, trying to steady his voice, trying not to show the effort these steps were taking, "because I was quickest to act when the Stone was discovered. I did not cower in darkness! If this Stone means so much to you, where were *you* when it was unearthed? As far as I could tell, you were nowhere to be found when your precious Stone became mine!"

"You wretched slug!" Praltuda bellowed. "My healers prolonged your pointless life and this is the gratitude you show? Fall down, like the maggot you are, and beg forgiveness for your insolence—before I crush you beneath my foot!"

"I will not bow to *you*, my *lord*," Ealon sneered. "I am a Prince of the great lands, son of High King Uther—and *you* will show me the respect the title deserves!"

"Your titles mean nothing—your *kingdoms* mean nothing here," Praltuda scoffed. "The Scrum were here before the entire line of Uther was spawned. Humans and their squabbles change with the seasons—but the Scrum endure, like the rock."

Ealon was ready to ignore the lord's rant...until he realized it had already stopped. Noticing the silence, he looked up to see the lord was staring at him.

"Cragga," Praltuda ordered. "A torch, to me."

Cragga hurried to the wall, near the dais, and pulled free a torch from its sconce. He then returned to the front of the dais, brandishing the flame before Praltuda, awaiting the next command.

"To the upstart," Praltuda said, quietly. "Hold it near his face."

Ealon looked at the torch uneasily as it came nearer.

"Tell me, young prince," Praltuda continued, almost sounding kindly. "What happened while you were in the varr, when you struck the Stone?"

"It shattered. It exploded in my face."

"...And you lost your eye, yes. So the stone touched you?"

Ealon was confused. First the lord ridicules him and now shows an interest in him? He answered hesitantly. "I suppose so, yes."

"Yes. You have the mark on you. I see it now."

"I do?"

"One of you—show him," Praltuda ordered. The other bearer—the one who wasn't Cragga—went to a banquet table, far off to Ealon's left, and returned with a clean, empty silver platter. Ealon looked at himself in it. He saw no mark, but he did notice the left side of his face was covered in a red blemish from cheek to hairline. "Do you see it? The triangle of red?" Ealon tried to lean closer and the healer raised the platter as well. The blemish had a triangular shape, but the narrow tip leaned to the left, like a windblown wave. "It is a tentacle. The tentacle of our master." Praltuda's voice grew as he raised himself from his throne. “It is the mark of the Dark Lord, known among you humans as Samael. He has surely touched you and made you his messenger. The Dark Lord lives—the Dark Lord is returning.”

The bearer lowered the platter, looking instead to his lord. As Praltuda continued his pronouncements, both this bearer and Cragga slowly sank to their knees. They raised their hands above them and joined into the chant. “The Dark Lord lives! The Dark Lord returns!” The shouting drew the attention of some guards, who ran into the room only to drop their spears and also join in on the chant. “The Dark Lord lives! The Dark Lord returns!”

Ealon looked about in confusion. Mockery, animosity, scorn, and now, suddenly, adulation, and always to the extreme. It was difficult to keep up with this conversation, adjusting to all its changes. But if there was one way to be won over it had to be this: seeing a roomful of strangers—a room full of brutish warriors—on their knees bowing to him. The jubilation was a bit much, but it was nonetheless easy to accept.

Then again, for all he knew, this so-called mark could just be a rash from whatever diseased loam they'd put on his face. What would happen when it wore off? Considering this lord's extreme reactions, Ealon would likely be accused of being a fraud and instantly sentenced to some horrible death.

Ealon told himself he would have to enjoy it while it lasted. He rather liked having a room full of supplicants chanting their veneration—even if, he had to admit, they were doing it through him rather than to him. And then again, if the mark *was* real, if he truly *was* an instrument of the Dark Lord...

“You must address our people,” Praltuda said above the din. “We will assemble our nations in the great hall. All the *Ūnna-kar* should hear your message—we have waited so long to hear it spoken!”

“Wait,” Ealon said. “You said ‘nations’? You mean, there are more of you?”

Praltuda nodded. “A great many more, all awaiting your instruction.”

The tense look of worry returned to Ealon's face, as he realized here was another wild development he would need to adjust to.

❦

ELLIS MADE his excuses after second dinner, much to the consternation of his family, who had been asking for a song. He deputized his brother Brander to sing in his stead, but since Brander couldn't hold a tune in a bucket, it had been a hard sell.

But as he stepped free of the low house and the round door closed behind him, he breathed deep of the cool night air and felt tension drain from his shoulders and pour out the ends of his fingertips. He loved his family, but there were times when the house made him feel claustrophobic. He was always happy to go home, but he was never there long before he felt the itch to be moving again, back to the road and its open spaces.

He felt a spring in his step as he found the road, just as the last bit of sunlight faded. Hearth—the great planet that Everdale circled—dominated the sky, however, and it was bright, flooding his road with a pale blue light that was more than enough to travel by.

As he walked, he found himself growing excited about the mysterious note in his vest pocket. It was a good and welcome feeling, since he'd spent most of the day feeling like a failure. Indeed, after his disastrous meeting with Bracegirdle, he'd gone home and covered his head with a pillow, ignoring his Aunt Tully's entreaties to rouse himself and help her around the Roost.

He remembered Kit's advice to ignore the note. It had been more than advice, really, it had been a command, but Ellis chose to interpret it as advice. Advice, after all, was easier to dismiss than a command.

He appreciated her care for him. Deep down, he knew she even loved him, in her own way. His heart ached a bit as he thought of her, and his hand went to his breast. She was his closest friend, and he was grateful for that. But he would have been more grateful to have her as a mate.

And that, he knew, was never going to happen. He had resigned himself to that the first time Kit had fallen in love...with another haffolk lass. From that moment, Ellis knew that he was as close to her as he would ever be. And on a good day, he was content with that.

But this was not a good day, and not good days had a way of

opening old wounds, the same way bad weather made Uncle Emmet's bones ache.

Lost in his thoughts, he did not see the road pass beneath his feet, nor notice when the country lane gave way to cobblestones and the first outlying buildings of the village. He was about to cross the third side street when a dark-hooded figure stepped around a corner, directly into his path.

Ellis nearly lost his balance trying not to bump into the figure. "Pardon me!" he said, but more as rebuke than apology.

Kit threw back her hood and drilled him with both dark eyes. "I thought I told you not to go tonight."

Ellis breathed a sigh of relief. "How did you know I would?"

"Because, with you, the only thing stronger than self-loathing is your curiosity."

Ellis moved his head from side to side. He wasn't sure he liked the sound of that, but it wasn't untrue.

"It's not a good idea," Kit said.

"How do you know? You have no idea who it's from or what it's about."

"Decent folk don't do business through anonymous notes and clandestine meetings in taverns."

"Decent folk *that you know* don't do business that way."

"That's a pocketful of fewmets and you know it," Kit said.

He didn't respond, because she was right.

"If you're determined to go, you'll not go alone," she said forcefully, as a statement of fact. She moved to stand beside him and they began walking together. She threw a sidelong glance at him, as if daring him to protest.

He did not protest. Instead, he weaseled. "How about this? You go in first, and set yourself up where you can see everything in the pub. I'll count to five hundred and follow you in. That way, it looks like I've come alone, but you can keep an eye on things."

She said nothing, which Ellis took to be a good sign. Finally, she said, "Count to six hundred, and lend me a shilling for a pint."

Ellis dug two shillings out of his vest pocket and put them in her outstretched hand. "Sorry," he said. "I'll pay you tomorrow. Promise."

"I'm not complaining," she said. "You had other things on your mind. It was a tough day."

"It was," he agreed.

The Slug and Lettuce Tavern loomed before them, filling the quiet village alley with an inviting golden glow and the sound of convivial voices. Snatches of a reel played on a concertina wafted out to them, pulling them in.

"Six hundred," Kit said. "Not a moment before."

"Six hundred," Ellis agreed.

She narrowed her eye at him in warning and then strode quickly to the door. Ellis backed up into the shadow of a nearby building as the round door swung open. He watched her descend the three stairs into the squat dugout before it swung shut again.

All haffolk buildings were the same—squat, thatched dwellings dug down as much as built up. Consequently, their homes and shops tended to stay cool in summer and warm in winter, without the need to burn too much coal.

When he reached six hundred, he stepped into the glow of the tavern again and made his way to the door. He opened it and was met with an instant rush of laughter, music, and warmth. It was inviting and homey. He stepped down into the pub and made straight for the bar. "Pint of Mallard's, please, Liza," he said to the barmaid.

Liza Silverberry winked at him and he blushed. She turned her back to him as she pulled his pint, and he couldn't help but notice the way her bottom filled out her dress in a way that pleased him. As she turned around, he noticed that she was pretty, too—not in the way that made his knees shake, but in a way that made him feel relaxed and at ease with himself.

"Here you go, love," she said, placing the pint on the bar with a generous smile. "Will ye pay now or will ye be drinkin' more?"

"I don't know if I'll drink more, but can I settle up with you later?"

"I'll be here all night." She winked at him and he suddenly felt lightheaded.

I could do worse than Liza, he thought. She's smart, she's got her own business, she's not hard to look at, and...she seems to like me. He cocked his head and watched her some more.

She noticed. "Are you going to drink that, or are you just going to spend the evening staring at my dugs?"

He blinked and looked away, aghast. Had he really been staring at her teats? He didn't think so, but in the moment he didn't trust himself.

Liza laughed at him. "Got you that time, love."

Ellis noticed he was sweating. "Yes...uh...got me," he said. He picked up his pint of ale and finally turned his attention to the room.

The first thing he noticed was Kit, one bemused eyebrow poised so high on her forehead he thought it might fly away. He quickly looked away from her and scanned the crowd.

And it was a crowd. He rarely went out to the pubs after dark, but many people did, and they all seemed to be here. If he needed to cross the tavern in a hurry, he would be hard pressed to do so, for it was something of an obstacle course for all the tables and benches and merry haffolk bodies—many of them in motion, dancing to the concertina's reel.

He peered into the dim reaches of the tavern and saw one figure who towered over the rest. A man? It was hard to see from this distance, but more likely a man than an elf. Ellis kept looking, but recognized everyone else. No one made eye contact with him, or if they did, it was no more than a nod and a raised pint in greeting. He nodded back and kept looking, but his eye kept returning to the tall, shadowy figure in the next-to-last booth—the only seat in the house large enough for a man.

Picking his path carefully, he made a circuit of the room, eventually making his way to the far corner. As he approached the man's table—and it was clear that it was a man, for as he got closer he could see the rounded ear of a human, not to mention the stubble of beard. The man was used to shaving, Ellis could see, but had not done so for a day or two. Elves did not grow facial hair, nor hair anywhere on their bodies save on their heads, or so went the old wives' tales. Ellis did not know if that were true, but the few elves he had caught glimpses of in Rhory were always smooth of face.

The man's eyes flitted up and met his own, and he gave Ellis a curt nod of recognition. It was only then that Ellis knew who it was.

"Osia?"

The summoner was not wearing his hat, and he had a cloak thrown over his robe, so Ellis did not see the stain on his shoulder. As he drew near, Ellis saw Jaq sitting on the bench beside his master.

"Sit, my little friend," Osia said, his swarthy face brightening in welcome.

"Did you..." Ellis fished the note out of his pocket.

"It was from me, yes," Osia said. "I do not know which of these cozy haffolk holes you live in, but I met a boy who swore he could find you."

"And find me he did," Ellis said. He placed his pint on the table and slid into the seat across from the summoner. "Truth be told, I was right nervous about who might show up, so I'm relieved to find it's you."

"Don't relax your guard too much." Osia looked around warily. "There are dark forces afoot, make no mistake."

"Dark forces, sir? I'm afraid I don't know what you mean."

Osia's face fell into a compassionate look. "And I hope you will never have to know. But...that seems unlikely."

Ellis blinked, not sure how to interpret what the man was saying. "Summoners are queer folk," he remembered his Aunt Tully saying, more than once. Most people were on their guard around them, if they met them at all. But Osia had rescued him and had brought him home. If not for this summoner, he might yet be rotting in a dwarfish prison. He shuddered at the thought.

"But there is no need to pounce on the carrion like a buzzard. We have ale before us and music to gladden the heart. I fear our hearts will need much gladdening in the days to come, so let us not forsake the gifts of the hearth while we have it. Tell me how it is with you, since your return from Ältremark."

Ellis had forgotten his troubles for a moment, but now they came rushing back. He quickly told Osia about his dashed hopes of being postmaster. He saw the summoner's brows knit together in concern. "What a disappointment, my young friend. I am very sorry for you."

"Beer!" Jaq ejaculated.

"Do you think that's wise?" Osia asked the bird.

"Beer!" Jaq repeated.

Osia pulled a small wooden bowl from some secret pocket inside his robe and poured some of his own ale into it. He put it down on the seat beside him. Jaq instantly dipped his beak into it.

"The thing that hurts most, though, isn't not getting the job," Ellis continued. "It's...it's the not-being-well-thought-of, if you know what I mean. I try very hard to do everything right, to make people happy. I just...I just want people to *like* me."

Osia pursed his lips and nodded slowly. He leaned over the table and said in a low voice, "The problem with wanting to be liked is that you can't do anything hard. Do you think as postmaster you could make everyone like you? Not a chance! You'd have to fire people, reprimand them, demand things from them that they wouldn't want to give. How would you do that without ruffling some feathers?"

Jaq cawed.

"Shh..." Osia commanded. "It is but an idiom." He turned back to Ellis. "You could not be postmaster and be liked by everyone, just as you cannot be a good courier and please everyone. Listen, my friend, and I'll tell you a great secret."

Ellis leaned over the table, too, cocking his head to hear better over the din of the tavern. "The truth is, you cannot control how other people feel...not even a summoner can do that."

"You can't?"

"No matter how hard you try. And if you try too hard...well, then you'll have no energy left for anything that matters. Mr. Sunderland, you don't *need* everyone to like you. You need to be the sort of person that you yourself respect. Some people will like that...and some won't. And you must be at peace with that."

Ellis blinked.

"You don't look convinced...or happy," Osia noted.

"I'm just...I'll need to think some on it, sir."

The summoner nodded. "Good lad. Brooding is good for the soul, I believe."

"Yes, sir." Ellis took a sip of his ale. "Begging your pardon, sir, but we don't see many summoners in the Dale. What brings you hereabouts?"

"Fire!" Jaq said.

"Everything is about fire with him lately," Osia apologized.

"What does it mean?"

"I shudder to think." Osia pulled a small flatcase from his robe. Ellis marveled at what other wonders the robe must contain. The summoner opened the flatcase with the flick of a fingernail that would be a little too long for a properly groomed haffolk in the Dale. From the case he gingerly pulled forth two *vakerbilds.* Ellis had seen one or two before at a display at the village hall, but he'd never been close enough to one to touch it.

"May I?" he asked.

Osia handed the *vakerbilds* to him. They were deep brown in color, and slightly fuzzy around the edges. But the image in the center was razor sharp. Ellis froze, and the *vakerbilds* dropped to the table.

"Are you all right, Mr. Sunderland? You look like you've seen a ghost."

Ellis noticed that he had stopped breathing. He forced himself to take a deep breath and looked at the summoner full in the face. "It's him."

"It's who?" the summoner asked, cocking his head.

"It's the...Inspector Brill. It's the man who stole the package, the stone," Ellis said, not daring to look at the *vakerbild* again.

"You are certain?" Osia asked, raising one bushy black eyebrow.

Ellis nodded vigorously.

"Look at the other one," Osia said.

"Do I have to, sir?"

"We want to be...very sure about this. Very, very sure."

"All right."

With shaking hands, Ellis picked up the *vakerbilds* and placed the one on top beneath the other. He looked at the second image. "That's the same man, sir. That's Inspector Brill. He's the man who stole my package. Or...his dwarf did."

"There is no doubt in your mind?"

"No, sir."

"You couldn't be mistaken? It couldn't be someone who looks a bit like him?"

"No, sir. I swear on the Red Horn of Arrunwolfe. That's the man... the very man."

Osia gently lifted the *vakerbilds* from Ellis' trembling fingers and replaced them in the flatcase. "You have done well, Mr. Sunderland."

"I hope that I have, sir."

"Because you want me to like you?" Osia smiled.

"Uh...I want *everyone* to like me," Ellis confessed, hunkering sheepishly.

"Now that's done, I have another item of business to discuss with you."

"Oh, yes?" Ellis brightened up.

"Now that you're not going to be postmaster...at least not yet..."

"Not ever, likely," Ellis interjected.

"The future coils like a snake, my friend. It's hard to predict the location of its tail."

"I suppose it is." Ellis noticed that it was difficult to argue with aphorisms.

"Do you mind if I smoke?" Osia asked.

"Not at all sir. If you've got some hearthweed, I've got my pipe," he pulled a gnarled, broad-bowled pipe from his vest pocket.

"Very good," Osia said, pulling a smoking kit from somewhere in his robe. The summoner opened the leather straps on a bag of hearthweed and gestured to Ellis to help himself. Then the man began to pack the bowl of a long clay pipe with a jagged mouthpiece.

"Fire!" Jaq called.

"We'll just use the candle here," Osia said to the bird. He took a deep pull at the pipe and closed his eyes, savoring its sweet, leathery taste. Releasing a small cloud of smoke, he said, "You say you are on probation now?"

"I am."

"For how long?"

"I couldn't say, sir."

"How much are they paying you?"

"Five guineas a week. Docked from ten."

Osia whistled and sat back, puffing. "What would you say if I were to put you on retainer, as a private courier? At, say, fifteen guineas a week?"

Ellis froze. "I think I didn't hear you right, Mr. Osia."

"I think you did. I'm offering you a better job. Of course, I can't guarantee how long it might last, so you'll need to weigh that against whatever job security you enjoy now."

"Precious little, sir," Ellis admitted. "Um...begging your pardon, sir, I wonder...what does a summoner need with a courier?"

"Ah..." Osia nodded. "Of course, you'd be under contract with my order and might be employed by any number of summoners. But I reckon for the time being, at least at first, you'll answer to me."

Ellis nodded, following. But then he realized the summoner had not actually answered his question. "Yes, that's reasonable, I think. But...*why* does a summoner need a courier? You go where you will." Ellis lit his own pipe.

Osia smiled. "Do you know this song?" he asked, and then began, half singing, half speaking:

"Linigan, Linigan,
More fit than fat
More dog than cat
More coat than hat
His vest made of sable.

"Linigan, Linigan,
Foe to none
Friend of the sun
Already won
Eager and able.

"Linigan, Linigan,
Moves through the trees
Nobody sees
Entirely free
Sleeps in the stable.

"Linigan, Linigan,
Light on his feet
Merry and meet
Always a seat
At the commonfolk's table."

Ellis sang the last line with him. "Of course, sir. Every haffolk in primary school knows that one."

"I need someone who is 'a foe to none,' someone who can 'move through the trees,' someone 'light on his feet.' You see?"

"I'm not sure I do, sir."

Osia sighed. "Let me speak plainly, Mr. Sunderland...Ellis. Would you do me the honor of allowing me to call you by your given name?"

"I would be very pleased indeed, sir."

"I'll make you a deal. I'll call you Ellis, you stop calling me 'sir.' Can we agree to that?"

"Yes, sir."

Osia smiled. "I can go where I will, but I'm suspected and noticed everywhere I go. A courier, especially a haffolk courier, is...well, not invisible, but near to it."

Ellis nodded. "People think we're beneath them, men do. And dwarfs."

"They do, sadly."

"People more often than not ignore us rather than acknowledge us, because to make note of us would be to...make us legitimate, somehow."

Osia nodded. "It's bad form to actively *discriminate* against haffolk in public, but quite acceptable to ignore them. The advantage to you... and to me, should you take this job...is that you can go almost anywhere and no one will stop you, nor even notice you. You can 'move through the trees,' and 'nobody sees.'"

"You need a Linigan," Ellis released a billow of savory smoke, nodding, his eyes distant.

"I do. I need someone who can evade prying eyes," Osia said. "Unlike here, apparently." Standing to his feet, he leaned over the table, and Ellis wondered whether the summoner was about to fall on him. But then, with a swift motion, Osia reached over Ellis' head into the booth behind him and effortlessly plucked Kit from the bench. She struggled in the air, writhing almost comically before the summoner dropped her beside himself, nearly on top of Jaq. The bird cawed in protest.

Kit's eyes were flashing fire. Her hand went to her longneedle but there was not room enough in the booth to draw it.

"You won't be needing that, little lady," Osia said. "Now...how much did you hear?"

"It's all right, Osia, sir," Ellis said. "She's with me."

Osia narrowed one eye at him. "Is she?"

"She's ready with a longneedle—"

"I see that."

"—and she...she protects me."

Osia pulled at his pipe and surveyed the young woman. "She looks like a scrapper."

"You can speak *to me*, sorcerer, but not *about* me," Kit informed him.

"Is she always like this, or did I just surprise her?" Osia asked.

"Uh...you *did* surprise her. But no...she's always like this."

"Are you deaf?" She struggled to draw her longneedle again.

"Are you sure we can trust her?" Osia asked Ellis.

"Absolutely, sir. I'd bet my life on Kit, sir."

"Kit. Short for...?"

"Kittredge. Kittredge Cornfeather," Ellis answered.

"Oh, great. Now the sorcerer has my name. Thanks a lot, Ellis."

Osia nodded. "Very well, then. I don't think we said anything damning aloud. Just...think about my offer, Mr. Sunderland. Yay or nay, I'll need your answer soon."

❧

"I'M TELLING YOU, cats have no place aboard an æthercraft," Ailwin said in elventongue.

"I have no quarrel with that, brother. I'm talking about space stations. You must allow a feline presence, or no self-respecting elf would bother going into space," Felærn replied.

"We do all right."

"We hate it. And if you were honest, you'd say the same." Felærn raised an eyebrow and dared his brother to cross him again. "Time for the 03:00 sweep."

The æthercraft *Eilandryl* was at rest at the far edges of the territory the Black Elves had claimed. Most elves were disdainful of humans and dwarfs, but Black Elves had never gotten on well with the Green or Brown Elves who traditionally ruled the elven worlds. Fiercely proud, they had dismissed the community of bright beings as beneath them and, as soon as their magic and technology had advanced far enough to take them, had claimed a world for themselves far from the meddlesome reach of their elven kin.

The æthercraft was quiet, being, as it was, on border patrol in the dead of night. The brothers had volunteered for watch duty together—partly because they enjoyed the quiet expanse, but mostly because they preferred their own company.

Ailwin touched a few nodes on his command console and sat back, watching the grid advance on the large viewscreen that filled one wall of the gleaming bridge.

At the center of the viewscreen was a blinking dot that represented Fondolyn Illasyntir, the planet the Black Elves had tamed and taken for themselves. The name of the planet had caused quite some consternation among the elven High Council. Fondolyn had been the name of a legendary elven city, while "Illasyntir" meant "primary" or "most important." It seemed a fitting name for a planet among the elves who lived there, but an affront to elven culture to everyone else.

The Black Elves cared little what their brethren thought. They cared even less what they did, so long as they steered clear of their claimed space.

At the far edges of the viewscreen, Ailwin watched a representation of the long-range scanner as it advanced through their territories. They'd claimed space up to seven parsecs around Fondolyn Illasyntir, but the scans were set for ten, just so they'd have some warning before an intruder crossed into their space.

Felæern jerked upright in his seat.

"What?" Ailwin asked.

"We've got something." He began touching nodes with an efficient haste.

"What? What do you see?"

"I...I'm not sure. It doesn't look anything like..." he trailed off, unable to make sense of what he saw on his console.

"Do you have a location?" Ailwin asked.

"Yes...972.649 through 895.186."

"*Through*? What do you mean *through*? No ship is that big. No *planet* is that big."

"I'm telling you, those are the readings I get," Felærn was as puzzled as his brother.

"I'm alerting the captain."

"Good." A moment later, Felærn said, "Can you get a long-range scope pointed in that direction? We need a visual on...on whatever this is."

"One moment," Ailwin's hands danced over his console. "We should have visual in...there."

Felærn looked up and his mouth dropped open.

"By the horn..." Ailwin's eyes were equally large as he studied the screen.

"What in the name of all that is holy...?"

Felærn could not comprehend what he was seeing. At first, it looked like a dark cloud was creeping up on them. It would not even have been immediately noticeable against the relentless dark of deep space, except that the stars behind it were occluded, creating a very long shadow.

"Zoom in," Felærn ordered.

The picture before them morphed, until the black band across the sky stretched from one end of the screen to the other. The band was slightly askew, but Felaern could see that, whatever it was they were looking at, it was not spherical. It was symmetrical, radiating out an equal distance from some central point. What they were seeing was vaguely disk-shaped, like a pie or a round of traditional journeybread, which they were viewing from the side.

"It's moving toward us...fast," Ailwin noted.

Just then the door to the bridge slid open and an elderly woman stepped out from the lift. Her skin was fair, but time had scored lines through her face, testimony to the millennia she had seen. Her black hair had turned gray, which she wore like a crown of wisdom. She nevertheless rubbed sleep from her eyes and yawned. "Why was I roused from my sleep?"

Felærn and his brother stood and saluted their captain, to which she gave a cursory response. "Quickly, before sleep overtakes me again," she said, an edge creeping into her voice.

"We have an intruder alert at coordinates 972.649 through 895.186."

"How could an intruder be that large?" she asked disdainfully.

Ailwin pointed at the viewscreen.

Captain Ildis Irryndir stepped closer, trying to understand what she was seeing. "It's just space," she said.

"No...there should be stars there. Whatever it is, it's very large, it's blocking our view of space, and it's headed our way at great velocity."

Captain Irryndir stood between their consoles, dead center to the viewscreen. "What is that?" she asked. She pointed to a dimly illuminated patch to one side of the black band. "Can you zoom in on that?"

"I'm almost at the edge of the scope's power."

"Push it to its limit, lieutenant."

"Yes, captain."

"That point you're indicating, captain," Felærn noted, "is at exactly the center of the object."

"Make an adjustment so that it's center screen, then," the captain ordered. "I like symmetry."

Ailwin nodded and a moment later the picture shifted again. In the center of the screen, they saw a roiling, crimson region. And at the center of that region was a mass of flailing tentacles. Lightning flashed out from its quivering center, briefly illuminating the space around it, including a ghostly black gossamer extending in all directions.

Felærn felt a severe chill, like a goblet of iced water poured down the middle of his back. "Is that...?" he began, but he could not finish the sentence. He looked at his captain.

Her eyes were wide, and her mouth began twitching. She raised her hand toward the screen, as if to push the image away. Her hand was shaking.

"Ialdaboth," she breathed, "The Oath-breaker."

"Ialdaboth?" Ailwin looked at his brother. "Isn't that the name of the elder god?"

"'*Samael, in Hearthentongue, the Doom of All Bright Worlds,*'" the captain chanted the ancient lay, "'*Saklas, in the Dwarfentongue, the Bringer of Death. Ialdaboth, in the reckoning of the elves, the Oathbreaker.*'"

The brothers locked eyes for a moment, then returned their gaze to their leader.

"How...fast...is the Dark Field moving?"

"4.3 parsecs a second."

"Begging the captain's pardon...I didn't think the elder god was... well...real," Ailwin said.

"You were born after the Days of Terror," Captain Irryndir said, not moving her eyes from the image of the roiling god. "How could you know?"

"We heard the stories," Felærn said. There was an edge in his voice, aimed at his brother.

"But they were just stories," Ailwin said.

"We wished they were just stories," the captain said, without a hint of rancor. Instead, her voice was soft, dreamy, as if remembering a pleasant, distant time. "And we told them as stories. If we'd told you as history...your tender minds would have been twisted by the trauma."

"What do we do?" Ailwin asked, his voice pitched high with an increasing panic.

"Do?" the captain said.

"Yes, what do we *do*?"

"Why, my dear boy," the captain's voice shook as she watched the roiling red patch growing larger on the screen. "We die, of course."

12

"Hot pot! Coming through!" Aunt Tully sang above the regular din of the family. Everyone scattered to get out of her way, but then followed her to the table like ducklings behind their mother. She set the piperpot of roast beef in the center of the table and wiped the sweat from her brow. She pointed at Uncle Emmet, who was already at the table, reading the weekly *Parchment-Crier*. "Don't ever let it be said I don't work as hard as ye do, especially as I do it every bleedin' day."

"Language," Emmet mumbled out of the side of his mouth. "Children."

"Bleedin' bleedin' bleedin'!" Aunt Tully shouted.

Everyone stopped in their places, frozen, and stared at her.

"An' did it hurt a single one of ye?" she demanded. "Anyone traumatized or anything?"

Even Uncle Emmet was looking at her now. Ellis wondered if he should intervene.

"Rules!" she turned on her heel. "I'm fed up with bleedin' rules—what you can say to whom, and when—" she went back into the kitchen.

The children looked at one another. They looked at Uncle Emmet.

He shrugged. "I don't know what's in your auntie's bonnet today, but it's a good bet she's going to want us around the table now, so let's not give her anything else to snap about."

Almost as one, everyone clambered into their seats. Next to Uncle Emmet was Agnes, the youngest. Towheaded and fair, she was spoiled by the whole family. Her uncle, especially, doted on her, and indeed she was barely separable from him when he was at home. On the other side of him was Brander, younger than Ellis and just finishing school. He was turning out to be a bit taller than most haffolk, with a perpetual cow lick that most of the Dale maids teased him about, but found irresistible. He was a bold sort, but also a little lost, not yet knowing what he wanted to do as a profession. Beside him was Beatrice, smart and responsible, but a good deal mouthier than most people cared for in a maid. She, too, was younger than Ellis, but older than Brander. The only one missing was Ellis' older brother Tivoy, but he must have smelled the roast because a moment later he opened the round front door and hastened to the table. He would be getting married soon, and as exciting as it was, Ellis knew he was beginning to grieve leaving the hearth.

"Where's your Auntie, then?" Uncle Emmet said, concerned.

"I'll see." Ellis leaped from his seat and headed to the kitchen.

He found her leaning against her chopping block, her face in her hands.

"I...Auntie, are you all right?" he asked.

"Why shouldn't I be?"

Ellis saw that she was crying. He glanced at the counter and saw the carrot salad and little potato pies, now getting cold. He felt an urgency to get them on the table before the others complained. But Tully's upset was clearly more important than the temperature of potato pies. He put his arms around her and squeezed. She was a large woman, and his arms did not reach all the way around her, but she leaned into him, his affection welcome.

"It's Tivoy, isn't it?" he asked.

She said nothing, which he took to be a yes. She'd been acting strangely ever since Tivoy had announced his wedding to Jackie Proudshingle last month. They were due to be wed in three weeks' time, and although the outward preparations were going smoothly, it was clear that Tully's interior preparations were not.

"He's just going to be downvillage, an easy walk," he reminded her.

"He won't be at our table," she almost wailed.

"Shh, Auntie, or we'll have the whole family in here."

"I'm sorry..." And then she started sobbing.

Ellis was uncertain what to do or say. So he simply held her while she cried it out.

"What? Is everything all right in there?" Uncle Emmet called through the kitchen door.

"Thank you, lad." Tully wiped her eyes on a dish towel. "We'd better get those pies on the table."

"Are you all right?" Ellis asked.

"I can manage for now."

"Do you want to talk about it later?"

"We'll see, love."

While Tully had always been a warm parent, she was usually focused more on the needs of her children than on her own. Rarely had Ellis seen her this emotional or reactive. It frightened him a little. "Let me help you, then," he said, picking up a tray of pies and pushing the kitchen door open with his back.

"Thank you, love."

Ellis placed the tray on the table and Beatrice began efficiently distributing them.

By haffolk standards, theirs was a small family, but Ellis knew they were close in a way that many other families were not. They were a comfort to him, and in his heart of hearts, he loved them all deeply.

He went back and held the door for his Auntie, who finally emerged, red of eye and sniffly, brandishing a basket of biscuits.

As soon as she sat down, Uncle Emmet intoned, "And now, let us give a sacrifice of silence in grateful thanks to the oyosii for our family and our meal."

Everyone stared at the food before them, savoring the silence, apparently giving the oyosii a passing thought. Then, as one, they began to tuck in.

For such a small number, they made a good deal of commotion.

Everyone started talking at once and there was a great flurry as biscuits, slabs of roast, and various condiments made their way around the table.

"I heard someone was making eyes at Ellis," Agnes said in a sing-song voice.

Ellis' eyebrows shot up.

"Someone named *Liza*," Agnes said. Everyone knew Liza, of course, as the village of West Farthingdale was a small one. Agnes was simply teasing him.

"There's nothing between me and Liza," he said, matter-of-factly.

Beatrice interjected, "But I hear tell she'd like there to be."

Ellis dropped his fork. "What? Where did you hear that?"

"From everyone," she said.

"Surely not *everyone*." Tivoy grinned, clearly enjoying Ellis' momentary fluster.

"Oh, all right. I heard it from several people," Beatrice said.

"Me, too," Agnes said, a little too quickly. Ellis guessed that she was perturbed that Beatrice was stealing her "news."

And it *was* news, to him. Had Liza been making eyes at him? He thought back to their interchange at the tavern. She'd been friendly, but had she been friendlier than usual, or friendlier than she was with others? He'd been attracted to her, but that was not the same thing as her being attracted to him. He cocked his head. She had called him "love," but everyone called everyone else "love" in the Dale.

"My boy, are you all right?" Uncle Emmet asked.

Ellis realized he had been staring at his plate. "Uh...yes. Yes, I'm fine."

"So...d'ye have any plans for this young lass, Liza, then?" Emmet asked him pointedly.

Ellis blinked, uncertain what to say. "Plans? No...no plans at all. I... no."

"Good," Emmet said, scooping a hulking piece of potato pie onto his fork. "'Cause I don't think yer Auntie could stand to lose another of ye."

At this, Aunt Tully emitted a tiny howl and turned from the table, dabbing at her eyes. Tivoy looked at her with what seemed like a mixture of horror and chagrin, while Agnes leaped out of her seat to embrace her auntie and comfort her.

Tivoy looked first at his uncle, then at Ellis, his eyes pleading for help. "'Tis not your fault," Emmet said to him. "You've caught yourself a fine maid in Jackie and that's a fact."

"She's a loud dresser!" Aunt Tully howled.

"She's a *stylish* dresser and that's all," Emmet rebuked her. He looked back at Tivoy. "She'll get over it. Once you and Jackie are on yer own, she'll come around—an' I mean, she'll come around yer hole-in-the-ground, more than Jackie will like, I reckon. An' she won't have a bad thing to say about Jackie's clothes then, as she'll want to be welcome."

Aunt Tully had gotten ahold of herself again. "I've ruined dinner."

"Dinner is delicious, Auntie," Beatrice said. "You've not ruined a thing."

"I heard you had a meeting with Bracegirdle," Brander said to Ellis, obviously trying to change the subject to something less volatile.

It was a bad choice. Ellis' face darkened and he looked down at his plate, which was suddenly three times less appetizing as it had been a moment before.

When he looked back up, he saw his Uncle's eyes were wide, and he guessed Aunt Tully had filled him in. He wished someone had told Brander. Well, why not him?

"What did I say?" Brander asked.

Ellis looked at his brother. "I'm on probation."

"Weren't you just off-world?" Tivoy asked.

Ellis nodded, twisting his lips to one side.

"I take it that didn't go well?"

Ellis shook his head.

"And now you're on probation?" Tivoy's face was full of concern. "I'm sorry, baby brother."

"Thanks," Ellis said. Tivoy was probably sincere, but he was probably also relieved to have the attention off him and the pain his upcoming nuptials were causing Auntie.

"How bad is it?"

"If I don't screw anything else up, I might earn back my route in a couple of years."

"No..." Brander was aghast. "Oh, Ellis, I'm so, so sorry. I had no idea. I just thought...you know, a slap on the hand."

"No, it was a pretty...confidential assignment. So...few people know the details. And I shouldn't talk about it."

"Of course," Uncle Emmet said. "We'll hear no more of it."

"I've got me a new job offer, though," Ellis said.

"From who?" Beatrice said with her mouth full, clearly unable to help herself.

"From a summoner, a Mr. Osia," Ellis said, trying to appear more chipper than he actually felt.

"That's mysterious," Tivoy said. "What's the job?"

"Uh...courier, I guess."

"You don't know what the job is, then? I mean, the details?"

"No."

"Oh," Tivoy said, but the tiny word seemed filled to the brim with judgment.

"I mean, he hasn't filled me in on...just what I'll be doing. The pay is good, though. Half again what I was making."

Uncle Emmet's mouth was full, so he jabbed in Ellis' direction with a fork full of roast in a fit of enthusiasm.

Ellis brightened a little at that.

"Yes, but think on it." Beatrice's face betrayed her suspicion. "You'll be in the service of a summoner, and who knows what dark intrigues you'll be forced to be party to."

"Dark intrigues?" Aunt Tully said, still dabbing at her eyes. For the first time, she seemed interested in what was being said, and she did not appear to like it. "Like what?" She looked at Ellis, a little fearfully. "That doesn't sound like the kind of thing decent haffolk should be involved in, does it?"

Beatrice shrugged, looking pleased with herself. She had sown her seed of doubt. Her job was done. Ellis scowled at her.

"Will you be going off-world again?" Tivoy asked.

"I don't know," Ellis admitted.

"Will Kit be going with you?" Brander asked.

"I...I don't know that either," Ellis said, now becoming truly worried.

"You don't know much about this job, do you?" Tivoy asked. Ellis knew he wasn't intending to be mean, and indeed, save for Beatrice, everyone seemed truly concerned for him. He knew they wanted him to succeed, but he did not always welcome their advice. He only wished they did not usually turn out to be right.

"Why would you even consider it?" Agnes asked him.

It was a mature question from such a young a girl, but he weighed it seriously. "I suppose I've always felt I was here to do something... important," he confessed.

"Important?" Uncle Emmet asked, reaching for another roll. "Whatever does that mean?"

"Being a courier *is* important," Tivoy asserted. There were nods of agreement around the table.

"I know, but..." Ellis was unsure how to articulate his response. "I guess I feel like I was always destined for some kind of adventure."

"Oh, pish on adventure!" Aunt Tully said, throwing her napkin down on the table. "You can never be sure of a hot roast or a dry bed or a warm hearth when you go chasing after adventures. Why would you even consider such a thing?"

Ellis didn't know how to answer that. "I-I-I don't know..." he stammered. "I hear the tales about Arrunwolfe—"

Ellis heard groans around the table. "Don't be too eager to be jumpin' into legends and old wives' tales, young lad," Uncle Emmet said with his voice of authority. He pointed his fork at him. "Besides that, there never was an Arrunwolfe, nor a dark lord, neither, I reckon. There's a Scar, sure enough, so we have to make up a story about how it got there—but that's all there is to your legends, my boy." He let that sink in a moment before narrowing one eye at him and adding, "Don't be too eager to throw yourself into fairy stories and fictions. Yer life is too precious. To us, anyhows."

Ellis felt his heart rise into his throat. He tried to swallow against the thickness of it, but it began to leak out his eyes. He sniffed and reached for his cup of wine. After sipping from it, he saw that every eye at the table was still on him, and he knew that every one of them loved him—even Beatrice. He nodded and felt awkward.

"Well, now that that's settled." Uncle Emmet turned to Aunt Tully. "Whatsabout dessert, then?"

"MAKE THEM STOP!" King Belorin cried, cradling his head. His elbows were on his desk, a great hulking slab of granite with gold streaks running diagonally through it.

"Shall I close the window, sire?" asked Taff Oakenwild, his secretary.

"There is no escape," Belorin growled. "If you close the window, we will roast. But if it is open, all we hear is their incessant yammering."

He pushed his stool back with a kick of his boot and went to the window. Looking down, he saw what looked like half his kingdom assembled in the cavern, creating such a din that the rock beneath his feet vibrated. "What do they want of me?"

"Was that a rhetorical question, sire, or do you wish to hear my opinion?" Oakenwild asked. Other secretaries might have asked such a question tentatively, but Taff was secure in himself in a way that Belorin admired. He was simply asking the question. Belorin simply answered it. "I want to know your opinion."

"Relations between High King Uther and our own High King Banniffe have been less than congenial of late. There is a growing suspicion that we have a less than equal role in the Mountain and Plain Alliance. There have been several opinions published in the newspaper of late—"

"There have?"

"Indeed, sire, saying that we are losing face, and therefore losing influence and, eventually this will lead to a loss of wealth."

Belorin chewed on a corner of his beard as he thought. "But they're not protesting about that."

"People are complex, sire, as you well know. There are the stated reasons, and there are the underlying, unspoken reasons. These are the real reasons, but they are rarely pointed to."

"So you're saying that this discontent has been simmering beneath my nose for a while, and this whole Fängelsten business just kind of made it...blow up?"

"That is my best guess, your majesty."

"How do we make it stop?" He was pacing now, in front of the window, his hands clasped behind his back.

"Since the problem, at its root, is the loss of pride, we must do something to restore the people's pride," Oakenwild said. The man's calm was almost maddening. He sat poised at his own desk—a much smaller, lighter, wooden thing facing Belorin's own. He had a quill in his hand, ready to scratch something out on the parchment that was perpetually before him. "This is only to stem the bleeding, of course. We must also work on the underlying malady."

"Damn your metaphors, speak plainly," Belorin commanded.

Oakenwild shifted in his seat and a pained look briefly crossed his face. "Very well. Since the Alliance is largely an affair between Kings Banniffe and Uther, there is little you can do about it at the diplomatic level. However, there is much you can do to change public opinion—both here and on Hearth."

"Like what?" Belorin stopped pacing.

"Perhaps our human friends need to be reminded how much of their own way of life and economy depend on dwarfish technology. A working installation at the planetary museum on dwarfish innovation and its gift to the universe might be a start. As the installation develops, the material can be packaged into a book, or perhaps a series of stage plays commemorating key events in dwarfish industry and development. We can then put the installation on tour, first in Ältremark, and then on Hearth—"

"This is a very long-range plan, if I am hearing you aright," Belorin grumbled.

"It is a long-range problem, your majesty. It is also one of many parallel streams we should be working."

"This is a very expensive plan," Belorin continued, as if he hadn't heard Oakenwild's response.

"There are many kinds of capital, your maj—"

"But what do I do about *them*, right *now*?" He pointed to the window.

Oakenwild looked toward the window, his red, wispy beard twitching from the slight breeze wafting from its direction. "I would suggest that you give them what they want."

"They want my head on a spike!"

"No, your majesty, I do not think that they do."

"You 'do not think that they do,' do you?" Belorin sneered. "Then just what *do* you think?"

"I think they want a head on a spike. But I'm fairly certain it does not need to be yours."

This arrested Belorin's pacing. His bushy eyebrows jumped. "It doesn't?"

"No, sire. They want blood, but I do not think it needs be *your* blood."

"Then whose?"

"Who is it who caused this whole mess?"

"I thought it was us," Belorin confessed, hand to his breast.

Oakenwild moved his head back and forth, equivocating. "It is good for a sovereign to take ultimate responsibility for what happens in his kingdom, that is true. But the fault is not yours alone. You, for instance, were not charged with delivering the Fängelsten."

"The haffolk?" Belorin lowered one eyebrow, the other remaining aloft. "Are you suggesting we feed them the blood of that idiot courier?"

"It will slake their bloodlust in the moment. It will satisfy their urge to save face. It will buy us time to address the deeper, underlying issues that are truly driving their ire."

Belorin pulled the bit of beard he had been chewing from his mouth and nodded. "It will make them stop yelling things outside my window."

"Precisely. People will go home—and more importantly, they will go back to work."

"Yes..." Belorin nodded. "Take a message, Taff. Let us search for that haffolk. We will find him, try him, and offer him up as sacrifice for the good of the dwarfish peoples."

"Best not to word it just that way, I think," Oakenwild held up one ink-stained finger.

"No, no, no. But we must cast the net wide. And call a lawyer, one that knows interplanetary diplomacy law. We need to know what our extradition rights may be, once he is found." He punched at the granite of his desk, relishing the momentary pain of it. "If it's blood they want...it is blood they shall have."

❧

MANY OF THE great castles had a landing pad as part of their structure, but Uther's sire had decreed the ætherport of Caer Trogan be set at a great distance. The Caer and the promontory on which it sat were nestled at the base of a crescent-shaped bay. The ships in its two harbors were cushioned from the rough ocean waves by two curving peninsulas, and the ætherport had been placed at the tip of southernmost one. Pilots complained about the occasional strong winds coming off the ocean, and passengers complained about the carriage ride necessary to get to or from the landing zone, but the location was chosen to keep air traffic from being a distraction or disturbance to the city. Ennisbrook suspected, however, that the elder king had simply been too superstitious of something crashing into the castle.

Emerging from the castle, Daevis Ennisbrook caught the attention of a waiting cab driver, climbed up onto the horse-drawn carriage, and was taken up the well-worn path to the ætherport.

He had been tasked with finding prince Ealon, and Estenlan being a big place it seemed more sensible to start with where the boy had been instead of where he might be now. He was accused of stealing something from a dwarf ship, which of course meant he'd gotten himself into space. Perhaps the prince had been more careful in covering his tracks, but Ennisbrook had a feeling Ealon had used the nearest ætherport, in haste or for simplicity's sake.

The horses took the tree-lined road at a fast clip. There was an attractive view of the bay to his left, but Ennisbrook looked at it without seeing it. The trees fell away as the cab reached the tip of the southern peninsula, and Ennisbrook discerned the whine of thruster engines was competing with the sound of the ocean. One large craft, gleaming and ridiculously top-heavy, was currently accepting passengers; and along the far perimeter Ennisbrook saw more ships, parked or moored or whatever these spacefarers called it.

Lines had been painted on the stones to keep people from straying too far into the landing zones. Ennisbrook followed their path to a low building on the south end. He bypassed the customs section and headed farther along. The first door he tried opened upon a cluttered and busy room, full of chatter and the percussive sounds of incoming messages. Since spaceflight was an innovation of the dwarfs, men had to rely on dwarfs to maintain the technology. Among the very busy dwarfs were a few listless humans. They looked apathetic and bored, sitting against the walls despite the activity. Some were openly napping. Ennisbrook could guess these were likely the younger sons of rich families, given comfortable jobs in exchange for some favor or donation to the royal family. *No wonder dwarfs keep their distance from humans,* Ennisbrook thought. *They see the worst of us.*

At the nearest desk sat a dwarf with a receiving horn to his ear. The top of his head was bald, but yellow hair sprang from the rest of his skull, as well as a full beard from his jaw. He looked up and did not seem pleased to see Ennisbrook. Heavy brows knitted as the dwarf peered over his spectacles.

"Why are you here? Are you lost?" the dwarf snapped. "Souvenirs are next door!"

"I have an inquiry about a ship that landed here a few days ago," Ennisbrook began.

"A few days—? We don't keep that information here! Get away with you, we're busy!"

"You don't keep track of incoming or outgoing flights?" Ennisbrook asked, genuinely confused.

The dwarf gestured angrily to his left, as if to say *next door!*, and proceeded to determinedly ignore the Enforcer. Ennisbrook stepped back outside and went to the next office. Within was a lone dwarf, sitting at a cluttered desk. The desks in the other office had faced forward; this desk faced the wall to Ennisbrook's right. And this dwarf looked similar to the other one, save this one had white hair.

It took a moment before this dwarf looked over and noticed his visitor.

"What do *you* want?" the dwarf snapped, as cranky as the first.

"I want information about an æthercraft that may have landed here a few days ago."

"That information is not for the public. I would prefer you to leave."

"I am here under the high king's orders," Ennisbrook answered, adding some weight to his voice.

"If this is truly the high king's request, he can submit it using the proper forms," the dwarf retorted.

"Are you blind?" Ennisbrook shot back, growing louder. He held his chain of office away from his chest and shook it. "I am the King's enforcer. I represent the King in his demands!"

The dwarf shook his head and clucked his tongue, as if witnessing a child's tantrum, and then turned to the great book on his desk. "Sorry. Can't help you. Please leave."

The Enforcer reached for the grip of his rapier. The dwarf's brow creased, not in surprise but in displeasure. "Threats will get you nowhere, son," he growled; but the Enforcer drew the blade out casually, placing it across the low counter between him the dwarf's desk.

In a gentler tone, ignoring what he had just done, the Enforcer said, "But you do keep that sort of information here...?"

The dwarf sighed, expressing his weariness at Ennisbrook's continued presence. "Yes. But if—"

"Would it be *that* book you have in front of you? And all the other books contain records of all the other landings and..." the word suddenly came to him, "departures, in the past?"

"Yes," the dwarf said warily.

"I see," the Enforcer said thoughtfully. He cast his eyes over the other books piled on the shelves lining the room. He leaned forward to get a better look; but in fact he just wanted to get closer to his rapier. With a quick tap of his fist on the pommel, the blade popped up. The dwarf let out a howl, looking at the bloody gash across his palm, just under his stubby fingers.

"*Förkärlek till heliga saker!*" the dwarf snarled. "Bastard of a human, look what you've done to me!"

"Yes, terribly sorry. You really should get that looked at," the Enforcer murmured, picking up his rapier and sheathing it disinterestedly. He stepped aside, letting the dwarf stagger out in search of help. As the door closed, Ennisbrook quickly went to the book and turned back a few pages. It was easy to recognize the routine of the same shuttles and deliveries going to and fro. He found one small craft that might be what he was looking for. Its landing was recorded, but he did not spot the same call sign further back. There was no note of this craft having left; it looked like the bay number of its current whereabouts was noted next to it. Ennisbrook headed back out, but just before he did he made a point to look for some kind of name plate. The dwarf's name appeared to be Grabbil Gragnaduh. Ennisbrook frowned at its oddity.

Back outside, the Enforcer strode to a line of ships on the western end of the clearing. As he grew closer someone called to him—a human. "Hie! You're not supposed to be out here."

"It's all right," the Enforcer responded, waving the man away. "I've got...clearance."

"Whose clearance?" The man had gotten close enough that they no longer needed to shout.

"Eh...the dwarf," Ennisbrook had forgotten the odd name already. "Grannida?"

The man's face cleared. "That's the name I wanted to hear, or near enough," he said with a smile. "Are you looking for a ship?"

"Yes, a small craft that landed a few days ago."

"Mmm. I bet I know the one you're after. A dwarfish box, but big enough to have an airlock. You can see it from here—facing us, between the two big boats." The Enforcer had continued his walk, and this man didn't seem to mind following along. "Whoever owns it seems to have dumped it here. Can't say I blame him. Something definitely fouled up in there. The smell is terrible."

"Is it?" the Enforcer replied, more a statement than a question. He was practically at the craft by now and his companion excused himself and continued off on his own.

The man was right—the craft was boxy, although its corners were rounded. The ship was plated in gleaming copper, as most dwarfish æthercraft were, and Ennisbrook could see streaks of green in the metal where it had oxidized. At the corners were endpieces made of a silver-like metal the Enforcer could not identify. There were two round viewing portals, not much bigger than a man's stretched-out hand, one on either side. It was clear this was more of a skiff than a craft meant to journey far or for very long.

Ennisbrook did not have much experience with spacecraft, but the outer controls seemed self-explanatory. He put his hand on a lever near the door, adding a little weight to it, and the door popped open a crack. He pulled it back and got a full blast of the horrible smell the man had been talking about. The Enforcer recognized it immediately. It was the smell of death.

He stepped inside, finding another door controlled by another lever. He yanked the lever up and this second door split in two, disappearing from in front of him. The smell was far worse now, and he was forced to cover mouth and nose with his left palm. Directly in front of him was a wall; it was dark to his right, but the front of the craft was obviously to his left. He walked past the wall and reached the forward cabin, which spanned the full width of the craft. There was a large front window and the seats where the pilot and...*other* pilot sit, with two seats behind for passengers. Between the seats and the rear of the cabin, a large brown stain scarred the floor. He recognized it instantly—dried blood. It was obvious a slaying had happened here, and Ennisbrook could not believe the landing crew had so easily dismissed it or ignored it.

The rear wall of the cabin was also streaked with the same brown stains. It looked like there was some kind of compartment cut low in the wall. He didn't see any controls, but Ennisbrook forced the panel open by sliding it. He was not at all surprised to find a body within. Crammed into the compartment was a dwarf. This one had wild red hair — it made a striking combination with the corpse's purpled face. The large eyes were frozen open, the mouth was fixed in a grimace;

black blood covered its chest and chin, where its throat had been slashed.

The story was that the prince had had a dwarf with him. This appeared to no longer be true.

❧

Osia closed the door to the room he'd rented at the Slug and Lettuce.

"Beer!" Jaq shouted in his ear.

"You've had enough—we both have."

"Beer!"

"You do *not* need a nightcap. You'll sleep ill enough as it is."

Osia pulled off his cloak, sending Jaq flapping until the bird landed on the desk. Jaq cawed in protest, but Osia appeared not to notice.

"That seemed to go well," he said.

Jaq cawed.

"Whether he takes us up on our offer remains to be seen, but I don't think we need be as pessimistic as all that."

Jaq cawed.

"You have an evil view of human nature...and haffolk nature, too, I suppose."

Jaq cawed.

"If you think that lad is an imbecile, you are not paying attention. He's *good*, not stupid."

Jaq cawed.

"I'll concede that he may well be naive."

Jaq cawed.

"Don't be getting all self-satisfied. You're insufferable when you're right about something."

Jaq cawed.

"I'm going to report...and then turn in. *You* may do what you like."

Settling himself in at the low desk, Osia adjusted himself awkwardly. Osia had rented the one room in the inn furnished with humans in mind, but whatever haffolk carpenter had done the job had not been quite clear on the scale of human anatomy. Osia's legs angled up higher than his hips as he sat in the chair, and even so, the desktop was lower than he liked.

Still, it would do. He pulled the velvet bag containing his seerstone from his robe and loosened the drawstrings. He placed the black stone on the desk before him, leaning it on the spine of a book to get a good angle. Then the summoner closed his eyes and sought out the Scar. Reaching forth with his mind, he connected to the world where speech through stones was common. The contact made, he opened his eyes and saw a swirling mist in the surface of the stone.

The mist curled about and gradually formed a face he recognized. The ghostly visage of Elsorin rippled, but quite noticeably yawned. "I am just about to turn in for the night, Osia. Let us be brief."

"Certainly, master. You did ask me to check in whenever I found something...notable."

"Indeed I did. And what have you found?"

"My worst suspicions have been confirmed. The thief of the Fängelsten is none other than Ealon, the second of Uther's sons."

If Elsorin had been sleepy before, he did not appear so now. "How... but...can," he spluttered. Finally, he found purchase on his thoughts. "Are you certain?"

"Do I have incontrovertible evidence? No. Nothing that would hold up in a Hearthen court. But I have an eyewitness."

"Is this witness credible?"

"I would bet my life on this witness, master."

"It's like that, is it? You are certain, then...in your heart?"

Osia nodded gravely. "I had suspected earlier, as the same witness had said he noticed the secret crest of the House of Summerfield on the thief."

"How do *you* know the secret crest of the House of Summerfield?"

"Elsorin, we are neither of us young. You can't do what we do very long without tripping over things."

"True enough. This is what makes us dangerous."

Osia smiled but did not comment further. "I met with Uther, to convey my suspicions."

"Did the old man throw you out on your ear?"

"He did."

"And did that surprise you?"

"Not at all, but it did advance my investigation. Without it, I would not have gained confirmation from the eyewitness."

Elsorin's ghostly eyebrows rose. "Well, then, I applaud your instincts."

"There is something else," Osia noted.

"Yes?"

"The eyewitness...he's special."

Elsorin narrowed his eyes. "What mean you?"

"I used the Sight with him, and...whatever is coming, he is a part of it. A significant part."

"Tell me of him."

"He is motivated by love and loyalty more than power or greed. He has a heart that is truly good."

"Sounds like someone who would not last a week in most æther-port towns," Elsorin grumbled.

"He is..." Osia fished for a word. Jaq cawed. Osia rolled his eyes. "Very well, Jaq. He is an innocent. He is immature. He is idealistic."

"And yet?" Elsorin interjected. "I sense there is a 'yet' coming."

"And yet...the Sight is never wrong. His heart is noble, and whatever is coming, we need him close to us."

"Who is he? A Hearthman, I presume?"

"A Dalefellow, actually."

Elsorin's head jerked back. "Are you telling me this 'special' person is a haffolk?"

"I am."

"Are you mad?"

"Master, have you ever gotten to *know* haffolk?"

"Of course not. That would be..."

"Beneath you?"

Elsorin blustered but did not articulate a response.

"I've offered him a job."

"What kind of job?"

"Courier."

"Whatever for?"

"To carry whatever we cannot."

Elsorin blinked. A long minute passed between them in silence. Finally, Elsorin said, "I hope you know what you're doing."

"Actually, I don't," Osia said. "But I am trusting my belly, which has rarely steered me wrong."

Jaq cawed.

"Jaq can think of a couple of instances," Elsorin raised one eyebrow.

"Jaq likes to peck at my patience."

"I would have stuffed and mounted that bird years ago."

Jaq cawed.

"Jaq says he loves you, too." Osia's smile faded. "What word on...on the *change*?"

"Only that every summoner with a fingernail's worth of real magic felt it. The elves' Order felt it, too, and I've had inquiries from the royal houses of Silnadin and Endilla."

"So the Green Elves and the Gray Elves know something is amiss. The Illendrafil?"

Elsorin shrugged. "The Black Elves keep to themselves, and their Order is not in communion with us. Even if they did feel something, they would not likely inquire of us."

Osia nodded. "I thought perhaps...something of this magnitude... they might reach out."

"They have long ago forsaken the company of bright beings. Whatever we may all be facing, they will face it alone."

"It makes me sad," Osia confessed.

Elsorin did not comment. Instead, he sniffed. "Where are you?"

"Everdale," Osia said.

"Of all the godsforsaken places—"

"Everdale is home to the haffolk, and like the haffolk themselves, full of hidden charms."

"I choose to take your word on that." Elsorin looked away, then looked back. "Stay close to your stone, Osia. The physic is trying to rouse Objor. We all know something has changed...something dire is afoot, but none know what it is or what can be done about it."

"I fear the worst. I fear the return of the elder—"

"Do not even say it aloud," Elsorin cut him off. "If there is guidance to be had, Objor will give it."

"And if he doesn't? If he dies before he can issue another oracle?"

"Let us offer our wine to the oyosii and pray that does not happen, for the good of all bright beings."

Osia nodded. "Master, tell me plainly. What do you fear is before us?"

"I dare not speak it, for fear that there may be a world on which it is already true."

"Even if there is, it will not come through the Scar unless we pull it through."

"I fear it is already here."

13

It had been a humiliating day at work. Ellis had been assigned mail sorting duty and never left the confines of the post office. For most of the morning, he could see Kit waiting across the street, pacing and glancing daggers at the building. Finally, she had given up and, he presumed, returned home.

It had been a long time since he'd spent a full day sorting mail, and he had forgotten how brain-numbingly tedious it was. He realized he had also been taking his job as an active, out-and-about courier for granted. "You never realize what you have until it's gone," his Aunt Tully was fond of saying, and he had never fully realized what she meant until just then.

He placed a letter in the proper sorting bin and went on to the next one, squinting to make out the scrawled address.

What was I thinking, hoping for postmaster? he scolded himself silently. He had reached for the highest job in the post office, but had plummeted to its lowest depths. *Let that be a lesson to you to curb your ambition*, the voice in his head continued.

He reached for another letter, but before he could read the address, a bell clanged. "Last one, then," he said, and put the letter in its proper place before turning and taking off his apron. He hung it on a hook beside the door, and with a nod and a wave to the few friendly faces that gave him the time of day, he left by the front door.

There was still plenty of daylight, but Ellis didn't have the heart for any sort of fun. He thought about going to find Kit, but decided he didn't want to be scolded. What did he want? "Supper," he said out loud, and that settled it. He turned left at the street and headed for home and hearth, food and family, comfort and coziness.

He had almost forgotten his troubles by the time the last of the village buildings receded behind him. He entered the canopy of trees that covered the road, enjoying the cool green light and the breeze, when suddenly he heard a twig snap.

He stopped. Except for the breeze, he heard nothing else. He turned around and faced the way he had come, and then he saw them. Stepping out from behind the trees where they had been hiding was Tubber Goodfoot and his friends Steffan Oatgrinder and Powdy Grumblethorn.

Tubber was a hand taller than Ellis, and taller than his friends too. He was also a good deal wider, which was why everyone called him, "Tubber." His real name was Aric, which he hated. Steffan and Powdy had been nearly inseparable from him since grade school. Only the postal service, it seemed, could come between them, and after hours they were still often to be seen together.

Ellis felt his heart sink into his stomach. This was not going to go well. Nor was he likely to emerge from this encounter without a black eye or two to show for it. He sighed, resigned to his fate. "What do you want, Tubber?" he asked, his voice heavy with resignation. "Just come and get it over with, will you?"

"Y'know, I'm curious, I am," Tubber said, hands behind his back, as if he were pacing in front of a class, about to give a lecture. "Jus' what could a young haffolk be thinkin', losin' a Very Important Item during a courier's run?"

"Yeah," Steffan agreed, as if he knew anything about it at all. Steffan washed dishes at a tavern in a nearby village called Peat. "What were you thinking?"

"Because you didn't just bring ig-, ignoma—"

"Ignominy?" Ellis offered helpfully.

"You didn't just bring shame on yerself, y'know. You brought shame on the whole Everdale Postal Service, upon the Royal Mail itself."

"Tubber, for gods' sakes—"

"How're people supposed to trust us, eh? An' you know what? You made the whole haffolk community look bad."

"I hardly think—"

"Humans already look down on us," Powdy interjected, "and dwarfs too. Now they have good reason to say we're not, uh... that....we're...."

"Irresponsible?" Ellis suggested.

"Yes, that's it. They're going to say we're *irresponsible*. That haffolk can't be trusted."

"That's number one," Tubber said. His hands were still behind his back, but now he walked straight up to Ellis, standing a little too close, directly in front of him, so that Ellis' nose was bumping into Tubber's collarbone.

"Tubber, a little space, please."

Tubber stayed put, having created the discomfort he was so obviously hoping for. Noticing that his hands had begun to sweat, Ellis nervously wiped them on his trousers. Tubber could best him all by himself, Ellis knew. The big brute didn't need any help from his friends to give him a licking, or a few broken bones, for that matter. Ellis' eyes darted to the trees, wondering if he were fast enough to escape them. Probably not, as Powdy had been the fastest runner in their school and hadn't put on much weight since. Ellis felt his heart start to pound in his chest.

"Number two," Tubber continued. "I wonder jus' what you had to say to Bracegirdle, then, eh?"

"About what?" Ellis asked.

"About me," he looked down, so that they were practically nose-to-nose.

"I didn't...honestly, Tubber, I didn't say anything to him."

"That's not what I hears. I hears you called me a *snake*."

"Uh...did I?" Ellis was beginning to panic. It *did* sound like something he would say, although he didn't remember saying it. Or didn't remember it, *exactly*.

"I think you was trying to scuttle my chances for the postmaster's job."

"Tubber, that's ridiculous," Ellis tried to sound calm and reasonable. "There's no way anyone would think you were a serious candidate for that job."

"And just what do you mean by that, eh?"

Ellis realized he had said the wrong thing, true as it was. *I was an idiot before, and now I'm going to be an idiot with multiple broken bones and fractures*, he thought. He watched Powdy making his right hand into a fist, pumping it and releasing it, and rubbing it with his left hand with obvious relish.

"Do you know how much of that fat postmaster's paycheck will be going into Spindlethorn's pocket now—*Spindlethorn's* instead of mine?"

"Tubber, it was never your money, it was never going to *be* your money," Ellis said, a little sadly. He looked at Powdy and nodded. "Please tell Astrid congratulations for me, won't you?"

Powdy looked a bit taken aback at that. The Grumblethorns and Spindlethorns were related houses, of course, as all the -thorns were, somewhere down the line. Although no haffolk were related by blood, family feeling ran deep. "Uh...I will. Uh...thank you."

"Never mind your cleverness," Tubber said, poking Ellis in the chest with the bent knuckle of his right forefinger. "What do ye have to say for yerself?"

"I say it's too bad that both of us are feeling disappointed that we didn't get the job. Rum luck, Tubber. But it's no good blaming me for it. I didn't undermine your chances, although you did try to undermine my own."

Tubber cocked his head, but didn't answer. Instead, a slow, wicked smile twisted his lip. "So you know about that, eh?"

"Well, I didn't know for sure who had filed the formal complaint, because it was anonymous. But I had suspicions. Suspicions you just confirmed, so...thank you."

"Oh," Tubber looked like he had just swallowed a bug. He narrowed his eyes. "Serves you right, you little humbletoken."

"Humbletoken? What does that even mean?"

"It means that by the time ye leave this road, yer goin' to be pulling yerself along home by yer one finger joint that still works." Tubber was rolling up his sleeve now.

"By the Horn, Tubber," Ellis said, raising his arms defensively as Powdy and Steffan closed in.

But instead of using his fist, Tubber surprised him, jerking his leg up with more alacrity than Ellis would have thought possible, and catching him in the stomach with his knee. Ellis bent over double, and Tubber brought up the other knee, catching Ellis in the face. Ellis heard his own nose crack before the pain hit.

"C'mon, ya swiving wealy-wink," Tubber shouted and spat. He raised his foot and cackled, aiming for Ellis' face.

❧

THE PORTER WAS certain he would not be needed on such a windy night. He backed into his small, dark alcove, hoisted himself onto a stool, and closed his eyes. Immediately, there was a pounding at the door. He should have known better. With a groan, he went to the door and slid back a small panel. Facing him he could make out three figures and three horses, almost as dark as the night. "State your business," the porter croaked, letting his irritation show.

"We come from Caer Eleanor, envoys of his majesty King Avantir. We seek an audience with King Melconnan, but for now we seek shelter from these sharp winds."

"It's the middle of the night!" the porter protested. "You can't just waltz up and ask to see the king—and certainly not in the middle of the night!"

"Please, good man," said another shadowy figure, stepping closer to the door. "I assure you Melconnan will be pleased to see me—in the morning, granted. We simply seek a room in which to stay for the night."

"And what makes you think my king would want to see the likes of you?" the porter sneered.

"Fool!" said the third figure, losing patience. "You speak to King Avantir himself!"

❦

THE MOUNTAINOUS, snow-covered land to the north was named Untwold on the maps but was commonly referred to as, simply, the Northlands. Melconnan was its king and his caer was found in the foothills, just below the snowline. The castle had been formed by delving into the rock, in the dwarfish fashion, but its outer structure was of rough stone, stacked into three walls. In a way, it resembled the pilings of a massive rockslide; but in spite of its rough appearance, it was as sturdy as a boulder, and Avantir at last felt a sense of security within its walls.

As Avantir had wagered, Melconnan was indeed pleased to see him, come morning, if a little surprised. "Your letter said you would be arriving a week from now," he said, as the two of them settled into comfortable chairs before a large fire. Melconnan would have loved to show off the rugged views, but it was too drafty to sit by a window. They were meeting in an inner chamber.

"That was a precaution, I'm afraid," Avantir answered, enjoying the aroma of his mulled wine. "I hope it did not put you out, but I don't want too many people knowing I'm away."

"Yes, of course. Especially after the terrible business with...with your son."

"You've heard of it?"

"Yes, yes, of course. So terrible."

"Well, that saves me having to tell it to you," Avantir said, and then sighed. "I suppose you heard the songs? '*The serpent with the poisoned tooth / sent slithering under Uther's roof.*' You've heard this?"

"Yes, and I don't believe it."

"Thank you."

"'*Wybrook then loosed its venomous snake / which Uther slew, for goodness' sake.*' What rubbish." Melconnan shook his head, and stroked his neatly trimmed ginger beard. "And I've heard the answer call too. Did you have a part in it? '*Careful you little ones, don't you run wild / King Uther's out hung'ring for another poor child.*' That sounds closer to the truth, I dare say."

Avantir raised his cup in Melconnan's honor.

"A rum thing it is," Melconnan continued. "A bloody rum thing. I don't mean to dwell on it, but I can't get over how this all happened. You try to put a halt to Uther's dominance, out on the field of battle, and beating you isn't good enough for him. He has to kill your son along with it. That's not war—that's outright murder. How is it not?"

"Yes, yes," Avantir whispered, his eyes becoming wet. "It is such a balm to me to hear you say this, to know we are in agreement. For I have a favor to ask you."

"And what is it, my friend?"

"I intend to strike at Uther. Not on the battlefield, no. I intend to take the battle to him."

"Ah, now," Melconnan began. He cleared his throat, suddenly uneasy. "This is dangerous talk. I agree something must be done, but..."

"I am confident there are other kings and lords who feel as you, and with the same passion," Avantir continued, ignoring Melconnan's hesitation. "The only problem is, I...well, some might consider my reactions to the...event as a bit, shall we say, excessive."

"I heard you set fire to your surrounding woodland."

"Yes," Avantir said, feeling suddenly uncomfortable, "that is so, though I'm not proud of it. And...because of that, I was hoping that you might represent me in the negotiations. I also request, if I am not asking too much of you, that I may stay here in the meantime, rather than in my own keep."

"Why, what is wrong with your castle?"

"It's not exactly presentable at the moment. The, um, desolation might lead people into questioning my judgment—although I assure you I am quite certain of my actions now. My grief overcame me, but now I am in full control of my faculties."

"I am glad to hear it. But who did you say is in charge of your castle? Your summoner?"

"That hag? No, I've had reason to question her advice, ever since that accursed battle. I will listen to her prattlings no longer; I've thrown her in our deepest gaol. The castle is being overseen by a stout heart named Querrin, a man I believe I can trust. "

"You know, there are some who might call destroying your woodlands the move of a clever tactician," Melconnan said, looking at his cup as if admiring it.

"Really? How so?"

"You have made your surroundings untenable," Melconnan answered. "It is possible that Uther, were he to discover you were away, might take the opportunity to lay siege to your castle. But now there is no cover for him, nor any greenery or wildlife to maintain his siege armies."

"Hm," Avantir said.

"And, by coming here early, and with such a small retinue, you have thrown Uther off your scent."

"Yes," Avantir said, with a rueful smile. "Aren't I the clever one?" It seemed like small comfort, but, when he considered it, it *did* amuse him to think his clumsy flailings might turn out to work in his favor. "Do you consent to assist me?"

"Of course, my friend," Melconnan said. "If that tyrant does not pay for what he did, then what is to stop him from attacking the loved ones of *any* lord or king?"

"Thank you, my friend," Avantir said, his eyes damp again. "With your permission I will write to the other kings and, if I may, ask them to meet here."

"Ah, as to that...you can write the letter, certainly, but I believe it would be best if the letters are under my name and seal. The less Uther might hear of your intentions, the better."

"Ah, yes. Agreed," Avantir said, taking a drink. "And once the nobles are assembled, we can discuss the best way to strike."

"Yes. Agreed," Melconnan said, downing the dregs of his cup. "A skewer in the eye is just what that swine needs!"

❧

Shards of bright pain obscured Ellis' vision, and his hand went reflexively up to his nose. When he drew it back it was covered in blood. Surrounded now by all three of the young haffolk, Tubber shoved him. At the same time, Powdy stuck his leg out and Ellis tripped.

Falling to the ground, Ellis curled into a protective ball, one arm over his eyes to shield away any more blows to his head. He kept waiting to be kicked, but instead he heard the flurry of wings, screams ripped from throats other than his own, and felt fresh blood strike his skin, raining down from above. Then he heard the scrabbling of boots on the gravel.

There was quiet again. And the wind. And the ache in his back and sides and nose.

"Blood," a bird said, in perfectly understandable Hearthentongue.

"Jaq?" Ellis asked.

"There, my dear boy, can you sit up?"

Ellis could not see, as the darkness surrounding him was thick, impenetrable.

"Osia?" Ellis asked.

"It is I. I am sorry I chanced upon those ruffians a bit too late. If Jaq had not insisted on just one more beer..."

"Beer!" Jaq said.

"...yes, well, we would have been here in time. It's all his fault."

Slowly, light began returning, a fresh, green glow filtering through the leaves. Ellis could see Osia in front of him, and Jaq beside him on the road. Osia's hand was on his back, now, supporting him.

"Does that hurt?" he asked.

"It...ah! Yes, a bit."

"Let's get you up, then you can lean on my arm. Do you think you can get home, or should I go on alone and get a cart?"

"I...I think I can make it."

Ellis leaned on the summoner's arm and found it reliable and solid. He began to shuffle in the direction of home.

"You were very brave, master haffolk," Osia said as they walked.

"I don't think I was, particularly." He glanced up at Osia. "You want an answer, don't you?"

"I'll be honest with you, Mr. Sunderland, I was on my way to meet you, to ask if you had made a decision. But this is not the time. No important decisions should be made in distress. The most important thing now is to get you abed and get your wounds tended to."

"You saved me," Ellis said.

"Tosh!" Osia said. "You were holding your own."

"In what possible world?"

Osia smiled at that, but most likely Ellis did not see it.

❧

Once Praltuda had determined the mark of Samael was emblazoned upon him, Ealon's treatment greatly improved. With the chanting still resounding behind him, he was escorted to a tunnel behind the dais, which led to a cave where the prince could reside in comfort. Animal skins covered the cold floor, as well as being hung on the walls as decoration. Large pots of hot coals also warmed the room. And, once Ealon was comfortable, young women were ushered in for his amusement. He was relieved to see they shared many of the features of human women, but with a much more muscular, athletic build. The coarse and hairy skin took a lot of getting used to, but in certain aspects, their hard faces and steely eyes held a savage beauty. And they were certainly more aggressive than the timid maidens he was used to at court. Their hygiene might be found wanting, but they made up for their deficits in other ways.

After what felt like three or four days, Ealon was escorted to another area of this subterranean world. He could tell by sound alone that he was nearing a vast and well-populated chamber. He was astonished upon entering a tremendous cavern, larger than even the courtyard of Caer Trogan, filled with Scrum. He reckoned this gigantic chamber must have once held an underground lake, since the floor was smooth and somewhat bowled. He was standing on a raised alcove, which served as stage. Praltuda was already there, nodding benevolently, along with guards and what might be Scrum dignitaries, if such a thing were possible.

The crowd was expectant but restless. Many torches lined the walls, and vast candelabra hung from the high roof, but single torches were scattered among the throngs, as if they identified certain clans or tribes. Occasional calls or whistles echoed above the din. Murmurs went up as Ealon appeared, and soon the Scrum began to stamp and shout, yelling slogans or demands. He became aware of drums beating out an insistent rhythm.

"The *Ūnna-kar* are assembled," Praltuda told Ealon, gesturing toward the masses. "They await your message."

Ealon was caught short. Not only was he suddenly unnerved at talking to so many people, he was unaware he *had* a message. Samael might have claimed an eye and left him with a skin rash, but the god had imparted nothing to Ealon while doing so. In fact, Ealon was worried he could not even remember exactly why he *had* gone through any of this—except for the fact he hated his father and his brother was a massive breeks-stain. But that would hardly be the makings of a rousing address.

Praltuda was waiting and the crowd was becoming louder. Ealon stepped reluctantly forward, to the crowd's delight. The drums grew louder but then ceased. All were now waiting for Ealon to speak, as was Ealon himself.

"My friends..." he began—and was surprised when the crowd sounded like they were jeering him. Did it offend them to be called *friends*? he wondered. He tried again with "My fellows...", which sounded weaker to him but found more favor. "I..."

As the echo died, Ealon realized he had no words to follow. If he had been touched by Samael it had not been in the ways of eloquence. He desperately wanted to flee the stage, but knew he could not. In fact he feared showing any cowardice in front of these Scrum would result in them tearing him limb from limb.

Random shouting had begun again, as the crowd resumed their unrest. Ealon needed to say something soon, and the only solution was just to start talking—whatever came out. "I am called Prince Ealon," he began. "My father is a great king—a great king of the humans." He expected this to get a derisive reaction and he played into it. "But I do not stand with *him* this day...I stand with *you*!"

The Scrum burst into triumphant shouts and howls, just like he had wanted. "The humans always talk of living in peace, but all they do is fight, right? They tear up the land with their wars and battles. The last battle I fought in, I don't even know why we were fighting. This is their legacy: death and destruction...but all built on weakness!" He was drowned in cheers again. "Built on weakness! While we ravaged over the land, you were forced to stay under it, am I right? But the days of the humans are over, my...my fellow warriors. For, I tell you, the old days are coming back!"

He wasn't sure this was the message they were wanting, but they cheered and hollered as if accepting it. "It is time to bring back the elder god, to go back to the way things used to be, to wipe away all the mistakes and disasters the humans have caused—and I am the one who can do it! The Prison Stone is broken, the door is open, the pathway from past to future is made clear. Samael himself can lead the way—and you, *you* can follow him. Escape these holes before they become your crypts. Together, we can rise up—above, to the surface. Reclaim the land for yourselves, the way it should have been—and can be again. It is not difficult to defeat the humans, and obviously, I know their ways!" The crowd howled once more; it appeared that Ealon was whipping them into such a violent frenzy that fights were breaking out among his audience. "Your great lord, in his wisdom, recognized that Samael left his mark on me." The crowd fell quiet at the name. "Upon my face is the sigil of...of the honored one. The great god touched me himself, leaving his emblem." Ealon no longer needed to shout, but his voice nonetheless grew louder as he continued. "Let that emblem be your shield... Come with me and it shall be your shield! *Follow me and it shall be your shield! RALLY BEHIND ME AND IT SHALL BE YOUR SHIELD! I...AM YOUR SHIELD!*" The Scrum throngs were ravenously howling again, raising their arms, brandishing weapons, shaking their fists. "*I AM YOUR SHIELD!*" Ealon cried, striding across the stage, eyes blazing. "*I AM YOUR SHIELD! I AM YOUR SHIELD!*"

He turned to look at Praltuda, whose mouth was open in a disconcerting but approving smile. Ealon smiled back, and then turned to face the crowd, shaking his fists in echo of their excitement. A chant rose up but he could not make it out. Whatever it was, soon the entire congregation was shouting it together. Ealon could not help smiling, in triumph as well as relief. He had done it. He had won them over. And in doing so, he realized, he had accomplished something he had not expected. He had gotten himself an army.

14

Tubber lifted his quill from the package with a feeling of satisfaction. He sat back and admired his handiwork. Would anyone recognize his handwriting? He had been careful to write with his right hand, which was not his way, ordinarily. The script had come out jagged, uneven, but legible for all of that. No, no one would trace this back to him. He grinned.

"Postage," he said aloud, and got up from his chair to retrieve some stamps. He'd been carrying mail long enough that he did not need to weigh it—instinctively he knew how many stamps he would need. He opened the wax paper envelope and pulled forth a sheet of the familiar stamps with the royal crown of Summerfield emblazoned upon them. He separated nine of them, and licked the back of the lot all at once, then applied them to the package in just the right spot.

But not *exactly* the right spot. He scowled to see that they had ended up slightly askew. "Well, that's all right," he told himself. He placed the package in a market bag, and made for a nearby postal bin.

As he walked, he thought about the bird that had attacked him—him and his friends. He felt at the place on his scalp where the swiving beast had ripped through his skin with its nasty beak—or had it clawed him? It didn't matter. He knew the bird, and that it belonged to the summoner who had come to town. Tubber had been surprised when the summoner and his demon bird had come to the aid of Sunderland, that oozing louse.

If he were honest with himself, he had to admit that it had scared him. Not only the surprise attack by the bird, but the fact that he'd crossed paths with a summoner at all. There weren't many that made Tubber feel that he was outmatched, but a summoner...he shuddered at the thought of it. Summoners were dangerous, unpredictable. And who knew the source of their power, anyway? Some say that summoners are secretly priests of the elder god, and who was Tubber to say that they were wrong?

After the attack, as they soothed themselves in the pub, Steffan had suggested they find a way to get Sunderland alone. That had started the gears in his head turning. Tubber did not consider himself a particularly clever man—nor did anyone else. But he was proud of the plan he had concocted.

It had taken some doing—there were several moving pieces, and everything had to fit into place just so for it to work, but he was confident. *It may, in fact, be the best plan ever,* he thought, and felt his chest swell with pride.

He moved through the market square and tipped his cap to the more prominent haffolk that he saw, the market bag hanging heavily from one hand. On the far side, he saw the postal drop, a large wooden box with a slot for letters and a bin for packages. Looking around, he made sure no one was looking at him. Then he realized that looking around was suspicious, so he looked at his shoes. Then he realized that was stupid. Why was he standing by a postal drop looking at his shoes? He quickly chastened himself, and taking a deep breath, concentrated on doing what he was there to do. He opened the market bag, pulled forth the package, and placed it in the bin. Then, he closed the lid on the bin, and walked away, whistling.

As soon as he was clear, he started chuckling. Sunderland would be surprised indeed. "Package for you, Mr. Massenbarrow," he said out loud. Then he chuckled again.

THERE WAS nothing Ennisbrook enjoyed about this assignment. His time and his talents were being wasted, playing this prolonged game of peek-and-seek with Uther's younger son. He was loath to voice an objection to his sire, of course, making his resentment all the more noticeable in his expression—already severe enough as was. He was forced into an aggravating dilemma, needing to approach people while at the same time driving them away from him. As he had said to himself already, he hated this assignment.

He had a strong feeling he could get a direct answer if he simply confronted the high king's summoner. It was no secret Liaga was like a teacher to Ealon. A few minutes with Liaga and he would learn all he needed to know about Ealon's whereabouts. But with equal certainty Ennisbrook knew Liaga would evade his questions and cloud any answers with half-truths. Of course Ennisbrook knew quick and effective ways of pulling the truth out of an uncooperative man, but it was likely Uther would frown at using them upon his summoner.

Thus, Ennisbrook was forced to what he liked least, to go into the town, seek people who might know Ealon, and ask them questions. Not even interrogate them—just ask them questions. Looking for clues and questioning commoners, like a sheriff searching for a lost dog. His newest hunch led him to the streets of Loaming, the seedy, rundown part of town southwest of the castle, outside the gates of Trogan proper. He had enough times seen Ealon loitering with the same delinquents, and he knew some of them and their families. He scanned both sides of the street as he walked, hoping to run into them, away from their homes. A crew like that would avoid the main city, so he ventured toward the seamier streets. Not only was he more likely to find whom he was looking for there, those were parts of town where he, as a soldier, was more comfortable.

As hoped, he spotted two youths arguing outside a tavern. By their attitude, it looked like they had just exited after a long visit. Both were lean; one was dark-haired and the other light. They had their coin purses out and were evidently arguing about money. As Ennisbrook got closer, he discerned the argument was about how much money they had left.

"I can't believe I'm bare," said the dark-haired one, opening the drawstrings on his coin purse wider, as if he would find more money in its depths.

"I can't believe it, either, since you had *me* buying every round!"

"I did not—and you drink twice as much, anyway!"

Ennisbrook was practically upon them now. He recognized the corn-haired young man as being of the Boselant family; the dark-haired young man was one of the Trowletons. Ennisbrook impressed himself in remembering his first name too.

"Hey, wait—did we get robbed in there?" Trowleton was saying, before they were interrupted.

"Rickant," said the Enforcer. "Rickant Trowleton. Don't you have better things to do in the middle of the day than standing in the mud outside a public house?"

"And what's it to you?" Trowleton began, as he unsteadily turned to see who was addressing him. Ennisbrook noticed in the youth a similarity with Ealon. Not necessarily in their face, but in their height, their build, the way they stood, and their air of condescension. Trowleton's companion, meanwhile, began to back away, looking wary of the Enforcer's rough countenance or perhaps the undeniable rapier at his side. Trowleton gulped, but then effected a false bravado.

"Whachoo walking with a sword for, mister? If you're here to rob us, you're too late. If you're the one who already robbed us, then I'll need to punch you." He glared, but the Enforcer's lined face made him gulp again.

Ennisbrook ignored him. "I'm looking for the prince. Do you know where Prince Ealon may be?"

"Never 'eard of him."

For a change, Ennisbrook was amused by this obstinacy. "The Prince, who lives in the great castle a short walk from here—you haven't heard of him?"

"What castle would that be, eh?" Trawleton replied.

Ennisbrook's amusement was short-lived. If he wanted obstinate answers he could have stuck with his first impulse and confronted Liaga. In a flash, the point of the rapier was under the young man's chin and all humor had left the Enforcer's voice. "Perhaps *this* will clear your head. If not, it will aid in *severing* it."

The threat achieved its intended effect. Trowleton regained his focus, while the Boselant boy had backed several paces away. "I repeat," Ennisbrook continued coldly and slowly, "have you seen Ealon?"

"I swear to you, sir, I have not."

"Do you know where he might be? Do you have favorite places you go to?"

He knew he had lost Trowleton already. The idiot had gone cross-eyed staring too intently at the blade tip under his nose. Ennisbrook looked over to Boselant, who, even at a distance, must have felt the threat as he began to stammer. "We go...frequently...we often go...the House...*to* the House..."

"Whose house?"

"The House of the Small Forest," Boselant answered, his hand reflexively gesturing over his shoulder.

"Small Forest," Trowleton dimly echoed, still staring at the blade point.

"The House of the Small Forest," Ennisbrook repeated, curious why the name was not familiar to him. "And it is that way?" he asked, gesturing with his chin to the street behind Boselant. The yellow-haired youth nodded.

Ennisbrook lowered his weapon and moved onward, deliberately forcing his shoulder into Trowleton's chest, pushing the boy aside. He could hear them arguing, behind him. He heard "the House" a few times, which pleased him. He might be on the right track if they were this out-of-sorts over revealing the name to him.

He passed a few storefronts, after which the street became no more than a path leading to the next small town. Following it into the forest, he walked for about ten minutes. He was beginning to wonder if perhaps the youths had foolishly had him on when he came to a clearing in which sat an impressive edifice. It was two-storied, pale yellow in color, and assembled after the fashion of the great country houses built a hundred years ago or more.

Ennisbrook instinctively felt that this was the place he was looking for, and cautiously walked around the side of it to assess its real size. It did not go very deep into its lot, which told him it was built to look like a great house, but was, in fact, hardly more than a large cottage. Ennisbrook could see a large fence behind the building, as if the proprietors had bought extra land. Coming back round to the front door, he tried the handle and found it open. With one hand on his rapier, he pushed the door inward and stepped inside.

The room he entered was full of comfortable couches. The walls were covered with the stuffed heads of many animals. To the right was a bar, behind which stood a barman with a thick black mustache. He looked up, but ignored the new visitor. Instead an older man with a pinched face and curly gray hair was immediately at Ennisbrook's side. "I would not have expected one such as you to visit us, kind sir," the man said in a suspiciously sweet voice. "What can I possibly do for you?"

"This place was recommended to me," Ennisbrook replied. "But I confess I don't know what it is for."

"Ah," said the man. "We are a humble hunting lodge. Though perhaps if my lord would follow me, I could better explain by showing you our grounds." He led Ennisbrook deeper into the house. Many of the rooms were closed, but he discerned the familiar sounds of men and women in passionate clutch behind the doors. *A sweeping interpretation of hunting*, Ennisbrook thought. He was led to a wooden porch behind the house, which looked out upon a long and rectangular yard, lined by the same wooden fence he had seen from the outside. The yard was wild with trees and undergrowth. To Ennisbrook's left, racks of bows and crossbows were affixed to the back wall. Farther along were large muskets. To his right, and noticeable from their squeaks and growls, were stacks of wire cages containing small animals.

"You hunt on the grounds of the lodge itself?" he asked.

The old man nodded. "We cater to the appetites of those who can't necessarily find time to delve deeply into the forests." With grunts and moans still in his ear, Ennisbrook knew they catered to other appetites besides. *Every man to his prey*, Ennisbrook thought. *It could be their motto*. "We bring the forest to them," the old man concluded.

While Ennisbrook stood there he saw a rabbit dart by and, far in the shadows, was pretty sure he could see a doe raise her head. Movement in the grass, however, revealed that the rabbit was on a tether, limiting its range of movement. For a moment Ennisbrook had grudgingly appreciated the idea behind such a business. He could even have recommended the place to his fellow soldiers for target practice. But now he saw that there was no need for skill here. All it honed was bloodlust, an indulgent way for disinterested youth to kill captive animals.

Which brought him back to Ealon. "As you may have recognized, I am a representative of the high king's court," Ennisbrook began.

"Yes, my lord."

"Tell me then, has his royal highness Prince Ealon been a patron of your house?"

"Yes, my lord. He has been here several times."

"Recently?" Ennisbrook asked.

"Yes, my lord. A few days ago."

Ennisbrook showed no reaction. "Do you recall any details of his visit?"

"As a matter of fact, I do," the old man said, hiding a sudden smile. "It was most interesting. He inquired about buying one of our animals."

"Did he?"

"Well, not buying, no; but his highness did inquire what an animal might cost if he *were* to buy it."

"Do you remember what animal in particular?"

"It was a goat, my lord."

"And did you ask why the Prince might be in need of a goat?"

"My lord, we cater to many different interests. It's not really my place to ask why people want the things they do."

"I can see that, yes," Ennisbrook said, before giving the man a nod and turning to re-enter the house.

"You will not be staying with us?" the old man asked, following him.

"No," the Enforcer replied, "it's not as much fun if your prey has no opportunity to flee. I thank you for your time though, my good man. You've been quite helpful." He nodded again and stepped nimbly down the steps and returned to the road.

There were three reasons why someone would want a goat, as far as

Ennisbrook could see. The first was best left unsaid, the second was for its milk and cheese and hair, and the third was for a sacrifice. Ennisbrook was not a pious man, but even he was aware of the many mentions of sacrifices — specifically, goat sacrifices — in the old stories. He had no idea why the gods would be in need of goats, but obviously they were partial to them, whatever the reason.

He pondered all this as he walked back to the town. Once there he hailed a carriage back to Caer Trogan and continued his mulling as it bounced along the cobblestones.

With the great kitchens of the castle at his beck and call, there was no reason Ealon would need to acquire his own goat's milk. One could say the prince was decent enough looking, objectively speaking, to win over plenty of young women in the castle or in the town, which struck down that *other* reason. What remained was the suggestion that Ealon must be plotting some kind of religious rite for reasons unknown.

Thus, Ennisbrook found he had one, simple, direct question for Liaga after all. Once back at Caer Trogan, he tracked down the summoner, stopped him in a corridor, and with no preamble asked him, "Where would you say is the nearest place for an animal sacrifice?" And when he saw the color drain from Liaga's face, Ennisbrook knew he was on the right track.

❧

AVANTIR WAS HEARTENED as the other kings and lords began to arrive. He remained in his suite of rooms, but Melconnan saw that he stayed informed. Late in the afternoon of the following day, Melconnan invited his guests to assemble in the great hall. He had intended to present a banquet, but his wife the queen had suggested that a standing meal be provided, seeing as they had business to discuss. Large platters of food were set on the great table, which the guests could pick at as they mingled. Although there were large chairs at the table, most everyone gathered before the large fireplaces at either end of the hall, trying to avoid the drafty windows. Turkey leg in hand, Melconnan moved about, welcoming them again, asking about any goings-on, making sure they were comfortable in their rooms, encouraging them to partake of the food.

After sending for Avantir, Melconnan gained everyone's attention and, waving the others to join him at the foot of the table, began a short speech. "I'm sure we've all heard about the unfortunate events at Wybrook. My friend, and a friend to all here, was forced to endure a great loss — the death of his son. Nay, let us call it what it is—the murder of his son."

The words elicited a slight murmur of discomfort, which Melconnan would not tolerate. "I do not choose my words rashly. I say it because it is true. Uther, the so-called purveyor of virtue and justice, insinuated himself into Avantir's court and wantonly snuffed out his son's life—with no more regard as if he were a...a..." Melconnan paused as he saw Avantir appear in the archway. "Ah, here is my friend now. Your Graces, I present to you Avantir, king of Wybrook."

The others walked toward Avantir to extend a hand. The old man seemed very touched at their looks of concern and their comforting pats on the arm. His eyes brimmed and shone in the firelight, yet Melconnan was relieved to see that Avantir did not succumb to his emotions.

"As you may have guessed," Melconnan continued, "it is no coincidence that he is here with us today. Uther's dangerous arrogance could befall any of us. There's nothing to stop him reaching into any of our courts, seizing any of our properties, claiming any of our lands, taking any one of our family—manhandling them, killing them...or worse." Melconnan studied the faces before him. He was not rousing anyone; they all looked at him uneasily, as if already knowing what he was about to ask of them. "Your graces, please," he said, more quietly but with all the earnestness he could, "how can I make you see that if we do not make ourselves heard, if we do not say, '*No... enough*,' if we do not make a stand, then there is nothing stopping Uther from doing this again...and again...until it is too late and we have become his slaves. What Uther did to Avantir is unpardonable. It is a sin that demands retribution."

At last he saw the words hit home. A few lords nodded, others lowered their heads, deep in thought. "And what does Avantir ask of us?" inquired King Wellingford of Torreldon, stroking as always his impressive mustaches.

"He...and I..." Melconnan continued, "ask your allegiance and your men."

King Harleyton of Fondritch, full of face and full of beard, sitting behind Wellingford, scoffed. "Avantir tried that already—and got his backside swatted like an insolent child. His army, I mean," Harleyton added, looking about uncertainly, swirling his skewer of pork in the air, "not the...the other thing."

Avantir held up a hand. "My lord is not incorrect. I acted rashly and ill-advisedly in that excursion. I hope that, by joining together, this can be avoided."

King Tarvenot of Gerfennen, a tall man with a severe expression, spoke up. "How do we know this cause is just? There are many who aver, and forgive me for saying so, that the child was killed in self-defense; that your friend here sent his son out as an assassin to kill Uther in his own household."

It was perhaps understandable that Tarvenot would be in a foul mood, for he had farthest to travel; but Melconnan minded this not. Tarvenot had always irritated him. "Those are stories," the king of the Northlands sneered. "Do you get all your information from idle talk and rumor?"

"I've heard it, too!" someone else said.

"Oh, aye. It's reached us, too," said another. "The bards."

Wellingford raised his voice above the din. "The verses have reached all of us. But why should we go by what the bards say?" He pinched the end of his mustache, contemplatively. "We have the father of the prince here before us. Tell us, King Avantir, did you turn your boy into an assassin set on killing the high king—don't be afraid to answer true, there are many who would applaud such a ploy."

"Yes," Tarvenot spoke again, running his fingertips over his dark and very thin mustache. "Was Prince Clendis sent to Uther with some poison squirreled away among his other things?"

Melconnan cast Avantir a worried glance. He was losing control of the argument, over a point that might cause his friend anguish. But

Avantir looked strangely calm. As he responded, he look above the crowd as if his answer was written on the wall. "My sirs. It is so."

"My friend," Melconnan interject, "you—"

Avantir continued. "Yes, Uther demanded that I send my boy to him, and I daren't refuse. But I feared that Uther, despite his oily promises, would make a hostage of him, and that he might hurt or torture my boy in an effort to ransom him. Yes, he had poison on him —which I told him to drink, if need be, at the first sign of menace, in order to thwart any of Uther's intended violations. The poison was intended for Clendis, not the high king."

Some shifted uncomfortably. After a moment Harleyton asked quietly, "Then...the boy took his own life?"

"No," Tarvenot said, equally quietly, "it is said he was stabbed in the heart by the high king's enforcer."

Melconnan cleared his throat before speaking. "Enough. There is no need to drag my friend again through his grief. The tavern talk is a fable Uther wants you to believe. I tell you, I know Prince Clendis, son of Avantir, was innocent, that Uther murdered him in retaliation for Avantir's declaration of war. Besting him in battle wasn't enough for Uther, he had to attack his opponent's family as well."

King Albingast of Kilgard spoke up. His baldness made his blue eyes blaze even stronger in his pink face. "Well, if Avantir was so easily bested, why should we let him lead our armies now?" he demanded, with neck muscles flexing

Melconnan answered. "King Avantir did not have the numbers to wage a proper assault. But we do...if we join together." He stared at the men again, seeing if his words were aimed true. "*If we join together*," he repeated, "I believe we will have enough men, enough strength to send Uther a message he will not soon forget."

"Do you wish to unseat him?" Tarvenot asked, sounding more worried than skeptical. "If we join together will we be setting *you* upon the throne? Is this your grand scheme, to have us all owing our allegiance to *you*?"

Melconnan stared at Tarvenot. The man touched his thin mustache so much, Melconnan thought, you'd think it was a disguise about to fall off. "As I said," Melconnan said, coldly, "I wish to send Uther a message. If he does lose the crown, so be it; but I—and I assure you, gentlemen—I did not call you here so I could exploit my friend's grief for my personal gain."

Melconnan was close to saying more, but he had to be a gracious host. He let the group's murmured admonishments speak for themselves. Tarvenot, graciously, gave a slow nod, conceding the point; but he did not look any less haughty, and his fingers still would not stray far from his thin mustache.

"I think the point has been made?" Melconnan asked, looking around for consensus. "We don't need to debate this further, do we?" He clapped his hands, calling in his scribe, who began keeping a tally of the soldiers each lord or king was willing to provide. The numbers were low, but they were still encouraging. All told, there were enough men here to provide an army of nigh five thousand men.

Uther had two thousand at his call, Melconnan figured, and a thousand or so serviceable civilians among his townsfolk—plus the reach to maybe drum up four thousand more. Avantir seemed pleased enough, by the looks of it, but Melconnan worried there were not enough, that they would be victims of another rout. He had hoped to strike soon and hard, but it appeared he would have to spread his net wider, dare to send inquiries to more of the peerage, even to Estenlan's own nobles, and spend his days waiting.

He shook the doubts away and played the host again. "Gentlemen, I thank you," he said. "We are on the cusp of something great and important, something I believe will benefit us all; and, on behalf of King Avantir and myself, I thank you for pledging to it. Ah, I see it is already eventide—it is too late for travel, yes? Please, reside with us another night, and you can begin your journeys home bright and early on the morrow."

The kings resumed chatting amongst themselves, returning to the table for more food. Melconnan walked over to where Avantir stood. "My friend," Avantir began, "you stated my case admirably and I thank you for being my advocate. Things have turned out exceptionally well."

"I am pleased you think so," Melconnan answered, "but I do not share your enthusiasm."

"And why is that?"

"We are pledged an army of five thousand, plus perhaps, at best, a thousand of whichever of your men are still able. But Uther can command an army of seven thousand or more. We don't have the numbers and, truth be told, I'm not sure we *have* the numbers we have. Meaning, that is, I wouldn't be surprised if more than a few of the lesser kings choose to forget this evening ever happened when the drums beat and the trumpets call."

"You think so?"

"I'd prefer not to, but I do."

Hands full with many selections from the table, the kings began to leave the hall and make their way to their rooms. Melconnan encouraged Avantir to retire as well—they would discuss matters in the morning. Avantir acceded and mounted the nearer of the two great stone stairways.

As it turned out, they saw each other only a few hours later. Avantir opened his door to find Melconnan holding two mugs of mulled cider. "There is news," Melconnan said, handing over a mug and entering Avantir's chambers.

"What? What is it?" Avantir asked, leading Melconnan to a table where they could sit.

"My men report there was a spy among us tonight."

Avantir's eyes widened. "You don't say!" His mug was raised halfway up but he set it down again.

"A runner was spotted, trying to leave the castle under cover of night. He was overridden and stopped before he could get far. He sits in my prison cell tonight, but he is not talking."

"You don't know who he works for?"

"He won't say. But he was wearing his household colors."

"Whose? Tell me. Is it Tarvenot?"

"He's—ha—it's funny you should say that. Tarvenot *is* a bit of a prig, isn't he?" Melconnan chuckled, not expecting to find humor in the situation. "No. He's Harleyton's man."

"Harleyton! The blackguard. Then Harleyton is *Uther's* man." Avantir shook his head. "I guess I shouldn't be surprised. Fondritch and Estenlan have been frequent allies...as has Torreldon." He looked up at Melconnan again. "You're sure you stopped his message going out? That Uther has no idea what we plan?"

"As far as we know. And Harleyton shan't send anything more—I've got him under lock and key."

"You put him in your gaol too?"

"No, no. I'm not Uther," Melconnan said. "He is restricted to his chambers, at least until I know what to do with him. Hopefully he won't cause a scene before the other guests leave."

"Do you think that's possible?"

"Possible, but unlikely. Instead of prison bars, we've given him a healthy sentence of laudanum for the time being. But let this be a reminder to us," Melconnan added, gesturing with his mug. "We travel on dangerous ground, my friend. There's no telling what pitfalls await us as we strike out on this path. We must be extra careful how we proceed."

❧

"SUNDERLAND!" Bracegirdle's voice thundered.

"By the Horn, what is it now?" Ellis put the stack of mail he was sorting to one side, and walked as swiftly as he dared to his supervisor's office. Poking his head in, he pretended cheerfulness. "Right here."

"I want you to take a wee break and run this down to Massenbarrow at the tavern." Bracegirdle held a package aloft.

"Me, sir?" Ellis asked. He felt his heart catch in his throat. He was being trusted with a delivery. He felt the sting of tears rise to his eyes, but he brushed them away impatiently.

Bracegirdle raised one huge, bushy eyebrow and glared at him through his spectacles. "It's a gift, Sunderland."

"The package, sir? We're not supposed to care what's in them."

"No, you dunderhead! The job. It's a gift. Don't muff it up."

"Oh." Ellis felt stung. "No, sir. I won't, sir."

"It should take you seven minutes to get to the tavern, two to find Massenbarrow, five to have a pint, and seven to get back. That's..."

"Twenty-one minutes, sir."

"I want to see you sorting mail once more in half an hour, and not a minute later."

"You're very generous, sir."

Bracegirdle held the package out to him, and Ellis took it, clutching it to his breast like a long-lost child. He was being given another chance! Ellis bit his lip, nearly overcome with emotion.

"Well, what are you just standing there for? The clock is ticking."

Ellis gave a quick bow and, still clutching the package gratefully, exited Bracegirdle's office. He grabbed his hat by the door and ducked out through the round door of the post office into the street.

He turned toward the tavern and proceeded at a brisk pace. Something seemed different. On the way to work, he hadn't noticed how the sunshine glinted off the metal studs of the ponies' livery. He hadn't noticed the effervescent liveliness of the people around him. He hadn't noticed the joy of the blood rushing through his own veins. His step became almost a skip.

I'll do this job with dispatch, and then Bracegirdle will give me another, he thought to himself as he walked. *I'll get my route back quicker than I hoped for!* He felt a tender flicker of hope catch fire and blaze within his chest. He would be a courier again.

Soon the tavern loomed before him. He wiped his boots and entered the round door, ducking into its chaotic interior. It was a different tavern from the one he frequented, the one Liza worked at, but he knew it well enough. Long Will Epperworthy would be at the bar, unless he missed his guess. And indeed, Will was there.

He was called Long Will because he was taller than any other haffolk in the Dale. He was also thin as a snapbean. Ellis pushed through to a space at the bar and waved to get Will's attention. Will nodded to acknowledge his presence and finished up with another customer. A minute later he turned to Ellis, wiping his hands on a bar towel. "Make it quick, Ellis, we've the second lunch rush upon us."

"Here to deliver a package to a Mr. Massenbarrow."

"Yeah, I know 'im. Stranger from Upper West Farthingdale. He's staying here at the inn. Room..." His eyes rolled to look at the ceiling as he thought. "...six, if I'm not mistaken. Big shouldered fellow, jet black hair. Wears a goose feather in his cap. Go on back through the kitchen."

"Thanks-in-a-bunch, Will," Ellis called over his shoulder, heading for the kitchen.

"Will ye have time for a pint?"

"Of course! Branwell's please."

"I'll pull it now for you, put it by the bell."

"You're a topper."

The kitchen was a dangerous obstacle course, as the two cooks and the coal boy rushed to fill the orders for second lunch and were not expecting to dodge a courier. Ellis nearly caught a faceful of sizzling bacon grease, but ducked just as the pan was being thrown back to the stove.

Ellis dove for the safety of the far door, pressed down on the wrought-iron handle and whirled into the quiet of the hallway. Down the hall a guest was letting herself into her room. Ellis moved quickly down the hall, looking at the cheery numbers painted on the doors.

"Five...and Six," he said, halting before a bright red door. He knocked with renewed authority. Nothing happened. He knocked again. He put his ear to the door, but heard only silence and the dim banging coming down the hall from the kitchen. Finally, he pounded on the door, but with no better results.

"Horn of blood," he swore. It was not an oath he used often in the presence of others, even friends. He felt awash with sudden panic. He turned and nearly ran back to the public room. Almost in a daze, he dodged the chaos of the kitchen, and wove his way up to the bar. There was his Branwell's, sitting underneath the bell, but he had not yet earned it.

"Ho, Will!" Ellis knew he was interrupting the barman at the busiest time of the day, but his anxiety got the upper hand.

Will scowled at him. *As well he might,* Ellis thought. "Will, it's urgent. Massenbarrow isn't in his room." Ellis had no idea if the package was urgent or not, but his own urgency was about to undermine his professional decorum.

"Don't know what to tell ye, Ellis. The man is free to go where he wants, isn't he?"

Will turned his back and began pouring a fresh pint.

Ellis breathed deeply, trying to quiet his pounding pulse. "All right, mate," he said out loud, although in the din, no one could hear him. "This is a minor setback. Ask around."

Ellis thought quickly about the immediate neighborhood. There was a blacksmith's across the road. Singehandle was the proprietor there, a haffolk with nine fingers, Ellis recalled. He'd see everyone going in and out the inn. And it being second lunch...he scanned the crowd.

"Blessed stars," Ellis breathed, and picked his way through the crowd as quickly as he could toward the blacksmith.

"Ho, Wynn," Ellis put a knee on the bench next to the man. Wynn Singehandle had a full pint in front of him, and was halfway through a side of roast duck.

"Ellis Sunderland," the man brightened. "What brings you here?"

"Delivery," Ellis said, pointing to the package still clutched to his chest.

"Oh, aye?"

"I'm looking for a guest at the inn, a Mr. Massenbarrow."

"What's 'e look like?"

"Uh..." Ellis struggled to remember Will's description. "Goose feather in his cap. Black hair. Big shoulders."

"Yeah, I seen 'im. Headed off toward the livery about half an hour gone."

Ellis clapped Wynn on the shoulder and offered his heartfelt thanks, then he made a beeline toward the door.

Once outside, he nearly broke into a run in the direction of the nearest stables. He made two loops around the buildings, but saw no one fitting Will's description. He saw a stableboy filling a trough and, out of breath, approached.

He wasn't really a boy, but closer to Ellis' own age. "Boy" was part of the job title, which, under ordinary circumstances, Ellis would have wondered about. Did it bother the young haffolk to be called a boy? But he had no time for such thoughts now. "I say, have you seen a Mr. Massenbarrow about?" he asked, panting.

"What's it worth to ye?"

Ellis bit his tongue to stop himself swearing and pulled a farthing from his pocket. He pressed it into the stableboy's hand, who pocketed it and grinned, showing Ellis his black and missing teeth. "Through there," the boy said, pointing to a low door Ellis hadn't noticed before. "Keep going back, the stables are long."

"Thank you, thank you!" Ellis called over his shoulder. He came to the door and yanked on the handle. It gave far too easily and nearly caught him in the forehead as he jerked it open. He had no time to wonder at the near miss, however, as he was busy calculating how many minutes had passed and whether he'd be able to make it back to Bracegirdle's office in time.

As he stomped past the stables, he was sorry he'd not gotten a chance to enjoy his ale. It was the least of his worries, but he was sorry nonetheless. The stables yielded no haffolk at all, let alone one with a goose feather in his cap. At the end of the hallway was a large barn door. Not knowing what else to try, Ellis pushed it open, and rushed into whatever room was beyond it.

It certainly looked like a barn. He heard the door close behind him with a bigger bang than he'd expected. Then he heard it latch.

Who had latched it?

Ellis spun around and saw Tubber standing with his hands behind his back, rocking on his heels, a wicked smile marring his goofy face.

Ellis' heart sank into a pit in his stomach. He clutched the package tighter. "Tubber, what in the name of the gods old and new..."

"You wanted a fair fight, did you not?"

"What?"

"Well, look here. I've not got me boys with me. And you've not got a wizard with you."

"Wizard" was a pejorative term often hurled at summoners. Ellis let it pass.

"Nor do you have a girl protecting you with her...widdle stick." He made a sour face, obviously disdainful of Kit's prowess. "This time, it's just you and me. A fair fight, eh?"

"Tubber, no. I...I don't want a fight at all."

"I'll even make you a deal. You clock me, fair and square, and I'll not hold ye responsible for losing me the postmaster's job. How does that sound, then?"

Ellis blinked. He lowered the package, looking at it suspiciously. "Tubber, is there even a Mr. Massenbarrow?"

But instead of answering, Tubber lifted his hands up in front of his face, curling them into fists with obvious relish.

Tubber was larger than he was. Ellis also knew that the young man had a good thirty pounds on him. He'd also grown up in the street, where he'd had to use his fists every day to survive. Ellis had gotten into exactly one fist fight in his entire life, and he'd lost that one handily. If it hadn't been for Kit...

...but Kit wasn't here. Ellis held the package by one corner and dropped it onto the straw. He sighed and resigned himself to his fate. "All right, Tubber. Let's get this over with."

He didn't know what else to do, and the prospect of Tubber's aggression finally being at an end was enticing—if he could trust him to keep his word. Yet what choice did Ellis have? Awkwardly, Ellis brought his fists into place and began to circle the barn, facing the bully.

Tubber spat on his fist, and pretended to polish it with his opposite hand. Then he grinned, so wide Ellis could see the gap where he'd lost a tooth in another fight not too long ago. In his mind's eye, Ellis could see Tubber's fist connecting with his own head, and saw his own head explode like a melon. He shook his head to clear the image and raised his fists. It seemed a useless and absurd gesture, a gesture not of defiance or aggression, but of capitulation. When Tubber swung, Ellis didn't even know enough to duck.

15

Obviously Liaga would never have been as obliging to explain where Asura Varr was, but his sudden taciturnity had been a strong indicator Ennisbrook was on the right track. The tomes he had consulted in the castle library contradicted each other, but a rough estimation was that the varr was located in the southern deserts. Daevis had suppressed a wry smile. The great forefathers had never been all that imaginative in their nomenclature: the Northern Wastes, the Southern Deserts, the Midlands, the Orchard. Even Estenlan itself. But, then again, the names were easy enough to remember and they got the point across. *A purity of simplicity*, he thought.

The name was simple enough but to get there was quite a distance for Ealon to cross, and Ennisbrook was once again curious what could compel such industry. Commandeering an æthercraft to go in that direction would be conspicuous, which would make a trip a long walk or ride for the prince. Ennisbrook, however, working at the king's wishes, had no trouble commandeering an æthercraft. As cover, he explained to the pilot and crew that he was chasing an escaped criminal. The thought of enabling the king's justice took the sting out of traveling to such an uninspiring location.

Far to the south, the verdant plains of Estenlan became dead fields and cracked, dry desert. There was no call to claim these dead lands. Although there existed an obvious visual boundary, no border existed on any map. These wastelands technically remained part of Estenlan, though they were of no monetary use or benefit to her.

Ennisbrook scanned the horizon, once the surroundings went from green to yellow. Shortly after the dead fields became barren desert, he spotted a slight rise on the otherwise flat horizon. He ordered the ship to fly as low as possible. As soon as he recognized that the hill up ahead was not an illusion, he ordered the craft to land. The Enforcer left the crew aboard the craft and took the remaining miles on foot.

As he neared the ridge he spotted a large gray lump. *Oh Ealon*, he thought at first. *What has happened here?* But the body was that of a horse, though it had been sliced open and its innards cleared out. There were many tracks, as if the animal had wandered aimlessly for a while. It had been undefended when attacked...if it had indeed been attacked. No teeth had torn out those organs; they had been sliced and severed by blades.

Ennisbrook had assumed the ground had risen here into a slight table, but in fact it was a circular ridge, like the crater of a volcano. Its cone was raised not much higher than the surrounding desert, though. It was the only discernible landmark, and the Enforcer felt it reasonable to assume this could be Ealon's target. He scaled the outside wall and slid down its inner side. The land was not bowled within the crater, but was as flat as the surrounding land and of a similar make—flat, dusty, with no scrub grass or life at all. The ground had a disturbing reddish brown hue, reminiscent of dried blood. Ennisbrook could not discern whether this was natural or brought on by shadow. He heard no wildlife around him, only a subtle wind. *By feel alone, this would be a good place for a mass grave,* he deemed.

The ground was darker a few yards away; he could almost see a circular pattern, dark streaks emanating from a central point, as if something had exploded and sent its remains equally in all directions. He saw bits of black grit amid the scorch marks. Had someone burst open a rock? He was doubtful rocks that could explode. Likely someone had taken a sledge hammer to it, but to what end? A geode, maybe? In the hope of precious crystals inside?

But why would such a thing interest Ealon? Ennisbrook wondered. *This is stuff for dwarfs.—Ahh, but that could explain why Ealon had a dwarf companion? But if so, why kill the dwarf before coming out here and performing this ceremony? Unless Ealon had learned all he needed from him...*

This was all conjecture, he admitted. He could talk to a summoner if he wanted invention and stories. He was working more on gut instinct, but the feeling was strong that Ealon had been here, that the star-shaped smear on the ground was evidence of the ceremony that had brought him here. But it was still just a feeling.

Sighing, the Enforcer rose from his crouch and looked up to the sky. The eastern edge was already growing dark. The crew of the æthercraft would likely wish to return home before nightfall. It was probably time to head back, despite the nagging feeling he should investigate further. The hunters who had stripped and cleaned Ealon's horse could be close by. There were no visible structures; they must be cave dwellers.

Ealon could be close by, just beneath him, Ennisbrook thought. Perhaps the cave-dwellers had him in captivity, as a trespasser. Perhaps this ground was sacred to them, living so close to it. In his younger days Ennisbrook might have charged down into the darkness, to effect a rescue all on his own. But he had grown shrewder and more cautious since then. He admitted to himself that he was hardly prepared to navigate unknown subterranean passages to confront what could be an uncountable race of cave warriors. It was best for him to get back to the æthercraft but return here in greater numbers. He glanced at the sky, to the black stain on the ground, and then across the flat circle of land to the ridge on the other side—and now he felt a different sensation...that he was being watched.

ELLIS FELL, nearly hitting his head on a wheelbarrow on the way down. Stunned, he looked at the straw for a few moments before he remembered where he was and what he was doing. Oh, yes. Tubber was about to pound his flesh into a mass of red, gooey mush. Ellis forced himself to rise, to get to his feet. He blinked, trying to regain his focus. Once again, he raised his silly useless fists in front of him.

Tubber nearly danced, hopping up and down, making little jabs into the air, letting Ellis know he was giving him a fair shake. *Playing with me, more like,* Ellis thought. As he regained his faculties, Ellis felt a mixture of sensations—on the one hand, adrenaline shot into his system, giving him a burst of energy, making time slow down, heightening his senses and his reflexes. It felt strangely euphoric, and the sheer intoxication of it took Ellis by surprise. On the other hand, however, he realized he was powerfully outmatched. Tubber was larger than he and far more skilled in the art of pugilism. And no one would be coming to his rescue now—not Kit, not Osia, not anybody.

Just then he heard a rustle of wings in the rafters. He spared a look upwards and saw a raven, looking down on him with one beady, black, intelligent eye. "Jaq?" Ellis said out loud. Hope leaped within him. If Jaq was here, could Osia be far behind? Maybe the summoner would come to his rescue after all.

"Fail!" Jaq screamed.

Ellis stumbled over a shovel handle, hidden beneath the hay. He didn't know what to make of Jaq's outburst, but it didn't sound good. *Anytime now, Osia*, he thought. He wondered if the summoner could hear his thoughts. Then he wondered if he could scream with his thoughts. He squeezed his eyes tight and thought as loudly as he could. But when he opened them again, Tubber was still there, giving him a queer eye.

"Did that last blow mess up yer head?" he asked.

"You wish," Ellis managed, with more defiance than he actually felt. *Fewmets, boy, you've really done it to yourself this time,* Ellis thought.

"Die!" Jaq screamed.

Ellis glanced warily at the bird, panic flooding him. If Osia was coming, he was certainly taking his time. Yet Jaq's ejaculations were not what Ellis would call encouraging or hopeful.

Tubber continued his dance, in a tight circle around Ellis. He was light on his feet, but closer, now, his jabs connecting more often than not. Ellis dodged as many as he could, blocked others with his fists and forearms, but some connected. Ellis lashed out with something between a block and a blow, and ended up hitting himself in the face with his own forearm.

For the life of him, he could not work out how he had done it, but he didn't have time to think it through, as Tubber was increasing his rate of attack, landing several blows to Ellis' upper chest and face. Ellis' felt a sharp sting on his lip, and quickly bringing his hand up, drew it away covered with blood.

"Fail!" Jaq screamed.

Ellis knew that one well-placed punch would, at the very least, break his nose, which had barely begun to heal from his last encounter. At most, it could flatten him, and that would be the end of him. It didn't help that Tubber seemed to have found a cheering accomplice in Osia's raven. "Traitor," Ellis hissed, sparing a quick glance at the bird.

For a moment, Ellis was consumed with self-pity. What had he done that had begun this run of bad luck? What gods had he offended? What stray word or action had set the universe against him? He didn't know. He longed for the time before he'd even put in for the postmaster's job. *Perhaps that was it,* he thought. *Perhaps I'm being punished for reaching beyond my station.* Whether that was true or not, he did not know, but it *felt* right. What had he been thinking? He'd been mad to think he even had a chance at it. He had reached for the gods' foods, and now his hand had been slapped. And then his head had been pummeled. And now he was about to be ground into the dust like a wood beetle. He struggled to return his focus to Tubber.

"Fail!" Jaq screamed again.

You're right, Jaq, Ellis thought. *I'm going to fail. I'm going to fail miserably. And then I'm going to die.*

But then another voice intervened, filling Ellis' brain with a new question: *Hey, now, what do you have that Tubber doesn't?* And he knew—smarts. Ellis cocked his head as a different stream of thoughts rolled out within him. His eyes moving quickly back and forth, he suddenly for the first time saw beyond Tubber to his surroundings. There were things in the barn—things he could use. The space itself, he realized, was a weapon that he could employ, if he used it aright.

Feeling just a morsel more hopeful, Ellis made good use of that hope. He sprang to his left, advancing tentatively. To his surprise, Tubber stepped backward. Taking a slight step to the right, Ellis advanced again, and Tubber took another step back, but in precisely the direction Ellis wanted him to go. *What's going on here?* Ellis wondered. Relief flooded through him as, for the first time, he thought he might have a tiny bit of control over his situation.

He blinked and wiped the blood from his mouth with the back of his hand. It was only then that he realized he was bouncing a little himself, and that he was breathing in hard, panting breaths.

It occurred to him that if he were too obvious about his attempts to "steer" the brute, Tubber would be on to him and his plans would backfire. So Ellis feinted backward, allowing Tubber to advance. The bully took the opportunity to take a swing at him, which Ellis successfully avoided with a quick step backward and slightly to the right. A thrill ran through him, and he felt his whole body practically buzzing with energy and keen awareness.

Behind Tubber, Ellis saw what looked to him like a closet without doors, filled with tools. He saw a pitchfork, a shovel, a long-handled hoe, and many other such things. He took a step forward, a little too quickly. It forced Tubber back, but Ellis just avoided losing his balance. He stumbled, but used the forward momentum to gain another foot or two. He realized that if his movements looked like erratic inexperience—which they largely were—Tubber would not be suspicious of his plans. So he took a swing, and went intentionally wide. Tubber stepped aside, but not in the direction Ellis was hoping.

"Blood!" Jaq cawed. "Bone! Blood!"

Ellis narrowed his eyes and stepped back, giving some ground but wheeling into the right position to force Tubber toward the tools. Unfortunately, Ellis was not watching his feet and he tripped over a large, wet clump of hay. He might have forced his foot through it, as he would through water or even mud, but gravity beat him to it. He fell, but fortunately onto the hay.

He expected Tubber to be upon him, kicking him again, but for some reason Tubber seemed bent on being a gracious—if coercive—opponent that day. "C'mon, ye weasel, get up and fight like a grown 'un," Tubber heckled.

Ellis rolled over, leaped to his feet and made to raise his fists again—but too late. Tubber took advantage of his distraction, stepped in, and landed a punch square on Ellis' jaw. Ellis heard a snap in his head, felt his neck twist around, and saw the floor coming toward him far too quickly. He succeeded in raising his arms to break his fall, only to have one elbow smash against the floor. Pain, blinding white, overpowered every other sense. A few moments later it subsided, but his elbow felt like it was on fire—searing blue fire that extended impossibly through the top of his head.

"Blood!" Jaq screamed, filling the rafters with the quick fluttering of wings.

Ellis opened his eyes and saw Tubber advancing on him again, but this time a pitchfork was in his hand. Ellis' eyes widened as he came closer. Tubber had discovered the tools, too, he saw, and this discovery seemed to supplant the bully's sense of pugilistic propriety.

Panic seized Ellis and he leaped to his feet, wobbling but erect. His eyes were wide as Tubber began to tease him with the pitchfork, making short jabs at his stomach and groin. Tubber's mouth widened into a wicked grin that made Ellis sweat ice.

His jaw throbbed, and when he tried to move it back and forth, he heard the sound of grinding and snapping in his head, and a sharp pain lit out from his chin to his ear. *That can't be good,* he thought. But he couldn't focus on that now. Tubber had become more aggressive with his thrusts.

"Die!" Jaq interjected.

Glancing behind him, Ellis saw a bucket hanging on a hook. Without any warning, he leaped for the bucket, which was just a bit too high for him. The motion caught Tubber by surprise, it seemed, and Ellis succeeded in toppling the bucket from its nail. It fell to the ground with a clatter and Ellis snatched it up, holding it by the rim with both hands, putting the bottom of it between himself and the tines of the pitchfork.

"Blood!"

It was a small shield, but effective. Tubber stabbed toward him, so hard that were it not for the bucket, it would have gored him easily. Instead, two of the tines punched through the bottom of the bucket, causing tiny points of light to appear in its depths, like the twin stars of Ellbaron. The action jarred Ellis' arms, though, which he'd been holding rigidly before him. When the tines connected, his wrists absorbed the better part of the shock, sending pain through both hands. He consciously bent his arms a bit to better absorb the thrust of the next blow, which was sure to come, and quickly.

Ellis knew he had to act fast, and he instinctively went on the offensive, stepping toward Tubber, bucket aloft, meeting the force of the pitchfork and pushing against it with all his strength. With a heave, he caught Tubber off balance, and pressed his advantage, forcing him back again. He heard Tubber swear, but also saw he was directing him exactly where he wanted him.

"Fail!" Jaq screamed.

Ellis saw the upraised blade of a hoe sticking out of the straw, its handle buried. He advanced again, driving Tubber back a step, his boot coming down forcefully on the hoe. As Ellis had hoped, the handle of the hoe swung up, but instead of catching Tubber in the back of the head, as he had hoped, it just missed and fell forward in Ellis' direction. Ellis was two paces away, and so did not get hit himself, but it was a near thing. Tubber noted the miss, and the look of disappointment on Ellis' face, and realized how close he'd come to being bested. Tubber's face screwed up, and his eyes hardened. He began to make short rabbit jabs at Ellis with the pitchfork, sending Ellis backward until there was no further he could go. Ellis hit the back of his head on the wood of the far wall and saw Tubber smile. Tubber raised the pitchfork over his head, grinning as he savored his kill.

"Die!" Jaq screamed.

Just as Tubber's muscles bunched for his downward stab, Ellis launched the bucket underhand, directly at Tubber's chin. It connected with a clang, and Tubber fell back a few steps, just time enough for Ellis to make a break for the opposite corner of the room.

"Fail!"

Ellis no longer heard the bird. Instead, he clutched at a board drooping from the interior wall and ripped it free, exposing a couple of nails in the far end. Positioning the board over his right shoulder for a swing, he faced the approaching Tubber again.

Tubber wasn't the cleverest courier in the post office, but he knew more about scrapping than Ellis did. He knew the pitchfork's reach was longer than Ellis' board, and he turned it around so that he would have something to swing as well.

Ellis was shaking as he stepped toward Tubber. To his surprise, Tubber did not step back. Ellis feinted a swing, bringing the board halfway off his shoulder, but Tubber didn't budge. The bully's smile had turned into a desperate sneer, and Ellis intuited that his enemy was no longer in the mood to play with him—he was ready to *end this*.

"Die!" Jaq screamed.

Ellis took aim for Tubber's jaw with the sharp end of his board and swung with all his might. It connected, but barely. Tubber let forth a howl, and Ellis could see two tracks of blood where the nails had torn at his flesh. Tubber's eyes clouded up like poison, and he let loose a howl of indignation.

"Die!" Jaq repeated.

Ellis brought his board back for another swing, but Tubber was too fast, catching him in the gut with the full weight of the pitchfork handle. Ellis felt like he'd been gored, even though nothing had broken the skin. In truth, he'd simply had the air knocked from him, but so powerfully that he sank to the floor. He raised his arm protectively, but Tubber brought the handle down on him again. And again. And again, until a faceful of hay obscured all else except the red bursts of pain, the sound of a screaming bird, and rapidly approaching oblivion.

EALON WOKE with little idea what time it was. All hours seemed the same in the Scrum caves, but he knew not to become too complacent. The celebrations after his speech might have been tremendous, but he was well aware action was still expected from him—more than just fist-shaking. The Scrum, emboldened by his message, had extended the range of their hunting to bring back as much meat as they could manage. They waited till all hunters had returned before skinning anything, resulting in a violent blood orgy that would have alarmed Ealon if he hadn't been the honored center of it. It had been too easy, after that, to sit back and receive their accolades, to honor more clans by taking their daughters into his bed. But it likely wouldn't be long before these warriors began to grow impatient with him, before they wanted to take this self-proclaimed Shield into war.

As he mulled this over, he saw a figure at the mouth of his cave: a Scrum messenger, no older than Ealon was. Ealon lifted the arm of the sleeping female off his chest. He had to admit he found the orc maidens more enticing when he was drunk and it was dark. They were shapely, but the amount of back hair was disturbing—and the less said of their faces, the better. He averted his eyes so as not to look at this one now. He slid away from her and rose from under the blanket of animal pelts. "*Hergut-sa*," the messenger said, using the epithet which Ealon had come to learn means "great shield," "there is someone in the varr. We thought you would want to know."

"Someone is out wandering above?" Ealon asked, pulling his trousers on.

"Yes, *hergut-sa*."

"I want to see them. Take me."

The messenger nodded and Ealon followed him through the tunnels. Up ahead he could see light hitting the wall to the left. They stopped, and Ealon was able to peer through a slit under a ledge of rock, looking out onto the circular plain. Near the ridge on the other side, Ealon could see a figure dressed in black. He watched as the figure walked slowly about, peering at the ground, digging at stones with his foot.

"I should have known," Ealon murmured to himself.

"Do you recognize him, *hergut-sa*?" the messenger asked.

"Yes," Ealon said. "In fact I do. He is one of my father's guard dogs, sniffing at my trail. I must say I'm impressed," he added, turning to address the messenger. "I did not expect to be found so soon, but perhaps it's good that I have. It might help speed things along."

"Yes, *hergut-sa*?"

"Bring Cragga and Grazzak to me. Looks like it's high time I paid a visit to my dear papa."

WHEN ELLIS OPENED ONE EYE, Bracegirdle was hovering over him. It occurred to Ellis that he had never seen his supervisor from this exact angle before, and it took him a moment to realize who he was. The elder haffolk's nostrils seemed to be enormous—and Ellis could see little tufts of hair descending from each—as well as the wattle hanging below his chin. *How—how did you get here?* he wanted to say. *Was it all a dream? Did I fall asleep at the office?* But attempting to move his mouth brought on an avalanche of pain.

"Hmmph, you're alive," Bracegirdle said aloud. "That's good, I suppose; although I doubt you'll think so tomorrow from the look of your bruises."

Ellis tried to open his other eye, but it seemed to be swollen shut.

"Just lie still. I've sent for yer uncle and aunt. They'll be wanting to take you home to nurse you, no doubt, and a visit from the physic seems in order too, unless I miss my guess." Bracegirdle straightened up, and it seemed to Ellis that the man was torn between compassion and...what? Anger? Contempt? "What I want to know is whether you delivered your package. Did Mr. Massenbarrow's package reach him safely before you were waylaid by whatever ruffians had it in for you?"

Ellis tried to shake his head, but a sharp pain shot through his jaw and he simply froze instead. "Unh-unh," he managed weakly, through an immobile jaw.

"No? Well, I'm very sorry to hear that, Mr. Sunderland, because you don't get a third chance in this post office. You, my dear boy—and I'm very sorry to say it—are fired." And with that, Bracegirdle reached into Ellis' pocket, withdrew his courier's passport, and placed it in his own pocket. Then he clucked his tongue in disgust and walked out of the barn, leaving Ellis staring at the ceiling with one eye through a gauzy haze of straw.

ELSORIN SQUEEZED the knuckles of his left hand with his right until they hurt, in a vain effort to rouse himself from the afternoon slumber that sought to overtake him. In front of him were two itinerate summoners seeking his assistance to resolve a dispute. It was the part of his job he most despised, and in truth, it bored him to tears.

"...it's not my fault Avantir burned down his own forest," Elia was saying. "And I feel for my sister summoner's plight. If it had happened to me, I would consider it a fell tragedy, and my heart goes out to her."

Elsorin was awake enough to anticipate the "but" that was coming. "But?" he said aloud, barely able to keep his eyelids aloft.

"But that does not give her the right to stake out new territory in *my* forest!"

"I never said it was permanent," Prouse protested. "I must go somewhere, and Havenford is nearby."

Elsorin snorted, waking himself up with a start. Slightly embarrassed, he smacked his lips and slapped at his leg, which had indeed succumbed to sleep. "Er...Summoner Elia. If your sister had come to you requesting your hospitality for a...defined time, would you have begrudged her?"

"Certainly not. But...she did not do that."

"Summoner Prouse, is there a reason you did not request such hospitality?"

"I did not think to impose—"

"You just thought you'd move in and set up shop instead."

"I took a residence, 'tis true. A room in a boarding house. Would you have me sleeping under the rushes?"

The door opened and his servant Riza entered, her mouse Kibit scurrying after her. Riza met his eyes and made quick jerking motions with her head.

Elsorin scowled at her, but her eyes widened and she repeated the motion with her head.

"Uh...summoners, I have heard your complaint and must...er... research my response. I will render my judgment after third bells." At that he rose and exited through the door Riza held open for him.

Once alone in the hall, he faced her. "What is it?"

"The sleeper awakes."

Elsorin's eyebrows jumped. "Does he?"

Instantly he turned toward the infirmary where Objor was being tended.

In his heart of hearts, he had not expected the seer to live after the psychic visions had so wracked him, weakening his heart. There was not another like him, and Elsorin scarce hoped for another audience, another morsel of wisdom from him since he had fallen into a coma.

Now, it seems, the old man may have one more vision in him, at the very least.

Proceeding through the arch that led to the infirmary, Elsorin noted the dread silence of the place. It reminded him more of a mausoleum than a place of healing. *But perhaps that is an indication of the liminal place the seer is in,* he thought, *between the world of the living and that of the dead.*

Elsorin paused at the door to the room where the seer lay, but Riza and her mouse moved past him into the room with none of his own reticence. He watched her approach the bedside and take his hand. Kibit chittered. Slowly Elsorin moved to join Riza as the old seer's eyes fluttered open.

"Greetings, old friend," Elsorin said, instantly regretting it. Objor never moved from the Throne of Vision. He must eat, but Elsorin had never seen him do so. He must, indeed, evacuate his bowels, but Elsorin had never witnessed the old man ever leaving the temple. They had never had a casual conversation. There was no way in which the revered elder could be called, "friend," yet Elsorin did feel a sort of affection for the old man, perhaps as a younger man might feel for a famous yet absent father.

The seer's mouth opened, and he strained to rise. Somehow Riza divined what he needed. She snatched up a cup from the bedside table and held it to his lips. He slurped at it greedily and then lay back again, staring contentedly at the ceiling. Elsorin moved so that he could more easily see the old man's eyes, and met them. The seer focused on him, recognized him, acknowledged him.

"Do not tarry, revered one. If you have a message, I pray you deliver it with dispatch." Elsorin winced at his own words, fearing they may be heard as unfeeling, even mercenary, yet a terror pricked at him, that the old man might be seized by another spasm of the heart at any moment, his counsel undelivered.

The old man's lips formed words before any sound emerged. Finally, however, he managed. "He has...returned. Our ancient enemy. The doom of worlds."

"I feared as much."

"He is coming."

Elsorin took the old man's other hand and held it, squeezed it. "I know."

"He is...hungry. And angry. He is also quite mad."

"Yes." Elsorin felt hope slipping away, as if everything he had worked for these many centuries was suddenly to be undone before his very eyes. He clenched his teeth.

"His herald is here, even now."

"The Lizard King?" Riza asked. "Surely he is dead. It has been centuries."

"He is the Lizard King," Objor insisted. "Spite is his food, and it has nourished him for lo these many years. He is the Lizard King."

Elsorin's head swam. It had not seemed real before. Samael, the Dark Lord—known to elves and dwarfs as Ialdaboth and Saklas—was a distant, remote entity, thrashing in his rage, unapproachable as the mystery of the first things...or the last. But if the Dark Lord's mouthpiece was present once more—the one being who communicated the will of the elder god, speaker of the Word of Doom—then the terror of ancient times was surely upon them again.

"My father—" Elsorin said. It was an honorific, of course. Elsorin doubted the old man had ever been human enough to enjoy the intimacies of love or even passion. Yet it seemed appropriate to address him this way. "—tell me what we should do."

"Despair," the old man croaked.

Elsorin felt a chill run down his spine, felt its iciness pool in his feet. He saw Riza's eyes, wide with fear.

"Do not tell me how to feel, my father," Elsorin objected. "Instead, tell me how we may avert this disaster."

Disaster was the wrong word. It felt too small. Yet Objor understood.

"I do not see it. I can see all possible worlds, I behold every possibility, and all things that may be. But I do not see any world on which you may prevail against him."

Elsorin clutched the old man's hand to his own breast and pressed it there. "Father, you may leave us, but you may not leave us without hope. Do you hear? I forbid it."

The old man's eyes opened again and held Elsorin's own. An understanding passed between them, but Elsorin could divine no practical or useful message from the gaze. When the old man spoke again, his voice was weak and tremulous. "I can offer you no great hope. But perhaps...perhaps there are small hopes."

"What does that mean?" Elsorin demanded.

"There is one who knows more than I," he said. "Go to him."

"To who? Who, father?"

"Eneld. If anyone will know what to do, it will be Eneld." His voice wheezed, and his eyes closed again.

"Eneld," Elsorin repeated.

"Does he mean the librarian?" Riza asked.

"He must," Elsorin answered.

"I think he sleeps," Riza said, her ear close to the old man's mouth, listening to his breathing.

"I fear he will not live long enough to see this doom," Elsorin said. "Would that we were all so fortunate."

16

Although out of bed, Cormoran did not feel quite awake. His breakfast had been laid out, at least, and it smelled pleasant to him as he sat down. But any restorative benefits to him were delayed as a young page pushed the door open and looked tentatively into the princely chambers. "Yes? What is it?" Cormoran asked aloud.

The boy entered the room, bearing a small square of parchment. Cormoran took it and the page backed away quickly. An audience, Cormoran saw, was being requested from from Daevis Ennisbrook. The sight of the name prompted the realization that Cormoran had not laid eyes on the king's enforcer for several days. Without looking at the page, taking more interest in lifting the cover off his eggs and enjoying the rise of aromatic steam, Cormoran said "Yes. Show him in"—and the page darted back to the corridor, scarcely closing the door behind him.

"Sir Daevis," Cormoran asked, when he heard footsteps reach the doorway, "may I interest you in some eggs? Some sausages?"

The Enforcer entered the chambers but did not respond. He stood at attention before Cormoran's small table. Cormoran looked up, noticing how Ennisbrook seemed to be staring at the gorgeous blues of calm sea and cloudless sky, without any form of appreciation for such a lovely morning. Sensing there was no interest in pleasantries, Cormoran continued, "And why do you wish to see me?"

"It is about your brother, prince Ealon."

"You've found him? Where is he?"

"I have found *of* him, your highness," Ennisbrook corrected.

"And, pray, what have you found?" Cormoran frowned. He had been in a fine mood, but Ennisbrook's reticence was threatening to sour it.

"I have reason to believe the young prince is meddling in...*something* with a dark and troubling purpose."

"Goodness. You sound like a market-day storyteller."

"Perhaps your summoner could explain it better, for I believe he is aiding Prince Ealon in this endeavor."

Cormoran wiped his mouth with a cloth. "My, you're full of accusations today." He'd meant it lightly, but Cormoran couldn't disguise the truth of it. "Have you brought this to my father?"

"You are the first I've spoken to."

"That's probably for the best. The king has been out of sorts of late."

"I am sorry to hear that," Ennisbrook said. "Is he unwell?"

"No...I don't think it's physical," Cormoran said, standing and dropping his napkin on the table. "But he hasn't been himself. He has been quarrelsome and quick to anger...which, now that I say it aloud, *is* like himself. Yet, it's different somehow." Cormoran stepped away from the table and led the Enforcer to the door. "He seems troubled. Ever since you left, in fact." The two of them stepped into the hall and approached the king's chambers. "It's as if he knew you'd be coming back with bad news."

Uther must have heard his son's voice. "Cormoran? Is that you? Come in here, boy!"

"Yes, sire," Cormoran called back. "And I have your enforcer with me."

"That blackguard?" the king spat. Cormoran cast a startled glance at Ennisbrook. The Enforcer had always been in the king's favor, and Cormoran was puzzled at this sudden change. Ennisbrook did not react at all.

When they reached the door, Uther was already pointing an accusing finger at his enforcer. "It is said that the poison was for Clendis, not for me! That's what they say. So tell me, enforcer: did you *kill* an innocent *boy*? *Eh*? Did you ruin my good name by *murdering* an innocent *child*?"

The Enforcer did not respond.

"'Look out for Uther,' they say. They don't sing about Avantir the coward now. Not any more. It's all 'Look out for Uther'—Uther the monster, Uther the child killer. By the horn! I've heard it in my own kitchens. Someone cried out, 'Look out for Uther,' but no one would own up to it. Mocked in my own kitchens, I am—because of you and your unending compulsion to slay things." Uther turned away in disgust, still muttering to himself. "*Look out for Uther / I tell you he's uncouth, sir*—what kind of rhyme is that?"

Then Uther quickly turned back to Ennisbrook. "You know what we should do?" he said, energetically shaking a finger at his enforcer. "Get your songsmiths to tell everyone how Avantir convinced his son to kill himself! For there's no better way to convince your townspeople that you're not an inept ruler who would blunderously sacrifice his own soldiers than to make yourself a grieving object of pity. Go! Go tell them that! Get *that* idea out there."

Cormoran was ready to leave, but Ennisbrook remained standing respectfully. But before Cormoran reached the doorway, a young page burst into the room. "Your majesty, your royal presence is requested in the throne room, sir."

"Eh? What? Who calls to see me?"

"The Royal Prince Ealon, your majesty."

"*Ealon*? Ealon has come home? Quick—out of the way, you two!" He pushed Cormoran and Ennisbrook aside in his haste to get into the hallway and down to the throne room. Cormoran and Ennisbrook exchanged a troubled look and then followed the king.

❧

Ellis awoke to the sound of tapping. It was dark, but there was the light reflected by Hearth—enough to see by, coating everything in a bluish hue. Reaching up, he felt at his face. His left eye was still swollen shut. He tried to pry it open, but winced in pain from the effort. "Fewmets," he whispered aloud.

It wasn't just the eye. Everything hurt. With his unmolested eye he glanced at the window. It must have been the branches of Old Man Oak outside, brushing against the glass. He groaned as he shifted in bed and tried to go back to sleep.

Sleep did not return easily, however. In his mind's eye he kept seeing images of Tubber's fist coming toward his face, over and over again. Cringing, he relived the impact of the pitchfork handle, then the ground.

In truth, he was not so badly battered as he might have been. He had plenty of bruises, but no broken bones. His eye was not permanently damaged, he had been relieved to hear. The physic said only that it would need a few days for the swelling to subside. Ellis was assured that even his jaw, sore as it was, would mend. He rubbed at it with one hand, wincing from the touch.

It hurt to talk, it hurt to eat, it hurt to stand, and it hurt to lie down. The physic had given his Aunt Tully some tincture of poppy—"two drops in his tea, morning, noon, and evening"—but Ellis hated the fuzzy feeling in his head and how sleepy it made him. Uncle Emmet, distressed at how life-threatening and cutthroat a job at the post office was turning out to be, had tried to convince him that sleeping was a good thing, but Ellis refused it. Yet, sleepless as he was this night, he was tempted to rouse one of his sisters and ask for a couple of drops, tea or no.

The tapping came again. His one good eye opened again, expecting to see a tree branch brushing the pane, but instead he found himself looking into the piercing eye of a raven. The eye looked right at him, and the bird tapped again more insistently, or so it seemed to him.

Is that Jaq? Ellis wondered. The last thing he wanted to see was that damn bird. *The traitor,* he thought. He thought Jaq would be on his side, not against him. And did that mean that Osia was against him, too? It must, but it was hard to fathom it. Ellis sat up. He cringed against the pain, gritting his teeth, but then instantly relaxing his jaw to relieve the pain he had just caused there. Groaning, he threw off the bedclothes and shuffled painfully to the windowsill.

Jaq's eye followed him and, as soon as Ellis had reached the window, flew away to a stout branch on Old Man Oak. He looked directly at Ellis and cawed. "Go away, you are a foul friend," Ellis said. He wished he had shutters to bang in the bird's face, but the window had none. Unfazed, Jaq looked back at him, and then hopped to another branch further away. Then he turned and looked back.

Ellis was confused. Did the bird want him to...what? Follow him? Ellis could hardly imagine going to the outhouse, let alone following Jaq wherever the bird wanted to lead him. Following Jaq was madness. Anything but hot compresses and chamomile tea and bedrest was madness. Besides, he was angry at the bird, and wouldn't want to give him the satisfaction of obeying him even if he was hale and able.

Ellis turned to go back to bed, but Jaq returned to the windowsill and resumed his tapping. This time it was louder and he did not stop. "Oh, piss and bonnets," Ellis swore. He was already having trouble sleeping and knew there was no way he would get any rest with Jaq's insistent rapping, so, with great effort and not insignificant groans, he drew his nightshirt over his head and reached for his trousers. Keeping his knees as straight as possible, he struggled to draw them on. Putting on a tunic and then a cloak were equal adventures in pain. Finally, he shoved his feet into his boots without the lubrication of hose, and not bothering to lace them, stumbled from his room.

Trying to be as quiet as he could, he let himself out the front, closing the great round, red door behind him, cringing as he heard the click—tiny enough, but booming against the silence of deep night. No sooner had he turned then Jaq fluttered onto the path before him. He cawed, and Ellis imagined he sounded pleased, although it was hard for him to tell, not knowing the language of birds as Osia obviously did. But Jaq hopped a few feet down the path, stopped and looked Ellis in the eye once more. *That I understand,* Ellis thought. Painfully at first, but then more easily as his muscles worked through their torpor, he followed. Soon, what pained him most was not his muscles but his pride. The bird had won, and despite himself, Ellis was doing exactly what the treacherous familiar bid him do.

Ellis glanced up at the great hulking semi-circle of Hearth, and beyond it, the looming, ragged edge of the Scar. The trees were sapped of their verdancy, appearing as black-and-blue shadows of themselves. Likewise, the green fields looked black. The effect would have been eerie had it not been such a familiar sight. The wind came in gusts, creating a sound like ocean waves as the leaves rose and fell and fluttered. But for all the windiness, it was not cold, and Ellis was glad of that.

He was expecting Jaq to turn right at the triple fork, toward the village, but instead the bird went straight onward, toward the burning ground—the place where the haffolk piled their refuse, and gathered once a month to set it alight and dance and drink in the light of its burning. Those were smelly gatherings, generally, the more so in summer, but Ellis was fond of them, and he thrilled to any reel played on fiddle and concertina.

"We've not got any trash to throw away tonight," Ellis said to Jaq, but the bird kept just ahead of him, hopping one yard, now two, always looking back to make sure the young haffolk was following. "Not that I would give you any, if I had it."

He was well and truly winded by the time he reached the burning ground. It appeared to be deserted, yet Jaq kept cawing, and Ellis kept following. The bird led him to a hillock where, legend says, the ancients had piled their refuse. Ellis always supposed it was this that had given the town elders the idea of storing their garbage here to wait for its monthly immolation. Jaq circled the periphery of the hillock, and as Ellis rounded it, he saw a familiar figure sitting on a broad, flat stone, staring up at the circle of Hearth.

"Ah, there you are, master haffolk," Osia said, looking down at him and grinning. His black hair was gathered at the back, and he looked in dire need of a shave. He removed the pipe from between his lips, and gestured to the stone beside him. "Sit, my friend, sit."

"I'm not so sure you *are* my friend," Ellis said. He was going to refuse to sit, but his limbs were stiff and weary. Once more putting pride aside, he painfully climbed up to sit next to the summoner, groaning as he did so. Jaq flew to the stiff patch on Osia's shoulder, and pecked once at the man's cheek. "Oh dear. You look worse than you did a couple of days ago," Osia said. "Did you get into yet another scrap?"

"As if you didn't know," Ellis said blackly. "As if you didn't egg him on."

"I think you misjudge me, my little friend."

"I do not misjudge your bird. You...I'm not so sure about."

"Oh dear, oh dear, oh dear," Osia mumbled, looking him over. "I wonder if you should not have stayed abed."

"Your bird is rather insistent."

"Hm..." Osia pulled on the stem of his pipe, and Ellis thought he saw wisps of smoke curl out of the summoner's ears. "That he is, that he is." He offered Ellis his bag of hearthweed, but Ellis waved it away.

"Thank you, but I don't have the stomach for it just now."

Osia replaced the bag somewhere in the depths of his robe. "You think I somehow set your attacker onto you?"

"I don't rightly know, sir. I do know that Jaq, your bird, watched the whole thing, and did all he could to aid him."

"Did he now?" Osia pulled at his pipe and narrowed one eye at the haffolk.

"Well...now that you mention it...no. But he did not cheer me on."

"Hm." Osia smacked his lips. "The things that matter most are often paradoxical. To go forward, you must sometimes retreat. To be pure, you must sometimes get dirty. To be strong, you must sometimes be weak. To taste the sweet, you must sometimes add salt."

"I'm afraid I don't know what you mean, sir."

"There is a voice inside you that tells you that you are weak, a coward...is there not?"

Ellis' shoulders sagged. "How did you know?"

"Because that voice speaks to all of us. That is how I know," Osia said, his voice tinged with kindness. "This voice must sometimes get louder in order for us to rebel against it."

Ellis cocked his head. "Jaq...made the voice louder?"

"Did he not?"

Ellis did not know what to think. It had not occurred to him that the bird's cruelty might actually have been in his service. "But to what end, sir? I still lost the fight."

"Yet you learned that you *could* fight."

Ellis did not respond to this. After several minutes passed with only the sound of the crickets in the air, Osia motioned at the looming planet above them with his chin. "You see that world?"

"Hearth? Why, yes sir."

"How many bright beings do you suppose dwell on it?"

Ellis shrugged. "Oh, I dunno, sir. Maybe a million or more. A good deal more than here on Everdale. Mostly humans, I would imagine, with a few thousand dwarf engineers, and a handful of elven visitors."

"What do you suppose it would take to kill them all?"

"What, sir? A mighty big army, I would imagine. Although...how you would get them there I couldn't say. But what a dreadful battle that would be."

"What if I told you they would all die at once? Instantly. And there would be no battle."

"Uh...I would say you were talking about the end of the world, I suppose."

Osia looked down at Ellis. "That is exactly what I am talking about."

Ellis pursed his lips and cocked his head. "I'm afraid I don't know what you mean, sir."

"I do not know what is around the next bend in my path—or yours, for that matter. There are no worlds in which the future is revealed in the present. I only know this. I must try to prevent the end of the world...of many worlds. Of your world, Mr. Sunderland. What I need to know is...will you help me?"

Ellis felt suddenly chilled, as the effects of his long walk began to subside. "I'm sure I...again, sir, I don't know what you are getting at."

"A few days ago I told you I needed a courier, that we—the summoners, that is—need a courier. Full time. We made you an offer. Have you, eh...have you thought about it?"

Ellis looked at his shoes. "I *have* thought about it, sir. And I talked to my family, and to Kit."

"And? Do you have an answer for me?"

"Well, now that I'm out of a job, it would make good sense," Ellis began.

"Did you say you were out of a job?" Osia asked.

"I am, sir."

"Because of the...scrap?"

"Aye, sir. Because of that."

"Mmmm," Osia pulled on his pipe again.

"And that's why I think I have to say thank you, Mr. Osia sir, but no thank you."

Osia's eyebrows jumped in surprise. "By the horn, young man, whatever do you mean?"

"I mean only that...to work for the summoners, sir, 'tis a great privilege. And it should probably go to someone a bit more..." Ellis fished in his mind for the right word. Responsible? Capable? Dependable? Then he found it. "...worthy, sir. You need someone more worthy than I."

Osia removed his pipe from his lips and scowled at the haffolk before him. Jaq cawed.

"Surely, my young friend, whether an applicant is worthy of a job is a discernment for the employer, not the prospective employee, is it not?"

"Begging your pardon, sir, surely 'tis both." Ellis' face fell as he thought. He could not look the summoner in the eye. "I mean, I must decide if I am fit for a job just as much as you must decide the same."

"And you believe you are not fit?"

"How can I be, sir?" Ellis looked away, at the sphere of Hearth, looming bluish bright in night sky. "I lost a Very Important Package and might at any moment be brought up on charges, or so I hear."

"By whom?"

"By the Royal Mail...or by the dwarfs...or by...I don't rightly know by whom, just...it seems just and right that it be so. I deserve to be punished." Before Osia could interrupt, Ellis rushed on. "And then Mr. Bracegirdle gave me another chance—a delivery to Mr. Massenbarrow. And I failed at that one, too. So I must conclude that while I have always been a courier, I must not be a very *good* courier, or I would not have performed so miserably."

"Do you think you are being a bit hard on yourself, Ellis?" Osia narrowed one eye at him.

"I do not, sir. I think that...well, prudence suggests, sir, that I not be trusted with anything very important. Not again."

"So you are saying 'no' to me?"

"I am saying you ought to find someone you can trust, sir, because I don't think that's me."

Osia nodded, placing the pipe back to his lips. "It pains me to hear it, Mr. Haffolk, but I will honor your decision."

"Thank you, sir."

"It's probably best if you return to bed and continue your recovery."

"Yes, sir. Thank you, sir."

Osia nodded, and Ellis rose, gave an awkward bow in the summoner's direction, and headed for home.

Before he reached the edge of the burning ground, however, he saw movement out of the corner of his eye. He looked to his left and saw a young woman—little more than a girl—hanging laundry on a line. The sun was shining over her shoulder—which was an odd enough sight to see at night, but what really caught Ellis' attention were her ears. This was no human girl, but an elf maiden. Ellis stopped, enraptured by the image. He had seen very few elves in his time, and none so beautiful. Her hair was as black as Jaq's feathers, but her skin was fair. Her motions were so fluid and effortless that it looked more like she was dancing than hanging laundry.

She looked up, and her eyes went wide.

"Oh, don't be frightened, miss," Ellis said, putting one hand up in a gesture of welcome. "I mean no harm, and I apologize for staring."

But it seemed to Ellis that she was not looking at him at all, but rather through him, as if what was causing her distress might be behind him. He turned around, and gasped as he saw what she saw.

He saw, but he did not understand. The sun was bright, but it was a reddish bright, casting a ceresian light on everything around, and Ellis realized it was not Hearth's sun he was seeing, but another, smaller, ruddy star. Still, it brightened the sky, except...Ellis looked back and forth, trying to comprehend what he was seeing. A quarter of the sky, it seemed, was shrouded in darkness—not like the darkness of rain clouds, through which the occluded light of day still filtered through—

but absolute darkness, the kind of darkness that even the light of the nearest stars cannot penetrate. And the darkness was growing.

"Horn of blood," Ellis swore. "What is that?"

Even as he wondered, it grew. Within seconds, it covered fully half the sky. Ellis heard a cry behind him, and saw the elven maid sink to her knees in fright, clutching at her breast and wailing at the sight of the sky. Ellis wanted to run to her, to comfort her, but something prevented him, something he did not understand. He whirled around again, feeling angry, defiant. He didn't know what he was looking at, but he wanted to place himself between it and the maid. If there was a way to protect her, any way, even if it meant his life, he would do it. He balled his hands into fists and walked toward the growing sea of black that threatened to engulf the sky, to swallow the stars, to eat the sun.

As he stared at it, summoning all his rage and courage, he saw that the blackness was not unbroken. In the middle of it, he saw a flare of red—like an angry eye in the midst of the storm. He squinted at it, but could not make out what it was. Whatever it was, though, it writhed.

The maid screamed, and Ellis whirled toward her. Covering her face in her hands, Ellis could see she was overcome by fear, by confusion, by despair. But then the black cloud edged out the red light of the sun. Ellis jerked his head up to see the sun disappear—not just blocked out, as in an eclipse, but annihilated, devoured. And suddenly it was night—absolute night. He could see nothing at all around him. All he could see was the roiling, angry eye at the heart of the darkness, and all he could hear was the screaming of the elf maid, until the screaming suddenly...stopped.

Ellis neither saw nor heard anything, nor felt anything until he sensed a calm presence, and felt a large, warm hand rest gently on his shoulder. He backed up, feeling the solid, safe presence of the summoner behind him. He leaned on him and felt Osia's body support him, felt the summoner's arm encircle his chest, hugging him and holding him until he felt he could stand again.

And then he saw stars—blessed, blessed stars. Once more he smelled the charred burning grounds, heard the cawing of Jaq. He stepped forward, out of Osia's embrace. Looking back at the summoner, he saw that the man had knelt in order to support him better. The man's eyes looked infinitely older than his face and sadder than Ellis had ever seen them.

"What was that?" Ellis asked him. "Was that a vision?"

"That was no vision. That truly happened. Just now."

Ellis turned and looked back at where the maid had been just moments before. "How did I—? Did you cause me to see that?"

"I did. Magic."

Ellis looked confused, then troubled again. "What was her name?"

"Teal. She was about to be married. Tomorrow. Tomorrow, she was to be married. But...there will be no wedding now."

Ellis turned and faced him, not bothering to wipe the tears from his cheeks. "Is this what you want me to help you with...to help you stop?"

"Yes." Osia stood and stared down at Ellis with as grim a face as he had ever seen on the summoner. "Every day that we delay the Dark Field gets closer to another planet."

"What is the Dark Field?"

"You have seen it," Osia said, motioning him toward the rock again where they had been sitting. Ellis followed. "It is the radiating influence of the elder god, Ialdaboth. Men call him Samael."

"Samael," Ellis breathed. He knew the name, but it was an evil omen to hear it spoken aloud. "So...is the Dark Field death?"

"No, my little friend. Death is a good and necessary part of life. 'It keeps all things in balance,' as the Oyosin never tire of reminding us. Death is a holy thing. This is not death."

"Is it nothingness, then?"

"No. Being and non-being depend on each other, they need each other to thrive. It is not non-being, or no-thing, as you call it."

"Then what is it?"

"No one really knows. I think of it as the complete and total absence of good."

Ellis nodded. It was a concept that raised more questions than it answered, but in Ellis' belly it felt right. "How can it be stopped?"

"I do not know," Osia answered. He met Ellis' eye and held it. Ellis felt the crushing danger in the simplicity of his words.

"And you really think...you need *me* to help you?"

"I don't think it, master haffolk. I know it."

"How do you know it, sir? If you don't mind my asking."

"I *do* mind. And I am a summoner, and the second among my kind. I know things others do not know and see things others do not see. And what I see, my dear friend, is that you are more capable than you feel."

Ellis sincerely doubted that, but he did not dispute it. "And we'll stop it?"

"I do not know. We shall surely try."

"She died, didn't she?"

Osia did not answer. Ellis knew the answer. She had not simply died, nor had she simply ceased to be. She had been claimed by evil. She had been eaten.

"All right," Ellis said. "I'll do it. I'll come with you. I want to help."

"Good lad."

"I don't feel very powerful. I don't feel very clever. I don't feel very important."

"Those are reasons why you are all the more likely to succeed."

"That makes no sense, begging your pardon, sir."

"Nevertheless."

Jaq cawed, and the sound broke through the spell of the moment, bringing Ellis back to himself.

"Uh...sir...I have a condition."

"Do you now?" Osia raised one eyebrow. "And what might that be?"

"Kit must come along as well."

"Kit? Do you mean the ruffian girl I caught spying on us in the tavern?"

"I do, sir."

"Certainly not."

Ellis looked at his feet. "Well, then, sir, I'm sorry to have wasted your time." Ellis pushed himself off the rock and began to walk away.

"And why should she be a condition of your employment?"

Ellis stopped and turned around. "Because she's my bodyguard. Because she goes everywhere I go. Because..." Ellis hung his head. "... because every time I've tried to do a job without her, it ended in ruin."

"She's your good luck charm, is she?" Osia took a pull on his pipe.

"Yes sir...I mean, no sir. I mean she's much more than that. She's... she makes things safe, sir. You might not like her...few people do. But when she's around, no harm comes to anyone, unless they're deserving it. That's certain."

Osia nodded and looked like he was thinking. "You do know...she will never love you. Not as you wish her to."

Ellis felt as if he'd been slapped. "And what do you know of that, sir?"

"I know that you keep a feather that fell from the band of her hat in a little pouch around your neck, right next to your heritage medal."

Ellis' eyes went wide. "You *do* see what others do not..."

Osia smiled grimly. "All right. I am not authorized to offer an additional salary—"

"And you'll not need to, sir. I'll split my own with her...as I always do."

"Hm..." Osia pursed his lips and narrowed his eyes. "We'll try her out...on a probationary basis, and for no additional salary. A haffolk bodyguard. Ha!"

Ellis grinned, scarcely able to believe his good fortune. "Uh...what does the job entail, then, sir?"

"You'll accompany me, and carry messages and letters and packages wheresoever they are needed."

"I can do that, sir. Me and Kit, I mean. When do we start?"

"There is a ship leaving Rhory at sunup, the *Tree and Pony*. Avoid any further injury and do not, by any means, be late. "

❧

UTHER ENTERED the throne room from its rear door, and as he walked around the thrones he encountered something he would not have expected to see. It looked like something from the arena. His young son was standing within a ring of guards, their spears lowered threateningly. And standing with his son were two muscle-bound brutes—hairy, bare-chested—ready to defend themselves with sling and club. They were not human. Could they be...orcs? But these were large for orcs. Could it be they were...? Uther clasped his jaw, pulling at his lower lip in disbelief.

"What is this? What is the meaning of this?" Uther thundered, but the guards did not put up their weapons.

"Is this the courtesy of Uther's house, father?" Ealon called. "Is this how my friends are to be treated?"

"Ealon," Uther began, short of breath. "My son, where have you been? What—what has happened to your face? And what is going on here—what are these beasts you have with you?"

"Allow me to introduce to you my companions, Cragga and Grazzak. They are *Ūnna-kar*, also known as the Scrum. You call them orcs," Ealon explained. "And I am their *hergut-sa*."

"What...what does that mean?"

"Oh, rest assured you will find out soon enough, my father," Ealon replied coolly. "All you need know is that everything will be changing soon. You and my *dear* brother were always too quick to dismiss my ideas and my suggestions, but soon you will see I can be a great leader after all."

"Of course, my son. Just have your friends lower their weapons..."

"When you have *your* friends put up their spears!" Ealon snapped.

"Yes, yes. Sir Cullion, call back your guard."

"Sir!" said one of the defenders. "We dare not. They mean you harm."

"Sir Cullion, if you would please—"

"There, Cragga. You heard the man," Ealon said, and suddenly the huge brute to the young prince's left grabbed a spear from a guard, swung it about, and lopped a guard's head off with it before goring the butt end into another guardsman.

"Ealon! No!" Uther bellowed, eyes bulging, face red.

As Grazzak turned to protect Ealon, a guardsman opposite charged at Cragga—who batted him aside with but a swing of Scrum forearm. Still clinging to the first guardsman, Cragga threw the decapitated body at the other side of the ring, scattering the other guards. Cragga now turned to face them, swinging one of their spears back and forth.

Uther, with Cormoran and the Enforcer behind him, stood

stunned, staring dumbly at the bloodshed on the throne room floor. Uther's mouth hung open, and when he found his tongue again, he spluttered, "What have you done?"

"I have shown you that I am serious," Ealon answered, stepping around Grazzak, advancing toward the dais and aiming the full extent of his contempt at the men who stood there. "I have shown you that you have trifled with me for too long." He swaggered up the steps, approaching Cormoran, standing in front of his older brother, and glaring contemptuously. "I have shown you that you have favored the wrong son. This one is...unimaginative. And weak."

Faster than Uther could see, his enforcer pounced—there was a blurry swirl of black in the air, and then Ennisbrook had Ealon by the back of his collar and was pulling him aside. Grazzak let out a roar and charged the dais, but Ennisbrook and Ealon spun about, facing forward, and revealing that Ennisbrook now had a keen knife edge at Ealon's throat. The Enforcer had his left arm around Ealon's chest, restraining the youth's arms; and with his right arm he held a blade to the left side of the young man's neck. Grazzak froze, but emitted restless growls as he studied the Enforcer, awaiting the opportunity to strike.

"Father, is this the way you treat your guests?" Ealon sneered.

"Daevis!" Uther barked. "Caution!"

The Enforcer had drawn blood—not much blood, but a blood of warning. The other Scrum, Cragga, advanced threateningly, wanting to stand alongside his companion, but he stopped short when he saw the intent in the Enforcer's glare.

Ennisbrook spoke, evenly and menacingly, through gritted teeth. "You will hand your weapons to what remains of our guard. You will do it—"

All eyes turned to the doorway as more men burst through the door. Any rescue Uther had envisioned was delayed, as these guards stopped and stared back, dumbfounded at the sight of the slain, the blood, the standoff with the orcs. An older page forced his way between the guardsmen, with a desperate announcement. "Your majesty...we are being invaded!"

In response, Uther descended the steps to confront his young son, still pinned against the Enforcer. "What further villainy is this?" Uther demanded. An evil smile spread Ealon's lips, but the young man gave no explanation. Uther was dispirited to think that the smile was caused not by recognition, but by satisfaction at his father's distress. *What have I done to make him hate me so?* he thought. In a quieter tone, he asked, "Is this not your doing?"

Uther braced for more arrogant and hateful and treasonous words. Ealon started to shake his head, but then remembered this might not be wise in his current predicament. Instead he said, simply, "No."

"Avantir!" Uther spat. "We are being invaded by Avantir—no doubt aided by our brother kings, swayed by his talk of betrayal." He pointed a finger at Ennisbrook. "*You* did this! *You* have brought this evil upon my house!"

The Enforcer's habitual reticence failed him. He spoke, without lessening his hold on Ealon. "There is indeed great evil come upon your house, my king, but I am not its source." He squeezed hard, making Ealon gasp and wince. The prince struggled to free himself, but Ennisbrook held him fast.

Uther could hear shouting from the hallway and from the windows, as if new information was being passed along, just out of his hearing. *Damn these muddy ears! Damn my age and this crumbling body! Damn everyone and everything in sight!* The captain of the outer guard spoke again, resuming his announcement now that the king was not distracted. "Your majesty, an æthercraft has landed in the courtyard. We fear it has caused much destruction."

"A ship in the courtyard?" Uther exclaimed, as if doubting his guards. "Why did we not hear that?" Uther demanded, but none around him bothered to point out there had been as much commotion inside the throne room as without. "An æthercraft, you say? Wybrook has no æthercraft of their own. Not warships, surely."

Uther felt dizzy. His world felt suddenly, hopelessly mad. Cormoran rushed to the window, opposite the one Uther typically sat in to watch the bay; he flung it open and leaned out to get a glimpse of the courtyard. "Orcs!" he yelled. "An æthercraft fills the courtyard and orcs are entering the castle proper! We're being invaded." He turned back to his brother, still struggling beneath Daevis' knife. "What possible evil has possessed you?"

The orc Ealon had called Cragga hissed. "If they be orcs, they be not *my* orcs." He turned back to keep an eye on Ealon. "No ships for the Scrum."

Uther heard a distant boom, and felt the stones beneath him shake. For a moment he feared the very foundation of Caer Trogan was about to crumble into the sea. Then there came the sound of men yelling and orcs shrieking, of close fighting near at hand yet just out of sight. Uther pointed at his enforcer and commanded, "Release my son and give him arms!"

Ennisbrook remained as he was. "Your majesty—"

Uther uttered a cry that might have been grief or frustration or rage, strode to where Ennisbrook still held the prince, and swung his fist hard at his enforcer's head. Ennisbrook did not flinch, but he obeyed the command and withdrew the knife at Ealon's throat, now adorned with a thin line of crimson.

Daevis stood, and moving quickly, took a sword from one of the fallen soldiers and slid it across the floor to Ealon, who scooped it up into a tight grip. He strode to stand with his Scrum, who moved protectively to either side of him. They stood once more with their rude weapons at the ready—not against Uther's men now, but against whatever invaders might at any moment burst in upon them.

Uther gathered up the train of his robe and ascended the dais. "If I am to die, I will die enthroned as befits a high king," he said. It was not clear to whom he spoke, but his voice was strong with dignity and resolve.

The sound of fighting faded, and with Uther poised upon his ancestral seat, a silence descended on the throne room. All within it seemed paralyzed, frozen, and it felt to Uther that this was a pivotal moment in time. At this moment, all outcomes lay before him. Perhaps his reign might come to an end. Perhaps he might be killed. In the next few moments, he might see his sons die before him, he might be taken prisoner, to be abused and humiliated by this opposing force. His soldiers might hold back the invaders before they could reach him. But there was no way to know the outcome until after this moment passed and he found out exactly what he was facing.

He had heard summoners talk like that, and he wondered vaguely if this is what they're thinking during their conjurings.

And then the moment was over. The noises in the hall grew louder. Uther heard the sound of a great beast slithering, or of something heavy being dragged. Then suddenly two orcs burst into the room. They surveyed its inhabitants, took note of their positions, and visibly relaxed. They instantly stood guard on either side of the door, longspears held stiffly at their sides, pointing to the ceiling. The skin of these orcs was different in shade from those accompanying Ealon, Uther noted. These too had rough skin, covered with course hair, but unlike the orcs in Ealon's company, these had a bluish glow to them.

These guards were standing at attention, and by all rules of propriety and protocol, this meant that someone of greater rank was soon to follow. A moment later another orc entered, but this was not a warrior. Uther's brows knit together as he tried to understand the creature before him. It was small, with one withered arm, and walked with a limp. The other arm, however, was strong and held fast to a standard low enough to pass through the arched doorways. Perched on his reptilian head was a colorful cap, which seemed at odds with the black satin and brown leather that made up the rest of his attire. *So, this is a herald,* Uther said to himself. *But of whom?* His eyes darted to the standard, and he felt a fist-sized ball of ice descend into his guts.

The standard showed a black crown, three equal tines rising like spires from its base, each ending in a cruel barb, like a hook set for a fish. The crown was set against what looked at first like the red corona of a sun, but as Uther studied it he saw that there were not rays of light radiating from the black crown—whatever it was looked more substantial, and at the same time more irregular. He scowled, squinting to see. Then he saw. They were tentacles. Red tentacles emitted by the crown, reaching into every corner of the standard. *Reaching even here*, he thought.

The herald struck the standard on the stone floor, creating a booming sound that filled the chamber. "All rise for His Majesty, King

Abraxis, Sovereign of the *Dunna-ar*, Lord of all the Orc Worlds, Herald of the Dark Field, Vassal King of the Great God Ialdaboth—known among dwarfs as Saklas, and among men as Samael. We speak for the elder god!"

None rose, as all but Uther were standing, but all held their breaths. Indeed, it seemed as if the room was devoid of air or æther, and it seemed to Uther that if he tried to draw breath his lungs would scream for lack of it.

The sound of shuffling became louder, or was it dragging? Uther still could not tell. But then, into the arched doorway, he saw movement. Emerging into the doorway he saw the great, stooped, lurching body of the Lizard King.

Uther's eyes widened at the sight of him, for he was massive. His limbs were three times the size of a man's, and he had to lower his head to pass through the arch. Once through, however, he was able to stand more naturally, yet there was nothing about him that Uther deemed natural. His skin was bright green, covered with scales that were delicate and fine and probably of great utility in warding off the blows of any weapons turned against him. His head was indeed that of a lizard's, proving the old tales true. He wore no crown, yet he did not appear less regal for lack of it. His eyes were slant with vertical, hazel-colored slits for pupils, tiny holes in either side of his oval-shaped head served for ears, and when he opened his mouth, drool spilled out onto the floor, rushing past what looked like thousands of tiny, spiked teeth.

His body did not look exactly human, but neither did it look reptilian. It was, instead, something horribly in between. Behind him a gigantic tail dragged on the stone—the source of the slithering sound at last revealed—stretching out from his hips as far behind him as his head stretched forward, providing exquisite balance from the fulcrum of his powerful back legs.

And yet, Uther noted, the Lizard King was stooped, his shoulders rounded from what he suspected was profoundly advanced age. *How old would this creature be?* Uther wondered, and realized that if the stories were true, and this was the same being who presided under the elder god in the previous age, he had over a thousand years. And somehow that looked appropriate to Uther. An elder king, vassal of an elder god. Uther did not doubt it.

King Abraxis was clad in black leather, not unlike Uther's enforcer, his feet shod in massive, oddly shaped boots. Covering his chest was a white tabard, emblazoned with the black crown and corona of crimson tentacles. He wore no gloves nor gauntlets, but instead, the long green fingers of each hand curled in upon themselves, as if twisted by age, yet each ended in a point that looked as deadly as a dagger.

Unconscious of what he was doing, Uther stood, but his rising was due to awe rather than homage. Moving in large, loping strides, Abraxis moved toward the throne. Uther expected Ennisbrook or Cormoran to step in front of their king, to block the Lizard King's path and prevent his approach to the throne of Hearth; but instead, Uther saw them both take a step back, standing now directly to Uther's left. To his right, Ealon and the orcs had also reflexively retreated a step. Uther's face darkened, and he faced the rival king defiantly.

Yet, as he got closer, Uther realized that the Lizard King did not meet his eye, nor indeed did he appear to take any notice of him at all. Instead of approaching the throne directly, he was moving diagonally across the floor, which made no sense according to any rules of protocol Uther had ever encountered. Where in swiving blood was the beast going?

Uther blinked, amazed at the magnitude of the creature's insolence as the Lizard King moved, incredibly, past his throne without so much as a nod or a bow or a met eye. Instead, the demonic sovereign simply slithered by him as if he wasn't there. He did not offer so much as an insult. Nay, this was worse. This was far greater scorn. The Lizard King simply ignored him.

Uther's fists balled into vibrating stones at the end of his arms, and he felt the blood rise to his face. Yet he was too wroth to form words as he watched the Lizard King pass in front of him, slouching across the floor...directly toward his son Ealon.

Incredulous, Uther watched as the Lizard King bowed curtly before the prince, lowering his great, aged head slightly, then resuming its proud elevation. "Your highness," he said, his voice thick and raspy, his consonants slightly mangled as if it took great effort to make his reptilian mouth form human words. "The *Dunna-ar* owe you their thanksss, and in my own person I welcome you asss brother-in-arms."

Ealon's boots seemed frozen to the stone beneath him. The orcs at his left and right had prostrated themselves, no longer at his defense. His eyes were wide and wild. Then, they shifted back and forth in short, jerky movements. His face broke into a tentative smile, but his voice shook as he spoke. "The...*Dunna-ar* are welcomed. And I w-w-welcome you, too...as a true brother to me, and a friend of my house and kingdom."

"Do you bring me a kingdom, then?" the Lizard King hissed.

"I bring you the *Scrum*, your majesty," Ealon said, his voice stronger, bolder now. He motioned toward Cragga and Grazzak, still on their faces before him.

"A limb, torn from our body, is restored!" the Lizard King exulted, lifting his snout toward the high ceiling.

"Uh...yes, your majesty."

"And you have ssset free our lord and god and masssster from his cruel prison," The Lizard King looked straight into Ealon's eyes, and Uther saw his son shrink a bit. "For this, all creatures of stout and cold heart will call you blesssed." He held out the "sss" in *blessed*, trailing off into a hiss.

"I am...honored, your majesty," Ealon said.

"Oh, Ealon," Uther said, the words erupting unbidden from his throat. "My boy, what have you done?"

But still the Lizard King ignored him. Instead, the beast laid one great, twisted hand on Ealon's shoulder and hissed, "We have much to discusss...." And then, incredibly, the Lizard King, along with the orcs of every provenance, along with Uther's recalcitrant son, simply disappeared into a haze of wispy æther.

A note from the authors:

THANKS so much for reading our book—we hope you enjoyed it, and that you will continue the story in The Dark Field.

And if you can, please post an honest review at whichever site you purchase books from. It doesn't have to be long, just a sentence or two with your feelings and opinions. It helps authors so much when you leave a review, and we'd be so grateful for yours! Thank you for taking the time, and thanks for reading!

—J.R. Mabry & Mickey Asteriou

Continue the adventure in the next thrilling novel in the Red Horn Saga:

THE DARK FIELD
By J.R. Mabry & Mickey Asteriou

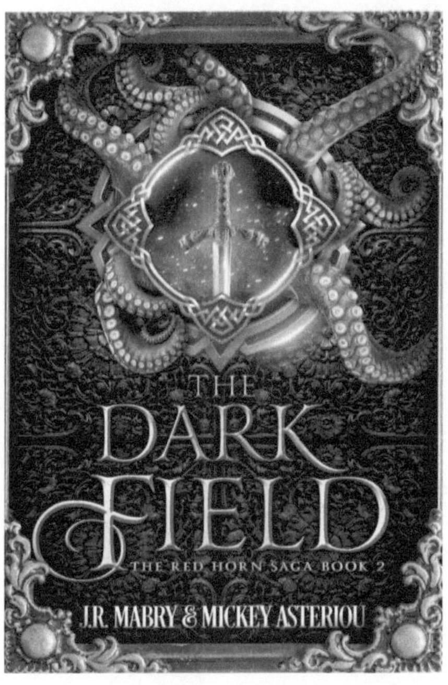

Only one woman knows how to save the universe from an ancient evil. But unless all bright beings are represented, she's not talking...

Get *The Dark Field* today!

AFTERWORD

BY J.R. MABRY

When I was in fifth grade, my mother and I went to a student-teacher meeting, only this time the meeting was with the principal. I think Mom was worried about it, because it's an ominous thing to be called into the principal's office. I don't remember being particularly nervous about it, as I didn't recall doing anything wrong. Afterwards, though, my mom seemed relaxed. "Do you know what he wanted to talk about?" My mother asked me.

"No," I said.

"Principal Asteriou has a son, but he has some trouble making friends. The principal has had his eye on you, it seems, and he thinks you and his son might get along. What do you think?"

"I'd like to meet him, I guess," I said, shrugging.

I don't remember the occasion of our meeting, exactly how it all worked out, but somehow me and Mickey got together. And his dad was right. We hit it off.

Mickey quickly became my best friend, and we had a fierce lot on common—especially a love for science fiction, fantasy, and writing. We had both been writing already, and soon we began writing together. Then, for some reason, our writing became kind of competitive. Nothing aggressive...well, a little bit aggressive. But I think it was healthy competition, over all. It kind of came to a head in eighth grade when we both entered a story into the annual school writing competition. This was going to solve it. The teachers would decide who was the better writer. I remember being extremely nervous about this, because deep in my bones I knew Mickey was a better writer than I. His story was much more mature than mine. Still, I had done my best and now it was just the waiting.

We tied. Can you believe it? It ended in a tie.

Our competition reached a fevered pitch many years later as Mickey and I set off to Europe together and kept battling diaries. We kept score of our numbers of pages written each day, trying to outdo each other. It was exhausting, because Mickey was a writing machine.

Over the years, long after my family moved way, Mickey and I kept in touch. One of the great joys of my working life is interacting with Mickey almost daily, since he works as the ebook-meister and occasional assistant editor for my publishing company, the Apocryphile Press and its various imprints, including Xenophile. He has helped me build it into the business it has become, and I'm grateful to him.

A few years ago, I turned from writing edgy spirituality non-fiction to fantasy and science fiction. I wrote the Kingdom trilogy, and the *Worship of Mystery*. It was always great to know I had at least one reader out there: Mickey. And sometimes I think I was writing just for him—because I knew he would read it.

Then I wrote the Oblivion Saga with B.J. West, my best friend from high school. It gave me the idea that perhaps Mickey and I could do something next. I pitched the idea to Mickey, and was so jazzed when he said he was in.

We began with an idea: "What if all the races in *The Lord of the Rings* were spacefaring?" We used a detailed map of Joseph Campbell's "The Hero's Journey" to construct our outline, and it just grew from there!

And now, two years, six volumes (counting the novellas), and nearly 2500 pages later, we're putting the finishing touches on our little collaboration. I am happy to say that we got this far without any major hitches, disagreements, or outright fights. We are still friends! And it's been a blast.

I hope you'll have half has much fun reading it as we had writing it. And if you really like it, please gift a copy to a friend. After all, I don't think it's a stretch to say that this series is, at its heart, all about friendship.

J. R. Mabry
Grass Valley, CA
December 29, 2019

DRAMATIS PERSONAE

HAFFOLK

Elias Bracegirdle | A haffolk of Everdale. Acting postmaster and Ellis' immediate supervisor at the post office.
Kittredge Cornfeather | A haffolk of Everdale. A bodyguard, friend of Ellis Sunderland.
Tubber Goodfoot | A haffolk of Everdale. The village bully. Given name, "Aric."
Powdy Grumblethorn | A haffolk of Everdale. One of Tubber's cronies.
Stephan Oatgrinder | A haffolk of Everdale. One of Tubber's cronies.
Liza Silverberry | A haffolk of Everdale. A village barmaid that Ellis fancies.
Ellis Sunderland | A haffolk of Everdale. A courier, friend of Kittredge Cornfeather.

HUMANS

Avantir | A human of Hearth. King of Wybrook, father of Clendis.
Daevis Ennisbrook | A human of Hearth. Enforcer to the high king of Hearth.
Elsorin Fairhaven | A human of Allo Torbitatha. Head of the Order of Arrunwolfe.
Osia Glenfallen | A human no fixed planet, originally from Hearth. A high summoner, second in rank. His familiar is Jaq, a small raven.
Imras | A human of Allo Torbitatha. Summoner and guest-master at Summoner's Keep.
Melasenvia | A human of Hearth. Deceased wife of Uther.
Objor | A human of Allo Torbitatha. A summoner, his familiar is the moth, Tepi. The oracle at Summoners' Keep.
Riza | Assistant to Elsorin. Her familiar is the mouse, Kibit.
Cormoran Summerfield | A human of Hearth. Prince of Hearth, and first son of Uther.
Ealon Summerfield | A human of Hearth. Prince of Hearth, and second son of Uther.
Uther Summerfield | A human of Hearth. High King of Hearth, and father of Cormoran and Ealon.
Liaga Thornheart | A human of Hearth. Summoner to the high king.

ELVES

Illuvium | An elf of Elderwood of the house Endilla. A noble, ambassador, and sometime friend of Eoche.
Eoche Silnadin | An elf of Isherwood. King of Isherwood, of the Sildadin, the Green Elves; father of Indiél.
Indiél Silnadin | An elf of Isherwood. Princess of Isherwood, daughter of Eoche.
Silla Silnadin | An elf of Isherwood. The King's sister. At one time an oyosin, but later became a member of the Order of the Scar.

DWARFS

Belorin | A dwarf of Yngremark. King of Yngremark, son of Belára, father of Brennar.
Brennar | A dwarf of Yngremark. Princess of Yngremark, daughter of King Belorin.
Orfek Gravelhorn | A dwarf of Ältremark in the employ of Prince Cormoran of Hearth.
Gürhilde | A dwarf of Yngremark. A stewardess aboard the æthercraft *Augmented Bovine*.
Taff Oakenwild | A dwarf of Yngremark. Secretary to King Belorin.

FAMILIARS

Jaq | A crow of no fixed planet. Familiar of Osia.
Kibit | A mouse of Allo Torbitatha. Familiar of Riza.
Tepil | A moth of Allo Torbitatha. Familiar of Objor.

ORCS

Cragga | An orc of Hearth, of the clan *Ūnna-kar,* commonly called the Scrum.
Grazzak | An orc of Hearth, of the clan *Ūnna-kar*, commonly called the Scrum.
Stargha | An orc of Hearth, of the clan *Ūnna-kar*, commonly called the Scrum.

OTHERS

Abraxis | Also known as the Lizard King, sovereign of the *Dunna-ar*, lord of all the orc-worlds, herald of the Dark Field, "The Speaker of the Word of Doom." Abraxis is a male *klarr*, viceroy to the Dark Lord, and commander of his hosts.
***Eilandryl*,** æthercraft from Fondolyn Illasyntir.

Oximorginon, a creature native to the æther. Possessed of great, leathery wings and internal air bladders, it is capable of flying at nearly the speed of light.
Samael, the Dark Lord. Also known as the elder god, *Ialdaboth*, and *Saklas*.

PLACES

Asura Varr | An ancient place of sacrifice, sacred to the elder god. Formerly the pit of a volcano.
Isherwood | Planet of the Green Elves. Ruled by King Eoche.
Trogan | Capital city of Estenlan and all of Hearth, and the seat of the High King.
Caer Trogan | The castle at Trogan, home of the high king.
Braka | Capital city of Yngremark, second planet of the dwarfs.
Fondolyn Illasyntir | Planet the Black Elves.
Wybrook | The country nearest Estenlan, to the North.
Elderwood | Planet of the Gray Elves.

GLOSSARY

Afril | Elventongue for a double-time march.
Alistair | A unit of measure used for æthercraft speed.
Anul | Elventongue for a metal pendulum that has been blessed by the oyosii.
Astrography | The art of reading maps of the aether
Brunöl | Dwarfish ale
Chel | Elventongue for a large, fluffy towel.
Crogsiunk | Literally "not an enemy" in Orcentongue; friend
D'race | a contraction of "mixed race," a Hearthen pejorative term for haffolk.
Dunna-er | In Orcentongue, the formal name for the smaller orcs.
Eildil | Elventongue for "soldier" or "sailor." Plural, *eildilla*. Plural: *Eildilla*.
Eildithas | Elventongue for "noble soldier"
Endilla | 1) The name of the reining house of Elderwood; 2) the ethnic group of elves resident on Elderwood, also known as Gray Elves.
Ellbaron | A constellation featuring two stars close together.
Elmirill | An elven stone of power.
Elu | Elventongue for "harmony," especially communal or cosmic harmony.

Eoh | Dwarfentongue for horse.
Fängelsten | Dwarfentongue name for the Prison Stone, the stone used by the summoners of the third age to banish Samael from the universe.
Gråstensten | Dwarfentongue term for a common gray kind of stone.
Hearthweed | A plant native to Everdale, smoked for recreation.
HRI | Hearthen Royal Intelligence
Hock | Orcentongue phrase, meaning obscure. Perhaps, "I see your point."
Hrrok | An elven liquor.
Hroshink togrok | Traditional greeting in Orcentongue
Hergut-sa | Orcentongue for "great shield"
Ialdaboth | Elventongue name for the Dark Lord, literally "oath-breaker." Also known among humans as Samael, and among the dwarfs as Saklas.
Illasyntir | Elventongue for "primary."
Illia | A healing balm found on Isherwood.
Illiana | Elvish for "healing herb," the dried, ground powder of a tree native only too Elderwood and its moons. Used by the Gray Elves as a sacramental hallucinogen.
Illendrafil | House of the Black Elves, native to Isherwood, but removed themselves to *Fondolyn Illasyntir* in the early part of the 3rd age.
Isunilir | "The darkening of the sun," a future mythic time, marked by the completion and healing of all things; the end of the world.
Kalc | Dwarfentongue for "chalice"
Kipper | Dwarfentongue for children, now used in Hearthentongue as slang.
Kipperset | Dwarfentongue for "babysit."
Klarr | The species the Lizard King belongs to.
Knulla | Dwarfentongue slang for the sexual act.
Miln | An Endilla religious ritual involving the psychoactive herb Illiana.
Min kära | Dwarfentongue for "my dear."
mitlak | Elventongue for a type of unbreakable metal.
Mörk kärlek | Dwarfentongue for "dark love."

Myanii | An aromatic bush found on elf worlds. A symbol of the oyosii, and used in harmony rituals.
Nir | A small elvish table.
Order of Arrunwolfe | The primary order of summoners among humans and dwarfs.
Order of the Scar | The primary order of summoners among elves.
Prison Stone | Hearthentongue for the Fängelsten, the stone used to keep the Dark Lord at bay.
Realgar | A kind of mineral.
Red Horn | Artifact from another universe, brought into String 257 by Arrunwolfe, opening up the Scar and creating an interdimensional portal for magic.
oyosin | The professional clergy who serve the oyosii (the gods). Employing simple rituals, they restore balance to nature and the communities of bright beings. Also known as "People of the Wood."
oyosii | The Elventongue name for "the gods," personifications of natural forces who strive to keep the universe in balance. This name is widely accepted on human and dwarf worlds as well, although humans may often also refer to them as "the gods."
Runeken | Dwarfentongue for "knowledge of runes"; an educated person is said to have "runeken"; also used in dwarfish rune mysticism to refer to an adept who has seen "through" the surface meaning of the runes to the mystical import below.
Saklas | Dwarfentongue name for the Dark Lord, "Bringer of Death." Also known among humans as *Samael*, and among the elves as *Ialdaboth*.
Samael | Hearthentongue name for the Dark Lord, "the Doom of All Worlds." Also known among elves as *Ialdaboth*, and among the dwarfs as *Saklas*.
Scrum | Informal name of the larger breed of orc; formal name, *Ūnnakar*.
Segla | Dwarfentongue for "sail."
Sfärer | Dwarfentongue for "explosive spheres." Singular form is *sfär*.
Silnadin | 1) The name of the reigning house of Isherwood; 2) the ethnic group of elves native to Isherwood, also known as Green Elves; 3) the name of the language spoken by elves on Isherwood.

The Song of the Scar | One of the two great epics. Composed in elvish, this is the earlier of the epics, depicting the coming of Arrunwolfe and the resulting doom.
The Song of the Stone | One of the two great epics. Composed in elvish, this is the later of the epics, depicting the banishing of the Dark Lord from the universe by means of the Fängelsten.
Swive, swiving | Hearthentongue slang for the sexual act.
Thantii | Elventongue name for a variety of bean that gives supernatural strength.
Tik | Dwarfentongue slang for a prostitute.
Tila | An elven musical mode, one of the "broken" modes.
Tillet | Elventongue for "child."
Tor | Dwarfentongue for a variety of rock that gets slippery when it is wet.
Tröghet | Dwarfentongue for "slowness."
Tur | A tall table, traditionally used by elven physics during surgery.
Ūnna-kar | In Orcentongue, the formal name for the larger species of orc. The informal name is Scrum.
Vakerbild | A square of copper upon which an image has been wrought using chemical means. Named for Jakob Vakerbild, the inventor of the process.
Vesse | A flower native to Isherwood, with a smell reminiscent of clove.
Vissa | An elven sparkling wine.
Woman of the Wood | See *oyosin*.
Wyyr | Elventongue word for werebears.

www.ingramcontent.com/pod-product-compliance
Lightning Source LLC
Chambersburg PA
CBHW020935310726
48980CB00007B/788/J

* 9 7 8 1 9 5 5 8 2 1 7 2 8 *